SWEET STITCHES

LEANNA STONE

PLAYLIST

Monsters - Ruelle
Sweet but a Psycho - Ava Max
The Hunted - Saint Asonia
Kill of the Night - Gin Wigmore
Bury a Friend - Billie Eilish
Feeling Good - Nina Simone
Begging for Thread - Banks
Heathens - Twenty-One Pilots
Teeth - 5 Seconds of Summer
Wicked Game - Ursine Vulpine
Paint it Black - Ciara
Mad Hatter - Melanie Martinez
Problem - Natalia Kills

For those who believe therapy is valid, but vengeance has better results.

INTRO & TRIGGER WARNINGS

Hey there, beautiful chaos lovers!

So, you're about to dive headfirst into my completely unhinged life, and honestly? I'm not sure if I should apologize in advance or just warn you to buckle up. Maybe both. Definitely both.

My name is Scout Prescott, though you might know me better as The Stitcher (yeah, I know, sounds like I run a quilting store, but trust me, it's way more stabby than that). This is the story of how I met the love of my life over a dead body and somehow found my happily-ever-after.

Listen, before we get to the fun stuff I should probably warn you about a few things. This story contains graphic violence, explicit sexual content (the really good kind), a LOT of murder, torture, emotional trauma (we're all works in progress), morally gray characters doing morally gray things, and well, serial killers being serial killers.

Oh, and there's psychological manipulation, lots of blood, substance use, and some very unconventional relationship dynamics. Also, we occasionally discuss child abuse and sexual assault, though never in graphic detail because some things are too dark even for me.

If any of that makes you want to nope right out of here, I totally get it. No judgment. But if you're still reading, then welcome to the club, you beautiful, twisted soul.

So buckle up, buttercup, settle in somewhere cozy, and prepare yourself for a love story that's equal parts sweet and sinister. You might find yourself rooting for the serial killers. Don't worry, we're the good guys.

Mostly.

XOXO
Scout

P.S. Seriously though, If you're squeamish about blood, creative violence, or the excessive use of the word "fuck," this probably isn't the book for you. Might I suggest literally anything else? Maybe something with puppies and rainbows? Though honestly, where's the fun in that?

ONE
SCOUT

If there is a hell, it's littered with cellphone alarms. And mine is screaming at me from somewhere under my pillow, vibrating like a taser having a panic attack. I crack one eye open and immediately regret every life decision that led to the Great Tequila Spiral of last night. I smack my phone screen three times to shut off the screaming banshee.

"Shut up," I croak at the phone, my voice rough.

After a good thirty seconds of aggressive whining into my pillow, I peel myself off the bed and stumble out to the hallway, wrapped in pink flannel pajamas covered in judgmental cartoon cats. And yes, I know they're judging me. I trudge down the stairs and make my way into the kitchen, hating the distance from my room to the coffee pot.

Somewhere between yawning like a feral gremlin and knocking over a potted succulent I named Kevin, I manage to pour myself a mug of strong coffee with an ungodly amount of caramel creamer. It tastes like sweet regret and childhood trauma, which, honestly, feels appropriate considering the amount of mental baggage I'm carrying. Turns out, when you lose everyone who's supposed to stick around, you learn to find family in the strangest places, even if part of you is always waiting for them to disappear, too. Hard to dream about happy endings when you're the monster in someone else's story.

I lean against the counter, elbows propping me up as I sip from my *Resting Stitch Face* mug, contemplating the choices that led me here. Namely, last night's drinking contest with Brayden. I am 5'2 ", made of rage and spite, and *still* somehow thought I could outdrink a 6'5" Southern boy built like a linebacker with a whiskey tolerance forged in hell.

Ten minutes and one existential crisis later, I drag myself up the stairs into my private bathroom, slap on an avocado face mask, and twist my hair into a messy bun that looks like it lost a fight with a blender. I stare at my reflection as my head pounds. Why did they have to make drinking seem so fun? Total bait-and-switch. 1 out of 10, would not recommend.

Phone in hand, I flop onto my bed and begin scrolling through my notifications, squinting against the screen's brightness like it's personally offending me.

Ugh. Twenty-two notifications and nothing even remotely interesting.

Delete. No, I don't want to update my screen time settings. I *like* being unhinged at all hours, thank you.

Delete. Oh look, a 20% off coupon for The Salty Dog, they gave me food poisoning last year. Bold of them.

Delete. Thunderstorms will begin around 2 pm. Great. Incoming frizz ball extraordinaire.

Delete. Donate to The Sterling Institute Disaster Relief Initiative. Ummm, not today.

Delete. Delete. Delete.

When I finally manage to get rid of every damn notification, I tap open the folder marked **"Totally Normal Date Night"** (because branding matters), and tap open *The Index*.

I scroll past a few typical duds:

"JEREMY, 49. RECENTLY DIVORCED. SELF-PROCLAIMED ALPHA. ENJOYS PODCASTS ABOUT 'REAL MASCULINITY,' HIS THIRD BOAT, AND 'YOUNGER COMPANY.'"

Not my type. Swipe left.

> "TROY, 33. WORKS IN PRIVATE SECURITY.
> LOVES TACTICAL GEAR. ENJOYS TEACHING
> PROPER DISCIPLINE AND HELPING WOMEN
> FIND THEIR PLACE. PREFERS A SUBMISSIVE
> WHO WON'T ASK TOO MANY QUESTIONS."

Gross. Swipe left harder.

Then, I see *him*.

> "NATHAN, 41. PASTOR & RELATIONSHIP COACH.
> ACTIVE ON SOCIAL MEDIA AND ALWAYS HAPPY
> TO 'MENTOR' WOMEN STRUGGLING WITH
> CONFIDENCE. BELIEVES 'EMOTIONAL
> BOUNDARIES' ARE A MYTH. MULTIPLE
> RESTRAINING ORDERS FROM FORMER
> PARISHIONERS. STILL INSISTS IT'S JUST 'A
> MISUNDERSTANDING.'"

I sip my coffee. My eye twitches.

Swipe. Right.

"You're mine, pastor boy," I mutter under my breath, marking the profile, and wait for my request to be approved.

Somewhere in the system, *The Operator*, a.k.a. Roman Kane, The Hollow's resident hacker prince and judgmental app daddy, would log my claim.

I wait for all of 10 seconds when a message from the Operator dings my messages.

APP DADDY

😑 He's all yours

ME

I smirk and lock my phone.

To outsiders, The Index looks like some sleek, ultra-exclusive dating app. Subdued interface. Clean lines. Artsy design. A fake homepage that promises "meaningful connections for discerning professionals."

But to those of us in *The Hollow*, The Index is a kill list in disguise.

Every "profile" is a target. Every swipe right is a claim.

And if someone else swipes too? Well, friendly interference is part of the fun.

I snort to myself, "Fucking MurderGram."

I stand to stretch, then I'm off to find my bunny slippers.

Correction: slipper. Singular.

After a quick forensic sweep of the bedroom, I find the other one under the bed. Soaking wet. Slobber-covered. Ear ripped clean off like it had been mauled by a teacup werewolf.

"Dammit, Brayden!"

Fueled by caffeine and righteous fury, I stomp down the hallway in one fuzzy bunny and one bare foot, leaving flecks of avocado mask in my wake like a furious guacamole fairy.

I don't even knock.

I kick Brayden Lockwood's door open like a cop in a rom-com. "Fucking Hell, Brayden! I swear to God, if your dog—"

Brayden appears shirtless in the doorway, his sandy hair mussed, eyes half-lidded, and still managing to smirk like a devil with Southern manners.

He smirks as he drawls. "Well, good mornin' to you too, Cupcake. Are you tryin' to be the next swamp monster beauty queen? 'Cause you nailed it."

I hold up the mangled remains of my slipper. "Your fucking hell-beast killed my bunny. Keep your damn mutt out of my room and away from my things. I better have new Bunny slippers on my bed by tomorrow or I swear to god—"

"Scout Prescott," he gasps, clutching his chest like a scandalized Southern belle at a garden party. "You take that back right now, darlin'. My sweet baby Tank would *never*—" His drawl stretches the word 'never' into about three syllables, dripping with mock outrage and protective daddy energy for his hellbeast of a dog.

As if summoned, his English Bulldog waddles into view, spots the slipper, and launches like a meat cannon. Brayden barely catches the ruined slipper before Tank yanks it out of his hand midair, whipping it back and forth like a chew toy with unfinished business.

I point. "Yeah. He would never."

"Well," Brayden drawls with that infuriating smirk, one eyebrow cocked as he sips from his *Dead Inside But Caffeinated* mug, "can't blame my boy for havin' a refined palate, sweetheart. Those slippers didn't stand a chance against his sophisticated taste. Kinda like you with that tequila last night." He winks, clearly enjoying my suffering a little too much.

I flip him my middle finger with extra flair. "Fuck off," I snap, then stomp back to my room, one slipper down, one kill claimed, and the distant knowledge that I still have a bloody job to do. Literally.

By early afternoon, I am no longer hungover or swampy. I've morphed into what could generously be described as "functionally adorable" in my bootcut jeans, fitted pastel pink tank top, and hot pink glitter belt, because subtlety is a scam and confidence is a weapon.

I leave my bedroom and start heading to my favorite place, the sunroom. As I walk down the hallway, I notice Tank still playing with the corpse of my poor pink bunny slipper. The little fucker.

"You'd better be happy that it's Tea time and I'm not a stereotype that kills animals." He snorts my way in return.

Tea time with The Watcher is sacred. Like Sunday brunch, but more British and less mimosa-fueled.

The Watcher, A.K.A. Lucien Hale, always has a fresh pot waiting, like some refined murder-butler ghost from another era. It's our daily afternoon ritual. The one constant in our chaotic lives of murder and mayhem. I've never missed it, not even when I was running on two hours of sleep or nursing a hangover like today's. Some things are just non-negotiable, and missing Lucien's carefully curated tea time is one of them.

When I enter the sunroom, he is already seated, dressed like he was about to give a eulogy and then steal the widow. Crisp white shirt, grey vest, and subtle cufflinks that probably cost more than my car. Dark hair perfectly in place, eyes the kind that see too much and give nothing back. A porcelain teapot steams on the tray, flanked by delicate cups and little plates of cookies that look too perfect to eat but taste like a hug and a threat all in one.

He gives me a slight nod and gestures for me to sit.

"I see we're bedazzled today," he said mildly, eyes flicking to my belt.

I sit with a dramatic flourish, cross my legs, and beam. "What can I say? Justice deserves sparkle."

He pours me a cup and grimaces as I add *three spoonfuls* of sugar and stir furiously.

"I still maintain that what you do to tea is a war crime," he murmurs.

I take a proud sip. "And yet here you are, harboring a fugitive of taste."

A small smile tugs at his lips as he shakes his head.

We chat about normal things like my latest embroidery project and his opinion on the new bistro downtown. When he asks about my day, I tell him all about Tank's ongoing vendetta against my slippers and dramatically recount my tequila showdown with Brayden. Lucien just shakes his head with that barely-there smile.

Tea time isn't about hunts or targets. It's about pretending, just for an hour, that we're regular people with regular problems. Not killers. Not monsters. Just a fussy British man and me sharing cookies and their day. He never pushes about my hunts, never pries into my methods. He just makes space for me to be Scout, not The Stitcher.

And in return, I try not to scorch the sugar bowl. At least not every day.

A short while later, I return to my room, curl up in my favorite chair with a fuzzy pink throw blanket, a second cup of tea (fewer war crimes this time), and the encrypted file drop The Operator sent me. Roman always labels them for me with something ridiculous like *"Church Boy Breakdown.zip"* or *"Sinfluence.rpt"*. What can I say? Sometimes, a little absurdity is the only thing standing between you and the abyss.

I open the file. Photos, court documents, social media archives, DMs, and sealed police reports that should've been burned. I have everything I need to build a profile. To understand the lie behind the smile. To confirm that the swipe is warranted.

And to make sure I stitch the truth into him before the end.

Somewhere, a charming, manipulative little pastor is preparing his next sermon.

Too bad he'll never finish it.

LATER THAT EVENING

I tug my curls into a quick high puff, touch up the gloss on my berry pink pout, and make my way downstairs, the scent of garlic and something roasted luring me in like a cartoon pie on a windowsill. It's rare that we're all here at once, but when we are, Lucien insists on something formal. *"To remind us that we're human, even if what we do isn't,"* he once said.

The table is set when I arrive, of course. Lucian doesn't half-ass anything. The mahogany dining table gleams under the warm glow of silver candelabras, each flame dancing like tiny funeral pyres. Crystal wine glasses catch the light, filled with a red so dark it could pass for blood in the right lighting. The china is pristine white with delicate gold trim.

Cloth napkins are folded into perfect triangles, and the silverware is arranged to perfection. But it's the little details that give it away. The way the steak knives gleam a little too sharply, like they've been recently honed. Even the centerpiece, a stunning arrangement of white lilies and dark red roses, feels ominous, like something you'd send to a funeral you personally arranged.

The vibe? Murderous family Thanksgiving.

Lucien sits at the head of the table, poised and polished in a charcoal vest and silver cufflinks, like he walked out of a gothic estate catalog. Roman is beside him, scrolling through something on his tablet and chewing absently. Ivy leans back in her chair, her long, dark braid falling over one shoulder. Brayden's already halfway through his dinner roll, offering me a wink as I drop into the seat across from him.

"Scout," Lucien says, "Pink again. How refreshing."

"I dress for the mood I want, not the reality I live in," I reply sweetly, unfolding my napkin. "So far, it's not working."

That earns a chuckle from Roman and a fond sigh from Lucien. My Bestie, Ivy, smirks behind her wine glass.

"You're like a walkin' glitter bomb in a funeral home," Brayden drawls with a wink, sliding the potatoes my way.

We eat like a normal family for about three whole minutes.

Lucien sets down his fork and folds his hands. "We have three new potential candidates for The Hollow," he says casually, like he's announcing dessert. "Roman's been tracking them."

Roman flicks his tablet screen toward Lucien. "I've narrowed it down. One's sloppy. One's arrogant. One's interesting."

"Define interesting," Ivy says, ever skeptical.

Roman reads from his tablet. "Precision kills. Symbolic signature. Excellent cleanup. No survivors. He's off-grid. No digital trail. And he's been doing this for at least a year."

Lucien's silver eyes scan the table. "Thoughts?"

Brayden leans back, tapping a finger against the side of his beer bottle. "If he's too neat, he's either got military trainin' or he's a psychopath."

Ivy raises an eyebrow. "Seriously?"

He grins. "What? I meant a *real* psychopath, darlin', not our special brand of crazy. Either way, count me out. Last thing I need is to babysit some ice-cold killer who probably alphabetizes his torture tools."

Ivy shakes her head. "After what happened with the last recruit? No thanks. I'm not ready for a repeat." Her voice drops. "Not making that mistake again."

Roman winces at that remark but says nothing. Lucien just hums and turns his attention back to his wine.

"I'll do it," I chime in, stabbing a piece of broccoli. "My schedule's pretty light right now. I've just one pastor to stitch up. Plus, I'm bored and Tank destroyed my favorite slippers, so I need the distraction."

Brayden looks offended on Tank's behalf. "Now hold on there, Cupcake. Tank was just helpin' you redecorate. Those slippers were an offense to good taste anyway."

"They were *pink bunnies*, you jerk," I fire back. "And I loved them."

"Seriously, Brayden, your dog is a nuisance. Did he snort up a bee? It's annoying." Ivy says.

Tank's currently sitting on the floor between her and Brayden, eyes locked on the roll in her hand, massive amounts of drool puddling on the floor as he doesn't stop snorting.

Brayden looks down at Tank and says, "Don't listen to them, buddy. They're just jealous that they'll never have a quarter of your charm."

I throw my roll at him as the bickering around the table continues. This is comfortable. We're just like any other family at dinner, well, except for the murdery part, but that's okay, right? All families have their quirks.

Lucien leans back and listens. Roman watches, throwing in a sarcastic jab here and there. And me? I'm just trying to figure out how I feel about someone else joining our broken little dinner table. But somebody has to do it, and it sure as hell shouldn't be Ivy. Not after last time. I was the new kid once, scared, alone, and probably more of a liability than an asset. She gave me a shot. Guess it's my turn to pay it forward.

TWO
SCOUT

THE NEXT MORNING.

The mansion is quiet in the morning hours, the kind of calm that makes the hardwood floors creak louder and coffee taste better.

I shuffle into the kitchen in a fuzzy robe patterned with strawberries and tiny cartoon skulls. Ivy's already there, curled up on the window bench with her legs tucked underneath her. Sipping from her favorite black mug that she cradles in both hands. Across it, in delicate gold script, are the words: "Prince Charming, My Ass."

Her dark hair is twisted into an elegant knot, and her robe is silk, black with deep red roses. It's draped perfectly like she rolled out of a noir film and into a Vogue cover. Her vibe is very *lounge singer meets licensed weapon.*

I'm the opposite, obviously. If I'm the storm, she's the sultry calm afterward, the kind that wipes everything clean and leaves nothing behind.

I grab my mug from the cabinet, my prized ceramic gem gifted by Ivy herself. It's white, obnoxiously glittery, and in bold pink letters it reads: "Bitches Get Stitches." There's a tiny stitched human heart under it. It's equal parts adorable and horrifying. I love it.

"Morning," she says without looking, her voice is low and smooth, like jazz on vinyl.

I grunt in return. I'm not fully human yet, not until coffee.

I pour myself a cup, dump in enough creamer to make a dentist scream, and join her at the window seat.

There's a peacefulness to mornings like this. Just us. No blood. No surveillance feeds. No plotting. Just caffeine and the quiet understanding of two women who've buried more secrets than a cemetery holds.

To anyone looking in, Ivy would be the picture of grace. Serene, elegant, still. The type of woman who belongs in a speakeasy, singing smoky ballads under low light. It makes it that much more unbelievable that she once used a severed penis as a brush to paint "WOLF" in blood above a dead man's bed.

That's the thing about Ivy.

She doesn't look like she could kill you. She looks like she already did and then wrote a poem about it.

I sip my coffee and sigh. "What do you think of the new potential recruits Lucien asked about?"

"I'm not sure what to think just yet," she replies, still watching the sunrise.

A soft chime sounds from my phone.

I swipe it open. One new notification in The Index:

New Assignment: Cotton Candy & Carnage

Target: Mr. Floss

Name: Deacon Thorne

Status: Shadow & Evaluate

Operator Note: *"You asked for it, you got it, Pink Menace, Mr. Floss is all yours. Full file incoming shortly. Don't let that pretty brain of yours get distracted. I like you alive and sarcastic, even if you are slightly annoying."*

I grin and show Ivy the screen.

She raises an eyebrow. "The Cotton candy guy? Seriously? That's the interesting recruit?"

"The very same. Tall. Creepy. Controlled violence. He leaves pink cotton candy in pedophiles' mouths like it's some twisted carnival." I say, as I wiggle my eyebrows.

"You look like a lunatic with a crush. I'm starting to worry that the insane amounts of sugar you ingest are causing you to become deeply unhinged." She responds.

I grin. "You're not wrong."

Ivy nods towards my phone, "So what's your plan?"

I scroll to the file labeled **Recent Routine Approximation**, Roman's weirdly formal way of saying *'here's everywhere he's been for the last two weeks, courtesy of hacked cameras, cell tower pings, and a complete disregard for privacy laws.'* It's a stitched-together breadcrumb trail of locations, timestamps, and movement patterns. Basically, it's stalker-level detail in the most delightfully helpful way.

One place pops up again and again at the same time every morning for the last five days.

I arch my brow. "I'm thinking I need to go out for coffee. Wanna join me?"

She smirks, "Sure. Nothing like a latte and light stalking to start the day."

We clink our mugs, our twisted kind of morning toast, and fall into silence. We're sisters in everything but blood, bonded over trauma, vengeance, and an alarming caffeine dependency. It's the comforting kind that only exists between two women who know what it feels like to clean blood out of silk and smile while doing it.

THE CAFÉ IS TUCKED between a sad florist and a preschool. The inside smells like burnt beans and broken dreams, but it's charming in that *"local hole in the wall"* kind of way.

Perfect.

I push the door open, the bell above it giving a cheerful little *ding!* as Ivy follows me inside like the sultry storm cloud. Her outfit is immaculate. Tailored black slacks, a deep charcoal blouse tucked just so, and a long coat that moves like it was stitched from shadow. Her dark hair's pulled back into a smooth, low twist, understated gold studs in her ears, and a watch that says *family money* without trying. She doesn't try to stand out, she just does, in that quiet, unbothered way that makes people straighten their posture without realizing it. Meanwhile, I'm dressed in my signature cropped tank, low-rise jeans, and my trusty pink glitter belt, which is to say, *fabulous*. People see a girl like me and assume I'm shallow. Clueless. A distraction. It's perfect for hunting my prey.

We order our drinks. A caramel iced latte for me, heavy on the caramel, because why not? A simple vanilla latte for Ivy. We head for a patio table with the best view of the street and a certain quiet corner where Mr. Floss himself is already seated.

Lightly tanned skin, jet black hair that looks effortlessly tousled. Sharp jawline. Simple black hoodie. Eyes down. Brooding like it's his job.

I laugh at something Ivy says, loud, bright, and a little obnoxious. It cuts through the morning like a sugar-laced slap, and that's when I see it: a flicker of movement from the far corner.

I know he heard it.

I know he looked.

Hook, line, emotionally unavailable murder machine.

We reach our table and sit, but I don't rush it. I stir my drink like I'm contemplating the meaning of life. Ivy sits across from me, sipping her latte like it's a sacrament. Her vibe is all femme fatale restraint. I'm sparkles and sass. We're opposites, and yet we orbit each other perfectly.

"He's watching us," she says without looking up.

"No, he's watching the world, *not* watch him," I murmur, stirring my iced latte with a hot pink straw. "But yes. He clocked us at the door."

I feel his gaze land on me again, just for a beat.

So I glance up and wink.

He blinks. A muscle in his jaw ticks. Then, just like that, he looks away.

I sip my drink with a satisfied hum.

"You're going to scare him off," Ivy whispers.

"He kills child predators with surgical precision. I think he can handle a wink."

We fall into a comfortable silence, watching the city move outside the café. A guy at the next table is reading the newspaper as if it were 1997. Ivy raises a brow.

"Who still reads those?"

"People who don't want their algorithms tracking murder porn," I reply casually, pulling out a bite of my chocolate croissant.

But then, a headline catches my eye.

"Body Found in Park – Police Stumped by Scene of Disturbing Brutality."

I frown.

The photo is mostly blurred out, but I can make out what I assume is a blood-soaked figure sprawled in the middle of what looks like... glass shards? The caption mentions a "garden-like arrangement."

I lean toward Ivy, gesturing toward the paper.

"You seen this?"

She glances over. Her expression doesn't change, but I know her well enough to catch the shift in her posture, alert, ready.

"That's a bit too close to home," she murmurs. "And it's definitely not one of ours."

"You need to loop in Roman," I say as I slowly rise from my seat. "And I've got to catch a sermon before I can go to the carnival." I flash Ivy a smile and wink.

She shakes her head as she tries not to laugh. "Well, that's one way to put it."

As we walk away from our table, I notice Mr. Floss practically drilling holes into newspaper guy with those steely eyes of his. "Well, well, well... someone's looking a little murder-y at the morning headlines," I whisper-sing to myself, biting my lip. "That's not suspicious at *all*, Candy Man. Not. At. All."

THREE

DEACON

The motel room smells like old carpet and cheap bleach. It's the kind of place no one remembers. There are no front desk questions, no cameras, and no noise. Just the hum of the mini fridge, the buzz of a dying light bulb, and the silence that's been my only company.

I wake up before the sun, not because I set an alarm; my body doesn't need one. Habit does the job. Years of training myself to sleep lightly and move quieter than a memory.

I stretch. Crack my knuckles. Roll out of bed without making a sound.

The room is stark, one table, one chair, and one cracked mirror that I avoid. My gear is packed in a single black duffel bag beside the bed.

I sit in the worn-out chair in the corner, staring at the screen in front of me. My laptop is untraceable, built from parts I stripped myself, and it's currently displaying my prey. The name in my crosshairs is Jeffrey Lorre.

Fifty-one. Substitute teacher. He should have been convicted of multiple counts of child pornography possession and solicitation but the douchebag walked free due to a technicality. One corrupted flash drive, one botched search warrant, and a slick lawyer who argued "violated rights" louder than the testimony of broken children.

He moved across state lines and started over. Quietly. Conveniently. He lives in a small rental off a dead-end road. No spouse. No kids of his own. Thank fuck. His record's clean... on paper.

But I've seen the forums he still visits. The message boards he scrolls through. The usernames he swaps.

He's still hunting.

He thinks he's safe.

He's not.

I've been in town for five days. Lorre keeps to a tight routine. Church three times a week, the grocery store at 7:15 a.m. on Saturdays, and a library two towns over, where the wi-fi has no filter. I've already mapped his home, his schedule, his routines. I know where he shops, where he works out. The brand of protein bars he keeps in the glove box of his truck.

He has no idea he's on borrowed time.

I shut the laptop and rub the back of my neck. My muscles are tight... too tight. The silence isn't restful anymore. It's suffocating.

I used to think solitude was the price of clarity. Now I wonder if I've mistaken isolation for control.

There's no one to talk to. No one who knows my real name. No one to ask why I keep doing this. Not that I'd actually answer them if they did.

I don't miss people. I miss noise that isn't mine. Laughter that isn't fake. A voice that makes me forget just how loud my head gets.

Sometimes... I wonder what it would feel like, just for a second, to have someone look at me and *not* see something broken or dangerous. Just a man.

I shake the thought loose. I can't have that, not like this. Thoughts like that don't belong here with me in the dismal space of my existence.

Most days, I observe. I sit in parks. Watch routines. Memorize patterns. Blend in.

If I walk past you, you won't remember me. That's the point.

I track my prey, log his schedule, and test his habits. I follow from a distance. Close enough to plan, far enough not to be noticed. Every move is purposeful. Every detail is absorbed.

But when I return to the motel each night, bag in hand, boots dusty, hoodie up, it's just me and the silence again.

I could be sleeping in a penthouse, bathing in stone tubs, drinking coffee ground from beans that cost more than this entire motel.

My family's money is old. Filthy. Endless. I could pay someone else to do this. Could vanish into a life of luxury and forget all of it.

But I don't. I won't.

Because people like Lorre slip through cracks built by wealth, power, and apathy.

So I sharpen the knives. Study the files. Memorize the pattern of his gait, the brands of his cereal, and the way he avoids looking anyone in the eye except children.

And I wait.

Not for justice.

For the moment he's alone. Vulnerable. Real.

Because that's when I remind him that monsters don't just live in closets.

I close my laptop, stand, and double-check my bag. Tools packed. Gloves. Knives. Burner phone. Backup plan. Exit route.

Tomorrow, he dies, and then I disappear again.

Because that's the job: find the monster, end him, and vanish before anyone even knows he's missing.

Rinse. Stalk. Kill. Repeat.

I pull on my hoodie, lock the door behind me, and step into the dark.

By 9:00 a.m., I'm sitting at a café three blocks from the motel. I order a plain bagel and black coffee with cash and no eye contact. I sit at a table in the back corner of the patio. Eat. Watch the sidewalk. Every shadow. Every license plate. Every pattern.

It's not paranoia when I'm hunting a monster. I don't follow close, just enough to confirm what I need. I've already marked my kill site, an abandoned warehouse he likes to walk past after dark. Private. Isolated. Easy to stage. Easier to clean.

I watch as Jeffrey Lorre walks into the café, just like every other day I've been here. He's so goddamn predictable. Same table. Same seat on the patio. Same bullshit disguise of "harmless old man with a newspaper." Wearing tan slacks and a weathered windbreaker like he's someone's retired uncle.

He doesn't look at the paper. Not really.

His eyes drift just past the top edge, fixed on the preschool playground across the hedge. The place fills up every weekday by this time. Kids tumbling off monkey bars, screaming over tricycles, teachers distracted by one meltdown or another. They run and laugh in the sun, too young to know that monsters don't hide under their beds. Sometimes, they sit on café patios pretending to read the paper.

He thinks he's being subtle.

My grip tightens around the ceramic cup in my hand. My other hand twitches, muscle memory trained by fury, not discipline. My fingers ache to reach for the blade tucked against my ankle. My entire body *itches* to end him. To feel the way his pulse kicks against steel for just one second before it goes still as his blood spills over my blade.

I've followed enough pedophiles to know the look. That vacant, locked-on stare. Not hunger, anticipation. Like he's counting the days until one of those kids wanders too far from the fence.

No one else sees it.

But I do.

And the worst part? He'll be back tomorrow. Just like yesterday. Just like every day before that.

Unless I stop him.

I gather my control to sip my coffee. It's pure shit. Weak, over-steeped, and lukewarm.

But it's predictable. Same table, same order, same cashier who doesn't look up when she hands me my change. Predictability is comfort when you live your life on the margins of society.

A laugh distracts me. It's sharp and obnoxious, and I glance over out of reflex.

She definitely doesn't belong here. Not with the quiet regulars and cheap coffee. Bright, careless, like someone who's never had to check over her shoulder. I was expecting a nuisance and found something... else. She doesn't belong here, but she doesn't care. And for some reason, that bothers me.

Not because she's subtle, she's *far* from it. Low-rise jeans. Caramel skin. Full pink lips. Glitter belt. Hips swinging, curls bouncing, like a living warning label. She doesn't match the world around her. Her laugh continues to cut through the noise of the café like a blade wrapped in sugar. She's small, bright, and moves like she owns the room as she walks to her table.

My eyes flick back to my prey. Still sitting, watching. He'll be here for another thirty minutes and leave once recess is over.

I glance back at Glitter Girl, and that's when she winks at me.

Unapologetic. Bold. Like I'm a challenge, she's already decided she'll win.

I blink once. Slow.

No smile. No reaction.

But internally?

I'm annoyed. Or maybe unsettled? The line between the two blurs when you've trained yourself not to feel either.

What the hell is she so sure of?

There's confidence, and then there's... whatever that was. She smiles at me like I'm some game she's already halfway through winning, and I didn't even know I'd been dealt in.

It shouldn't bother me. But it does.

Not because she's a threat, she's not. At least, not to me.

It's because people like her don't usually notice people like me.

Not unless they want something.

Focus, I remind myself.

I shift my attention back to Lorre.

He's still pretending to read the paper, eyes hovering just over the top edge to watch the preschool playground like it's cable TV. He's still sitting sideways in his chair for the best angle. Still sipping his coffee in slow, practiced intervals. Still imagining things I'd gut him for if I could see inside his head.

I watch his every breath.

I check her out of the corner of my eye. She's already looking away, talking to the tall, dark-haired girl with the glacier stare. They're laughing now. Whispering something over a shared pastry. She's already forgotten me. Good, because I've got a monster to deal with.

I finish my coffee. Leave a tip on the table. I slide my hoodie back over my head as I leave the café to sit in my car while I wait for Lorre to make his exit.

The rest of the morning is routine. I tail Lorre as he drives across town. Stops at a gas station. Buys a candy bar and a bottle of water. Smiles and chats with the cashier like he's just a nice guy. I can't wait to remove his mask and feel his blood pour over my fingers.

He doesn't know I've been in his house. Doesn't know I've watched him through his office window. Doesn't know I'll be joining him for an evening walk soon.

By mid-afternoon, I'm at the warehouse.

Abandoned. Quiet. Dust on dust. A perfect setting for removing a monster from the world.

His death will happen tomorrow night, but I'll prep everything today. The tarp. The tools. The lights. A single metal chair placed in the center of the room. No cameras. No witnesses.

Just him and me.

And the justice that the courts couldn't deliver.

FOUR

SCOUT

It's Sunday morning, and I'm standing outside St. Andrews Church, where Pastor Nathan Ashford is greeting the congregation as they filter in through the open doors. I have to say, he is charming at first glance, a boy-next-door smile, an expensive haircut, and hands that never seem to pray when they're supposed to. But I see the evil he keeps hidden, tucked behind his overly white teeth and that smooth, practiced voice that probably makes half the church ladies feel "blessed" in all the wrong ways.

I'm wearing a respectable pink floral sundress, paired with soft curls and a sweet little cardigan to complete the picture of innocence. Honestly, I look like I bake lemon bars for the church bake sale and say things like "*oh gosh darn*" instead of my usual *"go fuck yourself."*

Pastor Nathan is a pure waste of space. This charming "Man of God" is anything but. His file reads like your typical sadistic douchebag. Not only does he have numerous restraining orders, but he also has the bodies of several working girls buried beneath his facade. Of course, they aren't officially linked to him because, surprise, surprise, missing working girls are typically overlooked by police. But I don't miss a single one. I found all seven of them.

Literally *seven beautiful women* that this dick-shit decided didn't deserve to breathe anymore.

The church always moved him once the official complaints started to roll in. He was never in one place long enough for police to actually investigate. But I investigated them. I always do.

When it comes to my girls, I'm 100% all in.

I glance up at the building and let out a low sigh. White steeple. Stained glass windows. Pews full of people praying for guidance while this walking skin suit of a man preaches about purity.

I look down at my dress, brush an invisible wrinkle off the fabric, and take a deep breath.

"You're just going in for an introduction," I mutter. "Not an exorcism."

Then, lower: "Please don't let me spontaneously combust."

I take one hesitant step forward and instantly second-guess myself.

I mean, *technically,* I'm a good person. I just have a slightly unconventional career path. It's not like I kill innocent people. I kill the monsters. Abusers, killers. Men who treat women like objects and then toss them away when they're inconvenient.

That's gotta count for something, right?

I steal another glance toward the big double doors. "Okay, God, here's the deal; if you could maybe hold off on the lightning bolts and smiting things for like fifteen minutes, I'd really appreciate it. You don't even have to forgive me or anything. Just, you know, don't roast me alive in front of a bunch of senior citizens and Sunday school kids."

A woman in pearls passes by and gives me a polite smile. I smile back sweetly and wonder how many of his victims smiled just like that before he decided they didn't deserve to breathe anymore. Not on my watch. Not one more.

I take a deep breath and walk towards the entrance.

I step inside the church, blinking against the change in light. Everything smells like dust, hymnals, and wood polish. The sanctuary is warm, softly lit, and painfully beige, like God was going for "neutral farmhouse" on a budget.

I keep my posture delicate and respectful. Cross one ankle over the other. Smooth my floral sundress as I slip into the very back pew, not so far back that I look disengaged, just enough to stay unnoticed. Strategic devotion.

The congregation filters in around me. Mostly older folks, a handful of families, and two painfully earnest twenty-something women in identical sundresses. Pastor Nathan greets them all with that warm, polished charisma that makes him look like every church lady's fantasy of godly masculinity in a cardigan.

He glances toward me once mid-sermon.

I smile. Soft. Sweet.

Like, I couldn't possibly be planning to make his chest into the prettiest art project this side of a murder documentary.

The sermon is fine. Generic. A "lost sheep returns to the flock" special, complete with humble anecdotes and just enough tears in his voice to sell it. The woman in front of me sniffles quietly. My stomach rolls.

Every time he speaks, I hear the screams of the girls no one bothered to look for.

But I sit through it all, hands folded in my lap, nodding when appropriate. When he speaks of forgiveness, I press my lips together to keep from laughing.

When the sermon finally ends, I stand with the rest of the congregation, singing some hymn about washing in the blood of the lamb. The irony isn't lost on me. I might be the only person in this room who actually knows what it's like to be covered in blood, other than Pastor Nathan, of course.

I stay in character as everyone files out, keeping my movements small and unassuming. Sweet Scout. Harmless Scout. Definitely not going to embroider your chest cavity, Scout.

Pastor Nathan stands at the door, shaking hands, offering blessings, touching shoulders. Each time his fingers linger too long on a woman's arm, I feel my jaw tighten. I force myself to relax. Compartmentalize.

I linger near the vestibule, feigning hesitation. I wander just far enough down one hallway to look uncertain.

It doesn't take long.

"Lost, sister?" comes a smooth voice behind me.

I turn, blinking as if startled, and look up at Pastor Nathan Ashford. Up close, he's all charm and cologne. His smile is gentle. His eyes are calculating. He already thinks he owns me.

"Oh, um..." I force a breathy laugh. "I was just looking for the ladies' room."

"Of course," he says, tone like warm honey. "This way."

He walks beside me like a gracious shepherd, asking all the right questions.

"Are you new to town?" "Do you live nearby?" "Family in the area?" "Have you found a church home yet?"

Probing. Testing. Weighing.

I answer softly, voice laced with manufactured uncertainty.

"No, I just moved here recently. Don't really have anyone around, so I thought I'd... come here. Try to find a little peace."

I pause, then glance up through my lashes. "I'm not exactly good at... fitting in."

He chuckles, a low, private sound. "Well, you certainly fit here just fine."

Gross.

We stop outside the ladies' room. He gestures toward it like he's doing me some kind of holy favor. But then he leans against the wall and *waits.* Doesn't leave. Doesn't walk off.

He stays.

Outside the door. As if I might try to run away.

Could this bastard be any more creepy?

I duck inside, splash cold water on my face, check the stall layout, and mentally trace a potential escape route. Just in case. Because while I'm the predator, I'm never dumb enough to forget that men like him always think they're the ones holding the leash.

When I step back out, he smiles like we've shared something personal.

"Here," he says, pulling a business card from his coat pocket. He flips it over and scribbles a number on the back in smooth, confident pen strokes. "Just in case you ever feel lost."

I smile like a deer in headlights.

And take it.

Because monsters like him don't know what it feels like to be hunted. At least not yet.

I walk away, feeling his eyes on my back. The weight of his gaze makes my skin crawl, but I keep my posture relaxed. Sweet. Vulnerable.

Once I'm in my car, I let out a long breath and dig my nails into my palms.

"Seven women," I whisper to myself. "Seven."

I close my eyes and mentally shift gears. I need to establish myself as trustworthy but troubled. Someone who might need private counseling. Someone who won't be missed immediately if I disappear for a few days after he does.

The compartmentalization helps me stay focused. If I let myself feel the full weight of what these men do, what Nathan has done, I'd burn with rage until there was nothing left of me. So I separate. I organize. I create mental rooms where I can store different parts of myself.

When I'm done with this, I'll lock The Stitcher away again until she's needed. I'll go home and be the Scout who bickers with Brayden and drinks tea with Lucien. The Scout who isn't covered in blood.

But right now, I need to plan.

I start my car and pull out of the church parking lot. Pastor Nathan watches from the steps, raising his hand in farewell. I wave back with a bright smile.

Seven women.

Seven drops of blood spilling from the dahlia he'll wear over his heart.

THE FOLLOWING evening at the mansion, I'm holed up in my room, making sure everything is ready for the good Pastor. The final remnants of sunlight peek through my bedroom window in soft gold streaks, glinting off the shimmer of a pink body spray bottle and the glittery lid of an old lip balm I hadn't used in forever.

I sit cross-legged on my bed, surrounded by chaos.

My embroidery kit lay open beside me, scissors, silk threads, sterilized needles, a curved set for skinwork. Next to it was a folded stack of solid black clothing, pressed and ready. Loose-fit black cargo pants, long-sleeved black compression shirt, lightweight black gloves. My Combat Boots, freshly cleaned and shined, sit at the foot of my bed. Functional. Silent. Efficient.

It's a uniform of sorts. Not mine. Theirs.

I don't wear black because I'm grieving. I wear black because true monsters don't deserve color.

My real clothes are floral sundresses and rhinestone belts and fuzzy pink slippers (well, one slipper now). But this? This is the armor I need to descend into their rot.

The burner phone buzzes softly beside me. Roman had given it to me two days ago with a smirk and a warning: *"Try not to sext the creep, I just wiped it."*

I gave him a mock pout and blew him a kiss. "But then what would entertain that pervy brain of yours?" He rolled his eyes then. Mine roll now, as the screen lights up. I knew he would take the bait from that text I sent shortly after service had ended. God, he's so dumb. So easily manipulated.

> PASTOR PERV
>
> I was thinking of you today, little lamb. I hope peace has found you.

God. Little lamb. If I weren't planning to kill him, I'd need a shower just from that.

I wait a few minutes, let the tension simmer, then reply with exactly the kind of gentle vulnerability a manipulative monster like him can't resist.

ME

> I've been trying. It's just... hard sometimes. I feel like I'm drifting again. Ever since my parents abandoned me, I feel like I don't know where I belong.

I could practically hear him preening through the screen.

PASTOR PERV

> You always belong in the arms of the Father. But I understand how easy it is to lose your way. Would you like to talk? Sometimes it's easier with someone beside you.

Oh, would you look at that, he wants to meet me... shockeroo. Perfect.

I picked up my embroidery hoop and ran my fingers over the edge of the ring. Clean. Ready.

ME

> I don't want to be a burden. I know you're busy with the church...

PASTOR PERV

> Never too busy for you. You're not a burden, little lamb. You're part of the flock now.

I literally gag but I don't flinch. I just smile sweetly at the blood red thread as I pick it up to glide it between my fingers.

ME

> Maybe we could talk sometime soon? I don't know... I just keep feeling... lost.

There. Bait set. Sweet. Naive. Open to "guidance."

PASTOR PERV

> Come by the church tomorrow afternoon. I'll make time for you. We can speak privately. No pressure, just presence.

> I think you'll find what you're looking for.

My jaw twitches.

Afternoon is my tea time. And no matter how urgent the kill, no matter how filthy the target, I am not about to let this human skin suit interrupt my sacred ritual with The Watcher. Some things are just *off-limits.*

I type slowly, carefully.

ME

> Maybe later in the evening? It's easier for me once the day settles. I don't really want to be around too many people. After dark just feels... safer.

He takes longer this time to answer. Maybe he's recalculating. Maybe realizing I'm not quite as naive as I pretended to be.

PASTOR PERV

> Of course. Come when you feel most comfortable. You'll be safe with me, little lamb.

I lay the phone aside and stand, crossing the room to my closet. Hidden behind the ridiculous amount pink sweaters, shirts, and sundresses is a thick, rolled bundle of heavy cream-colored fabric, bound with an old black silk ribbon.

I pull it out gently and lay it across my bed. My fingers stroke the bundle and ribbon tenderly, lovingly. I slowly pull the ribbon free and unroll the fabric.

The Tapestry.

A personal chronicle. A stitched ledger of vengeance.

Each square space holds a Black Dahlia with jet black petals, red-tipped, outlined in white. Each flower has a date stitched above it in blood-red thread. The day the monster died. But the real story is in the petals.

Each petal bears a name. The names of the women the monster had hurt, silenced, and discarded. They are my girls. The ones who didn't make it out.

This isn't for show. This isn't just art. This is remembrance.

Each stitch is a promise kept. Each flower is a wound closed. And tomorrow, another bloom would be born.

I trace the blank space beside the last dahlia and grab my hoop. I take my time placing and stretching the fabric across it. The placement has to be perfect, my work has to be perfect. My girls deserve nothing less than perfection, and I will make sure they get it.

Nathan Ashford doesn't know it yet, but he has a date with the needle. And I never miss a stitch.

FIVE

SCOUT

The thing about predators like Pastor Nathan? They never expect the lamb to be holding the blade.

He thinks we're having a spiritual breakthrough. That's the real punchline. I had just finished "pouring out my soul" in his office about how I felt lost and adrift. No family, no community, no faith. I even fake a tear or two, which, for the record, I *crush*. Give me a fucking Oscar.

He offers to pray for me. I ask if we could hold hands. When he reaches across the desk with that smug, rehearsed smile, I press the syringe into his wrist faster than he can say *amen*.

One flick. One plunge. Paralytic delivered.

His expression shifts beautifully. I watch as he goes from holy confidence to confused disbelief, and then to fear. My favorite part. I hold his gaze the whole time, calm and sweet, as he tries to lift his arms and can't.

"You should probably sit," I say softly as he stumbles into his chair like a puppet with half-cut strings.

He manages a garbled "wh-what did you..." before his jaw starts to slacken. I shush him softly.

"Shhh shhh shh... No more sermons, Pastor. It's my turn to speak."

From there, it's all choreography.

I close the blinds, dim the lamp, and roll out my tools from my kit like I'm setting up a cozy little craft circle. The room still smells like wood polish, cheap cologne, and the faint musk of regret.

The Pastor's eyes follow my every move. I especially love the look of hope in his eyes when I grab my bag and walk out of the room into his private bathroom. I know his hope won't last for long. I grab my black cargo pants and the fitted dark top, making the mental shift to become The Stitcher. She's practical, serious, lethal. I quickly pull my soft curls into two boxer braids, tight against my scalp. No more bouncy, carefree girl, this is no place for her.

I step back into the room and watch as his eyes widen, and that beautiful moment of realization washes over his face. The lost little lamb has transformed into the wolf, and he's already bound for slaughter. I can't help but smile at the fear blooming in his eyes. It's that perfect instant when my prey realizes it wasn't a lamb following him, but a shark circling all along, and now his blood is in the water.

I lay him on the floor gently. "Can't have a nasty bruise mess up my canvas," I tell him as I reach into my kit to grab scissors. The Pastor's eyes widen as I flash the shiny steel tips against the light. I use the sharp point and lightly graze it from his forehead to his chin, just enough for him to feel it but not enough to leave any marks. I snap the scissors open and closed a few times, "Snip, Snip," I say, and I can tell by the way his eyes widen even further that my smile has crossed into something that would make normal people very, very nervous. What can I say, I enjoy being theatrical. He whimpers as the smell of urine offends my senses. Bingo! I look down at his crotch, turning back to laugh at him.

"Damn! You didn't even make it to the 'forgive me' part. That's gotta be so embarrassing."

I proceed to snip each button off of his crisp white shirt, parting the fabric to reveal my canvas of smooth white skin.

"Seven girls, Pastor," I say as I grab and begin to sterilize my needle. "Seven souls you used and discarded like trash. But I'm here for them." I tenderly trace the patch of skin over his heart, lean in, and whisper, "This is for my girls."

I chose my thread carefully, pure white, but it won't stay that way for long. It's the first stitch that always sets the tone. The skin gives just enough resistance to feel real. Human. Heavy.

I lift the flower patch I'd crafted in the stillness of last night. My black dahlia. Each petal curves with deadly precision, crimson tips delicately outlined in stark white thread. The perfect dark bloom hovers over his beating heart for just a moment before I pierce his flesh with my needle, securing my signature to his quivering skin, thread by thread, claiming him as my canvas.

He can't speak, but I know he's screaming inside.

I smile down at him.

"Don't worry," I whisper. "I'm almost done."

Midway through the third blood droplet, this one for Tanya Jenkins, twenty-two, found along the riverbank, my phone buzzes in my pocket. The vibration against my thigh makes me pause, needle hovering just above the Pastor's skin. I huff out a little annoyed breath. Timing, seriously? I wipe my bloodied gloves on my jeans before removing one to fish out my phone from my pocket.

"Sorry for the interruption, Pastor, this will only take a sec," I say as I check the notification.

It's exactly what I've been waiting for. A location alert pinging from the GPS tracker I'd magnetically slapped under Mr. Floss's car earlier today. While he'd been busy brooding over his black coffee, Ivy and I left the cafe early for a quick duck-and-plant maneuver in the parking lot. The little dot on my screen shows movement. Looks like he's hunting tonight too. My lips curl into a smile as I admire the precise coordinates.

My stomach does this weird little flip. Not nerves. Something else. Excitement? Curiosity?

I set my phone to the side and slip my glove back on to continue the last few pulls of thread. I glance down at the man beneath me. He passed out several times throughout the process, but he's waking up now. His puffy eyes and tear-stained face make my tummy flutter even further. I reach into my kit and pull another syringe. I tap against the cylinder. The final amount of paralytic needed to stop his heart and lungs.

"We're all done now, Pastor." I croon as I smooth my palm over the embroidered dahlia. The blood has begun to soak into the design, giving the petals and seven blood droplets life.

I stab the needle into the center of the dahlia, directly into his heart, injecting the final dose.

His eyes are glassy now, the light in them flickering. His breaths get slower and slower. I can tell we're close.

"You don't deserve this kind of beauty," I murmur as I caress the petals. "But my girls do."

He exhales one final breath.

I rise, clean my tools, and straighten the room. No panic. No mess. Just the calm after the storm.

Sliding out the back door into the cool night, I shiver and pull on my hoodie. I pull my phone from my pocket and tap open The Index, clicking to mark his file as complete. Roman will send the clean-up crew to ensure I didn't miss anything. I flip over to the file on Mr. Floss and click the location tracker. The pulsing red flame shows me exactly where I need to be. The icon moves slowly through an alley off the industrial district.

"Alright, Mr. Floss," I say, pulling up my hood and slipping into the dark. "Let's see if you're as neat and nasty as they say."

Twenty minutes later, I'm slipping into an alley next to an old abandoned brick warehouse. The beacon on my phone is my guide. Glancing around, I catch a faint glow coming from a window on the third floor. I make my way silently up the fire escape to the window.

"Found you, candy man," I say to myself as I watch him work through the grimy, cracked window. It's just him and the soon-to-be-dead guy slumped in a metal chair, zip-tied and whimpering. Why do they always whimper? Seriously, the "*Monsters*" almost always break down like little bitches. It's honestly kind of pathetic.

I shake my head to clear my thoughts and get back on task.

Mr. Floss. True Identity: Deacon Thorne. Appearance: I can't see his face right now, but damn, that body says a lot.

The man is a walking contradiction. He's six-foot-something of lean muscle and sharp angles, impossibly fluid for someone who looks so imposing. The same broad shoulders that caught my eye at the cafe now cut a lethal silhouette in that fitted black henley. His tactical pants hug thighs that could probably crush a man's windpipe, which, objectively speaking, is fucking hot in a terrifying way. He moves silently as a shadow, yet the tension in the air coils around him like he *brought* the darkness with him.

And the mask...

Oh, the mask. It's a fitted skull, sleek, matte black, bone-etched, with open eye sockets that reveal *everything and nothing* all at once. His eyes don't burn. They freeze.

The mask doesn't look store-bought. It looks like it was *designed for him* and the kind of fear it inspires is deliberate.

He stands over his victim now, calm as a still lake before a storm. No monologue. No flair.

Just a final moment.

The guy in the chair sputters something, probably begging, but I'm too far away to catch the words. Mr. Floss cocks his head, almost curious, then delivers a clean, efficient slice to the carotid. No sound. Just the immediate bloom of red.

The man jerks once. Twice. Then slumps.

Every movement he makes looks calculated. Efficient. My internal voice immediately says, "Beautiful." Which is a really weird thing to think about, a man slicing open someone's throat, but here we are. His mask should be terrifying, and it is, but it's the eyes that get me. They're Cold. Unblinking. Not dead... just emptied out, like there's no soul left behind them. And still somehow...

Nope. Nope. Not doing this. He's not hot, Scout. You have a job to do. Focus, bitch.

He kneels in front of the body like he's praying. Reaches into a small pouch on his hip. Pulls out a ball of classic pink cotton candy and gently places it into the dead man's open mouth.

And then... he waits.

The sugar begins to dissolve, sweet strands melting into the blood on the man's tongue, then slowly sliding down the chin in sticky pink drips. The effect is... horrifying.

And again, weirdly beautiful.

It's nostalgic. It's gruesome. It's performance art for the damned.

And it's my cue.

I slip through an open window for the room next to the one my target is occupying and maneuver through the dark silently until I'm in the hallway. The soft, glowing light spills into the hallway as there is no door to the room.

I lean against the doorway, cross my arms, and say, "Pink's my favorite color, ya know" my voice light and teasing like I'm commenting on a damn bakery window.

His shoulders and back stiffen, but he doesn't turn around. The seconds seem to drag on forever. My heart is beating so loudly in my ears, he's got to be able to hear it across the room. "Please don't panic on me, please don't panic," I repeat in my mind. I *really* don't want to have to kill him or fucking run. God, I hate running. Seriously, *loathe* it.

I see the faint twitch in his fingers, and my pulse quickens.

I smile slowly. Bright. Deadly. "So... is this a private art show, or can anyone get a taste? "

SIX

DEACON

The room is silent, except for the wet, dying gasps of a man who thought the worst thing in the world was prison.

He was wrong.

Jeffrey Lorre slumps. His body twitches in its final moments as blood pools beneath him. I cut him fast, clean, and right through the throat. No theatrics. No speeches. Just me, him, and the reckoning no courtroom ever gave him.

I crouch in front of his body, pull a puff of pink cotton candy from the pouch on my hip, and press it gently between his lips.

As the fluffy sugar hits his blood and saliva, it starts to melt, trailing down his chin in sweet, sticky ribbons.

Poetic justice.

Clean work.

Quiet.

"Pink's my favorite color, ya know?"

The voice hits first. Feminine. Light. Amused.

Not afraid. Not panicked.

And that alone makes her dangerous.

"So... is this a private art show, or can anyone get a taste?" she continues.

I don't turn right away. People don't interrupt me. Not here. Not mid-scene.

They run. They scream. They die. End of Story.

But she doesn't sound like she plans to do any of the three.

I straighten slowly, keeping my hands loose, my movements deliberate. Turning toward the sound, I finally get a look at the source.

And stop cold.

It's *her*.

It's the sorority girl from the cafe. Small. Pretty. Confident in a way that says she either knows something I don't or is just reckless enough not to care. Hood up. Boots planted. That smirk on her full lips looks like it comes with a warning label.

And for the first time in a long time... I'm not sure I'm the most dangerous thing in the room.

She's standing just inside the doorway, smirking like she's walked in on something mildly inappropriate but wildly entertaining.

My mind races. What the fuck is she doing here? Of all places, of all times.

My jaw locks, my blade steady in my grip. "You lost?" The words escape through clenched teeth, flat and cold as the steel in my hand. Her presence here, in this space, in this instant, goes against everything I know.

She tilts her head, mock-sweet. "You don't really look like the type to give directions."

"You don't really look like the type to need them," I grumble.

She grins wider at that. "Flattery won't save you. But keep going," she winks, "I like your voice."

"I like being alone," I reply, voice cool. "You're interrupting."

She shrugs, lifting her hand as if to inspect her nails. "I tend to do that."

There's a beat of silence. She removes her hood as she takes a few steps into the room, far too casual for someone walking into a crime scene.

"You got a name?" I ask, a slight tinge of a growl in my voice.

"The Stitcher." She says in a low whisper.

That stops me cold.

I don't flinch, but internally, every alarm I keep buried goes off at once.

The Stitcher.

Fuck.

The name hits like a bullet between the ribs. Not some street whisper or criminal folklore. She's a goddamn ghost story serial killers tell each other in the dark. The kind of legend you hear about third-hand because no one who meets her lives to tell you about it.

And she's fucking real. Standing right in front of me. Breathing. Smirking. Not a myth or a boogeyman story traded in the shadows, but actual flesh and blood.

Does that mean The Hollow is real, too? That it's not just whispers. Not just rumors designed to keep killers looking over their shoulder. *Fuck.* The society of shadows. The elite vigilante force that exists in nightmares. Killers who kill killers, leaving nothing but artful signatures and unanswered questions.

The implication of her presence crashes through me like ice water. If she's real, they're all real. And I've been operating in their world this entire time, thinking I'm invisible, while I was probably being watched.

This maniacal pixie with death in her smile looks at me like I'm one bad move away from becoming her next canvas. Like my blood would look perfect threaded through her sharp needle.

I keep my tone even. Controlled. Because when death comes wearing sunshine, you don't show fear.

"Cute name."

Her eyes flash like amber caught in sunlight, head cocked to one side. "I get that a lot."

I notice the curve of her smile, the subtle tension in her shoulders, and the way she's looking at me. She's cataloging me, too. The way my fingers rest near my pocket, how my feet shift slightly in case I need to move quickly. We're two predators sizing each other up across a kill site.

"Should I be concerned?" I ask.

A soft laugh bubbles from her throat as she closes the distance between us, the metallic scent of blood and sugar drifting into my space. "Not today. If I wanted you dead, I wouldn't have asked for a taste."

"That's... reassuring." The words scrape out. I'm not sure if I believe her.

"Isn't it, though?" Her laugh ripples through the silence.

My right foot slides back half an inch to lower my center of gravity. Not just in fear, more in preparation. I've survived this long by respecting dangerous things, not running from them.

"I've heard of you," I admit.

"Oh?" Her brows lift, eyes widening with practiced innocence that doesn't match the blood spatter on her boots. "Tell me, what have you heard?"

My tongue weighs heavily as I search for words that won't get me killed. "That you leave a mark. A very... specific one."

"What can I say? Sometimes a girl needs to make an impression." Her smile breaks across her face like dawn, bright and jarring against the cooling corpse between us, the copper tang of death hanging in the air.

"Is this... a warning?" I ask carefully as my fingers flex around the hilt of my blade. The last thing I need is to become a hunted man with The Hollow's shadow stretching behind me. Those kinds of ghosts don't stop until you're in the ground.

Her full lips purse as she presses a pink-tipped finger against them, eyes rolling upward as if in an overdramatic thought. "No. Just... an introduction."

"To what?" My weight shifts, shoulders dropping a fraction, a careful performance of ease that feels anything but.

"To a very exclusive network with excellent taste and a strict membership policy." The words float between us like she's discussing weekend brunch reservations, not standing over a cooling body.

"Ah. So you're networking." My voice falls flat as concrete.

"Exactly," sunshine breaks across her face again. "Murder, meet-cute, same vibe."

My eyes narrow to slits. "You recruit for them?"

Her grin transforms, she's all teeth now, sharp enough to draw blood. "Sometimes. When I find someone worth watching."

My gaze drops to the dead man's face, where the cotton candy dissolves into something grotesque. The sticky pink rivers carve paths through congealing blood down his slack jaw.

I see her move from the corner of my eye as she starts to circle me slowly, boots tapping lightly on the concrete. She stops once she's right in front of me, standing barely up to my chest. And then, like she has the right, she steps closer.

Too close.

I brace. My shoulders tense, muscles flex, but not from fear, from instinct.

Then her scent hits me.

It's not floral. Not sweet. Not musky. It's clean. Sharp citrus. And something warm. Like the first rays of sunshine after a summer rain.

Something that conflicts with a room full of blood and death.

She tilts her head. Her haunting amber eyes sparkle with amusement as she flashes that goddamn sunbeam from hell smile and nods toward the skull mask covering most of my face.

"Nice mask," she says lightly. "It's very 'don't talk to me unless you want to die.' Love that for you."

The sleek black card appears between her fingers, materializing from her hoodie pocket. No name graces its surface, just a faint embossed symbol I don't recognize. My eyes fix on it, something in my chest tightening at what it represents.

She holds it between us, her fingers handling the card with the same careful attention someone would give a live grenade. The fluorescent lights catch on her polished nails as they hover in the space separating us.

I remain rooted to the spot.

Every instinct screams to back away, create distance, but my boots might as well be cemented to the floor. She radiates heat like a small sun, her presence cuts through the room's chill like a blade.

She closes the gap, invading my space, her face tilting upward until her breath warms the exposed skin below my mask, her whisper curling behind my ear like cigarette smoke in a dark room.

"We should totally do this again sometime. Next time, you bring the victim, I'll bring the snacks." The words slide from her lips, husky and honeyed.

Not a request. Not even flirtation. It's a challenge wrapped in barbed wire and sprinkled with glitter.

I watch as she turns and slips out into the hallway, boots never betraying her movements, hoodie catching the low light like a spotlight following a girl who just set fire to the stage and vanished into the wings.

And then she's gone.

I stand there. Frozen. Silent.

One breath. Two.

Blood splatters onto concrete in a slow, steady rhythm, nature's metronome counting the seconds.

My fingers tighten around the card, as if it might disappear.

I just met the Stitcher and walked away breathing. She's got the kind of beauty and lethal grace that belongs on something with claws. The way a tiger is beautiful, right before it tears your throat out.

She could've sliced open my throat. She didn't.

Worse, she really saw me.

And I just stood there and let her.

I stare at the card, its edges digging into my palm.

It burns like a hex between my fingers.

"Let's do this again sometime..."

That's not an invitation. That's a bullet with lipstick on it.

And I hate the way my pulse quickens at the thought.

I stand over the corpse, watching pink sugar dissolve into crimson-soaked fabric, the cotton candy collapsing like a sweet, grotesque snow melting on hot pavement. And all I can think is:

What the fuck just happened?

My legs finally unlock. I slip out of the warehouse into the alley where night air cuts through my daze like a cold blade against skin. I tuck the card into my coat pocket, its edges scraping against my fingers, invitation or threat, I can't decide.

My phone buzzes against my thigh.

I go still.

No one has this number.

The screen glows accusingly in my palm. One new message.

THE OPERATOR

Hello, Mr. Floss.

Ice floods my veins. The contact name sits there, already saved. I never added it.

No photo. No number. Just those two words hovering on my screen.

My thumb slides across the lock screen and another message materializes before I can process the first.

THE OPERATOR

> Some things don't need to be seen to be known. The right place. The right time. 34.976177, -83.807990 – 11:15 PM.

The coordinates burn into my retinas, my heartbeat hammering against my ribcage. The message waits there like a loaded gun.

No app. No thread. No reply option.

Just *there*.

Watching. Waiting.

Tracking.

My neck prickles. I whip around, scanning the empty alley where nothing moves but my own shadow stretching across cracked concrete.

The card in my pocket feels heavier with each passing second.

The message stares up at me.

I don't know what waits at those coordinates. I don't know who or *what* will be there. But I know this: Who ever these people are?

They don't play fair.

And they don't ask twice.

SEVEN
DEACON

The road seems to end before it should.

No streetlights. No signs. Just trees and dirt and the sound of gravel crunching under my tires as I pull off onto what barely qualifies as a trail. According to my GPS, I'm less than a quarter mile from the coordinates.

According to my instincts? This feels like a trap.

Perfect place for one, too. Lake to the east. Woods in every other direction. Only one way in and one way out.

The Classic setup.

I kill the engine and step out into the cool night air, my boots sinking slightly into damp earth. Crickets hum in the distance, and a light breeze stirs the trees overhead. No human sounds. Just nature and the slow, deliberate thrum of my heartbeat.

I start walking.

I arrive over an hour early just to sweep the area. Nothing but squirrels, pine needles, and the growing certainty that I've lost my mind.

No movement. No hidden snipers. No red dots dancing on my chest.

Just me... waiting.

Five minutes before I'm supposed to be here, I approach the center point of the coordinates. My hands are steady. My mind isn't. Every nerve is braced, every muscle tight. And still, I walk forward.

They're already there.

She's hard to miss.

The Stitcher stands at ease, leaning against a moss-covered boulder like she's at a tailgate party. Fitted jeans hug the curve of her hips. A glitter belt shining under the moonlight. A cropped white tank clings to her curves with the phrase "Too Sweet to Die, Too Sharp to Bleed" stitched across it in pink thread. Her curls are wild and bouncing in the breeze, giving her an almost innocent look that doesn't match her reputation.

She's smiling, of course.

And beside her?

A man straight out of a gothic novel. Dark hair. He's wearing a tailored, dark coat. His hands are folded behind his back like he's waiting for something beneath his dignity to interrupt him. There's a grace to him that feels older than he appears.

His phone buzzes once. He checks it. Nods. But he still doesn't say a word.

I approach, slowly, carefully, the black card pinched between two fingers.

"I'm assuming this is where I turn in my homework," I say flatly as I raise my hand holding the card.

The Stitcher grins. "Only if it doesn't self-destruct in five seconds." She looks at her hand and starts counting off those seconds.

As if on cue, the card *flares*, no flames, no spark, just a hiss of heat and a soft whisper of disintegration as it crumbles to fine gray ash in my hand.

I blink in disbelief. What. The. Fuck.

"That part's my favorite," The Stitcher says with a gleam in her eye. "It's soooo dramatic."

Before I can ask *how*, the man beside her steps forward.

"Mister Floss," he says smoothly, a crisp British accent making it sound like a greeting *and* a judgment. "Or would you prefer... *Mister Thorne?*"

I stiffen. They know my name.

Of course, he's British. Only someone with that level of poise and passive condescension could make a serial killer's name sound like a punchline served with afternoon tea.

My teeth clench. I don't answer. He already knows it all anyway.

He continues, "My name is Lucien Hale. My family founded The Hollow."

Of course they did.

He gestures for me to come forward, not close, but present.

"We find those who hunt monsters. Not because we stop them... but because we are them. Controlled. Precise. Effective."

"Sexy," The Stitcher adds with a saucy wink.

Lucien lets out a small huff before continuing. "The Hollow doesn't recruit randomly. We watch. We listen. We wait."

"You passed the vibe check," The Stitcher says, twirling a curl around her finger.

"You've been vetted," Lucien continues. "Not just for skill, but for discipline. You kill with true purpose. That's rare for our kind."

"Why now?" I ask. My voice is low and flat.

Lucien's expression doesn't shift. "Because we believe you're ready to stop working alone. You have a choice."

"Choose right, and you get a family full of sarcastic psychopaths," The Stitcher chimes in. Her amber eyes flash as she rocks on her heels. "Choose wrong, and you still get to live. Probably. Maybe." She throws me an exaggerated wink, her lashes fluttering dramatically in a way that leaves me unsure whether it's a promise or a threat.

Lucien rolls his eyes but continues, tone level but weighted.

"Should you choose to join, you gain more than a code to follow. You gain resources. Support. Infrastructure."

He glances toward me, probably reading every flicker of doubt I'm trying not to let show.

"You'll have access to our encrypted database. It's what we call *The Index*. It's where our intel is collected, vetted, and updated by operatives across the world. Backgrounds. Patterns. Movement. You'll never hunt blind again."

He pauses as if to gauge my reaction.

"You'll also have the support of *The Operator*, our technical overseer. He handles digital security, communications, surveillance, and if needed, deletion."

The Stitcher leans in just slightly, eyes bright.

"He's the reason your phone didn't explode when that card disintegrated."

Lucien doesn't even pause.

"In addition to intel and infrastructure, you'll receive: financial assistance for essentials, safehouses in multiple regions, identity protection, and, should you choose it, a permanent residence at the Hollow estate."

"This place," The Stitcher sweeps her arm through the air like a demented tour guide, her eyes sparkling with mischief, "is basically a homicidal academy with fabulous snacks."

Lucien gives her a sidelong glance. She shrugs unapologetically.

"We offer sanctuary," Lucien continues, "not only from the law, but from those who would prey on us. We've built a network of support to ensure you can do your work without fear of exposure, retaliation, or interference."

"Also," The Stitcher adds, "there's laundry service. Which is a lifesaver when you're out here soaking shirts in sin every weekend."

Lucien's shoulders never shift as his gaze remains fixed on mine.

"You'll have direct access to encrypted transportation options. Medical care, if needed. Custom tools, weapons, and gear as assignments require."

"Oh, and birthday cupcakes," The Stitcher says brightly, pressing her palm against her chest. Her amber eyes widen with sincerity. "Not a lie. I make them myself."

Lucien's lips twitch at the corners, the ghost of amusement flickering across his otherwise stoic face as he gives the slightest nod toward her.

"What we offer is freedom. Structure. Protection. And the one thing none of us had when we started this alone was certainty. If you accept, you won't have to fight in the dark anymore."

I glance between them. "And if I say no?"

Lucien answers simply. "Then you walk away. No pursuit. No threat. Unless, of course, your path deviates."

The Stitcher's smile turns razor-sharp as she leans forward, amber eyes glittering. "Which is code for: 'don't start killing kids or nuns and we won't have to gut you later,'" she chirps, twirling a curl around her finger.

Lucien gives her a look and a slow, chastising shake of his head. She just smiles wider.

"Should you choose to join," he says, returning to me, "The Stitcher will serve as your probationary partner. She'll train you in our systems, protocols, and expectations. You'll work on assignments together, under surveillance."

I inhale slowly through my nose. My jaw locks.

Their eyes bore into me, waiting.

The offer hangs in the air between us while I digest each piece.

Intel. Gear. Protection. Housing. Custom weapons. Fucking cupcakes?

It's a hell of a pitch.

On paper, it sounds like a dream gig, assuming your dream involves arterial spray on your shoes, leverage over your darkest secrets, and a five-foot-two chatterbox with death in her eyes watching your every move.

I glance at Lucien again. He's a statue of composure. Refined. Polished. Powerful in that *old money, old pain* sort of way. Nothing in his delivery felt forced. Nothing about this feels like a trap.

But then again, most traps don't.

I shift my weight slightly, eyes flicking from Lucien to the unshakable grin the Stitcher's still wearing like it's part of her outfit.

This is insane, I think, even *for me.*

But my life hasn't exactly been built on stability and well-adjusted choices. I kill pedophiles and feed their corpses cotton candy. I don't exactly qualify for a 401(k), not that I actually need it.

Still...

"What's the catch?" I ask.

Lucien's expression doesn't change. But there's something in his eyes, something distant. Wounded. Old.

He exhales slowly, and the weight behind it feels heavier than anything he's said yet.

"There is no catch," he says. "Only purpose. The world is full of monsters, Mr. Thorne. We simply remove the ones no one else will."

His voice remains steady, but his eyes betray him; something flickers behind them, a shadow that passes like a storm cloud over still water.

And just like that, I get it.

Not the whole picture. But a glimpse. Just enough to see the truth beneath the tailored suit, the sprawling estate, and the impeccable manners.

He doesn't just lead this organization. Maybe something shattered him first. And instead of piecing himself back together, he forged those broken fragments into weapons.

I nod once.

The air hangs thick between us, silent and heavy with possibilities, the kind that settle into your bones and whisper that your life is about to fundamentally change. I've stood over bodies before, watched life drain from deserving eyes, but something about this moment feels more permanent than any kill I've ever made.

"When do I start?"

The Stitcher claps her hands together like she's just been handed keys to her favorite amusement park. Her eyes light up with a manic gleam that makes my instincts twitch. The chipmunk on meth starts counting her fingers dramatically, bouncing slightly on her toes as her entire tiny frame vibrates with barely contained excitement. She launches into one chaotic breath, words tumbling out in a rapid-fire stream that makes me wonder if she's ever heard of punctuation or if she just considers breathing a waste of valuable talking time. Her curls seem to dance around her face with each animated gesture, a physical manifestation of the hurricane of energy contained in her petite frame.

"Great! So... first things first, we're taking your car, obviously. I'm DJ'ing. If you drive like a psychopath, I will stab you. Two, we swing by your place so you can pack an 'I'm-joining-a-secret-society-of-murderers' bag. Three, we go to the mansion. Four, we check in with The Operator so he can digitally scrub your tragic little trail. Five, we get your blood-work and baseline psych profile, don't worry though, I already told them you're broody, emotionally constipated, and murder-curious." She fans out all five fingers and wiggles them, gracing me with a smile that promises homicide wrapped in cotton candy.

Lucien doesn't react.

I stare at her.

She beams up at me with a smile that's all teeth and bad intentions.

"Do you have any questions, Mr. Thorne?" Lucien asks.

"...Yeah," I grunt. "Does she come with a muzzle?"

"Nope," she fires back, deadpan and chipper. "But don't worry. You'll get used to it."

Fuck my life... What in the actual fuck have I gotten myself into?

I rub my fingers against my temple, already regretting every life decision that led me to the homicidal chatterbox in front of me.

"Do you *have* to ride with me?" I growl.

She tilts her head, curls bouncing like she's about to recite something cute, and instead drops, "Obviously. How else am I supposed to keep you company so you don't murder anyone just because you're lonely and under-caffeinated, and insult your driving in real time?"

My gaze locks onto her, words frozen in my throat.

Her grin stretches impossibly wider, dimples deepening like twin knife wounds.

The reality settles over me like a shroud. Her presence in my passenger seat is non-negotiable.

Lucien gives us both a nod and disappears back into the trees like he was never here at all.

And just like that, it hits me that whatever twisted nightmare I've stumbled into?

I'm already in it.

Balls deep. And the unhinged cupcake of chaos is calling shotgun.

EIGHT

SCOUT

I f I ever have to sit through another hour of absolute silence while a man aggressively grips the steering wheel like it insulted his dead grandmother, I might spontaneously combust.

Like seriously! I asked him questions, *normal* questions. Favorite color? Preferred brand of murder weapon? Go-to midnight snack? You know, the essentials.

And what did I get?

One-word answers. A grunt. Maybe two glances... *maybe.*

This man spent the entire ride looking like he was mentally filing a restraining order against small talk and human connection. But sure, let's pretend *I'm* the unhinged one.

By the time we pull through the gates of the Hollow mansion, I've had to physically stop myself from adjusting the radio ten times just to provoke him. I never *actually* said I'd smack him with a pink cupcake pillow until he spoke, but let's just say the energy was there.

We park in the long circular driveway in front of the estate, an old Southern monstrosity that gives *antebellum elegance meets serial killer sleepaway camp* energy. Ivy calls it "Southern Gothic chic." It's the Murder Mansion I call home.

Deacon climbs out, takes one long look at the mansion, and mutters something low. Probably about the number of columns. Or maybe about the fact that it's still standing, just like his emotional walls. I'm so going to break those.

I don't give him time to hang around.

"Come on, Candy Man," I say, as I walk toward the main doors. "Time to meet the Operator who can make your sad digital footprint disappear faster than your sense of humor."

He doesn't answer, but I hear the heavy footfalls behind me. At least he listens.

We step into the front hall, vaulted ceilings, warm wood paneling, a grand staircase, and just enough moody lighting to make you wonder if it's ambiance or a warning.

It's silent down the hallway as we make our way to Roman's control suite. The blue lights of his monitors spill into the corridor from under the door, creating an eerie glow on the floor. The ambient electronic hum grows louder with each step. Roman's digital kingdom awaits. I press my thumb against the glowing green panel next to the door frame, feeling the slight warmth as it reads my print. A soft ding confirms my identity, and the reinforced door slides open with a pneumatic hiss, revealing a cave of blinking lights and screens that would make the Pentagon's security team weep with envy. Roman sits at his desk typing. He doesn't turn from his screen as he says, "Evening, Scout." He glances down at his watch, the blue light catching the angular lines of his face. "Or should I say 'Morning'," he says smoothly, his fingers still dancing across the keyboard. "Took you long enough. Did you throw him out of the moving vehicle?"

"Not yet," I say. "But I've got six scenic cliffs mapped out with my name scrawled all over them just in case."

Deacon's steel gray eyes slide from Roman to me, a flicker of recognition crossing his face.

"Scout," he says, each letter dragging through his teeth like he's testing the flavor. "So that's your name."

My lips curl into a sideways smile, sweet with venom. "All you had to do was ask, Candy Man. Not my fault you've been playing the strong, silent type."

Roman swivels his chair toward us, his athletic frame unfolding with easy grace, projecting the quiet confidence of someone completely in control of his domain.

"Mr. Floss," he nods, the blue screen light casting shadows across his smirk. "Welcome to the black hole," he says as he turns back to his monitors.

"You're the Operator," Deacon says, his eyes narrowing to slits, tension radiating from his shoulders. "The one behind the messages."

"Guilty as charged," Roman replies, fingers already dancing across his keyboard, pulling up a fresh screen. "Now let's see just how deeply your digital roots go before we yank them out."

"You don't have everything on me already? Seems like you already know a lot," Deacon says.

Roman replies, "We have some, but I don't start digging to remove everything until it's worth my time to do so."

Turns out? The man's a ghost.

Roman pulls Deacon's online records in about ten seconds. It's not impressive; it's *frighteningly* sparse, which impresses Roman.

Roman's fingers tap across the keyboard as the scent of rich chocolate wafts through the air from his mug. His eyes narrow at the screen, the blue glow illuminating his furrowed brow.

"Well, you really are a ghost," he mutters, never breaking his rhythm as he types one-handed and lifts the steaming hot chocolate to his lips. The sweet aroma curls around us. "Even your burner phones have burner phones."

I perch myself on the edge of one desk, swinging my legs back and forth like a kid waiting for ice cream. The gentle thump of my heels against the metal cabinet fills the silence.

Deacon looms like a statue, his steel eyes tracking Roman's every movement. His jaw tightens with each click of the keyboard.

Every time his mouth opens with another question, each one short and dripping with distrust, I pounce before Roman can breathe.

"What's that for?" Deacon nods at the screen.

"Surveillance scrubbing. A.K.A. the digital lobotomy." My laugh bounces off the walls.

Roman's eyes roll toward the ceiling, but his fingers never pause.

"Why do I need biometric keys?"

"So you can open the door..." I wiggle my fingers in mock jazz hands, "Duh."

"Is this really necessary?" The muscle in his jaw twitches.

"Only if you want to live, Candy Man. Which, based on your life choices so far," I tap my chin thoughtfully, "seems questionable." My wink earns me a look that could melt steel.

Deacon's shoulders slump a fraction. He turns to Roman, exhaustion etched in the lines around his mouth.

"Is she always like this?"

Roman never looks up from his screen. "Not at all. Sometimes she's worse."

I purse my lips and blow Deacon a kiss, complete with a soft *mwah* sound effect.

Roman hands a pile of gear to Deacon and says, "You're officially plugged in. I've loaded up all contacts within the Hollow. Call anytime you need anything, and please, try not to break anything." His eyes drill directly into me for that last part.

"No promises, App Daddy." My laugh echoes as I slide off his desk, my shoes hitting the floor with a soft thud.

"Let's go, Candy Killer." I brush past him, my fingertip grazing the solid curve of his bicep. His expression hardens into something between annoyance and disbelief. Oh yeah, he's totally starting to warm up to me, I can practically feel his ice wall cracking beneath my fingertips. He follows me out of Roman's office. Our footsteps echo on the creaky floors as we walk through the hallway lined with ancient oil paintings whose eyes seem to follow our movement. The air smells like old wood and secrets. I begin walking up the stairs, "There are several bedrooms up here, complete with private bathrooms."

At the second-floor landing, I nod to the left, flashing a black key card similar to the one that disintegrated in his hand earlier.

"Your room's here. Right across from mine." My lips curl into a smile. "Convenient, right?"

Deacon's steel eyes narrow. "Convenient for what?"

"For yelling insults across the hall, duh." I toss him a wink that practically sparkles in the dim hallway light.

His face remains carved from stone.

God, I just love a challenge. I tap the card against the lock on his door, and it makes a small click as it unlocks. I hand him the card and say, "This is yours and it won't explode, in case you were wondering."

He drops his new stuff on his bed, and I take him on a quick tour because it's late and I'm tired. The Hollow's mansion is massive, equal parts historic charm and mayhem. I move fast. Deacon follows silently. Still broody. Still suspicious.

He doesn't ask questions, just keeps those haunted eyes scanning every detail like he's memorizing the blueprint in case he has to burn it down later.

Smart boy.

We pass the parlor, the library, and the kitchen because he needs to know where to get coffee. I'd hate to see what he's like in the morning uncaffeinated.

"And this," I gesture with a theatrical flourish as we enter the common room, "is Tank."

Brayden's overly spoiled English bulldog sprawls across the Persian rug like a sentient meatloaf. Between his jowls dangle the mangled remains of... my heart sinks. The last surviving piece of my bunny slipper.

"You're a monster," I whisper, my eyes narrowing at the slobbering beast, "A soggy, unapologetic monster."

Tank's nostrils flare with a wet, rumbling snort. He doesn't even blink, just stares back with those bulging eyes.

Deacon's gaze shifts between us, one eyebrow arching upward. "What's the deal with that?"

"I can't talk about it right now, I'm still devastated." My palm shoots up, blocking any further discussion.

Tank's jowls vibrate with a possessive growl around the formerly fluffy pink fabric, his wrinkled face somehow radiating smug satisfaction.

My fingers twitch at my sides as I drag my gaze from Tank's smug expression, my mind already cataloging the locations of his favorite toys, perfect casualties for my revenge. The pink fluff hanging from his jowls might as well be a declaration of war. I force myself to move before the mental blueprint of his destruction becomes too tempting to resist.

I take Deacon back outside to grab his things from the trunk of his car. There isn't much to carry in because the man packs like a serial killer on the run, which is fair.

I trail behind him as we walk back to his room, watching his shoulders tense with each step. "So... how are you handling this all?" My voice softens, the usual sparkle dimming just enough to show I'm actually concerned.

His shoulders rise and fall with a deep breath before he grunts. But answers, "It's a lot."

My teeth clamp down on my inner cheek to keep from rolling my eyes. The man gives me three words when I finally ask something genuine.

Fuck it. I'm not giving up yet. "Favorite candy?" I ask, my gaze drilling into the back of his head as if I could telepathically extract more syllables.

Nothing but the sound of his boots against the floor.

I huff, air blowing my curls off my forehead. "Okay, but like, you've *definitely* fantasized about stabbing someone while eating Sour Patch Kids, right?"

His stride falters. A muscle in his jaw twitches.

When we arrive back at his door, I lean against the frame, my hip cocked to one side.

I let out a soft yawn, my eyelids growing heavy. "Alright, Mr. Floss, I'm off to sleep. But I'll come by in the morning and show you how everything else works."

"It's Deacon," he mutters, the words barely escaping his lips.

My lips stretch into a wide grin, heart skipping. Victory blooms warm in my chest. Internal fist pump. Breakthrough!

"Deacon," I repeat, my voice wrapping around his name with unexpected softness. "Try not to miss me too much."

I slip into my room before he can respond, the door clicking shut behind me.

My fingers trace over tonight's pajamas, a matching short set in soft pink with little embroidered knives and cupcakes dancing across the fabric. Ivy's birthday gift. God, she totally gets me.

Cold water splashes against my face, minty foam swirls down the drain, and my curls spring into a ridiculous puff on top of my head. The mattress groans under my weight as I belly flop with a dramatic sigh. Tank may have torn my slipper to shreds, but my electric blanket hums to life beneath me, and an unopened pack of peach rings waits on my nightstand.

It's the little things.

My fingers instinctively dance across my phone screen, finding Deacon's contact, already uploaded courtesy of Roman's efficiency. I tap his name, pausing only to make one tiny adjustment to his contact info that's just for me.

> ME
>
> Soooooo... How's the serial killer suite?
>
> Smell like polished trauma and oak?
>
> You still brooding in the dark?
>
> Or did you crack a smile yet and die immediately after?

The little "delivered" turns to "read" beneath my barrage. Three dots appear, vanish, and appear again. My breath catches in my throat.

> CANDY KILLER
>
> Still brooding. Smells like guilt and mahogany.

My heart flutters against my ribs. *Oh my god, he actually has a sense of humor buried under all that brooding. Thank fuck.*

> ME
>
> Guilt and Mahogany is my favorite cologne. Very "I have a tragic backstory and a 3-step skincare routine."

> CANDY KILLER
>
> I regret responding.

> ME
>
> No, you don't. You love me already.

> Also, I saw the way you looked at me when you walked up in the woods. You were either impressed... Or just planning my murder. Either way: mood. 🫠

My thumb hovers over the screen, waiting.

CANDY KILLER

> Go to bed, stab-happy cupcake.

A laugh bubbles up and escapes my lips before I can stop it, echoing in my empty room. Great. The brooding serial killer is actually funny. Just what I needed to complicate my perfectly chaotic life. Classic Scout, find the most emotionally unavailable man in a hundred-mile radius and decide he's interesting. Fuck it. I'm enjoying this.

My cheeks ache from smiling as I drift off to sleep.

NINE

DEACON

I've been awake since 5:03 AM.

Not because of nightmares. Not because I'm restless. Because I'm in a new place, and in my experience, *new places get you killed.*

For the last three hours, I've traced every exit route, cataloged each distinct creak as footsteps pass my door.

This place is safe. I know that. Still doesn't mean I trust it.

My legs itch to escape for a morning run when a *bang* rattles my door.

Then another.

And another.

Not a knock, it's an invasion into my solitude.

I slide from the mattress, the hardwood is shockingly cold against my bare soles, and pull my knife from under my pillow. I tuck it into the back of my blue flannel pajama pants, just in case. I move to the door and open it.

There she is.

Scout. The Stitcher.

A hurricane compressed into human form, wearing pajamas covered in cupcakes and knives. Her curls explode outward in a wild halo, tangled and rebellious from sleep. Her eyes burn with the promise of violence, molten amber that should terrify me but somehow looks stunning instead.

This is not the sunshine-and-sparkles menace who cornered me in that warehouse last night. I expected the relentless chatter, the flirtatious barbs, the calculated chaos. Not this sleep-deprived gremlin with violence in her eyes.

She is, in a word, feral.

I lean against the doorframe, my lips curling up at the corners.

"Well damn," I murmur. "Did I miss the apocalypse, or is this just your natural morning glow?"

Her eyes shrink to amber slits, daggers of pure spite glinting behind heavy lids.

"You *were* going to get coffee," she snaps, irritation oozing from her voice, "but now I hope your soul shrivels into dust before you get any caffeine in your system."

A low chuckle escapes before I can trap it.

Something about the way she stomps around, that feral energy in those ridiculous cupcake-and-knife pajamas, tugs at something I thought had died years ago. She's feisty. I like it.

I snag the black tee from the chair beside me, the fabric cool against my skin as I pull it over my head, then trail after her thundering footsteps without comment.

The mansion breathes around us, the early morning is calm and quiet except for the rich aroma of coffee and the gentle tink-tink of metal against ceramic floating up from below.

A woman has already claimed her territory at the kitchen table, dressed like she murdered her way through a 1950s noir film and kept the wardrobe as trophies. Her long black hair falls over her shoulders in waves. She's holding a white coffee mug that declares:

"Happily Ever After is a Red Flag."

She looks up as we enter, one perfectly arched eyebrow climbing her forehead.

"Ah. So you're the new blood."

My mouth quirks at the corner. "Are you the caffeine dealer?"

Her crimson lips curl into a grin.

"Close enough. I'm Ivy. And just so we're clear," she tilts her chin toward Scout, who's decimating the creamer bottle with caffeine-deprived wrath, "she's useless before ten."

Scout's lips move against the rim of her mug, the sound a low, venomous hiss that might've been a curse or might've been *"he's not that hot,"* but I'm not gonna rise to the bait... For now.

Ivy lifts her mug to her mouth, the black wings of her eyeliner could cut glass, matching the edge in her voice.

"So," she studies me, her calculating gaze feels like she's deciding how long it would take to peel the skin from my bones, "are you the brooding kind or the silent-but-deadly type?"

"Is there a third option?" I ask, hoping my discomfort with her probing doesn't show through.

"Sure, there is." Her shoulders lift in a careless shrug. "Emotionally unavailable with an absurd jawline."

"I plead the fifth."

Her lips curl into a knowing smirk as she lifts the mug to her lips again.

Scout's spoon clangs against ceramic, clutching the handle like a lifeline as she hunches at the counter like a woman fighting vertigo.

"She doesn't achieve real speech patterns before caffeine," Ivy explains.

"Gathered that," I mutter.

Scout's eyes narrow in our direction, but the intended glare dissolves into something softer, more petulant.

"You two sound like besties," she grumbles.

"And you sound like someone tossed anger issues in a blender," Ivy fires back.

Scout's middle finger rises over her mug while her eyelids remain at half-mast.

The coffee pot feels warm against my palm as I pour the dark liquid into my cup. One sip and it hits. It's bitter, uncompromising, and midnight-black... perfection.

"Your handiwork?" I ask Ivy, motioning to my mug.

"Roman's," She gestures towards the hall. "I just threatened his life until he made it."

"So you're the one running this asylum behind the scenes."

"I'd say 'voice of sanity,'" she says, eyes gleaming, "but let's be honest, sanity's relative around here."

Scout finally slumps into a seat beside Ivy, drawing one leg up against her chest and coiling her arms around it. She looks simultaneously chilled, wrecked from last night, and ready to commit violence. The unholy trinity.

"Why are you both so awake?" she moans.

"Why are you still feral?" Ivy tosses back.

Scout lifts her mug with exaggerated slowness, tilting it to her lips for a theatrical gulp. A deep sigh escapes her afterward, as if oxygen has finally reached her bloodstream.

"Better," she murmurs. "Still homicidal. But better."

"So business as usual?" I mutter.

Her eyes narrow at me, but I catch that telltale twitch at the corner of her mouth. She's fighting a smile, unwilling to give me the satisfaction of landing a joke.

I'll take it.

Ivy reclines, legs crossed, her gaze dissecting me like I'm a specimen she's trying to classify, a potential threat, or just another broken soul Scout collected.

"You know," she says, "you're holding up better than most do on their first morning here."

"He's been haunting the house since dawn," Scout mumbles into her mug.

"I like getting a feel for where I am and making contingency plans," I say.

"You prefer your little man of mystery act," Scout counters. "It's draining."

"You're draining," I volley back, voice flat.

Her lips curl upward, victorious and wired on caffeine. The sight sends warning signals down my spine, worse than her anger ever could.

The bitter liquid warms my throat as I observe the two women, this strange morning ritual I've stumbled into.

Something about this place captivates me despite myself. Scout ricochets through space; Ivy slices through it. I'm caught in their orbit, trading barbs with one while the other watches with calculated interest.

Scout melts deeper into her chair, clutching her coffee like a lifeline. Ivy commands her space at the table, her sharp gaze pendulating between us as if monitoring two volatile chemicals that might react.

I return to my coffee, sitting back to observe them quietly. Watching usually gives me the best information for any situation. I study them. The two of them seem so different, chaos and calm. It's like they share an unspoken language that allows them to shift from sarcastic ribbing to a comfortable silence. It's a rarity I can't help but admire, like two forces of nature orbiting each other with practiced ease.

Ivy's gaze snaps back to me, catching me staring. Her eyes lock with mine, as if she knows what I've been doing while I watch them.

"So, Deacon," she says smoothly, "What's your story?"

"Which version do you want?" I ask. I'm not about to tell anyone my real story, especially not people who could kill me and not think twice.

"The one that tells me why you said yes to this place."

"Because Scout handed me a card and smiled like she'd memorized my medical records."

Scout straightens in her chair, the coffee finally hitting her system. Color returns to her cheeks as the caffeine works its magic.

"I *do* know your blood type," she says, batting her eyelashes with exaggerated innocence. "I guessed. I was right."

My eyebrow lifts as I study her face for tells.

She shrugs, the corner of her mouth quirking upward. "You just have O Negative vibes."

Ivy's laugh ripples into her coffee as she settles deeper into her chair, shoulders relaxing against the backrest.

"So you're a prepper," she says, eyes scanning me like I'm a puzzle with missing pieces. "Silent, observant, calculating. Definitely a planner."

"You make that sound like a bad thing." My fingers tighten almost imperceptibly around my mug.

"Not bad. Just..." Her gaze flickers over my face. "Hard to read."

Scout's fingertips trace lazy circles around the rim of her mug. "He brooded so hard in the car, I swear the temperature dropped ten degrees."

I grunt. "You talked enough for both of us."

"That's my job, sugarplum," she chirps, honeyed venom dripping from every syllable.

Coffee burns the back of my throat.

Ivy's expression doesn't change as she says, "You *did* not call him sugarplum."

Scout's face lights up like a child with matches. "It felt right."

"It felt criminal," I mutter, my jaw tightening until I can feel my molars grinding against each other.

Scout inches closer, her body tilting toward mine as her lips curl up at the corners, slow and deliberate. "What would *you* call me then, hmm?"

I look at her through the steam rising from my mug, the ceramic warm against my palms.

"Trouble," I breathe out.

A soft, pleased sound vibrates in her throat. "See?" She turns to Ivy, victory radiating from every pore. "He *likes* me."

"He tolerates you," Ivy counters.

"It's the same thing, but with emotional repression," Scout grins.

The kitchen dissolves into murmured words between sips from empty mugs and trailing sentences that hang in the air.

Scout's chair scrapes against the floor as she stands with an exaggerated groan, her arms reaching skyward like she's survived a battlefield rather than breakfast.

"Alright, boys and ghouls," she announces, flicking toast remnants from her sleep-rumpled pajamas, "we've got a long day of 'welcome to murder school' ahead of us, so I need at least a bra and real pants to emotionally handle it."

My eyes narrow over my coffee. "That's the most terrifying sentence I've heard today."

"Give it time, sunshine." Her lips curve into a smirk as she pivots toward the stairs, her curls bouncing with the movement.

I follow in her wake, keeping a deliberate three steps behind as Ivy's voice trails after us. "Try not to kill each other before lunch."

Scout's fingers flutter in the air, a dismissive wave without looking back. "Only emotionally, babe!"

Our footsteps fall into an uneven rhythm as we reach the second floor. The aged floorboards creak with every step. Scout's usual hurricane of energy has quieted to a gentle breeze, while I remain the still water I've always been.

We pause outside our rooms.

"So," she says, turning to face me, her amber eyes catching the morning light as they meet mine, glowing like molten honey against her sleep-flushed skin, "you survived the first breakfast. That's basically a graduation ceremony around here. Most people crack under the pressure of watching Ivy demolish four pieces of toast while explaining blood spatter patterns."

"What's the prize?" I ask, keeping my voice deliberately flat despite the unexpected warmth spreading through my chest.

"Me. Obviously." She winks with theatrical flair, fingers drumming a chaotic little rhythm against her doorknob, hips cocked to one side in that way that makes my brain short-circuit for a dangerous half-second. Her pajama shorts ride up just enough to reveal another inch of smooth thigh. "The grand prize is my continued sparkling presence and sharp wit. Limited time offer, very exclusive membership."

I arch a brow, feeling the corner of my mouth twitch. The wall I've built between myself and the world feels suddenly thinner in her presence, like she's found some invisible crack I didn't know existed.

"Lucky me," I deadpan, though there's less ice in my tone than I intended.

She grins, teeth flashing white against caramel skin, dimples appearing at the corners of her mouth like parentheses around a secret joke. Her eyes linger on mine for a beat longer than necessary, something unspoken passing between us that I'm not ready to name. But she says nothing else. Just turns and slips into her room with a graceful little pivot that somehow manages to be both innocent and devastating.

The door clicks softly shut, the sound echoing in the quiet hallway.

And the corridor falls quiet again, leaving only the lingering scent of her sleep-warm skin in the air, citrus and something uniquely her that my brain catalogs against my will. I stand there longer than I should wondering what the hell I've gotten myself into.

TEN

SCOUT

This time, I knock like a normal person.

No banging. No threats. No coffee bribery. Just two polite little taps while the words "please be naked" escape under my breath. The memory of his bare torso from this morning flashes through my mind, all sculpted muscle and smooth skin that makes my fingers itch to trace every line.

The door creaks open.

Deacon fills the doorframe, a black tee clinging to his broad shoulders, dark jeans hugging his narrow hips in ways that should be illegal. Droplets of water still cling to strands of his dark hair, and his face remains carefully unreadable, though something flickers behind those steel gray eyes.

"You didn't break my door. I'm shocked."

"Character growth," I chirp, bouncing slightly on my toes. "Also, Roman may have bet me five bucks I couldn't go a whole day without making you growl."

"You're already losing." His voice rumbles low in his chest.

"Then I'll just have to try again tomorrow," I grin up at him.

I pivot on my heel and stride down the hallway, my ears catching the soft fall of his footsteps behind me.

We duck into one of the smaller side lounges, a room with two chairs that have clearly never met each other before, a coffee table bearing years of mug rings, and Roman's pride and joy: a projector wall for Index briefings. I collapse into a chair and pull up the app with a few quick taps.

"Alright, Flossie," I slide the tablet toward him, my fingertips lingering on the edge. "Welcome to MurderGram."

"MurderGram?" he asks, his eyebrow raised.

"It's the Index!" Roman says loudly from the hallway as he walks by.

"It's MurderGram," I repeat, my smile sugary. "Just let me have this."

A sigh escapes Deacon as he sinks into the chair beside me, close enough that I catch the clean scent of his soap.

"So," I gather my wild curls into a loose puff, my fingers working through the strands as I explain, "The Index is our matchmaking service for vengeance. Every target gets vetted before being posted; some come from members, others from our informants. We dig deep. We verify the monsters. We don't kill on suspicion."

His jaw relaxes slightly as he nods. Something in his eyes softens, like it matters to him.

"All profiles are coded. We don't use real names in the open. If someone hacked this app, it would just look like a sketchy dating platform or some weird gig work. Our prey is hidden behind aliases and vague descriptors. Once you select a profile, Roman AKA the Operator sends you the full intel packet."

My finger swipes across the screen, profiles flashing by. "These douchebags are all from Chicago, which is where you and I are going. You can filter your options by area, which makes it easier for us to work together on jobs. I'm calling it 'Scout and Deacon's Excellent Adventure'."

One labeled **"Healer's Hands"** catches my eye, a surgeon whose white coat hides a predator, accusations of assault buried under hospital politics and power. My pulse quickens.

Another, **"Saint Nick,"** reveals a nonprofit director whose charitable smile doesn't match the growing list of volunteers who've vanished after working closely with him.

Then "**Coach Z**," whose wrestling mats have absorbed years of silent trauma from the young boys he's groomed and violated while everyone looked the other way.

Deacon's eyes narrow, his focus sharpening like a blade. His breathing slows as he studies each profile.

I place the tablet in his hands, our fingers brushing.

"Pick one that catches your eye. We're doing a two-for-one special, my choice and your choice. Consider it our first official partnership in the field. The Hollow likes to establish chemistry between members through shared work." I tap the screen, highlighting the profiles again. "Some teams stick with their first pairing for years. It creates a bond that's uniquely intimate when forged through this kind of work. You get to know someone differently when you're both elbow-deep in the same intestines." I wink.

His thumb slides across the screen, the blue light casting shadows across the planes of his face. The silence stretches as he concentrates on the profiles displayed on the tablet.

"That one," he finally says, tapping a profile titled **"Coach Z."**

"Oooo. What's his deal?" I ask.

"Zachary Phillips, a youth wrestling coach," Deacon reads from the tablet, "seen in the community as a saint who dedicates his life to helping young boys. Giving the illusion that he counsels and mentors them."

"And the reality?" I ask, my voice tight.

"He's psychologically manipulating and physically violating them behind closed doors," Deacon says, his voice flat but edged with restrained fury.

I nod slowly, watching the muscle in his jaw tighten.

That tracks with what I've come to know about Deacon.

"Creeps like him," Deacon continues, his voice dropping to barely above a whisper, "leave no marks. Just broken people no one believes."

The steel in his voice carries the weight of old wounds. His jaw clenches as he grips the tablet.

I gently retrieve the device, my fingers brushing his.

"Well, I'm picking Healer's Hands," I say, tapping my selection. "Four credible accusations, all from nurses. All buried by a hospital more concerned with their reputation than his victims."

"Are we taking them together?" He asks.

"Yes and no. We handle them one at a time. You'll shadow me first and see how I work. Then I watch you."

"I don't need babysitting." His shoulders stiffen.

"It's not babysitting," I say, rising from my chair as I roll my eyes. "It's... murder mentoring."

"That's worse." The corner of his mouth twitches almost imperceptibly.

"I like to think of it as professional development," I say, moving closer to him. "We all have our methods. You might even learn something."

"Like how to talk someone's ear off while they bleed out?" Deacon raises an eyebrow, but there's something lighter in his tone. It's the closest thing to playfulness I've heard from him.

"Excuse you, I'm extremely efficient." I tap the screen to send our selections to Roman. "My victims are usually too busy trying to process the fact that the bubbly sweetheart they underestimated is their grim reaper to do much talking."

"That's your strategy? Being underestimated?"

"Works every time." I flash him a smile. "You sure didn't think much of it when I saw you at the cafe. Besides, what's yours? Glowering them to death?"

He doesn't answer, but his eyes flicker with something, amusement, maybe. Hard to tell with Mr. Stoic.

"So when do we start?" he asks instead.

"We'll fly out tomorrow. Roman will send us the details via the Index. We can pick up any additional gear from him before we pack. I'll take Healer's Hands first. You can watch how I work, then we'll hit Coach Z after. We'll start investigating them once we get the files and go from there."

I stand and tuck the tablet under my arm, adjusting my crop top as it rides up slightly. "We need to get moving if you're going to be able to see everything before we head out. Murder Manor has got a whole lot of perks you need to check out."

Deacon stands as he says, "Perks at a place called Murder Manor. Let me guess, complimentary body bags?"

"Pssh, we're way more creative than that, Flossie." I wink at him and walk out into the hallway.

I LEAD Deacon through the mansion's east wing, past Lucien's prized collection of first-edition books and Roman's tech sanctuary.

"Down here is what we call the armory," I say, scanning my thumb on the digital panel beside an unmarked door. The lock disengages with a soft click. "It's not just weapons, it's everything we might need in the field."

The heavy door swings open to reveal a room that looks like a cross between a high-end spy shop and a surgical supply store. Glass cases line the walls, each meticulously organized and labeled.

Deacon's eyes widen; it's the most expression I've seen on his face yet.

"Impressive," he says, moving toward a display of knives arranged by blade type and length.

"Roman keeps everything cataloged. You check things out like a library." I tap a tablet mounted on the wall. "Scan your fingerprint here, select what you need, and it logs it to your profile."

Deacon runs his fingers over the scanner, watching as his profile appears on screen.

"Everything's untraceable," I continue. "The weapons are custom-made, with no serial numbers. The chemicals are pharmaceutical grade but sourced through shell companies."

He moves methodically through the room, examining cases of tactical gear, surveillance equipment, and what looks like an entire pharmacy's worth of medications.

"These sedatives," he says, pausing at one cabinet. "How fast-acting?"

"Depends on what you need." I join him, our shoulders nearly touching as I point to different vials. "This one works in under thirty seconds but leaves traces in the bloodstream for up to 72 hours. This one takes about two minutes but is completely undetectable after six hours."

"Useful."

"I prefer this one." I tap a small blue vial. "Tasteless, odorless, and the victim stays conscious but completely paralyzed. They feel everything I do and they can't move a muscle."

His eyes meet mine, they're dark and unreadable. "You like them to know what's happening."

It's not a question.

"I like them to understand why they're dying beneath my fingertips," I hold his gaze. "I need them to feel everything, even though it's only a fraction of what they've made others feel. Don't you?"

A moment passes between us, charged with something I can't quite name.

"Yes," he finally says.

I clear my throat and move toward another section. "Disguises are through here. We have everything from basic wigs to professional-grade prosthetics."

The disguise room is a theatrical wonderland. There are rows of wigs on mannequin heads, shelves of colored contacts, and drawers labeled with everything from "facial hair" to "scar tissue."

"Roman's the expert on this stuff," I explain, pulling open a drawer of identity documents. "He can turn you into anyone, different age, gender, ethnicity. The works."

Deacon picks up a driver's license with his photo, but a completely different name. "These are real?"

"Roman has connections at DMVs in twelve states. The IDs scan, the backgrounds check out." I shrug. "We don't cut corners here."

We continue through a room of surveillance equipment where I demonstrate our custom bugs and cameras, then to a small medical suite that could handle anything short of major surgery.

"And finally," I say, leading him down a short hallway, "Welcome to the workshop." I give my best impression of a prize girl on a game show.

The workshop looks like a cross between an art studio and a mechanical engineering lab. There are workbenches lining the walls, each equipped with specialized tools. A name plaque hangs on the wall of some of them.

"This is where we customize," I explain. "Weapons, disguises, whatever you need modified for a specific job."

I walk to my station, running my fingers over the embroidery hoops and spools of thread arranged by color. My name is engraved on a sign above the workbench. My sewing machine, a vintage Bernina, sits ready, needles organized in a leather case beside it.

"This is yours?" Deacon asks, picking up a half-finished piece of white fabric with black and crimson thread.

"Yes. It's my signature," I say, taking it from him carefully. "Everyone here has their method. Mine happens to be more artistic and takes a lot of prep."

He studies my face. "The stitching on your victims, it's not just for show."

"It's a memorial," I say quietly.

Deacon nods slowly, understanding dawning in his eyes.

"What about you?" I ask. "What's with the cotton candy?"

His jaw tightens. "Sweet things for bitter endings."

There's more to it, I can see it in the way his shoulders tense. As much as I want to dig in and see what makes him tick, I don't.

I drag Deacon away from the workshop; he's already plotting which weapons he'll need for Coach Z. The man clearly prefers blades, based on the way his fingers lingered over that custom butterfly knife.

"Come on, Candy Man. Tour's not over yet." I bounce ahead of him down the hallway, my glitter belt catching the light. "You need to see where we keep our bodies in peak murder condition."

He follows silently, but I've started to recognize the microscopic changes in his expression, the slight lift at the corner of his mouth that passes for amusement in Deacon-speak.

"Do you always narrate everything like it's a twisted real estate listing?" he asks as we round the corner.

"Only for the premium clients." I flash him a wink over my shoulder. "And honey, you're definitely premium."

I push open a set of double doors, revealing a gym that would make professional athletes weep with envy. Floor-to-ceiling windows line one wall, all bulletproof, I might add, overlooking the property's wooded acres. State-of-the-art equipment fills the space, everything from tread-mills and ellipticals to a complete weight section with machines and free weights. There's a separate area that holds yoga mats and balance equipment.

"This," I announce with a dramatic sweep of my arm, "is where we transform these killer bodies into, well, killer bodies." I grin.

Deacon steps inside, his eyes scanning the room with that calcu-lating gaze I'm starting to recognize. He doesn't just look. He's cata-loging, assessing, and filing away information.

"Nice," he says, moving toward the weight rack. His fingers brush over a set of dumbbells that go up to weights I couldn't lift if my life depended on it.

"Lucien believes physical conditioning is as important as technical skills." I hop onto a weight bench, swinging my legs. "Hard to chase down bad guys if you're winded climbing a flight of stairs."

Deacon nods, eyeing the sparring mats in the middle of the room. "You train in combat?"

"Three times a week with Brayden. He's always worried that someone bigger than me will get the upper hand." I roll my eyes as I pat the bench beside me. "I'm more scrappy street fighter with a side of 'stab first, ask questions never.'"

The corner of his mouth twitches again.

"Oh, and through those doors," I point to the glass doors on the far side of the gym, "is the pool. Olympic-sized, heated year-round. Lucien does laps every morning at five, says it clears his head."

Deacon walks to the doors, looking out at the sleek rectangular pool surrounded by tasteful landscaping. The morning sun glints off the water's surface.

"You swim?" I ask, joining him at the window.

"I used to. Competitively."

"Of course you did. With shoulders like that, you're practically screaming I'm a hot jock." The words spill out before I can contain them, and I feel warmth flooding my cheeks. Smooth, Scout. Really smooth.

He turns those steel gray eyes on me, one eyebrow slightly raised. "Hot jock, huh?"

A chime from our phones spares me from having to form a response, and I silently thank App Daddy for the divine digital intervention. I avoid Deacon's penetrating gaze as I fumble to pull my phone from my back pocket, nearly dropping it in my haste. My fingers leave nervous little smudges on the screen as I swipe up and tap The Index notification that's just appeared.

"That would be our files," I say, grateful for something practical to focus on instead of the fact that I just called him a hot jock to his face. I shift closer, but not too close, and tilt my screen toward him. "Here's how you access everything. Just tap here, then here, and voilà." I demonstrate the sequence, watching his long fingers mirror mine on his device.

His file name appears, predictably labeled with clinical efficiency:

File Name: Zellner, Marcus – Athletics Dept. (Flagged: Coach Z)

Internal Note: *"Pattern of reported misconduct involving minors. Current wrestling coach. Escaped charges due to a lack of physical evidence and community protection. Surveillance is ongoing.*

Mine pops up with sparkly font and emojis, because of course, it does.

"Mine has been 'Scout-ified,'" I explain with a small laugh, pointing to the ridiculous title that Roman has customized for me.

File Name: Gregory Stanton, MD. — 🔪 The Super Stabby Healing Adventure

Internal Note: *"Multiple internal HR complaints filed at two hospitals, all dismissed quietly. Pattern of inappropriate physical contact with nurses, medical assistants, and nursing interns under the guise of holistic 'healing therapy.' Known alias among staff: 'Dr. Healing Hands.' Believes he's untouchable due to tenure and connections."*

I spring off the weight bench, my hands fidgeting with the hem of my shirt as I look everywhere but at his steel-gray eyes. "Well, that's the grand tour," I announce, my voice a little too bright. "Any questions before we pack for tomorrow?"

Deacon looks around one last time, taking in the room that represents the culmination of years of careful planning and resources.

"Just one," he says. "How does someone like you end up in a place like this?"

The question catches me off guard. I've shown dozens of recruits around this room, but none have ever asked about me.

"Same way as you, probably," I answer, keeping my voice light. "One bad day too many."

I let his question hang between us for a moment, wondering how much of myself I want to reveal to this man I barely know but will soon trust with my life. There's something in his gaze that makes me want to tell him everything, my whole bloody history laid bare, but self-preservation kicks in.

"But that's a story for another time," I say finally, tapping my phone screen. "Preferably after several drinks and a successful kill."

He doesn't push, just nods once. I'm learning that's Deacon-speak for "understood."

"I should let you get settled in," I continue, backing toward the door. "You've got a lot to process, and we fly out tomorrow morning. Six AM sharp. Roman doesn't believe in sleeping in, even for murder trips."

"I'll be ready," he says.

"Your file has everything. The target's schedule, known associates, and vulnerabilities. Roman's thorough." I pause at the doorway. "And if you need anything else, I'm right across the hall."

Deacon's eyes meet mine, unreadable as ever. "I know where to find you."

Something in his tone sends a little shiver down my spine, not fear, something else entirely. I give him a two-finger salute and slip out of the gym, leaving him alone with his thoughts.

ELEVEN

SCOUT

I make my way through the west corridor, pausing at the tall windows that line the hallway. The afternoon sun bathes the grounds in honey-gold light, and I can see Tank romping through the garden, probably destroying Lucien's prized hydrangeas. That's not my problem. Brayden can get an earful later. He'll deserve it.

The familiar scent of Earl Grey and lemon reaches me before I even enter the sunroom, tea time, the most civilized part of our murderous little family's day.

I move into the glass-enclosed space with my usual dramatic flair, finding Ivy perched elegantly on the wicker settee, Roman typing away on his laptop at the bistro table, and Lucien arranging finger sandwiches and cookies on a three-tier stand.

"And how is our newest recruit settling in?" Lucien asks without looking up from his meticulous arrangement of cucumber triangles.

I flop onto the cushioned chair across from Ivy, kicking my feet over the armrest. "Just finished the grand tour. I left him to process his files and all the shiny new murder toys."

Ivy slides a cup of tea my way, already prepared with three spoons of sugar, just the way I like it. "And your impression so far?" she asks, her analytical mind clearly cataloging every detail.

"He's..." I pause, searching for the right words. "Different. He's not like our usual recruits."

"Different how?" Roman glances up from his screen, fingers still typing away on his tablet.

I take a sip of tea, buying time. "Okay, like most of our potential recruits are either too eager, like murder puppies, or they're freakin' terrified and trying to hide it. Deacon's not. He's just calm, like he's been doing this for his whole life."

"He likely has," Lucien remarks, finally joining us with the perfectly arranged tea service. "He strikes me as the type that has carried the weight of the world on his shoulders for a very long time."

Roman nods. "His digital footprint is practically nonexistent. Even for someone who's trying to stay hidden, it's impressive. Most people leave breadcrumbs without realizing it, but not him."

"What all did you find?" I ask, reaching for a sandwich.

"Nothing concerning," Roman replies. "Just nothing. Period. It's like someone went through and systematically erased him from existence. And not recently, years ago. That kind of deletion takes one of three things. A crazy amount of skill, deep government assistance, or a lot of money."

Ivy tucks a strand of hair behind her ear, her eyes narrowing slightly. "During breakfast, I noticed his hypervigilance. He catalogs the exits and analyzes threats. But he's not paranoid, he's just prepared."

"The way he moves," I add, remembering how silently he navigated the mansion hallways. "It's like watching a predator. Economical. Purposeful. And his kills reflect the same efficiency. They're clean. No unnecessary suffering. Just the removal of a threat."

Lucien sits down, crossing his legs with his usual grace.

"Unlike someone we know who turns murder into performance art," Roman quips, giving Ivy a pointed look.

She sticks her tongue out at him. "It's called having a signature, Roman. Some of us like to leave our mark."

I laugh and throw a cookie at him.

"And how does Deacon respond to your particular brand of chaos?" Lucien asks with a knowing smile.

I feel a flush creeping up my neck. "At first glance, you would think he's emotionless, but I'm starting to catch all these little tells. There's so much going on beneath the surface. Dry humor. Quick wit. He doesn't say much, but when he does..." I trail off, remembering our text exchange last night.

"She's blushing," Ivy announces to the room, a rare teasing note in her voice.

"Am not!" I protest, grabbing another sandwich to hide my face.

"The infamous Scout Prescott, flustered by our new candy man?" Roman closes his laptop, giving me his full attention now. "This I have to see."

"It's not like that," I insist. "He's just... interesting. Different."

"Different enough to make you speechless? That's a first," Lucien observes.

I roll my eyes. "Can we focus on the important stuff? Like the fact that we're flying out tomorrow to kill a child-abusing wrestling coach and a pervy Doctor?"

"Well, what's our current assessment of Mr. Thorne?" Lucien asks, ignoring my question, looking at each of us in turn.

Roman is the first to answer, "He's technically sound, security-conscious, and adapts quickly to new systems. I really have no concerns about his ability to maintain operational security."

"He seems very observant, controlled, and dangerous, but not unstable," Ivy adds. "I see no red flags in his psychological profile so far."

They all turn to me.

I sigh, setting down my teacup. "He's good. Really good. But there's more to him than the perfect killer robot routine. I just haven't figured out what yet."

Lucien nods, seemingly satisfied. "Then we proceed as planned. The first hunt is always a true test. Scout, you'll lead as discussed, and I can't say this enough, but you need to watch him carefully. Not just his skills, but his judgment and his instincts."

"And if he fails?" I ask the question hanging heavy in the air.

"Then you ensure he doesn't return," Lucien says simply. "But something tells me that won't be necessary."

I nod, suddenly feeling the weight of responsibility. I've shown dozens of potential recruits the ropes, but something about Deacon feels different, important.

"Don't worry," I say, forcing a grin. "I'll make sure the Candy Man delivers."

BACK IN MY ROOM, I flop onto my bed and stare at the ceiling, as I let out a long breath. God! What is it about Deacon Thorne that gets under my skin? I've worked with dozens of killers, some charming, some terrifying, some both, but none have made me feel so seen. Like he's looking right through my glittery facade and can see the darkness underneath.

A knock on my door jerks me from my thoughts, the sharp sound cutting through the quiet like a blade.

I jump off my bed, heart skipping as I pad across the floor to see who dared interrupt my mental spiral. I swing the door open, and my breath catches. Deacon leans against the door frame, his towering form nearly filling the entire space, those steel gray eyes looking down at me with an unreadable expression. His dark hair is more disheveled than usual, like he's been running his hands through it while thinking.

"I've got some questions," he says, voice low, the words more statement than request. No hello, no preamble, just pure Deacon efficiency as he brushes past me and walks into my room.

I try to ignore the way my pulse quickens as he steps into my personal space. "Well, hello to you, too. Please, do come in," I say to the empty doorway, shutting the door with dramatic flair. "I love it when tall, dark strangers invite themselves into my bedroom. Really saves time on the formalities."

The room suddenly feels smaller with him in it, his quiet intensity filling every corner. I return to sit on my bed, the mattress dipping beneath my weight as I cross my legs and pat the spot beside me, gesturing for him to take a seat. The invitation hangs between us, charged with something I know I'm not ready to name.

"What do you want to know?" I ask with a flirty smile, tilting my head to look up at him. My voice comes out huskier than intended, betraying the effect his presence has on me. Deacon might be all business, but I've never been good at keeping my sparkle contained, especially when I'm nervous.

Deacon remains standing, his gaze sweeps over my room, taking in the organized chaos of my space. Embroidery hoops hang on one wall in a deliberate pattern, my collection of glittery belts displayed on another. Sparkly things catch the light from my dresser top, while my black tactical gear peeks out from my half-open closet. The contradiction that is me, laid bare in decorative form.

"How many members live here?" he asks, finally settling his eyes back on me.

I bounce slightly on the mattress. "Six now, not counting you. There's Lucien, whose family, as you know, founded The Hollow. Roman, his nephew and our tech wizard, who can hack your life faster than you can say 'incognito mode.' Ivy, who's literally my soul sister and could poison you seven ways before breakfast without leaving a trace. Brayden, Tristan. And then there's little old me." I flutter my eyelashes dramatically.

He nods as he appears to process the information. His fingers tap against his thigh, once, twice, the only sign of restlessness in his otherwise still form.

"Are there other members? Working in different states or countries?"

I sigh, my smile fading slightly as I pick at a loose thread on my comforter. "Technically, no. The six of us are the 'official' Hollow members. Lucien's like the big daddy of our murder family. Roman handles operational-type stuff. The rest of us, me, Ivy, Brayden, and Tristan, we're the killers." I look up at him. "We have contacts, resources, people who help us in various ways, but they're not actual members. They don't know the full picture."

Something shifts in his expression, it's subtle, but I catch it. A slight narrowing of those steel eyes. "The Hollow," he says, voice low, "has been the rumoured boogeyman for serial killers. All that fear built by just four people? The math doesn't math, Scout."

"The Hollow's been around for generations. A lot longer than I have. There were more before," I say quietly, my usual bubbly tone subdued. "Some members died on a hunt. Some..." I trail off as I pick more aggressively at the thread until it snaps.

"Some what?" Deacon asks, his voice surprisingly gentle.

"Some lost themselves," my eyes lock with his. "They crossed lines. They started enjoying it too much, targeting people who didn't deserve it. They became the monsters they were supposed to hunt."

The silence stretches between us.

"What happens when someone loses themself?" he finally asks.

I stand up, moving to my dresser where I fiddle with a small crystal figurine, a hummingbird in mid-flight, wings crystallized in eternal motion, delicate yet powerful. The piece catches light in a way that sends rainbow patterns dancing across my wall. Ivy gave it to me on my first anniversary with The Hollow. "Small, fierce, never stops moving, and impossible to ignore," she'd said with that rare, genuine smile of hers. "Reminded me of someone."

I sigh as I respond, "Then the Hollow does what it was designed to do. We stop them from becoming what they despise most in the world."

"You kill them." Not a question.

"We do what's necessary." I turn back to face him, all traces of my usual playfulness gone. "That's the price of admission to this crazy life, Deacon. We all agreed to it when we joined. If any of us cross that line, if we become the predators instead of the hunters, we've authorized our own execution."

The weight of my words hangs in the air between us. I watch as he absorbs the information, his face unreadable, but his eyes spark with calculation.

"It's only happened twice since I've been here," I offer, my voice softer. "And as much as I hate that it came to that, they earned it. One started targeting homeless women for fun. The other one... well, let's just say you would have fed him a lot of cotton candy."

Deacon nods once, a sharp downward jerk of his chin. "Good."

The single word surprises me. Most people would be horrified, or at least concerned, to learn they're thinking of joining an organization with a kill switch policy for its members. But I guess Deacon isn't like most people.

"That's why we have the probationary period," I explain. "Why we partner newbies with veterans. It's not just about teaching you the ways of the Hollow. It's about making sure you truly understand what you're signing up for and that you're really one of us before you make the official commitment. That you can handle this life without losing your moral compass."

"Basically, you're my babysitter." The corner of his mouth twitches, almost a smile.

I grin, the tension breaking. "I prefer 'homicidal tour guide,' but sure."

TWELVE

DEACON

"Time for dinner," Scout announces, appearing at my doorway an hour later. She's changed into jean shorts and an oversized pink sweater that falls off one shoulder. The contradiction of her soft appearance against what I know she's capable of is jarring.

"Do you ever knock?" I ask, setting aside the tablet I'd been reviewing, Coach Z's file on.

"Nope." She pops the 'p' sound, leaning against my doorframe. "Knocking is for people with boundaries, and I don't believe in those. Besides, your door was open, which I know means you want me to stop by." She winks, "Now come on, Candy Man. Everyone's waiting."

I follow her down the curved staircase, watching how she trails her fingers along the banister. This house is her territory, her home, and I'm the intruder.

"Fair warning," she says over her shoulder, "family dinner can get chaotic. It's best to just roll with it."

The dining room is exactly what you'd expect in a mansion this size. The oversized table could seat twenty, a crystal chandelier, and artwork that costs more than most people make in a year. Six places are set at one end of the table.

Lucien sits at the head, the patriarch. Roman and Ivy are already seated, deep in conversation about something on Roman's tablet. The fourth person, a man I haven't met yet, looks up as we enter.

"Well, well. The infamous Mr. Floss graces us with his presence." His tone is mocking, eyes assessing me with barely concealed skepticism. Athletic build, short brown hair, sharp features. His southern drawl and posture are deceptively nonchalant, but the lethality oozes from him.

"Deacon, meet Brayden," Scout introduces with a dramatic wave of her hand. "Our resident asshole."

"Darlin, I'm the professional asshole," Brayden corrects, raising an eyebrow, "There is a difference."

"Potato, po-tah-to." Scout drops into the chair beside Lucien and gestures to the seat next to her.

I take the offered chair, as I take notice of the people sitting around this table. These people call themselves family, and I can see it's not just for show. There's something real here, a connection forged in blood and secrets. Some of the most dangerous predators sit around this table, yet they pass food and trade barbs like any normal family. Killers who've found their own, building something genuine amid the violence. It's unexpected. Contradictory. Oddly functional.

"So cotton candy, huh?" Brayden drawls, reaching for his bottle of beer with a lazy grin. "Nothin' says 'I'm a terrifying serial killer' like leavin' behind something you'd find at a county fair."

Scout's eyes narrow, but there's affection beneath her annoyance. "At least people remember it, Tooth Fairy. How's it feel knowing your badass reputation comes with the same name as a mythical creature who collects baby teeth?"

Brayden winces dramatically, laying his hand over his heart. "Low blow, Cupcake. You know damn well I didn't pick that name."

Roman snorts into his drink while Ivy presses her lips together, her shoulders quivering with suppressed laughter. My mind flashes to newspaper headlines I've seen, bodies discovered with molars missing, the Tooth Fairy's calling card leaving detectives baffled for years. This guy is a legend.

But looking at him now, this good ol' boy with his easy drawl and shit-eating grin, he's nothing like the cold-blooded monster I'd imagined. Then again, none of them are what I expected. Especially not

Scout. The notorious Stitcher, feared for her gruesome embroidery work, is this deceptively soft-looking woman whose wild curls and dimples hide the predator I know lurks beneath. It's jarring how her curves and those mischievous amber eyes can make me forget what those delicate hands are capable of.

"It's symbolic," Brayden defends, pointing his beer at Scout. "And effective. Unlike some people who need an entire arts and crafts session with their victims."

"Yeah, symbolically lame," she fires back.

"I can't even lie, I'm impressed. Out there," I motion towards the front of the manor, "people still whisper 'The Tooth Fairy,' you've got an insane body count." I try to keep the awe from creeping into my voice.

"See?" Brayden grins at Scout. "Someone 'preciates my artistry."

"Your artistry?" Scout scoffs. "You yank out teeth like a demented dentist. I create actual art."

"Darlin', I leave symbolic statements. You turn murder into some demented craft project."

"It's called staging, you amateur—"

"Children," Lucien says, his voice soft but commanding, "can we at least finish dinner before being subjected to the full extent of your bickering?"

Lucien presses a button on the edge of the table, and moments later, a server appears through a side door I hadn't noticed before. He begins bringing out plates of food. The spread is impressive: roast chicken, vegetables, potatoes, bread. Normal family dinner fare served on fine china that reminds me of life before I became Mr. Floss.

"So, Deacon," Ivy says as we begin eating, "Scout tells me you've picked your first 'date' in The Index."

I nod, cutting into my chicken. "I have. It seems straightforward enough."

"Straightforward doesn't always mean easy," Brayden warns. "Those 'easy' ones? They're the ones that'll have you diggin' bullets outta your shoulder at three in the mornin'. Trust me on that one."

I nod.

The conversation continues around the table, with everyone

discussing their "projects". It's somewhat surreal, discussing murders over dinner like they're business trips. But then, I suppose that's exactly what it is to them. To us now, I guess, maybe.

I scan the table, counting heads. Five of them. Scout mentioned six members, but only five are present. I make a mental note to ask her about the missing member later.

"We'll have the jet ready for your morning flight," Roman says, turning to me and passing over a small envelope. "Credentials, credit cards, burner phone. All untraceable."

"And I'll be your tour guide to all things murder," Scout adds cheerfully, bumping her shoulder against mine.

"Just what I always wanted, a cheerleader with deadly pom-poms," I deadpan, which earns a delighted laugh from her.

"He has a sense of humor!" she announces to the table. "Mark it down, everyone. The Candy Man made a funny."

"Careful, cupcake," Brayden warns Scout with a smirk, "he might actually keep up with you."

The rest of dinner passes with similar banter. I say little, observing instead. Lucien watches over everything with quiet authority. Roman keeps checking his phone. Ivy asks pointed questions about my background that I deflect. Brayden continues to tease pretty much everyone. And Scout, Scout fills every silence with chatter, drawing attention away from me whenever the questions get too personal.

It doesn't escape my notice that she's strategically pulling their focus whenever the questions get too personal. Using her chaos as cover for my adjustment period. Interesting. She's more calculated than she lets on.

The table goes quiet as dessert arrives, a towering chocolate creation with layers of mousse, ganache, and chocolate sprinkles. The server places one in front of Scout, and I watch as her entire demeanor changes. She goes completely still, eyes widening like a child on Christmas morning. Across the table, Roman says something to Ivy about the Glass Gardener.

"The Glass Gardener," I say, setting down my fork. "I saw that article in the paper yesterday. It's not my first time seeing that signature."

The table goes quiet. Five pairs of eyes lock onto me.

"What do you mean?" Roman asks, his casual tone betrayed by the sudden intensity in his gaze.

"I was hunting in Denver about eight months back. Stumbled across a similar scene in Centennial Gardens. The body was displayed in the center of Mirror shards, arranged like some kind of macabre garden."

Brayden leans forward. "You sure it was the same?"

"Hard to mistake." I take a sip of water, uncomfortable with the sudden attention. "The body was posed kneeling, head bowed, surrounded by broken mirrors arranged in rings. The shards were all angled to face the body and catch the light. It made the whole scene sparkle at dawn when I found it. Blood was everywhere. You could barely see any skin."

"Could you tell the kill method?" Roman's fingers hover over his tablet, ready to type.

"Honestly? It looks like death by a thousand cuts, but I would assume the killing blow was a sliced carotid. The body was the center-piece, male, mid-thirties. Whoever the Glass Gardener is, he's angry."

"That matches what was found in Freedom Park yesterday," Ivy says quietly.

"Victim information?" Brayden asks.

I shake my head. "Nothing on the news. I moved on. I had my own hunt to handle. But I remember thinking it wasn't random. The arrangement was too deliberate. Too artistic."

"Were there any markings on the body?" Roman asks, typing rapidly now.

"His chest was carved with some kind of symbol." I trace a circular pattern with my finger on the tablecloth from memory. "Similar to a sun with eight rays, but very rudimentary. I would say it was cut with one of the mirror shards."

Lucien's expression remains neutral, but his eyes sharpen. "And you saw this symbol clearly?"

"Yes. I got closer than I should have, probably. Professional curiosity."

"What about the glass?" Brayden leans in, his casual posture belying the sharp focus in his eyes. "Was it just scattered around, or did our artist friend have a method to their madness?"

"At first glance, it looked random. But when you got close to it, it felt intentional. I really didn't stay long to get anything more than that. The sun was coming up, and I did not want to be around for the early morning joggers. "

Scout, uncharacteristically quiet until now, tilts her head. "How'd you remember so many details?"

"I notice things. It's how I've stayed alive for so long." I meet her gaze. "And it was beautiful, in a disturbing way. Hard to forget."

"Did you take photos?" Roman asks.

"No. That would've been stupid."

"Ain't that the truth," Brayden agrees, leaning back in his chair. "Would've been a rookie mistake."

Lucien sets his napkin beside his plate. "Interesting that this killer has expanded territory. Denver to Atlanta is quite a leap."

"Could be a copycat," Ivy suggests.

"Not with those details," Roman counters. "The symbol Deacon described wasn't released to the press in the Denver case. I'd have to check our database, but I'm almost certain."

"You keep a database of other killers?" I ask.

"We keep track of the landscape," Lucien explains smoothly. "Knowledge has always been the most reliable form of protection."

"How do you think we knew about you?" Roman adds.

The server returns to clear our plates. Scout practically shields hers with her body, fixing the server with wide, horrified eyes.

"I'm not done with that," she protests, pulling the half-eaten dessert closer.

"My apologies, Miss Prescott," the server murmurs, backing away.

Ivy slides her barely touched dessert across the table. "Here. I'm full."

"This is why you're my favorite," Scout declares, eagerly pulling Ivy's plate toward her own.

Brayden rolls his eyes but pushes his plate toward her, too. "Take mine before you start eyeing it like a starving hyena."

"Your offering pleases the sugar goddess," Scout proclaims regally, adding his dessert to her growing collection. "Your life shall be spared."

He flashes a wink at her as the server leaves the room.

"Well now," Brayden says, his accent thickening as he settles back in his chair. "Since you've got such a good memory for details, what's your read on our glass-loving friend? One killer to another."

I consider the question. "Whoever it is, they're patient. That kind of display takes hours. They're not afraid of getting caught. They want the scene discovered, but only after they're long gone. The artistic elements suggest someone who sees killing as a creative expression, not just death."

"Like you with your cotton candy?" Scout teases, but there's no malice in it.

"Different. My signature is symbolic, a reminder. This person is creating an experience for whoever finds the body. They want a reaction."

"A performer," Lucien says thoughtfully.

"With a very specific audience in mind," I add.

Roman navigates through his tablet. "I'll cross-reference with similar cases nationwide. If they've moved once, they might have moved before.

"I want everyone to exercise additional discretion regarding this matter. There are too many... coincidences for my comfort." Lucien remarks.

Murmurs of agreement come from around the table before falling silent.

I get the distinct impression there's more to this conversation than I'm being told. These people have secrets within secrets, layers I haven't even begun to uncover.

And somehow, I've just stumbled into something bigger than I expected.

ROMAN LEAVES the dining room first, muttering about data analysis, then Lucien with a disturbingly graceful exit. Ivy slips away quietly, and Brayden announces he needs to check on Tank before bed. Their departures feel choreographed, practiced, like everything else in this house.

I remain seated, watching Scout twirl her dessert spoon between her fingers.

"So," I say when we're finally alone, "there were supposed to be six of you. Who's the missing member?"

Scout's fingers go still on the spoon. Something flickers across her face, a shadow I haven't seen before.

"Tristan." She sets the spoon down softly. "He doesn't always do family dinners, especially with new people."

"Doesn't like the new company?"

She traces a pattern on the tablecloth. "It's not personal. Tristan is extremely untrusting and protective."

"He's not a people person. I can relate."

"No, it's more than that." Scout's voice softens. "He's brilliant, like, scary brilliant. But he processes information differently. Multiple conversations, new faces, unpredictable interactions, it can sometimes overwhelm his system. He's fine once he has gotten to know you and feels like he has you figured out, but until that point, he tries to keep group interactions with new people to only when it's absolutely necessary. He and Ivy share a very tragic history. You'll meet him when he's ready, but sometimes he prefers to stay in his wing of the Manor."

"His wing?"

"East wing, third floor. Far removed from most of the bedrooms." She smiles, but it doesn't reach her eyes. "He's got an amazing workshop up there."

I study her face. "You care about him."

"I care about all of them." She fiddles with her napkin. "But yeah, I worry about Tristan. And I worry about Ivy."

"Ivy? She seems like she can take care of herself."

Scout hesitates. "She can, she's his step-sister. She's the only one he's always been completely comfortable with, but it's hard on her sometimes."

Understanding clicks into place. "That's why she seemed distracted tonight."

"It's the Anniversary of her Father's death. It made them both who they are today." A sad smile flickers across her soft lips. "It's pretty hard on Tristan."

"Did he kill him?"

"Oh god no. He watched his monster of a mother kill him. She destroyed the only person who ever truly loved him," she says, her voice dropping to barely above a whisper.

The weight of her words settles between us like a physical thing. Scout's normal sparkle has dimmed, replaced by something too close to the shadows I recognize from my own mirror. I don't like it.

"So," I clear my throat, "what's with you and sugar? Every meal I've seen, you practically mainline it."

Scout's eyes light up instantly. "Don't judge my relationship with sweets. Some people meditate. Some do yoga. I consume my body weight in sugar and choose violence."

There she is.

"Besides, Flossie, you're not exactly in a position to lecture me about my sweet tooth," she counters, leaning forward with a mischievous glint in those amber eyes.

I open my mouth to protest the nickname, but freeze as Scout picks up her spoon from her chocolate dessert, takes a bite, and closes her eyes with a soft moan that's borderline indecent. Something hot and unexpected flares in my chest. This woman is going to be the death of me.

"Careful, Stitch. You're dangerously close to making 'sweet tooth' sound like a kink." I raise an eyebrow at her, watching as she practically vibrates with glee at my observation. The way she talks about sugar is practically sinful, all breathless enthusiasm and intense devotion. It's like listening to someone describe their most intimate fantasies, except it's about caramel and chocolate. Something about her relationship with sugar feels almost voyeuristic to witness, the way she savors each bite with those little sounds of appreciation has my mind going in places I try and avoid. Not that I'm paying that much attention to how she eats. Definitely not noticing how her tongue darts out to catch stray sprinkles or how her eyes flutter closed when she takes that first bite of something particularly decadent.

Scout gasps dramatically, pressing a hand to her chest. "Did you just flirt with me? The Candy Man himself? I might need medical attention."

I feel the corner of my mouth twitch. "I'd offer CPR, but I'm afraid of what you'd do with the mouth-to-mouth part."

She throws her head back and laughs, a real laugh that seems to light her from within. "Oh my god, you do have a personality under all that brooding! This is revolutionary information."

"Don't tell anyone. I do have a reputation to maintain."

"Your secret's safe with me, Candy Man." She leans forward, elbows on the table, chin propped on her hands. "But now I'm going to spend all my time trying to bring it out of you. It's my new mission."

"Good luck with that."

"I don't need luck. I'm extremely talented." She wiggles her eyebrows. "Ask any of my victims."

"Is that before or after you sew flowers into their chest?"

"During, obviously. It's called multitasking."

The shadows have retreated from her eyes, replaced by that familiar chaotic light. Mission accomplished.

"I'm taking this with me." Scout scoops up the final dessert plate, balancing it in one hand as she stands. "We should get some sleep. Early flight tomorrow, and I still need to finish packing."

I push back from the table, noticing how the dining room's shadows have deepened while we talked. The mansion feels different at night. It's older, more secretive.

"By 'finish packing,' do you mean 'start packing'?" I ask as we leave the dining room.

"I feel personally attacked by that completely accurate statement." She licks chocolate from her spoon as we walk, leaving a trail of sprinkles behind us like breadcrumbs. "What about you? All packed and ready like the meticulous murder man you are?"

"It only takes me about five minutes to pack."

"Let me guess. One black duffel bag, precisely folded clothes, weapons hidden in false compartments?"

"Wrong. Two compartments. One for weapons, one for cotton candy." I grin as Scout nearly chokes on her dessert.

"Did you just make a joke about your murder signature? Who are you and what have you done with Mr. Floss?" She laughs.

The hallway narrows as we approach our rooms, forcing us closer together. Her shoulder occasionally brushes against my arm, each contact sending an unfamiliar jolt through my system.

"So tomorrow," she says, twirling her spoon, "Chicago. First stop is the safe house, then surveillance on Healing Hands & Coach Z, right? Figure out their routine, weaknesses, the usual?"

"I've already memorized Coach Z's schedule from Roman's file. He teaches until four, then wrestling practice until six. Home by seven except Thursdays when he stops at O'Malley's Bar."

Scout stops walking and stares at me. "You memorized all that already?"

"It's what I do."

"Impressive." She tilts her head, studying me with those amber eyes. It's unnerving the way she seems to see into the places I keep hidden. "Most people need notes or, you know, a second look."

"I'm not most people."

"No," she says softly, "you're definitely not."

We reach our doors, facing each other in the dim hallway. For a moment, neither of us moves. There's something in her expression I can't quite read, something beyond the mayhem and sugar high.

She steps back, breaking the tension. "Get some sleep, Deacon. Tomorrow we hunt together, and I need you sharp."

"I'm always sharp."

"Good." She walks backward toward the door, pointing finger guns at me. "Because I'm going to show you how The Stitcher works, and trust me, it's going to be one hell of a performance."

I watch her leave, feeling something unfamiliar stir beneath my ribs, something dangerous and alive that I thought I'd buried years ago.

THIRTEEN

SCOUT

A sharp knock rips me from a dream where I'm embroidering on clouds. I bolt upright, tangled in my chaotic nest of blankets, and nearly knock over the glass of yesterday's iced coffee on my nightstand.

"What time is it?" I mumble to my empty room, squinting at the red numbers on my alarm clock. 4:15 AM. Our flight's at six.

Another knock, more insistent this time.

"I'm coming! Ugh." I slide out of bed, my bare feet hitting the cold floor. I'm wearing my favorite sleep shorts with little cartoon devils all over them and an oversized t-shirt that reads "Stabby When Sleepy". Accurate.

I shuffle to the door, rubbing sleep from my eyes, and yank it open mid-knock.

Deacon stands there looking irritatingly perfect for this ungodly hour. His dark hair is slightly damp, like he's already showered. He's wearing a fitted black t-shirt that shows off arms that definitely didn't skip gym day and dark jeans that... Nope, not going there this early.

But it's what he's holding that makes me blink twice to make sure I'm not still dreaming.

In one hand, he's got an enormous travel mug that could double as a small bucket. In the other, a pink bakery box that can only mean one thing.

"Is that coffee?" I whisper dramatically.

"Extra large. with an insane amount of creamer." He holds it out like a peace offering. "And donuts. With sprinkles."

I take the coffee mug, inhaling the steam rising from it. "You brought me coffee AND donuts? With sprinkles?" I clutch the mug to my chest. "Are you trying to seduce me, Mr. Thorne? Because it's working."

His mouth does that almost-smile thing. "Figured you'd need motivation to get moving. Our car leaves in forty minutes."

I take a sip of the coffee and make an embarrassing sound of pleasure. "This is perfect. How did you know how I like my coffee?"

"I pay attention." He shrugs as if it's not a big deal.

Something warm that has nothing to do with the coffee spreads through my chest. "To me?"

"To everything." He opens the donut box, revealing a half dozen glazed beauties covered in pink frosting and rainbow sprinkles. "Roman said these were your favorite."

"Roman is a beautiful, beautiful man who will be rewarded in the afterlife." I grab a donut and take a massive bite, getting sprinkles everywhere. "But you," I say through a mouthful, "you might be my new favorite person."

Deacon raises an eyebrow. "Is it that easy to buy your loyalty? Coffee and sugar?"

"I'm a simple girl with simple needs." I lick frosting off my fingers. "Sparkly things, caffeine, and sugar, but not necessarily in that order."

He leans against my door frame, arms crossed, watching me devour the donut with an expression I can't quite read. His eyes linger on my mouth for a second too long before flicking away.

"Thirty-nine minutes now," he says.

"Ya know, you're very punctual for a serial killer."

"Professional courtesy."

I take another enormous gulp of coffee, feeling the caffeine hit my bloodstream like a welcome lightning bolt. "Fine, fine. I'll be ready. Just need to shower and grab my bag."

"You haven't packed yet, have you?"

I wave my donut dismissively. "Details. I work best under pressure."

"I'll wait downstairs." He says as he turns to leave.

"No!" I grab his wrist without thinking. His skin is warm under my fingers, and I feel his pulse jump. "I mean, you can wait here if you want. In case I need help deciding which knives to bring."

He looks down at my hand on his wrist, then back to my face. His eyebrow raises at me questioningly, "You want fashion advice on your murder weapons?"

"Maybe I just want the company." The words slip out before I can stop them. Oof, that's way more honest than I intended.

Something shifts in his expression, though, a softening around the eyes, a slight release of tension in his jaw.

"Fine." He moves past me into the room, careful not to touch me. "You've got thirty minutes, Scout. Not a minute more."

I salute with my coffee mug. "Sir, yes sir!"

As I dash around gathering clothes and toiletries, I'm acutely aware of his presence. He sits on the edge of my armchair, looking amusingly out of place among my explosion of color and chaos. His eyes track my movements, missing nothing.

"You know," I call from my closet where I'm digging for my favorite ripped bootcut jeans, "most guys who make it into my bedroom have very different intentions."

"I'm not most guys."

I peek around the closet door. "No, you're definitely not."

And for some reason, that feels like the most dangerous thing I've said all morning.

"Boom! Twenty-eight minutes. I win." I zip my last bag shut with a flourish, spinning around to face Deacon, who's been watching me pack with the patience of a man who's spent considerable time in surveillance positions.

He checks his watch. "Technically, you still have two minutes."

"And I'm going to use it to finish this donut." I pop the last bite in my mouth, licking the frosting from my fingertips.

Deacon's eyes follow the movement before quickly shifting away. "Is all of this necessary?" He gestures at my collection of bags, one large suitcase, a duffel, my embroidery case disguised as a vintage train case, and a sparkly backpack.

"Absolutely. A girl needs options." I pat my embroidery case. "And specialized equipment."

"We're hunting, not attending Fashion Week."

"Who says I can't do both?" I hoist my backpack over one shoulder and grab the handle of my rolling suitcase. "Besides, half of this is weaponry and supplies."

"The pink polka dot bag is tactical gear?"

"The polka dots are camouflage for the throwing knives, duh." I wink. "Nobody suspects the girl with the cute luggage."

Deacon sighs, a sound so subtle it's barely audible. He reaches for my duffel bag and embroidery case, adding them to his single black duffel.

"I can carry those," I protest halfheartedly, already knowing it's useless.

"You need a hand free for your coffee." He says it like it's the most logical conclusion in the world.

"My hero." I clutch the remaining donuts to my chest with one hand and my giant coffee mug with the other. "Saving me from the terrible fate of having to put down my breakfast."

"You're insufferable in the morning."

"Just wait until you see me on the plane. I get hyper at altitude."

The corner of his mouth twitches, not quite a smile, but something close. He shoulders both his bag and my duffel with ease, picks up my embroidery case, and heads for the door.

"After you," he says.

I roll my suitcase into the hallway, the wheels making a satisfying rumble on the hardwood floor. The house is quiet at this hour; everyone else is still asleep. Even Tank isn't up for his morning patrol.

"I hate being awake before the sun," I grumble, taking another gulp of coffee. "It's so unnatural."

"So is embroidering flowers onto men's chests while they're still alive."

I almost choke on my coffee. "Did you just make a joke, Mr. Thorne?"

"Stating facts."

"Uh-huh." I nudge him with my elbow as we reach the stairs. "I saw that little smile. You think I'm funny."

"I think you're a liability."

"A charming liability."

"A loud liability."

I lower my voice to a theatrical whisper. "Better?"

He shakes his head and starts down the stairs. I follow, trying to manage my rolling suitcase, coffee, and donut box while taking the steps. The suitcase bumps down each stair with a thunk-thunk-thunk that echoes through the quiet house.

"Stealth isn't your strong suit, is it?" Deacon asks without turning around.

"I can be stealthy when I need to be." I frown at my noisy suitcase. "This just isn't one of those times."

When we reach the bottom of the stairs, I see Roman waiting by the front door, tablet in hand. He's fully dressed despite the early hour, looking like he never sleeps.

"Good Morning, sunshine," I chirp. "Coffee?" I hold out my mug.

"No thanks, I prefer actual coffee, not liquid diabetes." He taps something on his tablet. "The car's outside, your flight's on time, and the weather looks clear."

"You're the best." I offer him the donut box. "Sprinkle?"

Roman takes one with a smile. "All information is in the app. I've loaded your cover identities in case you need them. Married couple, Emily and David Winters, you're in town visiting family."

"Married?" I wiggle my eyebrows at Deacon. "Hear that, honey? Better practice your adoring husband face."

Deacon's expression doesn't change. "I'll work on it."

Roman slides a manila envelope into Deacon's waiting hand. "The car will take you to the private airstrip. Another car will be waiting when you land." His fingers tap the packet's edge. "Keys will be inside it. The safehouse address is already loaded into your app."

I tip my coffee mug back, catching the last lukewarm drops before pressing the empty travel mug into Roman's palm. "Thanks for everything, tech wizard."

Roman nods. "Be careful out there. Both of you."

" I always am," I say, at the exact same moment Deacon says, "We will."

I flash a grin at Deacon. "See? We're already on the same wavelength. This marriage is off to such a great start."

The look he gives me could freeze fire, but I swear I see that almost-smile again.

As we head out to the waiting car, I can't help but wonder what it's going to be like spending the next few days with this brooding, dangerous man. Playing married. Hunting monsters together.

This is either going to be the best mission ever or a complete disaster.

Probably both.

THE PRIVATE JET'S engines hum beneath us as I settle into the buttery leather seat, kicking off my shoes and tucking my legs underneath me. Across the small cabin table, Deacon sits with perfect posture, scrolling through his tablet with clinical efficiency.

"You can relax, you know," I say, pulling my embroidery hoop from my bag. "Even serial killers deserve in-flight entertainment."

His eyes flick up briefly. "This is entertainment."

"Ooh, thrilling. Next, you'll tell me you read autopsy reports as bedtime stories." I arrange my threads in a neat row, blacks, reds, and a single strand of white for the signature detail. "Tell me what you think about Coach Z."

Deacon sets down his tablet. "Wrestling coach, thirty-two, single. Three accusations of inappropriate conduct from his former male wrestlers were all dismissed due to a lack of evidence or witnesses recanting."

"And what does your gut tell you?"

His jaw tightens. "He's guilty. The pattern is too consistent. The boys who recanted their stories all showed signs of intimidation."

I nod, threading my needle with black silk.

He continues, "The file shows he targets boys from unstable homes, troubled kids who need a father figure and are less likely to be believed." I start the outline of the dahlia, my needle piercing the fabric in precise, tiny stitches. "Alright, what's your plan so far?"

"I'll observe his routine, then take him during his evening workout at the high school after his last lesson of the day. The high school gym has several places with poor camera coverage."

I glance up from my embroidery. "You want to kill him at the high school gym?"

"Yes, I want to hurt him where he thought it was okay to hurt the boys." He says.

"Damn straight. There's something deeply satisfying about watching these monsters die in the same place they thought they were untouchable." My voice loses its playful edge for just a moment before I add, "Plus, easier cleanup with those gym showers, right? Practical and poetic."

I return to my embroidery and move to the intricate inner petals of the flower. "Mine will be a bit trickier. Dr. Greg Stanton, respected heart surgeon, pillar of the community, charitable foundation in his name."

"And serial predator," Deacon adds.

"Five women have come forward with claims of being drugged and assaulted after office hours. All nurses. All five were discredited. It was their word against his, or he paid them off. Plus, he's got that whole 'saving lives' thing going for him. But that doesn't account for the other four potential victims that didn't get a chance to say something."

Deacon's eyes darken. "Nine? If they didn't come forward, how do you know?"

My needle digs into the Dahlia with a satisfying puncture as I work. "There's a reason I wasn't packed this morning. I spent my time tapping our network." The silk thread slides through my fingers as I continue stitching. "Those other four victims? I'll confirm them before we take him. Two weeks gives me plenty of time to make absolutely certain before I make him bleed."

"The powerful protect their own." His voice vibrates low in his chest, the words rolling out like distant thunder.

"Which is why we exist." I hold up the embroidery hoop, examining my work. The black dahlia takes shape, each petal distinct and delicate. "He's careful, though. He doesn't leave a digital trail, only targets women who are vulnerable or can be paid off. Single mothers, women with crushing debt, and those with ill family members who have exorbitant hospital bills."

"Women who would have to weigh the option of getting justice or having a way to get their head above water financially."

"Exactly."

The flight attendant appears with two coffees, setting them on our table before discreetly retreating to the front cabin.

"My plan," I continue, sipping the fresh coffee, "is to catch him at a bar he cruises for nursing interns every week. If I play my cards right, I'll be able to get him alone."

Deacon watches my hands as I work the needle through the fabric. "You're good at that."

"What? The embroidery or the killing?"

"Both, I imagine, but I was referring to the embroidery this time."

I smile, as I reach for the red thread. "The embroidery came first. My gran taught me when I was eight. She said it would teach me patience." I tie a small knot at the end of the thread. "Turns out, she was right."

"And what about the killing?" He asks.

My fingers pause. "That came later."

He doesn't push, and I appreciate that. He asks, "What's with the dahlia?"

"Well, black dahlias symbolize betrayal and sadness." I start adding the red tips to each petal. "And of course, they're for Elizabeth Short."

His head tilts to the side as if questioning. "The Black Dahlia murder?"

I nod. "It fits. She was a beautiful young woman, that was brutally killed and discarded like garbage. Her killer was never caught." My stitches grow tighter, more deliberate. "Every Dahlia I embroider on these men, they're all Elizabeth Shorts. Forgotten. Dismissed. Their killers walking free."

"Until you find them."

"Until we find them," I correct, looking up at him. "That's what The Hollow does. We're the justice they never got."

Deacon's silent for a long moment, watching me work. Then he reaches for his coffee. "What about the coach? Do you have something prepared for him, too?"

"Oh no, Flossie. That one is all you."

The plane hits a pocket of turbulence, jostling us slightly. I steady my hand, continuing my stitches without missing a beat.

"Seems like you've done this a lot," Deacon observes.

"I've killed thirty-two times before you joined us." I finish the last red tip and reach for the white thread. "No one has ever met my needle that didn't deserve it."

"I don't doubt that."

I look up, meeting his steel gray eyes. "What about you? How many have you fed cotton candy?"

"Twenty-seven."

I whistle low. "And you've never been caught. Impressive."

"It's not about numbers."

"No," I agree, my voice softening. "It's not about numbers. It's about making sure that the monsters don't hurt anyone else."

The cabin falls quiet except for the soft hum of engines. I focus on the final touches of my embroidery. Each tiny white droplet that will soon turn blood red when I sew them onto Dr. Stanton's chest.

"We land in forty minutes," Deacon says, checking his watch. "You should finish that."

"I'm almost done." I tie off the last stitch, cutting the thread with my teeth. I hold up the completed black dahlia to show him. "What do you think? Personally, I think it's gonna look great on the good doctor."

Deacon studies my handiwork, that muscle in his jaw twitching slightly. "It's beautiful," he finally says. "And terrible."

I smile, tucking the finished piece carefully into my case. "That's exactly what it's meant to be."

FOURTEEN
DEACON

The car purrs beneath us as I navigate Chicago's busy streets. Scout bounces in her seat beside me, all restless energy even after the early flight. Her fingers tap against the window to some rhythm only she hears.

"You know what I just realized?" She turns to me, her amber eyes wide. "I know how many people you've killed, but I don't know your favorite color."

"Black."

"Boring. Try again."

I glance at her, one eyebrow raised. "It's an answer."

"It's a non-answer." She shifts in her seat, tucking one leg beneath her. "Come on, everyone has a real favorite color, even serial killers."

The GPS announces our next turn, and I follow its directions, considering her question.

"Dark blue. Like the ocean at night."

She claps her hands together. "Now we're getting somewhere! Mine's pink. Obviously."

"I never would have guessed," I deadpan, eyeing her sparkly pink belt and the matching nail polish.

"Was that sarcasm? I'm shocked." Her laugh fills the car, light and dangerous all at once. "What about music? Please don't say you're one of those 'I only listen to the screams of my victims' types."

I laugh, "No. I like Classical. Some jazz."

"Hmm. I can work with that." She fiddles with her phone, connecting it to the car's Bluetooth. "Any objections to Nina Simone?"

"None."

The sultry notes of "Feeling Good" fill the car. Scout hums along, her voice surprisingly melodic.

"What about you?" I ask, "Besides whatever pop stars use the most glitter?"

"Excuse you. My music taste is impeccable." She swats my arm playfully. "I like everything. Literally everything from classical to metal to K-pop. Music is music."

We drive in comfortable silence for a few minutes, Nina's voice washing over us. Her scent of citrus and sunshine mingles with the new car smell.

"Tell me something about Scout that isn't in your file," I say, taking a chance.

She tilts her head, studying me. "Are you trying to get to know me, Candy Man?"

I'm genuinely interested in her answer, but she doesn't need to know that. "We're supposed to be married. It might help if I know more than your body count."

Her smile grows wider. "Fair point, husband." She taps her chin thoughtfully. "Okay, something not in my file, hmmm, Oh! I know every line from The Princess Bride movie by heart. It's my favorite."

"Inconceivable."

She gasps, delighted. "Oh My God! I knew there was a human under all that brooding."

"Don't go spreading it around. I have a reputation to keep."

"Your secret's safe with me." She mimes zipping her lips, then immediately unzips them. "Your turn. Tell me something about Deacon that's not in your scary murder resume."

I consider what to share as I navigate onto the highway. Something that won't give too much away but isn't completely meaningless.

"I play chess."

"Like, casually? Or are you one of those people who study openings and read books about it?"

"I was ranked regionally. I had potential for national standing."

Her eyebrows shoot up. "You're serious?"

"Dead serious, but it was a long time ago. I used family connections to scrub those records when I decided some pieces needed removing from the board permanently."

She studies me for a long moment, then nods. "We should play sometime. I'm terrible, but I bet I could distract you into making mistakes."

"I don't doubt that for a second."

The GPS announces our exit in one mile. Scout stretches her arms above her head, her shirt riding up to reveal a sliver of caramel skin.

"So, Mr. and Mrs. Winters," she says, emphasizing our cover names. "How did we meet? We should get our story straight before we start surveillance."

"You decide. You're better at the details."

She grins, clearly pleased with the task. "We met at a coffee shop. Classic but believable. You spilled your coffee on my white dress—"

"Seems unlikely."

"—because you were distracted by how gorgeous I am," she continues, ignoring my interruption. "You insisted on paying for dry cleaning, I insisted on getting your number, and here we are, three years later, happily married and visiting Chicago for our anniversary."

"Why would I be carrying coffee without a lid?"

She rolls her eyes. "Fine. I bumped into you and made you spill it. Better?"

"That's more plausible."

"You're no fun." She pouts, but her eyes sparkle. "What do you think our married life is like, Deacon? Do we have a white picket fence and 2.5 kids?"

I take the exit, considering her question. "No kids. A modern apartment. You have too many shoes. I have too many books. We argue about the thermostat."

She laughs, it's genuine and bright. "Have you been thinking about this?"

"I was in your room and watched you pack. I know exactly what would happen."

"Spending twenty-eight minutes in my room with me is not enough to have it all figured out." She leans closer, her scent enveloping me. "Do we have a cat?"

"No, a dog. Better protection."

"What's its name?"

"Sir Bones."

"Wow," her laugh is half amusement, half disbelief. "Did you hurt yourself coming up with that one?"

I smile as I turn onto a quiet residential street. There's something about this pint-sized hurricane that catches me off guard. She's getting to me. It's dangerous. She's dangerous. I don't need complications, especially not ones with amber eyes and chaotic energy.

The safehouse appears ahead, a nondescript brick with a small front yard.

"Home sweet home," Scout says as I pull into the driveway. "Ready to play house, husband?"

THE SAFEHOUSE LOOKS like any other middle-class home at first glance. Outside, it's a simple one-story brick ranch with a manicured lawn and a white picket fence. Inside, a gray sectional couch faces a mounted television. A small coffee table sits in front, scattered with worn magazines, one of which sports a faded headline about some humanitarian award and a photo of smiling executives from a place called the Sterling Institute.

Just the perfect little place for Emily and David Winters to stay while visiting their family. It's Quiet. Unassuming. And fully sound-proofed.

I carry Scout's excessive luggage, four bags for a two-week trip, while she bounces ahead of me, inspecting every room like a kid at Disney World.

"Not bad," she says, flinging open the master bedroom door. "King bed, decent closet space." She peeks into the en-suite bathroom. "Ooh, and a soaking tub."

I set her bags down by the bed. "You planning to relax after we murder someone?"

"Self-care is extremely important, Deacon." She flops onto the bed, spreading her arms wide. "Where are you sleeping?"

"The guest room."

She props herself up on her elbows. "You sure? This bed is huge." She winks.

"Positive."

Her lips curl into a smirk. "Your loss. I've been told that I'm an excellent cuddler."

"I'll try to survive the disappointment."

I leave her to unpack and head to the kitchen. The safehouse is well-stocked, Roman's work, no doubt. The refrigerator contains pre-made meals, the pantry holds non-perishables, and the freezer has ice cream. Lots of ice cream.

Scout appears behind me as I'm checking out the options. "The pink container is mine," she says, reaching around me to grab the pint of strawberry cheesecake gelato from the freezer. "Touch it and die."

"Noted."

She grabs a spoon and hops onto the kitchen counter, legs swinging. "So, research time? I want to be ready for the good doctor."

I nod, retrieving my laptop from my bag. "Roman sent over hospital schedules, staff rotations, and building schematics."

"Boring but necessary." She hops off the counter, grabbing her bag and pulling out a pink sparkly laptop, which of course, is covered in stickers. "I want to know what makes the bastard tick. What drives him? How does he choose his victims?"

We set up at the dining table, our laptops facing each other. Scout immediately pulls her legs up into her chair, sitting cross-legged as she types.

"Dr. Greg Stanton," she reads aloud. "Fifty-two years old. Chief of Cardiothoracic Surgery at Chicago Memorial. Harvard Medical School graduate. Married once, divorced. No children." She scrolls down. "Blah blah blah, prestigious awards, blah blah, pioneering techniques."

"Focus on his routine," I say. "We need to know when he's vulnerable."

"I know how to do my job, Flossie." She sticks her tongue out at me. "But yes, let's see... He works Monday through Thursday, with surgeries scheduled primarily in the mornings. He's off on Fridays, Saturdays, and Sundays. He's on call but rarely goes in unless it's an emergency. He goes to his favorite bar on Friday nights."

I watch her face darken, the playfulness evaporating. This is the other Scout, the one who embroiders death with precision.

"Five confirmed victims," she continues, her voice harder now. "Three nurses who quit rather than report him after he provided them a hefty severance package for them to leave quietly. Two nurses who reported him, but the hospital paid for their silence. They get a lot of donations because of the Good Doctor, so you know they'll protect him. And a sixth nurse didn't report anything, but she basically disappeared. Moved to Miami according to records."

"Or she didn't move at all," I say quietly.

Scout's eyes meet mine. "Exactly."

She pulls out a small notebook from her bag. It's pink, with a black dahlia embroidered on the cover, and begins making notes.

Scout taps her pen against her notebook, frowning at her screen. "I need to check into this fifth victim. Miami sounds convenient. Too convenient." She digs her spoon into the strawberry cheesecake gelato and takes a massive bite, closing her eyes briefly in appreciation.

"I have to dig into his history more and confirm all five of his other victims, too, before I move forward. Need to be certain the count is right for my embroidery." She points her spoon at me. "It isn't just about killing these monsters, it's about acknowledging every single person they hurt."

I nod, understanding her logic. The cotton candy I leave isn't just a calling card; it's a reminder of childhood innocence destroyed.

"What about you?" She swings her legs under the table, her foot accidentally brushing against mine. "What's your game plan for Coach Z?"

I turn my laptop to show her the wrestling team's schedule I've pulled up. "His victims are the boys he coaches. I need to observe his patterns with them first."

"Smart." She leans forward, studying the screen. "Looks like he holds practice every day after school until 6 PM except on Thursdays."

"And private coaching sessions after that." I scroll down to show her the separate schedule. "One-on-one time with select team members."

Scout's expression darkens. "Bet those aren't just about wrestling techniques."

"No." The word comes out harder than I intended.

She studies me for a moment, spoon hovering halfway to her mouth. "This one's personal for you, isn't it?"

"They're all personal", focusing on the screen.

"You don't have to tell me," she says, softer now. "But I'm a good listener when I'm not talking. Which, admittedly, isn't often."

That pulls a reluctant half-smile from me. "I prefer to keep the past where it belongs."

"Fair enough." She takes another bite of gelato. "So, surveillance first? Or do you already know how you want to take him out?"

"I need to understand his movements first. His vulnerabilities."

She sets down her now-empty gelato container, closes her laptop, and stands. "I'm going to start with the potential sixth victim, the nurse who supposedly moved to Miami. If she's really there, great, if not..." She trails off, her expression grim.

"Do you think Stanton killed her?"

"It wouldn't be the first time someone escalated when threatened." She stretches, her crop top riding up to reveal a strip of caramel skin. "I'll see if Roman can dig deeper into her supposed relocation."

I turn back to my laptop, but Scout remains standing beside me.

"What?" I ask, not looking up.

"Do you ever relax, Flossie?" Her voice drops lower, a perfect blend of sugar and steel.

"Yes, I do. Just not around people I barely know." I keep my eyes fixed on my laptop screen, though I can feel her hovering presence like an electric current beside me. "Especially ones who have similar hobbies."

"We're supposed to be married, sharing a house and planning murders together. I'd say that's pretty intimate, wouldn't you?" The way she emphasizes 'intimate' sends heat up my spine.

I finally look up at her. "Intimate isn't the word I'd use."

"No?" She leans down, her face inches from mine, amber eyes burning with something dangerous beneath the mischief. Her scent, sweet with a hint of sharp citrus, floods my senses. "What word would you use then?"

"Temporary." My voice comes out rougher than intended.

She straightens, laughing low in her throat. "Oh, you're good. Very good." She heads toward the hallway, hips swaying deliberately, calling over her shoulder, "But temporary or not, we're partners now. And I always get to know my partners."

I watch her disappear down the hall, her curls bouncing with each step, the ghost of her nearness still lingering on my skin. Working with Scout Prescott is going to be complicated.

FIFTEEN
SCOUT

I pull up Stanton's file again, scrolling through the details Roman has collected. Five nurses have filed complaints, all buried in one way or another. His pattern is clear. Isolated after-hours meetings with a drink involved, roofie free of charge, naturally.

My jaw clenches as I read through victim statements. The ones that did report him couldn't remember much, thanks to the drugs he gave them. He's always been able to escape the consequences.

Until now.

I open my closet and pull out my special tapestry, running my fingers over the most recent addition, Pastor Nathan's black dahlia. I trace the embroidered names of his victims: Jasmine, Maria, Tanya, Samantha, Destiny, Amber, Crystal. Women that society deemed disposable. Women that I made sure would be remembered.

I place the dahlia that I've meticulously prepared for Dr. Stanton next to the tapestry. It's a rich, velvety black flower with blood red tipped petals. The stitching is perfect, if I do say so myself. I've spent hours getting the tension just right, making sure the thread won't snap when I'm working on a living canvas. I pick up the needle resting beside it, twirling it between my fingers. It catches the light just right, all shiny and eager for its big performance. God, there's nothing quite like the feeling of pushing it through skin, watching my victims lie perfectly still while I create my masterpiece right over their still-beating heart. Art and vengeance.

My mind wanders to Deacon. I wonder what he's doing right now? Probably organizing his weapons. I would bet money he's the type that alphabetizes his ammunition. And why is that so weirdly hot? There's just something about the way he moves, so controlled and deliberate, that makes my chaotic heart flutter in the most annoying way.

I wonder what's going on in that gorgeous head of his. He's all broody and mysterious with those rare half-smiles of his. God, it's like trying to have a conversation with a sexy brick wall sometimes, except now he's a brick wall that occasionally talks back. Progress!

I shake my head, mentally slapping myself back to reality. *Focus, Scout! Less drooling over Mr. Murder, more prepping for actual murder.*

I force my attention back to the files. We'll each take the lead on one target while the other shadows. I'll be showing off my skills first, then watching him work. This is about evaluation, about seeing if we can trust each other when blood starts flowing.

Which means I need to stop fantasizing about his jawline and start memorizing these surveillance notes. Priorities, girl. Priorities.

This is going to be interesting, to say the least.

As I head to the bathroom, I wonder if Deacon is still reviewing the files, too, or if he's still processing everything he's seen since we met. The mansion, the resources, his new colleagues? Partners? Whatever we are.

I hope he sticks around. There's something about him that fits here, despite his lone wolf vibe. Something that makes me think he might belong with us.

With me.

A SHARP KNOCK on the open door frame jolts me from my thoughts.

I spin around, heart skipping a beat, when I see Deacon's tall frame filling the doorway.

"Jesus!" I press a hand to my chest. "Make some noise when you move, would you? Like a normal human?"

His lips quirk up slightly at one corner. "I thought the knock was a noise."

"Before the knock, Flossie." I roll my eyes, subtly shifting my body to block his view of the bed where my tapestry lies unrolled. "You know, footsteps? Heavy breathing? The dramatic announcement of your presence?"

His gaze shifts slightly over my shoulder, then returns to my face with deliberate slowness. Something in those steel eyes tells me he's already seen everything on the bed. Great.

"You hungry?" he asks, hands sliding into his pockets. "Thought we could grab dinner. Scout the area."

I can't help the snort that escapes. "Was that a pun? Did Mr. Serious just make a Scout pun?"

"Pure coincidence." But there's that almost-smile again.

"Sure it was." I reach behind me, casually rolling up the tapestry and sliding it behind the pillows on the bed. "And yes, I'm starving. I'll be ready in like five minutes."

He nods, but doesn't move from the doorway.

"You got something on your mind, Candy Man?" I ask, crossing my arms as I turn to face him.

"What's that?" He points to the tapestry.

Straight to the point. Typical Deacon, no beating around the bush with this one.

"Just some needlework." I shrug, aiming for casual. "I like to keep my hands busy."

"Hmm." He doesn't push, but I can see I didn't answer the question to his satisfaction. He'll file it away for later, like everything else.

"Five minutes," I remind him, making a shooing motion with my hands.

He backs away from the doorframe, but not before giving me one of those looks.

"You should wear something warm," he says. "The temperature's dropping."

"Aww, worried about little ol' me catching a chill?" I call after him, batting my eyelashes even though he's already turning away. "You know, body heat is way more effective than sweaters!"

Then he's gone, silent as a shadow, but not before I catch the slightest tensing of his shoulders. Small victories.

I close the door and lean against it, exhaling slowly. I look at the bed where my tapestry peeks out from behind the pillows. I know he saw it.

The tapestry is my most private possession. It's the physical manifestation of every life I've taken, every woman I've avenged. It's all of my girls. It's not something I can share with just anyone.

But something tells me Deacon Thorne isn't the type to let mysteries lie. Especially not ones wrapped in embroidery thread and hidden behind pillows.

I push off the door and head to my suitcase. Dinner with Deacon. Surveillance of our prey. Just another night in the glamorous life of a serial killer.

I can't help but smile as I pull out a sweater. Who says murder can't be fun?

I GRAB my favorite cropped sweater from the closet. It's soft pink with a neckline that dips low enough to make things really interesting, and pair it with low-rise jeans that hug my curves perfectly. A quick touch of lip gloss, and Bam! I'm ready. I check myself out in the mirror that hangs on the closet door. Damn. I look good.

When I bounce into the living room, Deacon's already waiting, staring out the window. His back is to me, shoulders a broad line under his dark Henley. He must hear me because he turns, and for a split second, his eyes darken as they sweep over me. They drift from my exposed collarbone down to the strip of skin between my sweater and jeans.

The look vanishes so quickly, I might have imagined it, replaced by that controlled mask he wears so well. But I didn't imagine it. He just checked me out.

"This is your idea of dressing warmly?" His voice is flat, but there's a roughness at the edges.

I do a little twirl, letting my sweater rise just a bit higher. "What? It's so cute and it has long sleeves."

"It's forty degrees outside."

"That's what jackets are for." I grab my pink puffy jacket from the coat rack, sliding it on with deliberate slowness. "See? Problem solved."

His jaw tightens. "You're going to freeze."

"I'll be fine." I step closer, looking up at him through my lashes. "Unless you're offering to keep me warm?"

Something flickers in those steel eyes, heat, maybe frustration, definitely something he's trying to bury. He exhales sharply through his nose.

"We're going to sit and watch Stanton after we eat, we can't keep the car running while we're there," he says, all business now. "You'll be cold, distracted, inefficient."

I laugh, poking his chest with my finger. "Did you just call me inefficient? That might be the most offensive thing anyone's ever said to me."

His expression doesn't change, but I swear there's amusement hiding in the corners of his mouth.

"Just so you know, I've staked out targets in a bikini before." My fingers toy with the zipper of my jacket, leaving it deliberately halfway up as my shoulders rise in a casual shrug. The flash of bare skin between fabric catches the light. "But if this outfit's too much for you, just say so."

That gets a reaction, a slight widening of his eyes before he controls it.

"That was necessary for the job?" His voice is carefully neutral.

"Beach resort in Miami. The target had a thing for blondes in dark blue bikinis." I shrug, enjoying the way his gaze follows the movement. "I made it work."

I head toward the door, but pause with my hand on the doorknob.

"For the record, Deacon, if I'm distracting you that much, just say so." I flash him a knowing smile. "No need to hide behind lectures about being 'inefficient.'"

His expression doesn't change, but the temperature in the room seems to rise by several degrees.

Sixteen

Deacon

I tap my fingers against the steering wheel, eyes glued to the clinic's front door. A pizza delivery guy idles his scooter out front, scrolling his phone. A couple wait at a nearby bus stop, too busy arguing to notice much else. I'm trying to focus on the clinic's entrance instead of the woman beside me. Scout's been a tactical nightmare since we left the safehouse, deliberately brushing against me at the restaurant, dropping her napkin so she could bend over, flashing caramel skin with every movement, licking ice cream from her spoon with unnecessary enthusiasm. Suffice it to say, I can pretty much guarantee there is now a permanent zipper outline on my dick. Christ, if she keeps this up, I might need surgery to remove the goddamn zipper.

Two fucking hours of psychological warfare disguised as dinner. Two hours of trying to ignore her effect on me, and my body betrayed me anyway.

Now we're parked across from the Community Health Free outpatient clinic where Dr. Stanton works Wednesday evenings. Scout's curled up in the passenger seat, her legs tucked underneath her. One hand is tapping her thigh with the rhythm of the music on the radio, the other is playing with the hem of that ridiculous sweater.

"Well, Stanton's late," I say, breaking the silence.

Scout glances at the clock on the dashboard. "Oh my god, he's only like two minutes late. Some people have actual lives, you know."

"According to the file, he's worked every Tuesday evening for the past three years." I tap my fingers against the steering wheel. "People are creatures of habit."

Scout shifts, her knee brushing against the center console. "Not everyone's as obsessively punctual as you, Flossie. Besides, he still has eighteen minutes before I'd actually consider him late."

I ignore the nickname and check my watch again. Eighteen more minutes trapped in this car with her. Eighteen minutes of casual touches and that goddamn sweater. Torture would be more bearable than watching my self-control crumble like this.

The silence stretches between us, but Scout isn't built for quiet. She fidgets, adjusts the heat, checks her phone, then turns toward me.

"So, dinner was fun."

I don't respond.

"Seriously, are you always this chatty, or should I feel honored by all of this stimulating conversation?"

I shift my gaze briefly to scan the surrounding area before returning to the clinic entrance, deliberately ignoring her question.

"You know, most people consider it polite to answer a direct question," she prods.

"We're supposed to be focused on the job," I finally say.

She laughs, that bright sound that somehow manages to be both irritating and magnetic. "Oh please, we were at dinner, and now we're just sitting in a car watching nothing happen. Pretty sure the Hollow handbook doesn't forbid conversation between killings. Even serial killers get to talk about something other than murder occasionally."

I don't answer, but my mind drifts back to dinner. I could barely keep my eyes off of her. Every time she leaned forward, flashing her ample cleavage. Every time, she winked as she licked her dessert spoon. She laughed too loud, drawing eyes from across the restaurant. It feels like she's determined to get under my skin.

"For someone with a body count, you draw a lot of attention."

"Well, excuse me for enjoying my life between murders." She brushes invisible dust from her shoulder. "Sorry, I'm not carved from stone like you. Do you ever actually relax, or is that brooding thing hardwired into your DNA?" She reaches and turns the heat up.

I tighten my grip on the steering wheel. "I thought you wouldn't get cold in that sweater." I adjust my vent so it blows more towards her.

"Just trying to balance out your permanent frost, Candy Man." She grins. "Someone's gotta bring warmth to this partnership."

Nothing about Scout is subtle. Her casual approach to what we do unnerves me. The way she bounces from joking and flirting to planning murder with the same bright smile. It's like watching someone switch channels without changing expression.

"You should take this more seriously."

"Oh, I'm very serious about killing Dr. Grabby Hands." Her playful tone vanishes, replaced by something cold and sharp. "But I don't have to be miserable while I do it."

I glance at her, catching the flash of steel beneath all that sunshine. It's easy to forget she's killed thirty-two men with those delicate hands that now fiddle with the radio. She's deadly and graceful in the same moment, that's part of what makes her dangerous. She's impossible to ignore.

"How do you do it?" I ask, desperate for anything to change the direction my thoughts are heading.

"Do what?"

"Switch so easily. One minute you're..." I search for the right words. "All over the place. The next, you're focused."

She considers this, tilting her head. "Why compartmentalize? The world's fucked up. I can be both the girl who likes pink sprinkles and the one who puts down predators."

It's not an answer I expected, but it fits her. Scout exists in contradictions, dangerous and playful, chaotic and precise.

"A silver Lexus just pulled in," she says, straightening in her seat. "That's him."

I follow her gaze to where a man in his fifties, his salt-and-pepper hair visible even from this distance, walks briskly toward the clinic entrance.

"Seventeen minutes late," I note, checking my watch.

"Still within the fashionably late window." Scout pulls out her phone, snapping several photos. "He looks exactly like his picture. Smug bastard."

I observe the Doctor's confident stride, the way staff greet him with deference as he enters. "He walks like a man who thinks he's untouchable."

"They all do." Her voice hardens. "Until they meet me."

I watch as Stanton disappears inside. Scout settles back into her seat, her shoulder brushing mine.

"Tomorrow we'll follow him home, map his routine," she says. "Day after, I plan to be at his favorite bar. Get close enough to isolate him."

"And then?"

She smiles, but it doesn't reach her eyes. "Then I make him understand what those women felt. Helpless. Afraid. At someone else's mercy."

The clinical detachment in her voice is at odds with her playful appearance. This duality makes Scout dangerous, not just because she kills, but because I'm starting to want her. And wanting anything in this life is a liability I can't afford. Especially not someone who could slit my throat with the same hands I'm imagining wrapped around my cock.

I need to redirect my thoughts before they betray me completely. "Why embroidery?" I ask. "You mentioned your grandmother, but not why you chose that particular skill as your signature."

She glances at me, surprised by the follow-up. "Do you really want to know?"

"I wouldn't have asked if I didn't."

She laughs, shifting in her seat to face me. "Fair enough. After my parents died, I couldn't sleep and had way too much energy. Gran said I needed something to keep my hands busy." Her fingers drift to the hem of her sweater. "Turned out I was good at it."

"That doesn't explain why you use it to mark your kills."

"Because it's personal." Her voice softens. "Gran taught me that each stitch is deliberate. Time-consuming. I'm literally putting myself into the work." She absentmindedly lifts the edge of her sweater, her fingers tracing slow circles on the exposed skin of her stomach. "What about your cotton candy?"

I try to focus on her question, not the hypnotic movement of her fingertips tracing around her navel piercing. She clicks her nail on the small pink gemstone.

"It's... complicated."

"We've got time." Her fingers continue their lazy path across her skin. "Stanton's not going anywhere for at least an hour."

"That's not a story for tonight." My voice low.

"Oh, come on." Her fingers continue their lazy path across her skin. "I just spilled my tragic backstory. It's your turn in the sharing circle, Candy Man."

I force my eyes back to the clinic entrance. "Some things I keep to myself."

"Fine," she huffs, "Then tell me something else." She shifts in her seat, leaning closer. "Where'd you grow up? Got any siblings? When was your first kill? Do you have a favorite cereal? I'm not picky."

She's deliberately pushing my buttons. I don't think she's ever going to give up. Even when I don't answer, she just keeps coming at me, pure persistence and determination. The difference is, I think she genuinely wants to know. Not for leverage or advantage, but because she's actually curious about who I am beneath the silence. That's unsettling.

"Are you always this curious about your partners?" I deflect.

"Says the guy who just spent the last ten minutes interrogating me." Her smile is all teeth. "But to answer your question, only the interesting ones. And you, Mr. Floss, are very interesting."

Something about her makes me want to give her something, anything, even if it's not what she's asking for.

"I hate chocolate," I say finally. "Except dark chocolate-covered cashews."

Her eyebrows shoot up, clearly surprised I've offered anything at all. "Seriously? That's what you're giving me? Your candy preferences? But really, how in the fuck can you hate chocolate?"

"You asked for something. That's something."

She laughs, shaking her head. "Fine. I guess that will do. For now." Her fingers drift lower, tracing the waistband of her jeans in slow, deliberate movements that I know I shouldn't be watching. She blows out a hard breath to send a curl flying from her forehead.

"Do you have any siblings?" I ask, desperate to redirect my attention.

"Just the family at the mansion." Her thumb hooks into the waistband, exposing another inch of smooth skin. "Ivy's the closest thing to a sister I've ever had."

I grip the steering wheel tighter, my pulse hammering in my throat. Fucking hell. Twelve years of perfect discipline, and I'm coming undone because of fingers on skin? Focus. The clinic. The billboard in front boasts *Healing Hearts: Sterling Trauma Counseling Services.*

Trauma Counseling, huh? Sign me the fuck up. First session's just me explaining how I've memorized the exact curve where her hip meets that waistband and how hard I'm gonna bite down to mark it with my teeth. I need to think of anything but the way her thumb is hooking into that waistband. Fuck me, I need to stop these kinds of thoughts.

I shake my head and ask, "What happened to your parents?"

Her hand stops moving, and her voice goes soft as she says, "They died in a car accident when I was eight. A drunk driver hit their car, and it rolled. He walked away without a scratch. They didn't."

"Did you kill him?"

She smiles, a sharp edge to it. "No, but the alcohol eventually did. His liver knocked him off a few years later."

I nod, understanding the satisfaction of that karmic retribution. My eyes drift back to her hand, still tracing patterns on her skin. The movement is maddening, but it's not as over-the-top as her dinner performance, but for some reason, that just makes it so much worse. I shift in my seat in a poor attempt to alleviate the pressure on my throbbing dick.

"What about you, any family?" she asks, shifting in her seat. Her hand abandons her stomach, moving to fidget with the pendant hanging just above the neckline of her sweater.

I don't respond, watching as her fingertips roll the small charm back and forth against her chest. The pendant slides across her skin with each movement, drawing my eye to the curve of her breasts. I'm mentally mapping every inch she touches and imagining how warm and sweet she would taste. What the fuck is wrong with me?

"Stop," I snap, my control fracturing.

She blinks, her eyes widening with genuine confusion, head tilting slightly. "Stop what?"

Without thinking, I reach across the console and capture her wrist in my hand. My knuckles graze her breast as I pull it away from her chest."Stop. That."

Her eyes widen further as she realizes what she'd been doing. I'm leaning across the center console now, my face inches from hers, her wrist trapped in my grip.

"Oh," she breathes, a smile playing at her lips. "Was I distracting you, Mr. Floss?"

I should release her. I should pull back. Instead, I tighten my grip slightly, feeling her pulse quicken beneath my fingers.

"You know exactly what you're doing," I growl.

"Not this time," she whispers, her eyes dropping to my mouth before meeting my gaze again. "But I'm not sorry it worked."

I'm still holding her wrist, neither of us moving away. Her free hand comes up, hovering near my jaw without touching.

"I think," she says softly, "I'm getting under your skin."

Her tongue peeks out, wetting her bottom lip in a quick, subconscious movement that stops my breath. Time slows, each second stretching between us as I register every detail. The slight dilation of her pupils, the faint freckles across her nose visible only this close, the way her caramel-toned skin glows even in the dim car interior.

I'm still gripping her wrist, feeling her pulse hammering against my fingertips. The rhythm matches my own, too fast, too hard. Her chest rises and falls with each breath, the cropped sweater doing nothing to hide the curves beneath.

When did the temperature in this car rise twenty degrees?

"Deacon," she whispers, my name on her lips sounding like something I've never heard before.

Her fingertips brush my jaw with a touch so light that I can barely feel it, but it jolts through me like a live wire straight to my cock.

I should pull away.

I need to pull away.

But I don't.

Instead, I lean closer, pulled to her by something I can't fight. The scent of her fills my senses, sweet and warm beneath the lingering traces of her perfume. My gaze drops to her full lips as her eyes flutter half-closed, expectantly.

This is a mistake.

The thought crashes through the haze, sharp and cold. Attachments are dangerous. Distractions get people killed. I've survived this long by maintaining control, by never letting anyone close enough to matter.

Yet here I am, inches away from crossing a line I can't uncross.

I force myself to release her wrist, to pull back, putting distance between us. The loss of contact is physically painful, a sudden emptiness where her warmth had been. Scout's eyes open fully, confusion and something like hurt flashing across her features before she masks it with a smile.

"Too soon?" she asks, her voice light.

I turn away and fix my gaze on the clinic entrance where Stanton disappeared minutes ago. "We're working."

"Riiiight." She settles back into her seat, pulling her sweater down in a gesture that seems almost self-conscious. "Okay then, all business."

She turns to sit straight up, facing forward. Her eyes continue to scan the area.

I grip the steering wheel, trying to focus on the cold leather beneath my fingers rather than the lingering sensation of her skin against them. The silence stretches between us.

"I don't do this," I finally say, the words coming out roughly.

"Shhhh!" She dramatically presses a finger to her lips, eyes comically wide. "We're working here, Mr. Floss. Very serious surveillance happening. There is no time for personal revelations."

Christ, this woman. "Scout."

"What?" She snaps, her voice sharp-edged and clipped.

"I don't get involved." I keep my eyes forward, not trusting myself to look at her. "With anyone."

She shifts in her seat, and from my peripheral vision, I can see her studying my profile. "Why not?"

I choose my words carefully. "Attachments are liabilities in our world."

She studies her hands for a moment, the silence stretching between us. She doesn't look at me as she says, "Or they're what keeps you human."

I don't have a response for that. For years, I've operated alone, disconnected from everything. The idea that connection might be necessary rather than dangerous is unsettling.

"We should focus," I say instead. "Stanton will be finishing his shift soon."

Scout sighs as she says. "Fine. But this conversation isn't over, Deacon."

I say nothing but know it isn't. She's not going to let this go.

The car falls silent again, but the tension remains. I've spent years building ice walls to keep the world at a distance. And this menace has been attacking them with a pickaxe since the moment we met. And she's relentless, finding every hairline crack, every weak point. Every smile, every touch, every unfiltered comment chips away another piece.

The worst part? Some part of me wants her to succeed. It would be so much easier if I could dismiss her as just a simple complication, but it's been less than a week, and she's proving to be something far more dangerous.

She's becoming important.

And that terrifies me more than anything ever could.

SEVENTEEN

SCOUT

I'm on my second cup of coffee when the memories of last night come flooding back. The way Deacon's fingers wrapped around my wrist, the heat in his eyes before he pulled away. Warmth pools low in my belly. I press my mug against my lips, hiding a smile no one's here to see.

The kitchen in our safehouse is small but functional. The morning sunlight streams through the window onto the small table. I've already been up for an hour, but Deacon's door remains firmly shut. He's hiding from me, probably.

Men, or should I say emotionally stunted murder machines who can't handle a little sexual tension without going full hermit mode. Typical.

I take another sip, savoring the sweet warmth. The almost-kiss plays on repeat in my mind, the way his breath caught, how his pupils dilated when I touched his jaw. For a moment, I thought the infamous Mr. Floss was going to crack.

And then he didn't.

"Attachments are liabilities in this line of work," I mimic his deep voice, rolling my eyes as if I don't know the risks. As if I haven't seen what happens when this life goes sideways. Puh-lease.

But there's a difference between being careful and being dead inside. The Hollow works because we're a family. Don't get me wrong, we're dysfunctional as hell, but we're still connected. We keep each other human in a world where it would be easy to become the monsters we hunt.

I trace the rim of my mug, thinking. I'm not about to chase after him like some lovesick teenager. I don't do the push-pull dance, that game where he pulls away, I pursue, he shows interest, I retreat. That's bullshit for people who have time to waste, which I don't.

But.

The memory of his fingers on my skin sends a shiver down my spine. There's something there, something real beneath all his ice and my fire. There's something worth exploring, at least.

Plus, that look on his face when I catch him off guard? Priceless.

I drain my coffee and set the mug on the counter. I've made my decision. If Deacon Thorne thinks he can just pretend nothing happened, he's about to learn how relentless I can be when I want something. Or maybe "stubborn as hell" is more accurate. Not because I'm desperate for his attention, which honestly, I do want, but mostly because I hate unfinished business. And that moment in the car? Definitely, 100% unfinished, like a cupcake without frosting, and mama needs her sugar.

I head to my room, rifling through my suitcase for just the right outfit. We have surveillance on Coach Z today, Deacon's target, which means we'll be spending several more hours in the car together. Perfect.

I pull out a soft, clingy tank top in deep burgundy and pair it with my favorite jeans and lay it on the bed. Nothing too obvious, I'm not trying to look like I'm trying. Just enough to remind him what he walked away from.

The shower runs hot against my skin as I plan my approach. Deacon responds to confidence, to directness. He's spent too long in the shadows to know what to do with someone who stands in the light.

Lucky for him, I'm excellent at illumination.

I step out of the shower, wrap a towel around myself, and walk into the bedroom. Through my door, I hear movement in the kitchen. Well, well, well... it sounds like Deacon has finally emerged from his cave.

I take my time with my hair, letting my curls dry naturally, adding just a touch of product to keep them defined. I apply just enough makeup to highlight my eyes. A wicked grin spreads across my lips as my reflection stares back, conspirator to the chaos brewing behind my eyes.

Time to remind Mr. Floss that walls only work if both people agree to respect them.

I PAD barefoot into the kitchen in only a bath towel, where Deacon stands with his back to me, coffee mug in hand, as he stares out the window. His shoulders tense slightly, and he knows I'm here without turning around.

"Morning, partner," I say, keeping my voice casual as I reach past him for a clean mug, my arm brushing his. "Sleep well?"

"I wasn't sleeping, I was—" Deacon turns, words dying on his lips as his gaze lands on me.

His eyes widen slightly, the Deacon Thorne equivalent of a jaw drop, as they take in the towel wrapped around my body, secured just above my breasts. Water droplets still cling to my shoulders, one sliding slowly down my collarbone.

I pretend not to notice his sudden silence and focus instead on pouring coffee into my mug. "You were what? Planning? Brooding? Both seem equally likely with you." I add the perfect amount of creamer, stirring it slowly.

Deacon clears his throat, his eyes darting away before returning to my face with determined focus. "Reviewing the Coach Z file."

"Find anything interesting?" I ask as I turn and lean back against the counter. The towel shifts, sliding up to expose more of my thighs. I watch as Deacon's eyes track the movement before snapping back up, his jaw flexing as he clenches his teeth. I fight to keep my expression neutral, even as triumph threatens to curl my lips into a smirk.

"Nothing that we didn't already know." His voice has that tight quality, like he's measuring each word before releasing it.

I nod. "So, I've been thinking about what we could do for this stakeout. Since we're supposed to be married, maybe we should watch practice from the bleachers? The concerned parents considering the program for their non-existent son."

Heat flares in Deacon's eyes as he grips his coffee mug. "That could work."

"Great!" I beam at him, shifting my weight to one hip. "I figure we can head out in about an hour? That gives us time to prepare our cover details."

He nods stiffly, eyes now fixed on a point somewhere over my left shoulder. My gaze travels down his body, lingering where denim strains against an unmistakable bulge. My lips part slightly, the coffee cup suddenly unsteady in my hand. *Fuck that's big. Jesus, I didn't expect that size of situation in his pants. Get it together, girl. Stop staring at his dick like it's the last donut at a police convention.*

My eyes dart upward, catching the broad sweep of his shoulders just as his head begins to turn, saving me from being caught ogling his crotch. "Is something wrong?" The words drip sweetly as I lift the coffee mug to my lips, hiding my smirk behind the rim.

"No," he says too quickly.

"You seem tense." I step closer, looking up at him with exaggerated concern. "Is it about last night? Because—"

"It's not about last night," he cuts me off, jaw clenched.

"Oh, good." I place my free hand on his forearm, feeling his muscles tighten under my touch. "Because I'd hate for things to be awkward between us. We still have two monsters to eliminate, after all."

His throat works as he swallows. "Nothing's awkward."

"Perfect!" I squeeze his arm before stepping back. "Then I'll see you in an hour. I'm thinking jeans and a sweater for the stakeout. That should blend in with the other parents. What do you think?"

Deacon's eyes finally meet mine, a dangerous glint in them that sends a little thrill down my spine. "Whatever works."

"You're helpful as always," I laugh, setting my half-empty mug on the counter. "I'll go finish getting ready."

I turn and walk away slowly, adding just enough sway to my hips to make the towel's hem dance dangerously high on my thighs. Feeling his eyes burning into me with every step, I stretch my arms overhead in an exaggerated yawn, knowing exactly what that does to the towel's already precarious position. Just before I reach my bedroom door, I glance over my shoulder. Deacon stands frozen in the kitchen, coffee forgotten in his hand, watching me with an intensity that makes my skin tingle.

I flash him a bright smile and wink. "Don't forget to eat something. It's going to be a long day."

I close my bedroom door behind me, leaning against it with a satisfied grin. Deacon Thorne might think he's unreadable, but his eyes give him away every time.

Game on, Mr. Floss.

I FLOP onto my bed with a dramatic sigh, tossing aside the pink notebook where I've been scribbling observations from today's stakeout. What a complete waste of six hours. Coach Z showed up, ran practice, creepily adjusted some kid's stance with hands that lingered too long, then left. Nothing we didn't already know.

And Deacon? He might as well have been carved from stone. After my towel stunt this morning, I expected something. A crack in that perfect composure. A lingering glance. Anything.

Instead, all I got were monosyllabic responses and a laser-like focus on the surveillance. Even when I "accidentally" brushed against him while reaching for binoculars, he didn't flinch. Just handed them over without looking at me.

"Stupid, frozen, professional..." I mutter, kicking off my shoes and sending them flying across the room.

At least tomorrow night will be more exciting. Dr. Stanton likes to unwind at Martini Blue on Thursday nights. Hopefully, he'll be hunting for his next victim. I'm going to make sure he finds me.

I roll off the bed and open my suitcase, pulling out the outfits I've brought for this specific purpose. According to Roman's file, Stanton has a type. He likes petite women who look younger than they are, who seem vulnerable but not timid. Women who drink fruity cocktails and laugh too loudly. Women, that he can pay off or disappear if they wouldn't be missed.

Women like me, minus the "won't be missed" part. The Hollow would rain hellfire if I ever disappeared.

I lay the options across my bed, studying each one:

Option one is a blue dress. It's flirty, with a sweetheart neckline that makes me look innocent.

Option two is a black skirt and pink top, playful but still sophisticated,

Option three is a green dress. It's an attention-grabbing, satin cocktail dress that hugs me like a second skin, and it's so short that if I breathe wrong, my ass is definitely falling out

I hold the green dress against me, turning to check my reflection in the mirror. Ding! Ding! We have a winner. It's perfect victim material. Stanton won't be able to resist—

A sharp knock on my door interrupts my thoughts.

"Just a second!" I call, laying the green dress at the foot of the bed.

I open the door to find him standing there, still in the same jeans and dark grey t-shirt from our surveillance, looking annoyingly put-together despite the long day. His steel-gray eyes immediately take in the clothes scattered across my bed.

"Planning a fashion show?" he asks, one eyebrow slightly raised.

I lean against the doorframe, crossing my arms. "Just getting ready for tomorrow night. Dr. Stanton has an appointment with The Stitcher, and I need to look the part."

Deacon's eyes narrow slightly as they move from the clothes back to me. "The part of what, exactly?"

"His type," I say with a shrug. "Vulnerable. Easy prey."

Something flickers across his face, before his expression settles back into neutral. "You're using yourself as bait."

It's not a question, but I answer anyway. "That's how it usually works. Get close, gain trust, strike when they're vulnerable." I tilt my head. "Why? Is there a problem with that?"

"Sounds a bit risky," he says, voice flat.

I roll my eyes. "I'm a professional. I'm the Stitcher, remember? I know what I'm fucking doing."

"And what happens if something goes wrong?"

"If it does, I'll handle it. It's what I do. But this time, I have you, partner." I tap his chest with my index finger. "You can be my backup, if it makes you feel better?" I drag my nail down his chest as I say, "Or did you have something else in mind?"

He steps back and doesn't answer immediately, just studies me with that intense gaze that makes me feel like he's reading every thought in my head.

"What's the plan?" he finally asks.

"I meet him at the bar, play the part, get him to invite me somewhere private, and then," I make a stitching motion with my hand. "The Stitcher does her thing."

"And what do I do?"

I smile up at him. "You watch from a distance, follow us when we leave, and you can step in if things really go sideways. Which they won't."

Deacon nods once, still looking at me with that unreadable expression. "We should discuss the details."

"Sure," I say, stepping back from the doorway. "Come on in. Just don't touch my clothes. I have a system."

As Deacon enters my room, I can't help but wonder what's really going on behind those steel-gray eyes of his. Is he really concerned about my hunt, or is there something else making him suddenly so concerned with my plans?

Either way, tomorrow night is going to be more interesting than I thought.

EIGHTEEN
DEACON

I've been in this booth for forty-three minutes, nursing the same whiskey neat while tracking every movement in Martini Blue's dim lighting. The ice has long since melted in my glass, but I don't care.

All I see is Scout.

She's wearing a green dress that clings to her curves as if it were painted on, stopping high enough on her thick thighs to be illegal in several states. Those fuck me heels add four inches to her height and miles to her legs, making her calves flex with each step. Her hair falls in wild curls around her shoulders, catching blue light from the bar's neon signs.

She looks nothing like the woman who barged into the warehouse with a smart mouth and black boots.

She looks like prey.

But I guess that's the point.

Dr. Stanton noticed her the moment she walked in. I watched his eyes track her movements, watched him straighten his tie and smooth back his salt-and-pepper hair. He's exactly as his file described, mid-fifties, distinguished, with the confident posture of a man who's never faced consequences for his actions.

Scout orders something pink and fruity, pretending to study the drink menu while perfectly positioning herself in his line of sight. Three minutes later, he's beside her, leaning in too close to be professional.

"Is this seat taken?" His words don't reach me, but I can read his lips from here.

Scout turns, all wide-eyed surprise, and shakes her head. The movement makes her curls bounce, and she tucks one behind her ear, a practiced gesture of vulnerability.

She's good at this. Too good.

I take another sip of watered-down whiskey, keeping my expression neutral despite the tightness in my jaw.

This is the job. This is what we came here to do.

So why does my hand keep drifting toward the knife in my boot every time he leans closer to her?

Stanton orders her another drink. His hand drops something into the glass in a practiced move as he passes it to her. Scout giggles, a sound I've never heard from her before, and touches his forearm lightly.

Rage floods my vision as I grip my glass.

I've killed twenty-seven people. I've watched the light fade from their eyes without blinking. I've stood over their bodies and felt nothing but the satisfaction of justice served.

But watching Scout laugh at something Stanton says makes me want to tear across this room and rip his throat out with my bare hands.

Stanton's hand moves to her lower back. Scout leans into the touch, angling her body toward him. They're playing the same game, except she knows the real stakes.

"You're a surgeon?" She sounds impressed, voice pitched higher than normal. "That must be so difficult. I can barely handle nursing school."

Stanton smiles, all false modesty. "It takes a special kind of person to hold someone's heart in their hands."

The irony would be amusing if I weren't fantasizing about putting my knife through his throat.

Scout touches his chest, fingers lingering over his heart. "I can only imagine."

She's marking where she'll embroider her signature later tonight.

The Black Dahlia with red-tipped petals, one blood drop for each victim.

I should be focused on the mission. Instead, I'm counting the inches between his hand and the hem of her dress, calculating how quickly I could cross the room if he moves that hand any higher.

Scout catches my eye for a split second. It's a professional check-in, nothing more. But in that brief moment, I see past the act to the hunter beneath. Her eyes are clear and focused. She's in complete control, but that doesn't help to calm my erratic thoughts.

I watch as Stanton leans in, his lips brushing against her ear. Scout's eyes widen with that perfect mix of surprise and intrigue. Her smile unfurls slowly across her face as she nods, fingers wrapping around her glass. She lifts it to her mouth, but the liquid barely touches her lips. My chest loosens, tension draining from muscles I hadn't realized were coiled tight. She knew the bastard's little powder trick.

Minutes tick by as Scout's performance evolves. Her words slur slightly. Her focus drifts. Her body sways with vulnerability.

The doctor slides off his stool, offering his steady hand. His fingers curl possessively around her waist as she rises. Her steps falter, ankles wobbling in those death-trap heels as he navigates her toward the exit. She collapses against him, all helpless prey.

My fingers dig into the table edge as I start to rise, blood rushing in my ears. Then Scout's gaze finds mine through the crowd, one deliberate wink cutting through my panic like a knife.

Perfect victim. Perfect bait. God, she's good.

I wait exactly forty-five seconds before following, leaving cash on the table. The cool night air hits me as I step outside, clearing my head slightly. I spot them half a block ahead, walking down the street.

Scout's laughter carries back to me, high and breathless. Stanton's arm is around her waist now, his hand resting dangerously low on her hip.

I follow at a distance, keeping to the shadows. My footsteps are silent against the wet pavement, years of practice making me a ghost in the night. Every muscle in my body is taut, ready to spring.

Stanton's hand slides lower, cupping Scout's ass with possessive fingers. The sight sends a surge of something primal through me, not jealousy, I tell myself. It's just disgust at watching a predator who thinks he's found easy prey.

Scout giggles, leaning heavily against him as they turn the corner into the alley where he parked his car. Away from streetlights. Away from cameras. Away from witnesses.

Perfect.

I quicken my pace slightly, rounding the corner just in time to see Scout stumble dramatically, nearly taking Stanton down with her. He laughs, that condescending chuckle men like him use when they think they've won.

"Careful there, beautiful," he murmurs, steadying her with both hands on her waist. "Let me help you."

The darkness of the alley swallows them, but my eyes adjust quickly. I watch as Scout's hand slips into her purse, the movement so smooth that Stanton doesn't notice as she pulls the syringe out. He's too busy staring at her breasts, at the way her dress shifts with each exaggerated breath.

"You're so strong," Scout slurs, her fingers tracing his jawline. "A real lifesaver."

Stanton preens under the attention, completely missing the steel that enters her eyes. "I save lives every day, sweetheart. Maybe I'll show you my technique."

I slide my hand inside my jacket, fingers wrapping around the cold metal of my knife. Just in case. Just a precaution.

Scout doesn't need my help, I know this. I've seen her file. Thirty-two kills, all clean, all deserved. She's more than capable in this situation.

But as Stanton pushes her against the brick wall, his mouth hovering over hers, his hand sliding up her thigh, something inside me snaps.

I step forward, emerging from the shadows like a nightmare.

Scout's eyes flick to mine over Stanton's shoulder. Not panicked. Not pleading.

Amused.

She winks at me, and I realize I've just tried to step in for absolutely nothing.

Dr. Stanton lurches backward, fingers clawing at the tiny puncture in his neck while Scout twists the cap back onto her syringe with a practiced flick of her wrist. The paralytic is already working its way through his system.

His gaze locks with mine. Pure terror floods his features, eyes bulging, face contorting. His jaw works uselessly, opening and closing without sound, like a goldfish dumped from its bowl as his body slides down his car's exterior until his ass hits asphalt.

I force myself to breathe, to stay where I belong. Scout knows what she's doing. This is the plan. The carefully choreographed dance of predator becoming prey. But watching Stanton's manicured hand slide lower, watching him lean in to whisper something that makes her giggle that fake, hollow laugh, it awakened something primal and vicious inside me that I've kept carefully locked away.

My hand drifts unconsciously to the knife in my pocket, thumb tracing the familiar ridge of the handle. One quick movement. That's all it would take. One clean slice across his throat. I've done it before. Made men disappear without a sound. Made them pay for their sins without the luxury of confession. Every cell in my body screams to cross the distance between us, to make him understand with brutal clarity what happens to men who think they can touch what's mine.

I freeze. *Woah, where did that come from? I've never felt this level of possessiveness. Why am I reacting like this over her?* The thought comes unbidden and fierce. I've never felt this protective instinct for anyone. It's unwelcome. Dangerous. A liability.

Scout points at Dr. Stanton sprawled on the asphalt, her finger jabbing toward his crumpled form as her lips curl into a suggestive smirk. "Since you're so big on interfering... You could save me the trouble and put him in the trunk."

I'm sitting in Dr. Stanton's office in the Community free clinic, watching in awe as Scout stitches the Dahlia to his body. The needle glides through his flesh with precision that would make the surgeon jealous, if he weren't on the receiving end of it, that is. Each puncture draws more tears from his frozen face. She is utterly terrifying and absolutely stunning as she works, her amber eyes narrowed in concentration, the tip of her tongue peeking out between her lips. The dim fluorescent lighting casts shadows across her face, highlighting the wicked gleam in her eyes and the delicate curve of her jaw.

The saucy green dress from earlier has been replaced with the outfit I saw her in that first night: low-rise black pants hugging her hips, a black compression shirt, black gloves, and boots. Caramel skin glows against her ash-blonde streaked boxer braids that sway with each methodical stitch she places into Dr. Stanton's chest.

She is definitely an unhinged multitasker as she talks to the good Doctor, her voice bubbling with the same enthusiasm someone might use discussing their favorite show rather than explaining to a serial predator why he deserves this fate. Her fingers never falter, even as she gestures dramatically with her other hand, detailing exactly how many women he's assaulted and killed. He destroyed lives figuratively and literally.

"This one's for Naomi," she says cheerfully, pushing the needle through another layer of skin. "And this pretty little stitch? That's for Kristin. You remember her, don't you, Doc? She's the one you claimed relocated to Miami." She giggles, the sound both melodic and chilling in the sterile room. "But we both know the real story behind that one." Her gloved finger traces the finished petal, leaving a faint smear of blood in its wake. A smile slices across her face, sharp and terrifying, like a predator savoring the moment before the kill. "She laughed at that pathetic excuse for a cock in your pants." Her bottom lip juts out in mock sympathy, eyes glittering with cruelty. "Poor widdle feller, can't handle the truth? I'm gonna be honest with ya, Doc, she was right." Her gaze flicks dismissively between his legs, nose wrinkling. "From where I'm sitting, grub worms are bigger." A sadistic laugh tumbles from her full lips.

I should not be so turned on from watching her sew in his skin, the red thread forming perfect petals against his pale chest, but I most definitely am. My jeans strain against the length of my rigid cock, the denim's seam digging mercilessly into sensitive flesh. I shift in the good

Doctor's plush chair, hoping to relieve the pressure. There's something hypnotic about the way she works. She's confident, skilled, and completely in her element while delivering vengeance one stitch at a time. Every muscle in my body tightens with primal hunger as I watch her count out blood droplets beneath the flower, one for each of his victims, including the two nursing students police never connected to him.

My breath catches as she looks up at me and smiles, a predator pausing mid-hunt, before she returns to her grisly artwork with lethal focus. God help me, I've never seen anything more beautiful than Scout Prescott with blood on her hands and vengeance in her smile.

NINETEEN

SCOUT

The ride back to the safehouse is excruciating. I'm floating on that perfect post-kill high, the one where justice feels like warm honey in my veins and every nerve ending tingles with satisfaction. But the car is thick with tension. Deacon's thumb drums restlessly against the steering wheel as he navigates the crowded Chicago streets.

I sneak glances at his profile. He's all sharp angles and a clenched jaw. His forearms flex every time he adjusts his grip, the muscles rippling beneath his tanned skin. I've seen this before, the way some killers come down from the adrenaline rush after a kill, but this feels different. It feels personal.

When we finally pull into the garage of the safehouse, I can't take the silence anymore.

"You gonna tell me what's got you wound tighter than my embroidery thread?" I ask, unclicking my seatbelt.

Deacon kills the engine but doesn't move, just stares straight ahead through the windshield.

"Was there a problem with how things went down back there?" The words tumble out with an edge of frustration. Silence from him is nothing new, but this feels different.

"That's not it." His voice is gravel and steel.

"Then what?" I tilt my head, studying him. "Did I steal your thunder? Was the Candy Man feeling left out of playtime?" My lips curve into a deliberate smirk. "Or maybe you just couldn't resist seeing my handiwork up close and personal?"

He turns to me then, steel gray eyes piercing through the darkness of the garage. "You know that's not true."

"Do I? Because crashing my party isn't exactly your style, Flossie." I lean closer, invading his space. "So either you didn't trust the plan, or you didn't trust me. Which is it?"

"I trust your abilities."

I fold my arms across my chest. "Then what the hell is your deal? You've been radiating death vibes since we left Stanton's office."

Deacon's jaw works, like he's chewing on words he doesn't want to say. Finally, he exhales sharply. "I reacted... unprofessionally. When Stanton put his hands on you, I wanted to remove them. Permanently."

"Excuse me?"

"It wasn't about the job." He stops, shakes his head. "It was a lapse in judgment. It won't happen again."

I blink at him, processing. "Wait. Are you saying you were... jealous?"

"Not jealous." His voice is firm. "Territorial. There's a difference."

The confession hits me like a punch to the gut, stealing my breath. I wasn't expecting that level of honesty from him.

"Territorial," I repeat, testing the word. "Of me?"

"It doesn't make sense." He runs a hand through his dark hair, frustration evident in every movement. "I don't get attached. I don't do this." He gestures vaguely between us. "But watching him put his hands on you, even knowing it was part of the plan."

"Made you lose control," I finish, leaning forward slightly. "That must be terrifying for someone like you."

His jaw tightens. "Yes." The word comes out like a confession.

I lean back against the passenger door, studying him. The admission hangs between us, heavy with implications. "So you weren't worried about me being able to handle myself."

"Scout." His eyes lock with mine, intense and unwavering. "I've seen your work. I know exactly what you're capable of."

A slow smile spreads across my face as I inch closer. "So what exactly bothered you?" I'm pushing now, deliberately testing the cracks in his perfect composure.

"Not bothered." He shakes his head, but his eyes darken as I move into his space. "I wanted to be the one to make him pay for touching what's—" He cuts himself off abruptly.

Something dangerous shifts between us, like that moment when you've pushed too far and can't decide if you're about to get kissed or killed. I've never seen the perfectly controlled Deacon Thorne struggle for words before. It's intoxicating.

I can practically see him fighting against whatever this is between us, that dangerous current that's been buzzing since I first spotted him in that café.

"I don't want this," he finally admits, his voice strained as he grips the steering wheel. "I don't do attachments. They're liabilities."

"And yet," I lean closer, deliberately invading his space, "you want me," I say it like a challenge, a dare.

His jaw clenches. "It's a mistake."

"Is it?" I reach across the console, my fingertips hovering just above his forearm. "Because I think you're just afraid of what happens when you let go of all that perfect control."

"Scout." My name comes out as a warning, low and dangerous.

"Deacon." I mimic his tone, but can't keep the smile from my voice.

"This isn't—"

"Smart? Professional? Part of the plan?" I finish for him. "I've never been great at sticking to plans."

His eyes darken as they drop to my lips. "I've noticed."

The post-kill high still simmers in my veins, making me reckless and hungry for whatever comes next.

I shift toward him, my movements slow and deliberate like a panther closing in on its prey. "You know what I think?" I whisper, leaning into his space. "I think you've been fighting this since the moment we met."

His jaw tightens, but he doesn't pull away when I reach out, trailing my fingers along the sharp line of it.

"I see the way you watch me," I continue, my voice a silken purr as I slide my hand to the back of his neck. The words feel like stepping off a cliff, bold and terrifying all at once. "When you think I'm not looking." I lean closer, my lips a breath away from his. "I wonder what else you do when you think I'm not looking."

Something dark and hungry flashes in his eyes, and hope flutters dangerously in my chest. Maybe this time he won't pull away.

"You can keep pretending you don't want this," I murmur against the corner of his mouth, not quite kissing him. My heart hammers against my ribs as I put myself completely on the line. "But we both know you're going to break eventually. Why not now? Why not with me?"

His hand shoots out, fingers tangling in my hair as he yanks me toward him. The center console digs painfully into my ribs, but I barely register it as he pulls me half into his lap.

"You have no idea what you're asking for," he growls against my mouth, the last thread of his restraint snapping.

When his lips finally meet mine, it's not gentle. It's not sweet. It's a collision, inevitable and explosive. He devours my mouth as his hand slides to the back of my neck, fingers tangling in my hair as he pulls me closer. I grab his shirt, fisting the material as I kiss him back with equal hunger.

He tastes like mint and danger, and I can't get enough. I bite his lower lip hard, drawing a growl from deep in his chest. The sound vibrates through me, settling low in my belly as the metallic taste explodes on my tongue.

"Inside," he mutters against my mouth. "Now."

WE PRACTICALLY FALL out of the car, unwilling to break contact for more than a few seconds at a time. The short walk to the safehouse door becomes a stumbling dance of hands and lips and breathless laughter when I nearly trip over my own feet.

Deacon pins me against the wall the moment we're inside, his body hard and insistent against mine. The hard ridge of his cock presses against my stomach through his pants. His hands frame my face, thumbs tracing my cheekbones as he stares down at me with an intensity that makes my knees weak.

His mouth finds my neck immediately, teeth grazing the sensitive spot below my ear. I gasp as pleasure shoots through me, my hands sliding under his shirt to feel the ridges of muscle beneath warm skin.

"For someone who doesn't do attachments," I manage between shaky breaths, "you're very good at this."

He chuckles against my skin, the sound dark and delicious. "I didn't say I don't do this part."

"Just the feelings part?" I pull back slightly to look at him.

Something shutters in his eyes, walls visibly reinforcing. "The attachment part complicates things."

I trace my fingers along his jaw, fighting the sting of his words. Of course, attachments complicate things. They always do, especially when people leave. "Good thing this isn't complicated, then."

His eyes darken at the challenge in my voice. His hand slides up to cup my throat, thumb pressing against my pulse point.

"Nothing about you is uncomplicated, Scout," he growls, his mouth hovering just above mine.

The admission seems to break something loose in him. His next kiss is deeper, more demanding, like he's trying to consume me. My body answers his with equal desperation, my leg hooking around his hip, pulling him to me.

My hands find the hem of his shirt, yanking it upward with urgent need. He breaks the kiss just long enough to help me pull it over his head, revealing the sculpted planes of his chest and abdomen. My fingers trace the defined muscles, exploring every ridge and valley before my nails carve crescents into his bare back, leaving trails of red as I mark him.

He growls against my mouth, his hands finding the bottom of my shirt. In one swift motion, he pulls it over my head and tosses it aside, his hungry gaze devouring the sight of my lace-covered breasts.

"Fucking perfect," he mutters, before his mouth descends to my exposed skin.

When his knee drives between my thighs, my breath catches. The hard pressure against my swollen clit sends lightning through my veins, and I can't help the low moan that escapes as I rock against the firm muscle of his thigh, chasing that sweet, maddening friction.

His mouth drops to my collarbone, teeth scraping over the sensitive skin. In one fluid motion, he captures my wrists, forcing my arms upward until he pins them against the wall above my head. The cold surface presses against my bare back as his fingers tighten around both wrists, his grip like iron. His free hand snakes downward, a trail of fire following his touch until he reaches the heat between my thighs. The heel of his palm presses against my pussy, creating delicious friction as he cups me through my pants.

"Fuck, Deacon," I gasp, grinding against his palm as he controls the pressure with precise, torturous skill that makes my legs tremble.

"Fuck," he groans, his voice breaking as his fingers slide roughly against the heated, wet fabric. "Your pussy is soaked for me, Kitten." His teeth scrape against my collarbone, leaving goosebumps in their wake. "I'm going to bury my face in your cunt until I've had my fill of your sweet cream."

Damn. The obscene things he's saying send heat spiraling through me. I never imagined the king of one-word answers could be so goddamn explicit.

"More," I moan, my voice breaking as my hips buck against his palm. "I need more." His fingers move with maddening control, giving me just enough pressure that I'm grinding helplessly against his hand. My thighs tremble with each movement, electricity building low in my belly as my body chases release. The tension coils tighter, sparks shooting up my spine as the edge hovers just beyond my reach.

His hand pulls from between my thighs, leaving me cold and aching. A desperate whimper tears from my throat as my hips chase his retreating touch.

"You're not going to cum without me inside of you," he growls, his steel-gray eyes burning into mine.

The possessive edge in his voice makes my heart clench. I know better than to read more into this than what it is, but God, I want to pretend, just for tonight, that someone might actually want to stay with me.

His fingers trail upward, finding the button of my cargo pants. He pops the metal button and pull the zipper with excruciating slowness. Above my head, my fingers twitch and strain against his iron grip, every nerve ending screaming to feel his skin beneath my hands.

His mouth crashes against mine, stealing both breath and thought. His tongue delves deep, claiming every corner while his hand slips beneath the loosened fabric to find my bare, aching center. His long fingers tease my entrance, just the tip breaching me before retreating. My hips buck and chase the sensation, betraying my desperation. When his fingers glide upward to circle my clit, my body shudders with need. The kiss breaks, and his forehead presses against mine, our shared space filled with the harsh rhythm of his breathing, each exhale hot and heavy with want.

"You've been playing with fire since we set foot in this place." His breath is hot against my ear as his voice drops to a dangerous whisper that makes my insides liquify. "Time to burn, Kitten."

My body trembles beneath his touch, inner walls clenching desperately around nothing as his fingers trace deliberate patterns across my swollen clit. Methodical. Relentless. One moment pressing hard enough to make my vision blur, the next barely there, a ghost of contact that leaves me chasing the sensation. His fingertips glide through my slick folds, gathering evidence of how badly I want him. Each ragged breath tears from my lungs, my chest heaving as he continues his exquisite torture.

"Do you want to cum, little minx?" The question vibrates from deep in his chest, his voice a dark caress against my skin.

I could lie. I could play tough. But the truth spills from my lips instead. "Yes," I gasp, arching into his touch. "Please, Deacon."

The plea surprises me. I never beg. I never let anyone reduce me to this, desperate and aching and completely undone. But here I am, laid bare in every way that matters.

His pupils dilate at my plea, something primal flashing in those steel-gray eyes. Two fingers plunge inside me, stealing the breath from my lungs. My lips part in a silent cry as he captures my mouth with his, his tongue invading with the same merciless rhythm as his fingers curling against that perfect spot deep within me. The rough heel of his hand grinds against my sensitive flesh while his fingers twist and curl in my pussy, sending electric currents racing through every nerve ending.

My wrists fall free as his hand trails down to my bra. His fingers find the front clasp effortlessly, a quick flick, and the material parts like curtains, cool air kissing my exposed skin as my breasts spill free. The rough pad of his calloused palm scrapes against my sensitive flesh as he claims one breast, his thumb circling my hardened nipple before flicking across the stiff peak, sending lightning straight to my core.

"Perfect," he growls, his warm breath ghosting across my skin before his tongue flicks over my sensitive nub. His mouth captures my nipple, the wet heat enveloping me as he sucks, teeth grazing just hard enough to make me gasp.

Heat coils tight in my belly, muscles clenching and unclenching as the pressure mounts, threatening to shatter me from within. Sweat beads across my flushed skin, dampening the wisps of hair at my temples while my temperature skyrockets. I close my eyes, moaning as my body dances on the edge of release. His mouth releases my nipple with a wet, soft pop.

"Eyes on me," he growls, the words rumbling from deep in his chest.

My eyes snap to his, drawn by the rough command that leaves no room for refusal. Steel gray eyes bore into mine, searching, demanding, as his hand leaves my breast to glide up my body. Those long fingers wrap around my throat, encircling the delicate skin. My pulse hammers against his palm as he flexes, applying pressure that steals my breath away. The room narrows to just his face, just those eyes, as the edges of my vision begin to blur.

His forehead meets mine, steel eyes burning into me as he growls. "Now, Kitten. Cum for me."

His palm grinds against my swollen clit while his fingers twist and scissor inside me, finding that perfect spot that makes my vision spark.

"Deacon," I gasp, the name tearing from my throat as lightning crashes through me. My inner walls clamp down on his fingers, pulsing and gripping like they never want to let go. My nails carve half-moons into his bare shoulders, marking his tanned skin as every muscle in my body pulls taut. Tremors wrack through me, my chest heaving with each broken breath.

My head falls back against the wall as his grip loosens on my throat. His fingers slide free of my throbbing pussy, glistening with my cum. He raises them between us, examining what he's done, what he's pulled from my body. Steel eyes capture mine, holding me hostage as his tongue traces the moisture on his fingertips.

"You taste so fucking good," he murmurs, voice rough with hunger.

His palm slides up from my throat to cradle my jaw, calloused fingers pressing into my cheeks with just enough force to make my breath catch. "Now open that saucy fucking mouth," he growls, the command vibrating through me.

My lips part instinctively. He drags his wet fingers across them, painting me with my own release before pushing them past the threshold of my mouth. "Suck them clean, Kitten."

I seal my lips around his fingers, my tongue swirling against his skin, tasting myself on him. His eyes darken, pupils blown wide as he watches me suck, his gaze locked on my mouth.

He withdraws his fingers slowly, then closes the distance between us. His tongue traces the curve of my lower lip before claiming my mouth completely, exploring its depths.

"Mmmm," he rumbles against my lips, "tastes even better."

His hands slide along the curve of my hips and below to palm my ass with possessive heat. He lifts me effortlessly, my body responding instinctively as my ankles cross behind the solid plane of his back. The hard length pushes against my center, the friction sending electric currents through my already overstimulated nerves. A moan escapes me, unbidden and raw, as his cock drags perfectly against my swollen, aching flesh.

I wrap my legs tighter around his waist, pressing my core against the hard ridge straining against his pants. My hands fumble with his belt buckle, desperate to feel him without barriers.

"I need you inside me," I whisper against his mouth, nipping at his lower lip. "Now."

His eyes flash with primal hunger as he carries me toward the bedroom, his grip tight enough to leave marks I'll admire tomorrow. We barely make it three steps when a shrill electronic wail cuts through the heated air between us.

TWENTY

SCOUT

The shrill alarm slices through the heated moment like a bucket of ice water. I groan, burying my face against Deacon's neck, my body still thrumming with need.

"Ignore it," Deacon growls, his lips finding my pulse point.

His teeth graze the sensitive skin of my neck, just enough pressure to send electricity racing down my spine. A shudder ripples through me, my knees nearly buckling as his mouth works that sensitive spot. Heat pools low in my belly, and I have to bite my lip to stifle a moan. My fingers curl against his bare chest, torn between pulling him closer and doing what I know we have to do.

"God... fuck," I whimper, my voice catching between want and reality. With every ounce of willpower I possess, I push against his chest, reluctantly creating space between us. "We can't. That's not a sound you ignore."

His brows furrow.

I wiggle until he sets me down, immediately missing his heat. "That's an all-call alert. Everyone in The Hollow gets it simultaneously."

Deacon's warmth envelops me from behind, his calloused hands sliding to my hips like they belong there, even if he doesn't believe it yet. He tugs my pants up in one fluid motion, fingers brushing against the curve of my waist as he secures the button. Without pause, his hands slide up my bare ribs, leaving goosebumps in their wake. He gathers the cups of my bra, still hanging from my shoulders, and guides them back into place before snapping the front clasp with a soft click.

The Index app flashes red, demanding attention.

"Fuck," I breathe, scanning the alert. "It's the Glass Gardener. They've struck again just outside of Atlanta."

Deacon's demeanor shifts instantly. The hungry lover vanishes, replaced by the calculating killer. He moves beside me, reading over my shoulder. "That's not far from the compound."

"No, it's not." I swipe rapidly through the screen, pulling up more details. "But the alert isn't bringing everyone home, so the scene was only close enough to warrant extreme caution."

Images populate my screen, shattered mirror shards arranged in a grotesque garden around a body. The sun symbol carved into the victim's chest is identical to what Deacon described from Denver.

"This is the exact same signature," Deacon says, voice tight. "Down to the placement of the larger shards."

"Roman's tracking pattern recognition." I swipe through more photos, each more disturbing than the last. "Five kills in the last eight months can be linked back to him. The locations are all over, though."

A second alert pings, this one with a different tone.

"That alert is just for us," I explain, opening the new notification. "Shit. Coach Z booked a one-way flight. He's leaving in two days."

Deacon's jaw tightens. "He's running."

"Or hunting somewhere new." I meet his eyes. "Either way, your timeline just got accelerated."

"Tomorrow night then," he says without hesitation. "We take him tomorrow night."

I nod, mind already racing through the logistics. "I'll contact Roman, have him compile Coach Z's movements for the last forty-eight hours. We need to know if he's spooked or just relocating."

The heat between us hasn't disappeared, but it's been redirected, channeled into the focused energy that comes with planning a kill. I straighten my clothes, trying to ignore how my body still aches for his touch.

"I should..." I gesture vaguely toward my room.

"Yeah." His eyes darken briefly, reminding me of what we've just interrupted. "We both should."

I take a step toward my bedroom, then pause. "Deacon?"

"Hmm?"

"This isn't over." I hold his gaze, making sure he understands I mean more than just Coach Z.

A ghost of a smile touches his lips. "No, it's not."

I retreat to my room, the phantom sensation of his hands still burning on my skin. The alerts from The Index glow ominously on my phone, two very different threats demanding our attention. The Glass Gardener is moving closer to our territory, and Coach Z is preparing to slip away.

Both need handling. Both require a focus I can barely muster with my body still humming from Deacon's touch.

I take a deep breath, willing my racing heart to slow. First, we plan. Then we kill.

And after that? After that, I'm finishing what we started against that wall.

My FINGERS STAB at the phone screen like I'm trying to murder it. Morning sunlight pours through the window, offensively bright and cheerful when I feel anything but.

"Stupid Roman with his stupid efficiency," I mutter, squinting at the latest message from our tech guru. It's barely seven in the morning, and I've already exchanged twenty messages with him about Coach Z.

> Any unusual cash withdrawals?

I type.

The response is immediate:

> None. Credit card activity was normal until yesterday. He purchased a one-way ticket to Tallahassee for $742.

I growl at my phone, chugging the coffee Deacon silently placed beside me ten minutes ago. He's been moving around the safehouse kitchen with quiet efficiency all morning, the sounds of cooking weaving between his methodical preparations for tonight while I handle intel gathering. I ask Roman.

> Gym schedule today?

> Regular Thursday routine. Morning practice 8-10. Private sessions 3-6.

"He's not acting like someone who's running," I announce to the room, voice still gravelly with sleep. "No cash withdrawals, keeping his regular schedule."

Deacon looks up from where he's arranging items on the kitchen counter: zip ties, duct tape, knives, and a small bag of pink cotton candy. "He doesn't know we're coming."

"Exactly." I stretch, my oversized sleep shirt riding up my thighs. Deacon's eyes flicker to the exposed skin before deliberately returning to his prep work. The tension from last night still hangs between us, electric and unresolved.

My phone pings again. Roman sent a detailed schedule of Coach Z's day, including the names of the three boys he has private sessions with this afternoon.

"Look at this," I say, sliding my phone across the counter. "Last private session is with Jamie Winters. Kid's been seeing him three times a week for the past month."

Deacon's jaw tightens as he studies the screen. "That's our window. After the last session, before he leaves the gym."

"What are you thinking?" I ask, stealing a sip from his coffee mug since mine is empty. It's black and bitter, just like his soul, I think with amusement. I gag. *God, how can he drink this?*

"We'll be direct. Wait until the kid leaves and catch him in his office."

Deacon's voice is calm and methodical. "I don't think he'll be expecting trouble."

I nod, watching him organize his tools with military precision. "Do you need any help?"

"No, I'm almost done." He pauses as his eyes meet mine. "Will you be there tonight?"

"Obviously." I roll my eyes and tap my fingers against my temple. "I'm your partner on this, remember? Besides, someone needs to make sure you don't mess up your cotton candy placement."

The corner of his mouth twitches. It's almost a smile. "Of course, I wouldn't want to disappoint my adoring fans."

"Exactly." I grin, momentarily forgetting my morning grumpiness. "The aesthetic is half the statement."

My phone buzzes again. Roman sent blueprints of the high school gym and adjacent offices.

"Service entrance here," I point out, zooming in on the screen. "Minimal security cameras, and Roman can loop those anyway."

Deacon leans over my shoulder to look, his chest pressing against my back. The casual intimacy sends a shiver down my spine that has nothing to do with murder planning.

"Coach's office is isolated," he notes, his breath warm against my ear. "One exit to the hallway directly across from the locker room and one window facing the back lot."

"Perfect killing location," I murmur, leaning back slightly into his solid frame.

For a moment, we stay like that, my back against his chest, both of us staring at the blueprint but hyper aware of each other's proximity. Then Deacon straightens, returning to his methodical preparations.

I turn my eyes back to my phone and type a quick request to Roman for any security patrol schedules at the school. My brain feels foggy, caught between planning tonight's kill and replaying last night's interrupted moment against the wall.

"You should eat something," Deacon says, sliding a plate with toast and eggs in front of me.

I stare at the perfectly prepared plate, something warm and unexpected blooming in my chest. He wasn't making this for himself. When was the last time someone just... took care of me like this? "You made me breakfast?"

"Can't have you passing out from caffeine overdose and hunger tonight." His tone is practical, but there's something softer in his eyes.

"Thanks," I mumble, suddenly aware I'm still in my oversized sleep shirt with messy hair and morning breath. Not exactly the seductive image I'd planned for our morning-after.

Except it isn't morning-after anything, thanks to that damn alert.

I stab at my eggs, wondering how we're supposed to navigate this strange new territory between us while simultaneously planning a murder. The juxtaposition would be funny if it weren't my actual life.

THE EVENING AIR hangs heavy with anticipation as we approach the service entrance of Kennedy High School. My heart thrums with the familiar pre-kill rhythm, not quite fear, not quite excitement, but something electric that dances between the two.

"The camera loop is live," I whisper, checking the notification from Roman on my phone. "We're invisible."

Deacon nods, his movements are fluid and silent as he works the lock. His entire demeanor has shifted since this morning. Gone is any trace of the man who made me breakfast. In his place stands a predator, focused entirely on the hunt.

The lock clicks, and we slip inside, darkness swallowing us whole until our eyes adjust to the dim emergency lighting. The school smells like every high school ever, disinfectant barely masking teenage sweat, with undertones of floor wax and desperation.

I check the Index app on my phone, where Roman has set up a live feed from the security cameras he's hacked. "Coach Z is still in the locker room. Across from his office."

Deacon's eyes meet mine, steel gray hardened with purpose. "Jamie Winters?"

"Left ten minutes ago." I swipe through the feeds to confirm. "Roman says we're all clear."

A short nod, then Deacon reaches into his black duffel bag and pulls out the skull mask I'd seen once before on the night I watched him kill Jeffrey Lorre. The mask is simple but haunting. It's matte black with bones etched onto it and hollow eye sockets that somehow make his actual eyes more intense, more predatory.

He slips it over his face, and my breath catches.

There's something wildly intoxicating about this version of him. The controlled killer with death in his hands and ice in his veins. His broad shoulders seem more imposing, his height more threatening, his presence consuming the narrow hallway we're standing in.

We move down the empty corridor, our footsteps silent against the polished floor. The gym looms ahead, it's a cavernous space with bleachers pulled back against the walls and basketball hoops hanging like silent sentinels in the darkness.

I hang back and press my body against the cold concrete wall. Deacon's the star tonight, and I'm just here for the show.

"I'll stay here," I whisper, gesturing to the shadowed alcove near the equipment closet.

Deacon nods once, sharp and precise. The skull mask transforms him into something otherworldly, a reaper in human form. He moves with such liquid grace that I wonder if he's even touching the ground. His body melts into the darkness beside the locker room doors, becoming one with the shadows.

The locker room door swings open, spilling fluorescent light across the polished floor. Coach Z emerges with his keys jangling in his meaty hand. He's taller than his file photo suggested, six-foot-something of former athlete gone to seed, with a barrel chest and thick neck. He's whistling something tuneless, utterly unaware that death waits just inches away.

One heartbeat. Two.

Deacon moves so fast I almost miss it. One moment, he's a shadow; the next, he's materialized behind Coach Z like a nightmare. His arm locks around the coach's throat in a textbook blood choke, pressure on the carotids, not the windpipe. No sound, no struggle, just the sudden panicked widening of Coach Z's eyes as his oxygen supply gets cut off.

The coach's keys clatter to the floor as his hands claw uselessly at Deacon's forearm. His legs kick out, but Deacon has positioned himself perfectly, using the larger man's weight against him. Within seconds, Coach Z's struggles weaken, his eyes roll back, and his body goes slack.

Deacon catches him before he hits the ground, controlling the descent with the same precision he's shown in everything else. Not a sound. Not a wasted movement.

I stay frozen in my alcove, watching as Deacon drags Coach Z back through the locker room doors. After a moment, I follow, keeping to the shadows.

The locker room reeks of sweat and cheap body spray. Deacon has already dragged Coach Z to lie in an open area between rows of lockers. He moves to grab a metal folding chair from against the wall, setting it in place next to an unconscious Coach Z.

He positions Coach Z in the chair, the man's head lolling forward like a broken puppet. From the duffel come zip ties. They're black, heavy-duty, and impossible to break. Deacon secures the coach's wrists to the chair's metal arms, then his ankles to the legs.

Throughout it all, Deacon moves with methodical efficiency. There's something mesmerizing about watching him work, like witnessing a master craftsman or a surgeon. Every motion has a purpose, and nothing is wasted.

I watch, transfixed, as Deacon retrieves another metal folding chair from against the wall. The scrape of metal against tile echoes through the empty locker room as he positions it directly in front of Coach Z's slumped form. Instead of sitting normally, he turns the chair backward, the metal backrest facing the unconscious predator.

From his duffel, Deacon pulls out a knife that makes my breath catch. The blade is wicked, at least seven inches of gleaming, razor-sharp steel with a serrated edge near the hilt. The handle is matte black, perfectly balanced in his gloved hand. There's nothing ornate or flashy about it, just like Deacon himself, it's designed purely for lethal efficiency.

He straddles the backward chair with casual grace, folding his muscular arms across the metal backrest. The knife rests on his forearm, the blade catching the harsh fluorescent lights with every subtle movement. Despite the predatory intensity radiating from him, his posture appears almost relaxed, like a hunter so confident in his kill that he can afford to wait patiently.

The skull mask transforms him completely. Through the hollow eye sockets, his steel-gray eyes track every twitch of Coach Z's body with unwavering focus. The contrast between his seemingly casual posture and the deadly intent in those eyes sends a shiver down my spine that has nothing to do with fear.

Coach Z begins to stir, a low groan escaping his lips as consciousness returns. His head lolls forward before jerking upright, confusion giving way to panic as he realizes he's restrained. His eyes dart wildly around the locker room before landing on the skull-masked figure sitting calmly before him.

"What the fu—" His words die in his throat as his gaze fixes on the knife gleaming on Deacon's forearm.

I press myself deeper into the shadows, not wanting to distract from Deacon's moment. This is his kill, his justice to deliver. But I can't tear my eyes away from him, the controlled power in his stillness, the absolute command he has over the situation without saying a single word.

There's something intoxicating about watching Deacon work. I feel heat bloom across my skin despite the locker room's chill. My breath quickens as I watch Deacon tilt his head slightly, studying Coach Z like a scientist might examine a particularly interesting specimen. The movement is subtle but somehow more terrifying for its restraint.

The knife catches another flash of light as Coach Z struggles against his restraints, the zip ties cutting into his wrists as panic sets in. Deacon doesn't move, doesn't speak, just watches with those penetrating eyes behind the skull mask, the blade a silent promise of what's to come.

I've never been more fascinated, or more aroused, by anything in my life.

TWENTY-ONE

DEACON

I sit perfectly still, watching Coach Z's panic escalate with each passing second. The room fills with nothing but the sound of his labored breathing and the metallic creak of the chair as he struggles against the zip ties.

Let him stew. Let the fear build.

I've studied men like him for years. Predators who hide behind positions of authority, using their power to access victims who can't fight back. I know exactly what Coach Z has done to those boys, what he was planning to do to Jamie Winters before leaving town.

"Coach Zachary Phillips." My voice comes out lower than usual, distorted slightly by the mask. "Wrestling coach. Mentor. Monster."

The knife feels perfect in my hand as I slowly lift it from my forearm, letting the fluorescent lights catch the blade. Coach Z's eyes lock onto it, his pupils dilating with terror.

"I don't... I haven't... please, I don't know what you want." His voice breaks on the last word.

I tilt my head, studying him. "That's interesting. You don't know what I want." I lean forward slightly, the chair creaking beneath me. "But you know exactly what you've done."

"I haven't done anything!" His voice rises to a desperate pitch.

The knife twirls between my fingers, a flash of silver that pulls his gaze like a magnet. "How many boys, Coach? How many young boys trusted you? How many young boys did you put your filthy hands on?"

His face drains of color. "That's—that's not true. Who are you? Is someone paying you? I can pay more—"

"Money." I let out a soft, humorless laugh. "Always the first offer. As if that would ever be enough."

I stand slowly, still holding the knife where he can see it. His eyes never leave the blade.

"Let me tell you what I know about predators like you, Coach." I circle behind him, my voice never rising above a controlled murmur. "You start small. A touch that lasts too long. A comment about physical development. Creating situations where you're alone with them."

I complete my circle, coming to stand directly in front of him now. "You convince them it's normal, that it's for their improvement. That they're special."

"Please," he whispers, tears beginning to streak down his ruddy face. "I have a family."

"You're a liar." I bring the knife closer to his face, not touching him yet, just letting him feel the proximity of the blade. "Did Michael Fernandez mention his family when you cornered him in the equipment room? Did Ethan Davis talk about his mother when you told him what would happen if he ever spoke up?"

His eyes widen at the names, confirmation I don't need but appreciate nonetheless.

"How—"

"I know everything about you." I crouch down to eye level. My skull mask is inches from his sweating face. "Every boy. Every threat. Every life you've poisoned."

The knife flashes again as I stand to my full height, towering over him. I can feel Scout's eyes on me from the shadows, but I remain focused on the trembling man before me.

"Please don't kill me," Coach Z sobs, his earlier bravado completely shattered. "I'll do anything. I'll turn myself in. I'll confess everything."

"No." The single word drops between us like a stone.

"Please, no, I promise." His words dissolve into incoherent pleading as tears and snot run down his face.

My shadow stretches across him as I close the distance, legs braced apart like a predator about to strike, shoulders squared in a way that makes Coach Z's pupils dilate, his face contorts in pure terror, a wailing sound escaping him as a dark stain spreads across the front of his pants. The acrid smell of urine fills the space between us.

I look down at him, this pathetic shell who held so much power over others. Now reduced to what he truly is, a coward facing the consequences at last.

"They were children," I say, my voice deadly quiet. "And you were supposed to protect them."

I move directly behind Coach Z, gripping the knife with practiced ease. The blade catches the harsh fluorescent light as I bring it around to hover in front of his face. His terrified eyes cross as he tries to focus on the metal edge just inches from his nose.

"Do you know what the worst part is?" I whisper near his ear. "You'll never feel remorse. Not really. Men like you never do."

A movement in the shadows catches my attention. Scout has crept closer, her amber eyes wide and luminous in the dim locker room. She's leaning against a row of lockers, her chest rising and falling with quickened breaths. There's something primal in her gaze, a mix of fascination, excitement, and arousal, all rolled into one intense stare.

I lock eyes with her across the room. Something electric passes between us, a silent acknowledgment of what we are, what we do. What we're about to do.

"Please," Coach Z whimpers, oblivious to our silent exchange. "I'll do anything."

My free hand shoots up to grab a fistful of his thinning hair, yanking his head back to expose his throat. I don't break eye contact with Scout as I position the blade.

"You already did everything," I tell him, my voice is deadly calm. "This is just the consequence."

In one swift, powerful move, I drag the knife across his throat. The blade slices clean and deep, opening him from ear to ear. Blood erupts in a crimson spray from his throat, spattering across the concrete floor.

The gurgling sound he makes is brief, a wet, choked attempt at a scream that dies in his severed windpipe.

Scout's lips part slightly as she watches, her pupils dilated with a dark hunger I recognize all too well. Her fingers curl desperately around the metal locker's edge as if fighting for an anchor. A flush creeps up her neck to her cheeks, and she shifts her weight from one foot to the other, unconsciously pressing her thighs together.

I maintain our eye contact as Coach Z's struggles weaken. His body jerks and twitches, blood pumping out in diminishing pulses as his heart fails. I can see Scout's reaction to every spasm, every spray of crimson. The way her breath catches, how she bites her lower lip.

When Coach Z finally goes still, I release his hair, letting his head drop forward. Blood continues to drip from the gaping wound, pooling on the floor beneath the chair. The metallic smell fills the room, sharp and coppery.

I step back, still watching Scout. She pushes herself away from the lockers and moves toward me with fluid grace, like a predator approaching prey. There's a wildness in her eyes I've never seen before or perhaps never allowed myself to notice.

She watches intently as I place the cotton candy in Coach Z's slack mouth, positioning it so it will slowly dissolve with the blood still trickling from his throat.

She stalks forward with lethal grace, amber eyes locked on mine. There's something feral in her gaze, hungry and unrestrained. Her lips part slightly, the tip of her tongue darting out to wet them as she closes the distance between us.

"Scout," I say, my voice a growl of warning.

She doesn't respond. Just keeps coming, step by deliberate step, until she's close enough that the fluorescent lights cast shadows across her face, highlighting the sharp curve of her cheekbones, the dangerous glint in her eyes.

The air between us crackles with something electric and dangerous. Blood pools around Coach Z's body, the pink cotton candy in his mouth slowly dissolving into a sickly sweet mixture.

"We need to go," I manage, my voice rough. "Roman's loop won't last forever."

She doesn't respond. Just keeps coming, deliberate step after deliberate step, until she's close enough that I can smell her perfume beneath the metallic scent of blood. Her gaze never leaves mine, amber eyes dilated with a hunger I recognize because it's mirrored in my own body.

"Scout," I try again, "we need to—"

Her hand shoots out, pressing firmly against the front of my jeans where my body has already betrayed me. The touch sends electricity straight up my spine.

My breath catches as her fingers trace the outline of my erection through the denim. The skull mask suddenly feels suffocating, but I don't move to remove it. Something about the anonymity it provides makes this moment feel surreal, as if it's separated from reality.

Any protest I have dies as she increases the pressure of her palm.

"You want this as badly as I do, Mr. Floss," Scout whispers, her eyes never leaving mine through the mask's eye holes.

She's right. The control, the power, the vengeance, it's always been an aphrodisiac. I've just never allowed myself to acknowledge it, much less act on it. But Scout sees through every defense I've built.

"Let me have this," she says, her fingers already working my belt buckle with practiced ease. "Let me have you."

The rational part of my brain screams that this is insane, we're at an active crime scene with a corpse three feet away. But rationality has no place here, not with Scout looking at me like I'm her next meal.

The belt comes loose with a metallic clink. Her fingers move to my button, then my zipper, the sound unnaturally loud in the quiet locker room. I stand frozen, letting her take control, my hands clenched at my sides.

Scout drops to her knees before me, seemingly unconcerned about the blood that's now seeping into her pants. The sight of her there, looking up at me with those wild eyes, nearly undoes me completely.

She tugs my jeans down to mid-thigh, and my erection springs free, painfully hard. A small smile plays at the corner of her mouth as she takes me in, her hand wrapping around me with confident pressure.

"I knew you'd be like this," she murmurs, her breath warm against my sensitive skin. "So controlled on the surface, but underneath..."

I swallow hard, unable to form words. The blood from Coach Z continues to spread across the concrete floor, congealing at the edges, a dark frame for Scout's kneeling form. The contrast should be disturbing, Scout's beauty against the backdrop of death, but instead, it feels like the most honest moment I've experienced in years.

This is who we are. This is what we do. There's no pretending otherwise.

Scout's eyes hold mine as she leans forward, her lips parting. The skull mask limits my peripheral vision, narrowing my world down to just her face, her eyes, her mouth. Everything else, the body, the blood, the risk, fades away until there's nothing but Scout and the sensation of her touch.

Scout's mouth closes around my cock, warm and wet, and my head falls back with a groan that echoes through the empty locker room. My hands find her hair, tangling in those caramel-streaked curls as she takes me deeper. The skull mask suddenly feels suffocating, but I don't care.

"Fuck," I hiss through clenched teeth as Scout hollows her cheeks, creating a suction that sends shockwaves through my body.

She pulls back, dragging her tongue along the underside of my cock before circling the head. Her amber eyes never leave mine, watching my reaction through the mask's eye holes. There's something almost predatory in her gaze, a challenge, a claim.

"Mmmm," she moans around my throbbing dick.

The picture we've created is twisted beyond reason, Scout kneeling in the slowly spreading pool of crimson, Coach Z's body slumped in the chair beside us, his dead eyes staring sightlessly at the eroticism before him. The pink cotton candy in his mouth has dissolved into a sickly sweet mixture with his blood, dripping down his chin in sticky rivulets. The metallic drip of blood hitting concrete punctuates the wet sounds Scout makes as she takes me into her mouth.

Her hands slide around to grip my ass, nails digging into the flesh hard enough to leave indentations. The sharp pain only heightens everything else. The heat of her mouth, the sight of her lips stretched around me, and the gruesome setting we've chosen.

My hand tightens in her curls, holding her in place as I lean back, pulling my cock from her lips. "Give it back," she commands, her amber eyes darkening with predatory intent.

"Open your mouth," I growl, my voice barely recognizable. "I'm going to fuck your throat."

A wicked smile spreads across her face. "Then fuck it," she challenges, opening her mouth and sticking out her tongue in invitation. "As much as you can give me."

My hands tighten in her hair, holding her head steady as I thrust forward. Scout moans around me, the vibration sending a jolt of pleasure up my spine. Her nails dig deeper into my ass, urging me on, demanding more.

I oblige, setting a punishing rhythm that has her eyes watering. But she doesn't back away. If anything, she pushes forward, taking me deeper as I hit the back of her throat.

The obscene sounds fill the locker room, the wet, sloppy noises of Scout's mouth, my harsh breathing, and underneath it all, the steady drip-drip-drip of Coach Z's blood hitting the concrete floor. His glazed eyes seem to stare through us, a lifeless witness to our depraved communion.

Scout's throat constricts around me as she swallows, and my control fractures. I thrust harder, chasing the building pressure at the base of my spine. Her hands move from my ass to my thighs, fingers pressing into the muscle hard enough to bruise.

The fluorescent lights flicker overhead, casting strange shadows across Coach Z's pallid face and Scout's flushed one. In this moment, the line between beauty and horror, pleasure and violence, blurs beyond recognition.

"Scout," I warn, my voice strained as I approach the edge.

She responds by taking me impossibly deeper, her nails now raking down the backs of my thighs. My balls tighten painfully as the pressure builds to an unbearable peak. Scout's throat works around my cock. The combination of pain and pleasure, death and desire, pushes me over the edge. My vision blurs at the corners as the most intense orgasm of my life tears through me.

"Fuck," I growl, gripping her hair tighter as I pump into her mouth. "Take all of it."

My hips jerk forward uncontrollably as I empty myself down her throat. Scout moans around my cock, her eyes never leaving mine as she swallows everything I give her. A small trickle of cum escapes the corner of her mouth, sliding down her chin in stark contrast to the blood surrounding us.

I pull back, breathing heavily, and rip the skull mask from my face. The cool air hits my sweat-slicked skin as I haul Scout up from her knees. Her lips are swollen and glistening, her eyes wild with desire.

My tongue traces the corner of her mouth where my cum leaked out, licking it clean before I capture her mouth with mine, tasting myself on her tongue. The flavor is bitter and primal, heightening the already electric connection between us. She responds with equal fervor, her hands fisting in my shirt, pulling me closer. Our teeth clash, the kiss more violence than tenderness. The metallic scent of blood fills my nostrils, mingling with the musky smell of sex.

I press my forehead against hers, both of us breathing hard. For a moment, we stand there, suspended in time, a scene of death and desire with Coach Z's body as our horrific audience. My breaths are ragged as the words scrape out of my throat, raw. "Christ, Kitten. You're going to be the death of me."

Scout hums in agreement, reaching down to tuck me back into my pants with surprising gentleness. Her fingers brush against my oversensitive skin, making me hiss through clenched teeth. She zips me up, fastens my belt, and steps back, her eyes scanning the room.

"We need to clean up," she says, voice husky with her own arousal.

Reality crashes back in. We're standing in a high school locker room with a dead body and a steadily expanding pool of blood. Roman's camera loop won't last forever.

I pull latex gloves from my pocket and snap them on. "I'll wipe down anything we touched near the body. You get over by the gear."

Scout nods, already moving toward our duffel bag. She pulls out sanitizing wipes and begins methodically cleaning any surface we might have contacted. I retrieve my knife from where I'd set it down, wiping it clean before returning it to its sheath.

We work in efficient silence, moving around Coach Z's body like it's simply another piece of furniture. His head lolls forward, the pink cotton candy now a grotesque, blood-soaked lump in his gaping mouth.

His eyes stare sightlessly at the floor, forever frozen in his final moment of terror.

Scout packs the last of our supplies into the duffel. "Done."

I scan the room one final time. Nothing left but Coach Z and the evidence of his final moments. The blood has begun to congeal at the edges, turning darker, thicker. In a few hours, it will be a tacky, brownish mess. But that's not our problem. Roman's already arranged for the janitor to arrive early tomorrow. Better than having some student stumble across this.

"Let's go," I say, shouldering the duffel bag.

Scout leads the way, moving silently through the empty hallways. The school feels different now, darker, somehow complicit in what we've done. Our footsteps echo softly against the linoleum floors, the only sound in the stillness.

We reach the side exit we used to enter, pausing to check that the coast is clear. Scout pulls out her phone, taps the Index and marks the Coach Z file as complete. She pulls up the live camera feeds outside of the building and flashes the screen towards me.

"Clear," she whispers, pushing the door open.

The night air hits us like a slap, cool and fresh after the blood-scented locker room. We slip out into the darkness, moving quickly across the empty parking lot to where our car waits. Scout tosses me the keys, and I catch them one-handed.

As we pull away from Kennedy High School, leaving Coach Z's cooling body behind, neither of us speaks. The tension between us has transformed, shifted into something I don't have a name for yet. All I know is that nothing will be the same after tonight.

TWENTY-TWO

SCOUT

The drive back to the safehouse is silent but electric. My body still hums with adrenaline and arousal. The image of Deacon slitting Coach Z's throat is burned forever into my fucking eyeballs. I can't stop replaying it, the precise movement of his hand, the blood spray, and the way his eyes never wavered. Perfect control in perfect chaos.

"You're staring," Deacon says, his eyes fixed on the road.

"Oh please! Like anyone with functioning eyeballs wouldn't be staring at you right now." I shift in my seat, the fabric of my pants creating delicious friction. "The way you handled that knife, god, it was like watching a damn artist."

He grips the steering wheel. "I've had practice."

"It shows." I lean closer, breathing in his scent. He smells of sweat, blood, and something uniquely him. "You didn't hesitate. It was like you were spreading butter on toast, except the toast was Coach Z's throat and the butter knife was, well, an actual knife."

"Neither did you." His voice drops lower. "You never even looked away once."

Heat floods my cheeks. "I like seeing you work."

We pull into the garage of the safehouse, and the automatic door closes behind us with a soft mechanical whir. When Deacon kills the engine, the silence feels heavy.

I look down at my clothes. The spatters of Coach Z's blood have dried to a rusty brown on my pants. Some is smeared on my hips from Deacon's hands when he gripped my hips. The sight doesn't disgust me, but I suddenly feel the overwhelming need to wash it away.

"I need a shower," I announce, pushing open the car door. "I've still got bits of Coach Z on me."

Inside, I head straight for the master bathroom, peeling off my blood-spattered clothes and dropping them in a pile on the tile floor. The bathroom is all sleek marble and glass, with a shower large enough for four people. I turn the water as hot as I can stand it and step under the spray.

The water runs pink at first as it rinses away the blood on my skin. I close my eyes, letting the heat seep into my muscles. My body is still humming with energy from the kill, the encounter in the locker room, and the tension that's been building between us since we arrived at the safehouse. Maybe even before that.

I reach for the washcloth hanging on a hook and squeeze body wash onto it, working up a lather. The scent of the citrus soap fills the steamy air as I begin scrubbing my arms, my shoulders, and my neck. I need to erase every trace of Coach Z from my skin.

The glass door slides open behind me.

I don't turn around. I know it's him. I can feel his presence like a physical weight. The shower suddenly feels smaller, the air thicker.

"Scout." He just says my name, and it sends a little spark straight to my reckless heart.

I turn slowly, water cascading down my naked body. Deacon stands there, still fully clothed, his t-shirt and jeans darkened with Coach Z's blood. His eyes track the rivulets of water running down my breasts, my stomach, and between my thighs.

Without a word, he steps into the shower, clothes and all. The water immediately soaks through the fabric, plastering it to his muscled frame. He takes the washcloth from my hand, his fingers brushing mine.

Then, to my surprise, he sinks to his knees on the shower floor.

"Deacon—"

"Shh." He presses the cloth to my hip, beginning a slow, methodical cleaning. His touch is reverent, almost worshipful, as he moves the cloth in small circles across my skin.

I brace myself against the shower wall, watching him through half-lidded eyes. His movements are precise and thorough. He has the same controlled energy he showed with the knife now channeled into his touch on my body.

He works his way down one leg, then the other, his breath warm against my wet skin. When he reaches my feet, he lifts each one gently, washing them with unexpected tenderness.

"Flawless," he murmurs, almost to himself.

Water streams down his face, dripping from his eyelashes and his lips. His clothes cling to him like a second skin, but he seems oblivious to it.

He works his way back up, the cloth sliding over my calves, my knees, and my thighs. His eyes meet mine as he reaches the apex of my legs, and I can't suppress the shiver that runs through me.

My hands fist at my sides as Deacon moves the washcloth with deliberate slowness between my thighs, his touch is both reverent and possessive. The water cascades around us, steam filling the space between our bodies, but the intensity in his eyes makes my core clench with need. I'm burning up and it has nothing to do with the temperature.

His hands grip my thighs, applying firm pressure outward, a silent command my body instantly obeys. The rough texture of the cloth glides over my sensitive folds. His movements are methodical, thorough, just like everything else about him. He takes his time, washing every fold, every curve, his eyes locked on mine as if gauging my reaction to each stroke.

The washcloth moves in gentle circles, rinsing away soap and sweat, but drives my arousal higher. I bite my lip to keep from begging him for more than this clinical touch. His face remains impassive, but his eyes burn with something primal.

When I'm completely clean, he tosses the washcloth aside with a wet slap against the tile. His hands replace the cloth, palms sliding up my calves, my thighs, as his thumbs trace every scar and crease.

"Deacon," I whisper, my voice barely audible over the shower spray.

My pulse races so fast I feel dizzy, and every nerve ending in my body is on fire.

He doesn't respond. Instead, he leans forward, pressing his mouth to my hipbone. His lips are hot against my water-cooled skin, like touching a flame to ice, the contrast makes me shiver all the way down to my toes. His teeth graze the curve of my hip, followed by the soothing pressure of his tongue, and holy hell, I might actually combust right here in this shower.

I thread my fingers through his wet hair, tugging lightly. He growls against my skin but doesn't yield to my silent plea. Instead, he moves his attention to my stomach, trailing kisses across my soft abdomen while his hands grip my thighs.

His mouth traces a path along the underside of my breasts, across my ribs, down to the opposite hip. Everywhere but where I fucking want him. It's fucking torture, in the best way. Each kiss and nip brings me closer to the edge without offering release.

"Please," I gasp, my hips instinctively rocking forward.

He pulls back just enough to deny me contact, his breath hot against my inner thigh. "Not yet."

His hands slide around to cup my ass, kneading the flesh as his mouth continues its maddening journey across my body. He licks a droplet of water from the crease where my thigh meets my torso, so close yet deliberately avoiding my center.

I'm trembling now, my entire body wound tight with need. The steam fills my lungs, making each breath feel heavy and insufficient. Or maybe that's just the effect of his hands, his mouth, and his eyes that never leave mine even as he worships my body.

His tongue traces patterns on my inner thigh, moving higher before diverting to my hip again. My legs quiver with the effort of remaining upright as he continues this sensual assault, bringing me to the brink without ever touching where I desperately need him most.

Just when I think I might collapse from sheer frustration, his strong hands grip my hips firmly, pressing me back against the cool tile wall of the shower.

"Hold on," he growls, his voice rough with desire.

Before I can respond, he lifts me effortlessly, positioning my thighs to rest on his broad shoulders. The new position leaves me completely exposed to him, my back supported by the wall, my core directly in front of his face. Water streams down between us, but his eyes remain locked on mine, dark with hunger.

"Remember what I promised you?" His breath ghosts over my heated pussy, making me shudder.

I try to remember through the haze of arousal. "What—"

"I told you I'd bury my face in your sweet cunt." His words are a physical caress, making me clench with need. "And I always keep my promises."

He presses his face firmly against my pussy, inhaling deeply. The intimacy of the gesture makes me flush with heat that has nothing to do with the shower's temperature. His eyes close briefly as he hums in appreciation before opening again, pinning me with their intensity.

"You smell delicious," he murmurs against my flesh.

Then his tongue makes contact. A slow, deliberate lick from bottom to top that has me arching against the wall. His hands tighten on my thighs, holding me in place as he explores me with agonizing thorough-ness. He's licking me like I'm the world's most delicious ice cream cone that might melt if he doesn't get every single drop. So fucking slow and deliberate, and god, how does he know exactly where all my nerve endings are hiding?!

"Deacon," I gasp, my fingers tangling in his wet hair. "Please..."

He pauses, looking up at me from between my legs. "Please, what, Scout?"

"Fuck, I need you," I manage. I don't fucking care what I have to beg for at this point.

Something changes in his expression, a tightening around his eyes, a flaring of his nostrils. My desperate plea seems to snap something loose in him. The controlled, measured pace vanishes as he dives back in, devouring me as if he's been starving for this exact taste.

His tongue flattens against me, making broad strokes before circling my clit relentlessly. I can practically feel my eyes rolling to the back of my head. He alternates between gentle suction and firm pres-sure, reading my body's responses, somehow knowing exactly what makes me tick, like he's got a freaking roadmap to my pleasure points.

My hips buck against his face, but his grip keeps me exactly where he wants me.

I can't stop the sounds escaping my throat, moans, whimpers, and his name repeated like a prayer. The steam swirls around us, the shower's spray creating a private world where nothing exists beyond this moment, this sensation, this man worshipping between my thighs.

His stubble scrapes deliciously against my sensitive skin as he angles his head to reach deeper. His tongue thrusting deep inside my pussy. He slides it up to curl around my clit as one of his hands leaves my thigh, and I feel his finger teasing my entrance before slowly pushing inside. The dual sensation of his tongue on my clit and his finger curling inside me has me seeing stars.

"Don't stop," I plead, my head thrown back against the tile. "God, Deacon, I will fucking kill you if you stop."

He chuckles and adds a second finger, stretching me as his tongue continues its relentless assault. My thighs begin to tremble against his shoulders, my inner walls clenching around his fingers as tension builds low in my belly. I'm climbing higher, closer to the edge with each stroke of his tongue and each thrust of his fingers.

The combination of the hot water, the steam, and Deacon's mouth on my pussy creates an overwhelming sensory experience. My skin feels hypersensitive, every nerve ending alive and firing. His free hand grips my ass, squeezing possessively as he pulls me even tighter against his face.

He devours me with single-minded focus, as if this is the only thing that matters in the universe. My pussy and his tongue. The intensity in his eyes when he glances up at me is almost frightening in its rawness.

My back arches against the cold tile as Deacon works me closer to the edge. His fingers pump in and out with perfect rhythm while his tongue circles my clit like it's his favorite freaking candy. I'm so close I can feel my inner walls starting to pulse around his fingers.

"Deacon," I gasp, tugging at his wet hair. "I'm going to—"

He growls against me, the vibration shooting straight through my core. His teeth graze my clit. The sensation walks that exquisite line between pleasure and pain, making my thighs tremble against his shoulders.

"Oh my god," I whimper as he continues this sweet torture, alternating between harsh nips and soothing licks.

His teeth scrape along my sensitive folds, catching and tugging lightly before his tongue soothes the sting. The dual sensations are so fucking overwhelming. Soft and sharp, then gentle and rough. My arousal is soaking his tongue, his fingers, running down his wrist as he works me into a frenzy.

I'm right there, my muscles tensing in anticipation of release, when suddenly he fucking pulls back.

I cry out at the loss, my hips chasing his mouth desperately. But his strong hands hold me firmly in place against the shower wall.

Deacon looks up at me from between my thighs, his eyes dark and possessive. Water streams down his face, dripping from his lashes, his lips glistening with my arousal.

"I want you to fall apart, kitten," he growls, his voice rough with desire. "I want to feel you cum on my fingers, taste you on my tongue. Give it to me. Now."

Before I can process his words, he presses his open mouth against me again. He seals his lips around my entire center, creating suction while his tongue flutters rapidly against my clit. At the same time, his fingers curl upward, finding that perfect spot inside me that makes my vision blur.

The combination of sensations is too much. The suction of his mouth, the vibration of his tongue, and the pressure of his fingers stroking me from within. The orgasm hits me like a freight train, radiating outward from my core to the tips of my fingers and toes.

"Deacon!" I scream, my back arching off the tile as waves of pleasure crash through me. My thighs clamp around his head, but he doesn't let up, continuing to work me through each pulse of my orgasm.

My entire body convulses as he draws out my pleasure, extending it beyond what I thought possible. Stars explode behind my eyelids, and for a moment, I swear I black out from the intensity.

When I finally come back to myself, my legs are trembling uncontrollably. Deacon gently lowers me until my feet touch the shower floor, but his arms remain around me, supporting my weight as my knees threaten to buckle.

He presses his forehead against mine, our breathing synchronized in the steamy air. His clothes cling to his body, completely soaked through, but he doesn't seem to care.

"You're magnificent when you come undone," he murmurs, his voice a reverent whisper against my lips.

I cling to Deacon's shoulders, my legs still quivering beneath me. The water continues to cascade over us, though it's cooling now. I can barely stand, my body completely wrung out from the intensity of what just happened.

"I can't feel my damn legs," I mumble against his neck.

His chuckle vibrates through me. "Good."

He reaches behind me to turn off the shower, and I shiver when the water stops, partly from the sudden chill and partly because holy crap, my body is still recovering from that orgasm apocalypse. Without the hot spray hiding everything, I'm standing here naked as fuck while he's still in his clothes, soaking wet clothes I might add, that cling to every muscle like they're painted on, which is honestly a crime against humanity because why is he still wearing ANYTHING?

"You're overdressed," I point out, gesturing at his soaked clothes.

"Irrelevant," he states, his eyes never leaving mine.

He steps out of the shower first, grabbing a large fluffy towel from the rack. Instead of handing it to me, he holds it open, a clear invitation. When I step forward, he wraps it around my shoulders, using it to pull me against his chest.

Mr. One-Word-Answer is back, but I can't really complain when those few words come with him wrapping me up like I'm something precious.

His hands move over the towel, rubbing gentle circles across my back, my shoulders, my arms. The soft friction of the fabric against my oversensitized skin makes me shiver again, but not from cold. Every touch feels magnified, like my nerve endings are still firing at maximum capacity.

"Turn around," he instructs softly.

I comply, too boneless to argue. He works the towel down my back, over the curve of my ass, drying each leg with methodical care. His movements are efficient but gentle, reminiscent of how he washed me earlier, but somehow even more intimate.

When he finishes with my back, he turns me to face him again. The towel glides over my collarbones, down between my breasts. His touch is clinical now, focused on the task of drying me rather than arousing me further, but my body responds anyway, nipples tightening as the soft fabric brushes over them.

"You're beautiful," he says matter-of-factly, as if stating that water is wet or the sky is blue.

I should have a witty comeback. Something flirty or dismissive or both. But exhaustion is setting in, the adrenaline from both the kill and our extra activities rapidly leaving my system. All I can manage is a sleepy smile.

Deacon seems to notice my fading energy. He wraps the towel around me again, tucking it securely under my arms. Then, without warning, he scoops me up, one arm behind my knees and the other supporting my back.

"I can walk," I protest weakly, even as my head drops against his shoulder.

"I know."

He carries me from the bathroom to the bedroom, his wet clothes leaving a trail of droplets on the floor. The bedroom is dark except for the faint glow from the bathroom light. He lays me gently on the bed.

The mattress dips beneath his weight as he sits beside me. He unwraps the towel and continues drying me, his touch feather-light as he blots the remaining moisture from my skin. When he reaches my hair, he works with surprising gentleness, squeezing out the excess water and combing through the tangles with his fingers.

"You're good at this," I murmur, my eyes growing heavier by the second.

"I have many skills," he replies, a hint of amusement coloring his voice.

"Mmm, you certainly do." My words slur slightly with fatigue. The post-kill crash is hitting me hard.

Deacon finishes with my hair and pulls back the covers. I roll obediently onto the sheets, too tired to even feel self-conscious about my nakedness. He draws the blanket up over me, tucking it around my shoulders with unexpected tenderness.

"Sleep," he commands softly, brushing a strand of damp hair from my forehead.

I catch his wrist before he can pull away. "Stay."

Deacon hesitates, his expression unreadable in the dim light. The muscle in his jaw tightens as he looks down at me, still holding my wrist.

"Not tonight, Kitten," he says, his voice a low rumble. "You need sleep."

I want to argue, but my eyelids are so heavy, and my brain can't think of anything other than the softness of my pillow. The post-kill crash, combined with the intensity of everything else, has drained every ounce of energy from my body.

"Fine," I mumble, attempting a pout that probably looks more like a sleepy grimace. "But we're not done with this conversation."

A ghost of a smile touches his lips. "We're not done with a lot of things."

He gently disentangles my fingers from his wrist, placing my hand back on the bed. The mattress shifts as he stands, and I immediately miss his warmth. The room feels colder without him next to me, despite the blanket tucked around my shoulders.

Something shifts in his expression, a softening around the eyes, perhaps, or a slight relaxation of his perpetually tense shoulders. He leans down, and for a moment I think he might change his mind and stay after all. Instead, he brushes his lips against my temple, the contact so light it might be a dream.

"Sleep well, Scout," he whispers against my skin.

I want to respond, but my body has other ideas. My eyes close of their own accord, and I feel myself sinking deeper into the mattress. The last thing I register is the soft click of the door as Deacon leaves, and then I'm drifting, floating on the edge of consciousness.

In that hazy space between waking and sleeping, I realize something that should probably terrify me: I'm falling for the Candy Man, hard and fast, with no safety net in sight. The scariest part is how much I want this to be real, even knowing monsters don't deserve happy endings.

TWENTY-THREE

DEACON

The morning light slants through the kitchen blinds, painting stripes across the granite countertop. I cradle my second cup of coffee between my palms, letting the warmth seep into my skin while Roman's voice crackles through the speaker of my phone.

"Coach Z's body was found by the school janitor this morning." Roman's typing clicks in the background. "The local news is already running with the Cotton Candy Killer angle."

"What about Stanton?" I take a sip of the black coffee, savoring its warm bitterness.

"His office staff found him and called the police. They're piecing together his connection to the missing nurses. Our girls' embroidery is getting attention."

The memory of last night floods my senses. Her skin under my hands. The taste of her. The way she came apart against my mouth.

"Deacon? You still there?"

"Yeah." I clear my throat. "What about our exit plan?"

"Flight's already been changed. The private jet leaves the airstrip at 2 PM. You can leave the keys in the car. I've got someone picking it up."

I flip bacon in the cast iron skillet, watching the fat render and curl. Next to it, pancake batter sizzles on the griddle, regular ones for me, chocolate chip for Scout. I don't usually cook for others, but it seemed practical. Efficient. It has absolutely nothing to do with the way she moaned when I tasted her last night.

"I've updated everything in the system," Roman continues. "Lucien wants a full debrief when—"

A feral growl echoes down the hallway, followed by the shuffle of bare feet against the hardwood. I recognize the sound immediately.

"Hold that thought, Scout just woke up," I tell Roman as I lower the heat under the bacon.

I grab a clean mug and fill it with coffee, adding the exact amount of creamer I know she likes. She stumbles into the kitchen just as I finish stirring.

Scout is definitely not a morning person. She's adorably disheveled like a murderous gremlin. Her hair is tangled in chaotic spirals, her eyes half-lidded, and she's wearing an oversized t-shirt that barely reaches mid-thigh. The sight of her bare legs sends heat coursing through my veins, but I keep my expression neutral as I extend the mug toward her.

"Coffee?" I offer it like a peace treaty.

Scout blinks at me, then at the mug, as if she's trying to process what she's looking at. After a few moments of confused staring, she takes it from my hand, causing our fingers to brush against one another. The contact sends an electric current up my arm.

"You're a god," she mumbles as she brings the mug to her lips.

She takes a long sip, eyes closing as the caffeine hits her system. A soft moan escapes her throat, almost the same sound she made last night when I—

"Sounds like someone got her coffee," Roman's voice cuts through my thoughts. "Good morning, Scout."

Scout's eyes snap open, finally registering the phone on the counter. "Roman? Why are you in our kitchen at this ungodly hour?"

"It's 9:30. Some of us actually have to work before noon."

"Like I said. Ungodly." She takes another sip as she leans against the counter. She's holding the mug like it's a lifeline.

I turn back to the stove and begin flipping the pancakes onto our plates. "Our flight's been moved up to this afternoon. You need to get packed up."

Scout grunts in acknowledgment as she moves to sit at the small kitchen table. She's watching as I place the bacon next to the stacks. Her eyes widen slightly when she spots the chocolate chip pancakes as I slide the plate toward her.

"Are those..."

"I figured it would feed your sugar addiction."

She stares at the plate, then at me, a slow smile spreading across her face. "You made me chocolate chip pancakes?"

I shrug, uncomfortable with her scrutiny. "It's just breakfast."

Scout cuts into the stack, dragging a piece through the maple syrup I've set out. She pops it into her mouth and makes a noise that should be illegal outside of a bedroom. The sound goes straight to my dick.

"Oh my god," she moans, loud enough that I'm certain Roman can hear every decibel. "This is better than sex."

"I sincerely hope not," Roman chuckles through the speaker. "Otherwise, you've been doing it wrong."

Heat crawls up my neck. I shoot a glare at the phone while Scout nearly chokes on her pancake.

"Jesus, Roman," she sputters, cheeks flushing pink. "I'm eating. I don't want to know anything about your sex life."

"Just stating facts," Roman replies, the smirk evident in his voice. "Anyway, flights at two. Don't be late."

The phone beeps as the call disconnects, leaving Scout and me in sudden silence.

I settle into the chair across from her. She's hunched protectively over her plate like someone might steal her pancakes. The domesticity of the moment feels strange, dangerous even. I've spent years avoiding all attachments, keeping people at arm's length. Yet, here I am, making chocolate chip pancakes for a woman who watched me kill a man, then let me taste every inch of her in the shower.

"So, what else did Roman want?" Scout asks between bites, not meeting my eyes. Her voice is carefully neutral, stripped of the playfulness I've come to expect from her.

I recognize the tactic immediately. I do it myself. She's compartmentalizing and building her walls. Last night's vulnerability has been locked away, replaced by professional distance. Part of me is relieved. Attachments get people killed in our world. The other part...

"Just the usual," I reply, matching her tone. "Flight details. News coverage of our handiwork. "

She nods, stabbing another piece of pancake. "That makes sense."

The silence stretches between us, filled only by the clink of silverware against plates and the sound of slurps as she drinks her coffee. I watch her from beneath lowered lashes, noticing how she avoids looking directly at me and how her shoulders remain tense despite her casual posture.

"These are really good," she finally says, gesturing to the pancakes with her fork. "I didn't peg you for the cooking type."

"There's a lot you don't know about me."

Her eyes flick up briefly, a slight frown on her face as she says. "Apparently."

I take a bite of my own food and consider my next move. I could push, ask about last night, demand we address whatever this is between us. But the guarded set of her jaw tells me she's not ready. And truthfully, neither am I.

What happened in that locker room and in the shower once we returned to the safehouse complicates things. Complications lead to mistakes. Mistakes lead to death. I've survived this long by keeping it simple.

Yet, nothing about the dangerous woman sitting across from me is simple.

"I'll clean up here," I offer, breaking the silence. "You should get packed. Roman mentioned something about a storm system moving in. It might affect our flight if we don't get ahead of it."

She nods as she drains the last of her coffee. "Thank you for breakfast." She stands, hesitating for a moment like she might say something more, but doesn't, then turns and heads back toward her room.

I watch her go, fighting the urge to follow. To press her against the wall like I did last night and taste the maple syrup on her tongue. Instead, I gather our plates and move to the sink, letting the scalding water burn away the thoughts that I know I shouldn't be having.

The truth is, I don't know what happens next. With Scout. With

The Hollow. I came here looking for resources, not relationships. Not a family. Not her.

But the way she looked at me in that locker room, eyes dark with desire as I slit Coach Z's throat, no one has ever seen that part of me and wanted more. No one has ever understood the predator beneath my skin and invited it closer instead of running.

I scrub at the cast iron with more force than necessary, my mind racing. The Hollow offers everything I've been searching for: infrastructure, intelligence, and support. A way to be more effective in my hunt. But Scout, she offers something I never wanted. Something I'm not sure I can afford to have.

The pancake batter has dried onto the griddle, requiring extra elbow grease to remove. I focus on the task, grateful for the distraction. One problem at a time. First, we finish the job. Get back to the mansion. Debrief with Lucien. Then I can decide whether to stay or go.

Whether to lean into whatever this is with Scout or walk away before it's too late.

Water drips from my hands as I dry the last dish and put it away. In the distance, I hear Scout moving around her room, the soft thud of her suitcase hitting the bed. She's giving me space, just as I'm giving her space. Both of us circling each other, neither willing to acknowledge the gravity pulling us together.

For now, that's enough. It has to be.

THE WHEELS TOUCH down with a gentle bump, jolting me from my thoughts. Beside me, Scout doesn't stir. She's been asleep since we reached cruising altitude, curled into herself like a cat. One hand tucked beneath her cheek, the other still loosely clutching her blanket. Her face in sleep is so peaceful, her light snores are a soft rhythm to my ears. My gaze drops to her lips before I force myself to look away. God, she's such a beautiful menace. The memories of last night threaten to surface, but I shut them down immediately. I can't afford to want her. I've buried enough already to know I couldn't survive losing one more thing that matters.

The pilot announces our arrival at the private airstrip outside Atlanta, his voice crackling through the cabin speakers. Scout shifts but doesn't wake. I consider letting her sleep another minute, but we need to move.

"Scout." I keep my voice low, not touching her. "We've landed."

Her eyes flutter open, momentarily unfocused before sharpening on my face. For a split second, I see something flicker in her expression, something warm and open that makes my chest tighten. Then she blinks, and it's gone.

"Dang, that was fast." She stretches, arching her back like she's working out kinks. "Did I sleep the whole time?"

"Like the dead."

She grins as she says. "That's appropriate, considering."

We gather our things in silence and disembark the plane.

The evening air hits my face as we descend the stairs. The sun hangs low on the horizon, painting everything in shades of amber and gold. A black SUV waits for us about fifty yards away, its windows tinted dark against the setting sun.

"Home sweet home," Scout mutters, more to herself than to me.

The hair on the back of my neck prickles. Something doesn't feel right. I scan our surroundings. It's a wide open space with minimal cover, a few small maintenance buildings to our left, and a small cluster of trees in the distance. I don't see any immediate threats, but something feels off.

"Where's the driver?" I ask, noticing the empty front seat of the SUV.

Scout frowns. "That's a good question. Let me check with Roman."

She pulls out her phone and makes the call. I keep my eyes moving, tracking any potential threat while listening to her side of the conversation.

"Hey, it's us. We're at the airstrip, but there's no driver." She pauses. "What do you mean he should be here?" Her voice sharpens with concern. "No, the car's here, but it's empty. No, we haven't actually looked inside it yet. Okay, I'll check."

She hangs up, shoving the phone back in her pocket. "Roman says the driver should be here. He hasn't heard anything about him leaving."

"Something isn't right."

"Makes two of us." She glances at the SUV, then back at me. "Maybe he stepped away for the bathroom?"

I gesture to the empty lot and field, shaking my head. "Where would he have gone?"

She glares at me. God, she's adorable.

"Roman's checking the GPS on the driver's phone now." She shifts her weight, hand drifting toward where I know she keeps a knife. She creeps towards the vehicle.

I follow, our footsteps are silent on the tarmac. The air feels charged, like the moment before a thunderstorm breaks.

As we draw closer to the SUV, I notice the driver's door is slightly ajar. Scout is three steps ahead of me. She moves with practiced efficiency around the vehicle.

"The outside of the car is clear," she murmurs, peering through windows and checking underneath the chassis in smooth, practiced movements. She moves around to where I'm standing and pulls open the driver's door. She leans in to inspect the interior.

I scan our surroundings while she works. The empty airstrip stretches out before us. It's eerily quiet except for the distant hum of the idling plane. A flash of light catches my eye. It was just a brief glint from the grassy area near a small cluster of trees about a hundred yards away. It's low to the ground, almost hidden by the tall grass.

"Keys are in the ignition, and I don't see any signs of struggle. Everything here looks clean except for the distinct lack of driver," Scout says as she steps away from the SUV. She turns to find me staring intently at the distant tree line. "What?"

I don't immediately respond, my focus locked on that spot where I saw the flash.

"Deacon?" Her voice pulls me back.

"Did you see that?" I ask, nodding toward the trees.

"See what?" she asks, her eyes following to where I'm staring.

I narrow my eyes, focusing on that spot where I saw the flash of light. There it is again. Just a brief sparkle, like sunlight catching on metal. My instincts are screaming at me that something isn't right.

"It's over there," I nod toward the trees. "Don't you see it?"

Without hesitation, I reach down and pull my knife from my boot, a seven-inch tactical blade with a serrated edge.

Silently, I start to move across the tarmac toward the grassy area, keeping my body low.

Scout falls in behind me without question, her footsteps nearly silent. We move in perfect sync, as if we've been partners for years instead of days. I can feel her presence at my back. Steady and watchful.

As we get closer, the grass parts to reveal what caused the reflection, and recognition hits me with a jolt. My steps falter for just a moment.

Mirror shards. Dozens of them, arranged in a deliberate pattern around a central point. The pieces catch the setting sun, sending fractured light in all directions. And in the center, a naked, bloody body, positioned on its knees, head bowed forward as if in prayer.

My blood runs cold. It's identical to the scene that I found in Denver eight months ago. Every detail, the precise arrangement of the glass, the positioning of the body, and even the way the light plays across the gruesome display.

"Well," Scout says beside me, her voice is filled with dark amusement despite the horror before us, "I think we just found our driver."

She moves to step closer, but I catch her arm, holding her back.

"Don't," I warn, my voice tight.

Scout stills. Her head tilting slightly as she studies the grotesque display before us. Her eyes narrow as if she's inspecting a piece of art rather than the body of our driver.

"Jesus," she breathes. "It's exactly like you described at dinner. It's so beautiful."

I nod, my eyes scanning the area around us with renewed urgency. "We really don't need to be hanging out here, the killer could still be nearby."

The body kneels in a grotesque parody of prayer, surrounded by a perfect circle of mirror fragments. Each shard is placed with meticulous precision, creating a sunburst pattern that radiates outward. The victim's skin has the waxy pallor of recent death, and even from here, I can make out the carved symbol on his chest, a stylized sun with eight rays.

"I'm calling this in," Scout says, already pulling out her phone. "Roman needs to know the Glass Gardener is here."

"You can do that from the car. We need to get out of here. Now." I place my hand over her arm, pulling her towards the empty vehicle.

She doesn't argue, matching my pace as we sprint across the tarmac. My eyes scan our surroundings with each step, the open field, the tree line, and the distant hangar. The killer could be watching us right now.

"You think they're still here?" Scout's voice is steady despite our pace.

"Don't know. I don't really want to find out, either."

We reach the SUV in seconds.

"I'm driving," she calls out, already sliding behind the wheel.

I throw our bags into the back seat before jumping in beside her. The SUV's engine roars to life as Scout turns the key, her movements quick.

"Buckle up," she warns, shifting into drive.

The tires squeal against the pavement as Scout floors it, sending us lurching backward. The gravel sprays behind us as we tear away from the scene. The SUV fishtails slightly before Scout gets it under control.

I pull out my phone and click to call Roman. He answers on the first ring.

"We've got a situation," I say. "The Glass Gardener. He was here."

"What?" Roman's voice sharpens. "Are you sure?"

"Positive. The driver's dead. It was the same signature. The mirror shards are arranged in a sunburst, the body positioned on knees, and the sun symbol is carved into the chest. It's an exact match to what I saw in Denver."

Scout takes a sharp turn onto the main road, her eyes flicking between the road ahead and the rearview mirror. Tension radiates through her entire body.

"Jesus Christ," Roman mutters. "Are you both clear?"

"For now. Scout's driving. We're heading..." I glance at Scout.

"Manor," she says firmly. "We're going straight to the manor. I checked the car over, it's clean. No obvious tampering or tracking devices. "

"Did you hear that?" I ask Roman.

"Yeah. I'm sending an alert through the Index now. I'll call everyone back in." I hear rapid typing in the background. "What's your ETA?"

Scout glances at the clock. "Forty-five minutes if I push it."

I relay this to Roman, who grunts in acknowledgment.

"Then push it and stay on main roads," he instructs. "No stops unless absolutely necessary. I'm tracking your location. If you see anything suspicious—"

"We'll call," I finish for him.

"Good. And Deacon?"

"Yeah?"

"Watch your backs."

The call ends, and I pocket my phone. Scout's already merging onto the highway, pushing well above the speed limit.

She nods her head, eyes fixed on the road. "The timing's too perfect. The Glass Gardener showing up right before we land? Do you think they were waiting for us?"

My thoughts exactly. "Or they're sending a message."

"To who? Most people don't know The Hollow is real."

I lean back in my seat, considering this. "Eight months ago, I stumbled across one of their scenes in Denver. Another scene is found, days after I get to town, and now they show up here, right as we arrive?"

"Could be they've been tracking you," Scout questions. "Maybe they don't like another killer on their turf."

"Maybe." But something doesn't add up. If they wanted me dead, why not just take me out? Why the elaborate display?

Scout weaves through traffic with practiced ease, putting distance between us and the airstrip. Her driving is aggressive but controlled, each lane change calculated.

The setting sun casts long shadows across the dashboard as we race toward the manor, toward safety. But safety is an illusion I stopped believing in long ago, especially now that it feels like someone is arranging bodies like love notes just for me.

TWENTY-FOUR

SCOUT

I've never been happier to see the manor's wrought iron gates. My fingers ache from gripping the steering wheel so tightly the entire drive, constantly checking the rearview mirror for any cars that might be following us.

"Home sweet murder home," I mutter as the gates swing open automatically, Roman's security system recognizing the SUV.

Deacon sits beside me, a study in controlled tension. He hasn't said much since the call with Roman. His eyes were constantly scanning our surroundings, his body was coiled like a spring, ready to release.

We grab our bags and hurry inside. The manor feels different, the usual relaxed atmosphere replaced with something heavier, more urgent. The moment we step through the door, I know exactly where we're going.

"Follow me," I tell Deacon, heading straight for the East Wing. "The emergency alert means that everyone needs to go to the War Room as soon as they get here."

"The what?"

"You'll see."

I lead him through the manor's elegant corridors, past the sunroom and library, deeper into the East Wing where Tristan's quarters are located. Deacon follows silently, and I can barely hear his footsteps behind me.

We stop in front of what appears to be an ordinary section of wall. There isn't a door, no markings, nothing to suggest anything unusual. Just expensive wallpaper and a small digital panel that most would mistake for a thermostat.

"Watch and learn, Mr. Floss." I press my thumb against the biometric scanner on the panel. A soft blue light traces the outline of my thumb.

"Identity confirmed: Scout Prescott," a disembodied female voice announces softly.

The panel slides silently into the wall, revealing a hidden entrance, and a staircase descends deep under the manor. The murmur of voices drifts up from below.

"After you," I gesture to Deacon, whose eyebrows have risen slightly, which is basically the Deacon equivalent of looking impressed.

"Hidden panic room. That's smart." He steps through the entrance, and I follow, the panel sliding closed behind us.

The stairs lead us down to The Hollow's most secure space, what we affectionately call the War Room. As we descend, the voices grow clearer. They're tense and focused.

"—tracking patterns across six states now," Roman's voice carries up the stairs. "The timing can't be coincidental."

We reach the bottom of the staircase and step into a room that looks like a cross between a high-tech command center and an upscale conference room. Large screens cover every wall, displaying maps, data feeds, and surveillance footage. A long mahogany table dominates the center, surrounded by ergonomic chairs.

Every member of The Hollow is already seated at the table, a tablet in front of each one. Roman stands at the head, hands splayed on the surface as he leans forward, analyzing something on the nearest screen. Lucien sits to his right, face grim. Ivy and Brayden occupy seats on the opposite side.

And there, in the corner next to Ivy, sits Tristan.

My breath catches slightly. It's been months since I've seen him outside his quarters. Tall and broad, Tristan's tan face is partially obscured by dark blonde hair that falls past his jawline. His fingers tap a rhythmic pattern on the table's surface, but his eyes are sharp and observant. He notices our entrance immediately.

"Scout. Deacon." Lucien acknowledges us with a nod. "Take a seat. Roman was just bringing us up to speed."

We slide into the two empty chairs. I notice Deacon studying Tristan with subtle interest before focusing on Roman.

"As I was saying," Roman continues, "we now have confirmation of Glass Gardener kills in Denver, Dallas, Chicago, and now here. The pattern suggests they're following something, or someone." His eyes flick briefly to Deacon.

"Show them what you found," Lucien instructs.

Roman taps something on his tablet, and one of the screens changes to display a series of crime scene photos. Each shows the same distinctive arrangement, mirror shards forming a sunburst pattern around a kneeling victim, the sun symbol carved into their chest.

"According to everything we've found so far, the Glass Gardener has been an active serial killer for at least eighteen months," Roman explains. "But here's where it gets interesting." He swipes to a new image. It's a map with red dots marking various locations. "These are all of the confirmed kill sites. Notice anything?"

I lean forward, studying the pattern on the screen. The dots form a rough line across the country, moving from west to east.

"I saw a lot of these locations as confirmed Mr. Floss kills when I was researching you," I say.

"Are they following me?" Deacon asks.

I glance at his face, searching for any reaction beyond the emotionless mask he wears so well. Nothing. Not even a flicker of surprise crosses his features.

"We would need to confirm that theory," Roman says, typing rapidly on his keyboard. "I've been compiling data about the Glass Gardener since you called about the dead driver."

Another screen illuminates, displaying a detailed timeline with dates, locations, and names.

"These are Deacon's confirmed kills over the past eighteen months," Roman explains, pointing to the list of eleven names running down the left side of the screen. "And these," he gestures to five dates highlighted in red, "are the Glass Gardener's known victims."

A digital map in color-coded pinpoint marks each location.

I lean forward, my elbows on the table. "Holy shit."

Each Glass Gardener kill occurred in the same city as one of Deacon's targets, the dates falling within the time he was there. The pattern is unmistakable.

"Denver, Dallas, Chicago, now two in Atlanta," Ivy reads aloud, her voice tight. "Always within days of Deacon's arrival."

"Hold up now," Brayden drawls, leaning back in his chair with that easy confidence of his. "Y'all are seein' patterns where there might not be any. Five kills trailin' Deacon across the country? That's either one hell of a stalker with a twisted admiration problem, or we're connectin' dots that don't belong together. Wouldn't be the first time two of us hunted the same ground without knowin' each other." He crosses his arms, his drawl deepening as he gets more thoughtful. "Seems a bit too on-the-nose to me, if I'm bein' honest. Real life ain't usually that tidy."

Deacon shakes his head. "No, it's too consistent. They're either tracking me or—"

Lucien interrupts, "Or maybe they're using you to select their hunting grounds."

Silence falls over the room, the only sounds are the soft hum of computer equipment and the rhythmic tapping of Tristan's fingers.

Tristan's deep, gruff voice cuts through the tension in the room. "The body count is off." His fingers continue tapping their pattern on the table, but his mismatched eyes remain sharp and focused on the data displayed before us.

"There are eleven kills for Deacon and only five for the Glass Gardener," Tristan continues. "If they're following him, why not match every kill? What makes these five people special?"

"That's a good question," I say as I look back at the screen, trying to see any pattern in which of Deacon's kills triggered a Glass Gardener response.

"Maybe Brayden's right and they're not following Deacon," Tristan suggests, his voice low and measured. "Maybe we're just reaching for an easy answer."

Roman frowns as he scrolls through the data. "What do you mean?"

"Correlation doesn't equal causation," Tristan replies, tucking a strand of hair behind his ear. "The Glass Gardener could be tracking something else entirely that happens to intersect with Deacon's movements."

I watch Deacon's reaction carefully. His jaw tightens almost imperceptibly.

"No," Deacon says finally. "It's got to be me that they're following."

"But why?" I ask the question that's been burning in my mind since we found the driver's body. "Why follow you specifically? And why leave these displays?"

"Y'know what this looks like to me?" Brayden drawls, leaning forward with his elbows on the table. "This fella's tryin' to say somethin'. Like leavin' a love note, but with bodies instead of paper." He cocks his head, that easy smile nowhere to be seen. "Question is, who's the message for? You, Deacon? All of us? 'Cause whoever's on the receivin' end of this little pen pal situation's got themselves a mighty persistent admirer."

Tristan's tapping stops abruptly. "You're right, Brayden. It's personal."

All eyes turn to him.

"The sun symbol," he continues, pointing to the screen. "It's not random. It means something specific to the killer, and likely to whoever they're sending the message to."

I look back at Deacon, who remains frustratingly unreadable. "Does the sun symbol mean anything to you?"

His expression doesn't change. "No," he says simply, "but that doesn't mean it isn't important to him."

Roman doesn't look convinced. "We need to consider all possibilities. If the Glass Gardener is tracking Deacon, then we need to understand why. And if they're not, if there's some other connection that we're missing, we need to find it before they strike again."

"We need to cast a wider net," Lucien says as he looks to Roman. "It's possible the Glass Gardener likely has other victims we don't know about, ones that weren't publicized or connected to their signature."

I chew on my bottom lip as I stare at the pattern of red dots blinking across the digital map. The five known victims follow Deacon's path like a trail of breadcrumbs. But it feels wrong somehow. It's too pretty and too obvious, like it's a beautifully wrapped present. That doesn't happen in this life.

"Roman, can you search for similar MOs in unsolved cases?" I ask. "Maybe ones that are missing the mirror arrangement or the sun symbol, but with other matching pieces?"

Roman nods as he continues to type. "I'm already setting up those search parameters. I'll run it through every law enforcement database in North America."

"Hold up now," Brayden drawls with that signature smirk. "Even your tech wizardry can't sweet-talk every police database in the country at once. That's gonna be like herdin' cats."

Roman doesn't look up from his screen. "I don't need to. The Index already maintains backdoor access to VICAP, NCIC, and most state-level crime databases. I just need to refine the search criteria."

"You should look for victims found in kneeling positions with multiple cuts," Deacon suggests, his voice calm despite the tension in the room. "Something like that would be unusual enough to flag in most homicide reports."

"And mirrors or glass," Ivy adds. "Even if it wasn't arranged in the circular pattern, the presence of broken mirrors at a scene might be noted."

I scroll through the pages on my tablet, reading through the data that Roman has shared with all of us. But something continues to niggle at the back of my mind. It's like a pattern within the pattern, maybe? I'm not sure. The dates, the locations, and the victims themselves, like I'm missing something. I can feel it.

"What about all the victims?" I ask. "Is there anything that ties them together?"

"Far as I can tell, they're all guys," Brayden drawls. "But that's about where the similarities end. Different ages, different looks, different day jobs. Seems like our mirror-happy friend ain't too picky 'bout who he turns into art. He just needed 'em to be in the wrong place at the wrong damn time."

"The driver was Hollow support staff," Lucien points out. "While they aren't fully aware of what exactly we do, it could still potentially suggest the Glass Gardener knows about us."

An unsettling silence settles over the room. If the Glass Gardener knows about The Hollow or its locations, we're all possibly at risk.

"Or they just saw an opportunity," Tristan counters as his fingers resume their rhythmic tapping. "The driver was alone in an isolated, rural area. Maybe they didn't know his connection to us."

"I'll be honest," Deacon says. "I thought the Hollow was an urban legend until the Stitcher waltzed into my kill scene. So I have a really hard time believing that someone actually knows about anything to do with The Hollow."

I'm not convinced. The timing is too perfect. The Glass Gardener struck just before we arrived. They knew we'd be there.

Roman's tablet pings softly. "First results are coming in. I've got five potential matches in the past two years. All are unsolved homicide cases with victims in kneeling positions and broken glass at the scene."

"Where?" Deacon asks sharply.

"Portland, Oregon. Minneapolis, Minnesota. And," Roman pauses, his expression darkening. "Savannah, Georgia. Three weeks ago."

My stomach drops. "Savannah? That's less than four hours from here."

"It's like they're creeping closer," Ivy says.

"Roman, can you show Deacon's movements for the past two years with these new potential Glass Gardener sites?" I ask.

Roman nods as he begins manipulating the data points on the large screen. The map transforms, adding new layers of information as he overlays Deacon's movements with the potential Glass Gardener kills.

"Interesting," Roman murmurs, zooming in on the Portland location. "The Portland victim was killed four months before you arrived there, Deacon."

Deacon replies. "I've never been to Portland before that hunt."

"Minneapolis," Roman continues as he highlights another dot on the map. "You were there last February, but according to our records, you didn't kill anyone there."

"Correct, I was hunting someone," Deacon confirms. "But ultimately they didn't fit my code and I left without making a move on them."

"And Savannah?" I ask as a chill runs down my spine.

Deacon shakes his head. "I've never been to Savannah."

Well, shit, there goes that idea. The neat pattern we thought we'd found isn't so neat after all.

"So it's obviously not as simple as following Deacon's kills," Ivy says, tapping her pen against her tablet.

Tristan shakes his head, hair swinging gently with the movement. "I think we're grabbing at the easiest explanation because it's comforting to have an answer, even if it's wrong." His fingers resume their rhythmic tapping against the mahogany table. "Deacon's kills correlate with some Glass Gardener victims, but not all. That's not a pattern, that's a coincidence with exceptions."

I watch Deacon's face for any reaction, but he remains emotionless as ever, only the slightest tightening around his eyes betraying him.

"So what are you suggesting?" I ask.

Tristan's mismatched eyes meet mine directly. "We need more data before we make any more assumptions. The Glass Gardener could be tracking something else entirely that occasionally intersects with Deacon's movements. Or they could be following someone else in The Hollow. Or it could be about the victims themselves."

"He's right," Roman says, scrolling through data on his tablet. "We don't have enough information yet to draw solid conclusions."

"I'm with Tristan on this," Brayden says. "But 'til we figure this out, nobody should go anywhere alone." He gives Deacon and me a pointed look. "This Glass Gardener just killed someone close to The Hollow. Either he knows about The Hollow, or he's watchin' Deacon close enough to pick off people around him." He shrugs one broad shoulder. "Or hell, maybe we're seein' connections that ain't even there. But I ain't willin' to bet anyone's life on that hunch."

"That's fair," I say, even though the thought of being locked down in the manor makes my skin crawl. "It really sucks, but I get it."

Don't get me wrong, I love my Murder Manor, but being trapped here is not my idea of a good time.

Lucien nods gravely. "Until we understand what we're dealing with, we need to prioritize security and safety."

"I'll continue analyzing the data," Roman says, his eyes never leaving the screen. "I'm expanding the search parameters to include any homicides with ritualistic elements involving glass, mirrors, or sun imagery. If there are more Glass Gardener kills we haven't connected yet, I'll find them."

He looks up, his expression unusually serious. "Until further notice, no one leaves the compound alone. All hunts are suspended unless absolutely necessary, and then only with full team backup."

Well, this is gonna suck, but the tone of Roman's voice tells me this isn't negotiable.

"What about active hunts?" Ivy asks, her voice is calm but concerned.

"Roman and I will review each case individually," Lucien answers. "Some hunts may proceed with additional security measures, however, most will be postponed."

I glance at Deacon. His face gives nothing away, but there's tension in his shoulders.

"Should we consider movin' operations temporarily?" Brayden asks, his expression serious. "If this Glass Gardener knows our location, stayin' put might be givin' him the advantage."

"No," Lucien says firmly. "The manor still remains our safest option. The security system here is unparalleled, and we have several contingency plans in place. Moving operations now would only make us more vulnerable to an attack."

This isn't the first time the Hollow has been threatened, but this feels different. Like it's more personal, somehow.

"We'll reconvene tomorrow morning after Roman has had time to process more data," Lucien says, rising from his chair. "I know I don't have to remind you, but in the meantime, stay vigilant. Report anything unusual, no matter how insignificant it might seem."

Whatever connection exists between Deacon and the Glass Gardener, if there even is a connection, I'm certain of one thing. We've only scratched the surface of a much deeper mystery.

TWENTY-FIVE
DEACON

I watch as Scout leaves the War Room with Ivy and Brayden, her curls bouncing with each step. She doesn't look back. The three of them are huddled close, already deep in conversation as they disappear up the staircase.

The weight of the meeting settles on my shoulders. Connections that aren't connections. Patterns that break down under scrutiny. A killer who might or might not be following me. It's a lot.

Roman remains hunched over his laptop. Lucien stands by the video monitors, staring out with that thousand-yard gaze that suggests he's seeing something none of us can. Tristan has already slipped away, silent as a ghost.

I need air.

Without a word, I exit the War Room and wander through the manor's labyrinthine corridors. The opulence still feels foreign, all this polished wood and gleaming metal, the tasteful art and soft lighting. It's nothing like the bare-bones motels and abandoned buildings where I've spent most of the past six years. It reminds me of my childhood, but that's not a wound I want to open right now.

My feet carry me toward the back of the house, where a set of

French doors stands partially open. Cool evening air slips through the gap.

The terrace stretches wide. It's bordered with stone balustrades and dotted with carefully arranged furniture and plants. Beyond it, the grounds of the estate roll away into twilight, the treeline a wall against the evening sky.

I step outside, letting the door close silently behind me. The temperature has dropped since we arrived, and the bite in the air feels clarifying after the stuffiness of the War Room.

Eight cities. Five scenes match my movements. Three that don't align.

What the hell does it mean?

I move to the edge of the terrace, resting my hands on the cool stone railing. Mountains rise and fall in the distance, painted in fiery oranges and deep reds that bleed into golden yellows. Fall in North Georgia transforms the landscape into something that belongs on a postcard or hanging in some art gallery.

I notice none of it.

The Glass Gardener. Such a pretentious name for a killer. The mirror shards arranged like petals around the body. The rudimentary sun symbol carved into the bodies. All that effort for what? To send a message? To create art? To satisfy some twisted need for meaning?

The Hollow thinks they might be following me. Or following someone else who occasionally crosses paths with me. Or following some pattern we haven't identified yet.

The uncertainty is maddening.

I breathe in deeply, filling my lungs with the crisp evening air. It smells of distant rain.

For six years, I've operated alone. I've made my own decisions and followed my own rules. The only person at risk was me.

Now I'm entangled with these people. And with her.

My thoughts circle back to Chicago. To Scout's skin under my hands. To the way she looked at me when I killed Coach Z. Her eyes weren't filled with disgust or fear, but with something darker. Something that matched the hunger inside me.

I push the thoughts away. Attachments are liabilities. I know this. I have always known this.

Yet here I am, standing on the terrace of a mansion full of people, worrying about what happens next. Worrying about them. Worrying about her.

I grip the stone balustrade, its cold surface anchoring me to reality. Until recently, I was a ghost. A shadow that moved through the world without connections, without attachments. I killed monsters and disappeared before anyone knew I existed.

I take a deep breath of mountain air. This place is a fortress; Roman has made that blatantly clear. But fortresses can become prisons just as easily as they can become sanctuaries.

The smart move would be to disappear. Just cut ties and return to the solitude that's kept me alive this long.

But the thought of leaving Scout behind twists something in my chest. Something I thought died years ago.

I run a hand through my hair, feeling the tension knotting at the base of my skull. This isn't me. I don't do this. I don't stand around contemplating feelings like some lovesick teenager. I eliminate threats, period. Clean. Efficient. No complications.

But Scout...

Her face flashes in my mind, her amber eyes alive with mischief, that knowing smile when she caught me watching her. The way she looked in that bar, playing the perfect prey while being the most dangerous person in the room, other than myself.

"Fuck," I mutter, the word disappearing into the mountain air.

This is exactly why I've always worked alone. Love is just another word for having something that can be taken from you. I learned that lesson when I was fifteen, standing over Sarah's grave. I swore then I'd never let myself care again, not when caring means giving the world something to take from you. I dedicated my life to vengeance for her. Swore to her I'd destroy every predator so no brother would ever have to stand over his little sister's grave the way I was the day we buried her.

I pace the length of the terrace, my footsteps soundless against the stone. Professional detachment has kept me alive for six years. Twenty-eight kills, including Coach Z, and not a single mistake. Because I never let myself get distracted. Never let myself want.

Until now.

I stop pacing and press my palms flat against the stone railing, leaning forward until my shoulders strain.

This is temporary. A partnership of convenience. Once we figure out who this Glass Gardener is and why they're shadowing me, I'll go back to working alone. Back to the quiet. The control. The safety of solitude.

But even as I think I'll leave, I know it's a lie.

There's something about Scout that pulls at parts of me I thought were dead. Her chaos to my order. Her light to my darkness. The way she fills silences that I didn't even realize were empty.

There's something about being here too. Being part of something larger than myself, that feels disturbingly like belonging.

One hunt. One woman. That's all it took to make me question everything.

I close my eyes, focusing on the distant sounds of the estate, the rustle of leaves, the faint calls of night birds.

Professional detachment is safe. It's what I know, what I've relied on.

But it's also lonely. Cold. Empty.

And Scout... Scout is anything but.

My hands grip the railing, decision made. For now, I'll stay. I'll help them figure out this Glass Gardener situation. I'll do my job.

But Scout... Scout is a complication I can't afford. Whatever happened between us in Chicago needs to stay there. I need to maintain distance. Focus.

Even if every instinct in my body screams otherwise.

A deep rumble intrudes on my solitude, "It's beautiful, isn't it?"

I don't startle at the voice behind me. I sensed someone approaching, but I am surprised by who it is. Tristan stands a careful distance away, his hands tucked into the pockets of his hoodie. His eyes don't meet mine, instead focusing somewhere beyond the mountains.

"Yes," I answer simply, though I haven't really been looking at the view.

Tristan nods. "I come out here when the house gets too loud. Not with noise, but with..." He gestures vaguely with one hand. "Energy. Emotions."

I stand quietly beside Tristan, letting the silence stretch between us. There's something different about him compared to the others, a stillness that feels like the calm before a storm.

"I'm Tristan," he finally says, his voice low but clear.

"Deacon," I reply.

He nods once, "I know." His eyes remain fixed on the mountains, never meeting mine. He inhales deeply before saying, "You're wondering if you should stay or go."

It's not a question. His observation catches me off guard.

"I'm considering my options," I say carefully.

Tristan's lips curve slightly but it's not quite a smile. "I felt the same way when I first arrived. Like I was standing on the edge of a cliff, unable to step back or jump forward."

I study him from the corner of my eye. His posture is rigid and controlled, but there's an energy radiating from him, like a live wire insulated but still humming with dangerous current.

"What made you decide?" I ask.

Tristan pauses for several moments, his gaze fixed on the horizon. The silence between us isn't uncomfortable, it's contemplative, like he's arranging his thoughts into perfect order before speaking them aloud.

"She watches you," he finally says, the words soft. "When you're not looking."

I keep my expression neutral, that wasn't what I asked him, though something shifts in my chest. "Scout watches everyone."

Tristan shakes his head once, a short, decisive movement. "Not like this." His fingers tap against the stone balustrade in a rhythmic pattern. "Her eyes follow you differently. Like you're a puzzle with missing pieces."

I don't respond. I don't confirm or deny. But Tristan doesn't seem to need my participation.

"You watch her too," he continues, his voice almost clinical in its observation. "When she's talking to others. When she laughs. When she moves across a room, your body shifts toward her like you're connected."

My jaw tightens. I'm not used to being the one observed and analyzed. "Is there a point to this?"

Tristan's lips curve slightly. "True connection is rare in our world. Genuine connection, not the kind we manufacture for hunts or to maintain an illusion." He glances at me briefly, his eyes meeting mine for just a fraction of a second before darting away. "It's... fascinating."

"We're partners," I say flatly. "Temporarily."

"Is that what you tell yourself?" There's no mockery in his tone, just genuine curiosity.

The mountain air suddenly feels too thin. I've spent years cultivating invisibility, training myself to leave no impression, no connections. Yet this man I've barely met has stripped away those defenses like they were nothing.

"You didn't answer my question," I remind him, steering us back. "About why you stayed."

Tristan goes still, his fingers ceasing their tapping. For a moment, I think he won't answer at all. When he speaks, his voice has dropped to something just above a whisper.

"I stayed because leaving meant losing the only thing that truly mattered to me." He turns slightly toward me, though his eyes remain fixed on something in the distance.

"And the truth is, we would burn down the world for the things that matter to us." His voice is calm, matter-of-fact, despite the violence of his words. "I would become the very thing I hate. I would sacrifice anything for them, my freedom, my sanity, my soul."

The intensity behind his words is staggering. There's no dramatic emphasis, no theatrical delivery. Just the simple, devastating truth of how far he would go.

"That's your answer, Deacon Thorne." Tristan steps back from the balustrade. "We stay for what matters, who matters to us. And we become whatever we need to be for them."

I watch Tristan's profile against the autumn sky, weighing his words. There's a conviction in them that feels both familiar and foreign. A clarity of purpose I once had.

I don't say anything, I can't.

Tristan doesn't wait for a response. He doesn't need one. His statement was meant to force me to confront something I've been avoiding since the moment I saw her wink at me across that café.

He turns to leave, his movements precise and methodical. At the terrace door, he pauses without looking back.

"The question isn't whether you should stay or go. It's how far are you willing to go for the woman who holds your heart?"

The door closes behind him with a soft click, leaving me alone with the mountains and the dying light and the uncomfortable weight of his words.

TWENTY-SIX

SCOUT

I trace patterns in the condensation on the window, watching raindrops race down the glass. Seven days of Murder Manor house arrest has everyone on edge. Seven days of analyzing the Glass Gardener's kills. Seven days of avoiding Deacon's eyes across rooms.

The gardens below blur through the rain, turning the manicured hedges and flower beds into watercolor smudges. Even the weather seems to match my mood. It's gray and unsettled. Trapped.

A low drawl cuts through the quiet, smooth as whiskey and twice as dangerous. "If you stare any harder, you might burn a hole through the glass."

I don't turn at Brayden's voice. His reflection appears in the window as he approaches, hands tucked into the pockets of his bootcut jeans. Always the picture of a southern playboy, even when we're prisoners in our gilded cage.

"Maybe that's the plan," I murmur. "Escape route."

"Awww, now Scout, you know you don't want to escape me." He winks and flashes his signature grin. I roll my eyes but say nothing.

He moves to lean against the wall on the opposite end of the bay window seat, arms crossed. "You've been quiet."

"Everyone's quiet. We're all playing the world's most fucked up game of Clue."

"That's not what I meant." His voice drops lower. "You haven't cracked a single joke in three days, and Tank misses the sound of your voice at breakfast."

I shoot him a look. "Tank's deaf in one ear and sleeps through breakfast."

"Fine. I miss it." Brayden studies me, his usual smirk softening into something genuine. "What's going on, Cupcake?"

The fucking nickname, stupid and affectionate, breaks something loose in my chest. I pull my knees closer to me.

"Nothing's going on. We're locked down because some mirror-obsessed psycho might be stalking one of us. Isn't that enough?"

"Bullshit." Brayden nudges my foot with his. "I know you. This ain't just about the Glass Gardener. This is something else."

I rest my forehead against the cool glass. The truth sits heavy on my tongue, wanting release but terrified of the consequences. Brayden and I have always been the ones who talk. The ones who joke through the darkness of what we do. But this feels different.

"I want him," I finally whisper.

Brayden doesn't immediately respond. When I glance over, his expression hasn't changed. There's no shock, no judgment.

"And?" he prompts.

"And nothing. We killed, we fucked around with each other, and now we're playing strangers." The words tumble out harsh and clipped. "End of story."

"That don't sound like nothing, darlin'."

I press my palms against my eyes. "It was supposed to be nothing. That's how this works, right? We're killers, not lovers. Attachments get people killed."

"Is that what he said, or what you believe?"

The question hits too close. I drop my hands and glare at him. "Does it matter? You know our life. You know what happens to people who get too close."

Brayden leans back, studying me. "So this is about protectin' him? Or yourself?"

"Both. Neither." I shake my head, frustrated by my inability to articulate the storm inside me. "He doesn't do relationships, Bray. We don't do relationships. We're not supposed to get normal things in life."

"Because?"

"Because I'm The Stitcher," I snap. "You're the fucking Tooth Fairy. We're goddamn serial killers, Brayden. Normal people don't exactly line up for that."

"Deacon ain't normal people, cupcake."

The simple truth of that statement hangs between us. Deacon isn't normal. He's like me. He's damaged, dangerous, and devoted to a cause bigger than himself.

"That's the problem," I admit quietly. "He understands. He watched me kill Stanton and looked at me like I was beautiful. He killed Coach Z, and I wanted him right there, with blood still on his hands."

I swallow hard, voicing the fear I've been avoiding. "What if this isn't just sex? What if it's something I can't walk away from?"

Brayden's expression softens. "Would that be so terrible?"

"It would be fucking terrifying." My voice cracks. "I don't know how to do this, Bray. I don't know how to want someone who could disappear any day. Who could decide The Hollow isn't for him? Who would rather be alone than with me?"

"None of us knows how to do this," Brayden says gently. "You think Lucien planned to lead a family of killers? You think any of us expected to find people who see the darkness and stay anyway?"

He reaches across the space between us, squeezing my hand. "Maybe instead of decidin' what it can't be, you should use that pretty little head of yours to figure out what you want it to be."

I stare at our joined hands, at the tiny scars that mark both our knuckles, badges of our shared life.

A small tear tracks down my cheek, leaving a cool trail against my skin as the words tumble out barely louder than a breath. "What if I want something impossible?"

Brayden's smile turns wry. "Scout, we kill people, monsters. We're part of an underground network of vigilantes. We live in a mansion with security that would make the government jealous." He squeezes my hand again. "Impossible is kind of our specialty."

I laugh despite myself, wiping away the tear with the back of my hand. "Since when did you get so wise?"

"Now I've always been wise, darlin'. You were just too busy blowing shit up to notice." Brayden's southern drawl thickens when he's trying to make me smile. It works.

"Do you really think there's a chance?" I ask, hating how small my voice sounds.

Brayden shifts against the window seat, leaning closer. "I think Deacon Thorne has been watchin' you like a man dyin' of thirst looks at water. And I think he's just as confused about it as you are."

"He doesn't seem confused. He seems distant." I trace another pattern in the condensation, this time a tiny dahlia. "Ever since we got back, he's barely said ten words to me."

"That's because Mr. Floss don't know what to do with feelin's that don't fit into his neat little boxes." Brayden's eyes gleam with mischief. "Trust me, I've seen the way he looks at you when you're not lookin. Man's got it bad."

"How bad?" I can't help asking.

"Bad enough that Ivy and I have a bet goin' about how long before one of you cracks."

I smack his arm. "You're betting on my love life? That's low, even for you."

"Love life? Is that what we're callin' it now?" His eyebrows shoot up in mock surprise.

"Shut up." I pull my knees tighter to my chest. "It's not. I don't know what it is."

"That's the thing about feelin's, they don't come with instructions."

We sit in comfortable silence for a moment, watching the rain intensify outside. The gardens have disappeared completely now, obscured by sheets of water cascading down the glass.

"What if he leaves?" I finally voice my deepest fear. "What if I let myself feel this and he just walks away?"

Brayden's expression turns serious. "Then you'll hurt like hell. And I'll be here with a sundae and a shovel to bury his body."

"Bray!"

"Kiddin'. Mostly." He winks. "Look, none of us know what tomorrow brings in this life. We could get caught. We could get killed. The world could end. But that's true for everyone, not just us."

He reaches into the bag beside him that I hadn't noticed before. "Now, enough of this sad talk. I got you a little somethin' to put that smile back where it belongs."

He pulls out a pair of fuzzy pink bunny slippers, complete with floppy ears and little embroidered eyes. They're so ridiculously perfect and exactly what I need in this moment. My throat tightens.

"To replace the ones that Tank murdered," he explains, handing them to me.

I take the slippers, running my fingers over the plush fabric. "They're perfect. Thank you."

"Don't thank me yet. Tank already tried to steal one while I was puttin' them in the damn bag."

I laugh, the sound breaking free from the tightness in my chest. As I look up from the slippers, movement in the doorway catches my eye.

Deacon stands there, his tall frame filling the entrance to the sitting room. How long he's been watching us, I don't know, but something in his expression makes my heart skip. His eyes meet mine across the room, intense and unreadable.

"Speak of the devil," Brayden murmurs, following my gaze.

For a heartbeat, no one moves. Then Deacon nods once, a barely perceptible dip of his chin, before turning and disappearing down the hallway.

"See?" Brayden nudges me with his elbow. "What'd I tell you? Man's got it bad."

I clutch the bunny slippers to my chest, staring at the empty doorway. "Or he thinks I'm ridiculous."

"Scout," Brayden's voice turns gentle. "That man didn't look at you like he thinks you're ridiculous. He looked at you like he's afraid of how much he wants you."

I swallow hard. "So what do I do?"

"You put on your new bunny slippers," Brayden says as he stands and stretches. "And you decide if he's worth fightin' for.

I slip my feet into the fuzzy pink bunnies, wiggling my toes. "And if I get my heart broken?"

"Then you'll still have kick-ass bunny slippers." Brayden grins. "And a family who loves you, psychotic tendencies and all."

Twenty-Seven

Deacon

I stand frozen in the doorway, watching as Brayden hands Scout those ridiculous pink bunny slippers. Something twists in my chest at the sight of her face lighting up. A small, genuine smile breaking through the shadows that have haunted her eyes since we returned to the manor.

Seven days of lockdown. Seven days of avoiding her gaze across rooms, of stepping back when she steps forward. I pretend I don't feel the pull between us growing stronger with each passing hour.

And here she sits, cross-legged in the window seat, cradling those absurd slippers like they're precious. Something about the vulnerability in that gesture makes me want to cross the room and—

I catch myself. This is exactly why I've been keeping my distance. These feelings are a liability. A distraction. A weakness I can't afford.

When Scout's eyes suddenly lift to mine, I feel exposed, like she can see straight through the walls I've carefully constructed. For a heartbeat, I can't move. I can't breathe. I can't look away.

Then my survival instinct kicks in. I give her a curt nod and turn away, my footsteps quickening as I put distance between us.

"Deacon."

Roman's voice stops me in the hallway. He's coming towards me down the hall, looking at a tablet as he walks.

"Hey, man," I say.

He stops in front of me, eyes focused on the tablet as he types. I narrow my eyes. "Did you need something?"

"Actually, yes." His lips quirk, then his eyes lift to mine. "I've been analyzing the Glass Gardener information and found something you should see. It's in my data room."

The change in topic is a relief. "Lead the way."

Roman gestures down the hall. As we walk, I feel the weight of his sideways glance.

"What?" I finally ask.

"Nothing." He shrugs. "Just thinking it's interesting how you've been avoiding Scout since Chicago."

"I'm not—"

"Save it." Roman holds up a hand. "I'm not Lucien or Ivy. I am not here to coax you through your trauma."

We enter the data room, Roman's domain of screens, servers, and technology. The main monitor displays a map with red pins marking several locations.

"These are all the confirmed Glass Gardener kills so far," Roman explains, pointing to the screen. "Nine in total over the past two years."

I study the pattern. "They're all over the country. No kills are in the same area twice, except for Atlanta."

"Yes, but look at the timeline." Roman clicks a key, and dates appear next to each pin. "Only six of them correlate with your movements over the same time frame."I lean closer to the screen, studying the pattern of red pins scattered across the digital map. The dates next to each location tell a story that doesn't add up.

"See this kill in Phoenix?" Roman points. "You were in Minneapolis that week. And this one in Portland happened while you were in Boston."

"So it's not about me," I say, relief washing through me.

"Not directly, at least." Roman clicks through several screens. "But there's something else that's bothering me. Look at the victimology."

The screen fills with nine photos. They're all men of different ages, races, and backgrounds.

"Nothing connects them," I observe. "Different professions, different cities, different social circles."

"Exactly." Roman nods. "Which makes the ritualistic nature of the kills even more puzzling. Most serial killers with this elaborate of a signature typically target specific types that fulfill some psychological need."

"Unless the ritual itself is the point," I suggest. "Maybe the victims are just convenient vessels for whatever message the killer is trying to send."

Roman gives me a considering look. "That's actually really insightful."

I shrug. "I've spent a lot of time thinking about how killers think."

"Speaking of thinking, " Roman closes the Glass Gardener files and turns to face me directly. "Your entrance to The Hollow hasn't exactly been standard."

I tense, sensing the shift in conversation. "Is that a problem?"

"Not necessarily." Roman leans against his desk. "Typically, we have a longer probationary process, but the Glass Gardener situation fucked things up a bit. We've reviewed all of Scout's debrief, and everything looks solid."

My brows furrow as I look at him, unsure of what he's saying.

"What I'm saying is that you passed, and I'm asking whether you intend to stay."

The question catches me off guard. Seven days ago, I might have had a different answer. But now—

"I haven't decided yet," I say, the lie tastes bitter on my tongue.

The truth is, I don't know if I want to leave or not. Not just because of Scout, though she's a gravitational force I'm struggling to resist, but because for the first time in years, I don't feel alone in this fight. There's something powerful about being surrounded by people who understand the darkness without judgment. People who stand beside you in solidarity.

Roman studies me for a long moment. "Well, while you're deciding, there's something you should know."

His tone shifts, a subtle edge entering his voice that makes me straighten.

"What's that?"

"Whatever's going on between you and Scout needs to get figured out." His eyes harden. "Fast."

I open my mouth to deny it, but Roman cuts me off with a raised hand.

"Save it. I've seen the way you two have been with each other. The tension is affecting everyone."

"It's not—"

"It's exactly these kinds of distractions that create mistakes," Roman interrupts. "And mistakes get people killed in our line of work."

His words hit hard, targeting my deepest fear. "I know. Why do you think I've been trying to avoid it?"

Roman's voice drops lower. "I don't care if you two fuck each other senseless or never speak again. Just resolve it."

The crudeness of his statement sparks anger in my chest. "That's between me and Scout."

"No." Roman steps closer. "Nothing in The Hollow is just between two people. We're a system. A machine. Every part affects the whole."

There's something in his eyes now, a cold calculation that lets me know that this man isn't just a tech genius.

"Let me be perfectly clear, Deacon. I am loyal to The Hollow above everything." His voice is quiet but carries the weight of absolute certainty. "My family has dedicated their life to it and I have lost more to it than you will ever know. And I can tell you with absolute certainty that I will remove anything, or anyone, that threatens its integrity or capabilities."

It's more of a promise than a threat.

"Do you understand what I'm saying?" Roman asks.

I hold his gaze, refusing to be intimidated. "I understand perfectly."

"Good." Roman turns back to his computers, dismissing me. "Because I'd hate to lose someone with your particular talents."

I leave the data room with Roman's warning echoing in my head. He's right about one thing. I need to resolve whatever this is with Scout. The question is how, when everything inside me is at war.

Because the truth I can barely admit to myself is that I'm not just afraid of getting her killed.

I'm afraid of how much I'm starting to need her.

THE HALLWAY STRETCHES BEFORE ME, silent and oppressive. I need to clear my head, work through the tangled mess of feelings I've been avoiding since Chicago. Maybe the gym? Some physical exertion might help burn off this energy.

As I round the corner toward the east wing, I hear it. Loud thuds and grunts echo down the corridor. Then a voice cuts through the noise.

"Oh, you goddamn motherfucking asshole!"

Scout.

I quicken my pace, instinct kicking in before reason can catch up. The double doors to the gym stand partially open, and I push through them, ready for—

I stop dead in my tracks.

Scout and Brayden circle each other on training mats in the center of the room. She's wearing tiny hot pink athletic shorts that frame her wide hips and hug her round ass in a way that makes my mouth go dry. Her breasts are barely constrained by the matching sports bra, bouncing slightly with each movement. Her caramel skin glistens with sweat, curls pulled into a fluffy ponytail that whips around as she dodges Brayden's advance.

"That's the best you got, Tooth Fairy?" she taunts, dancing back on the balls of her feet.

Brayden, shirtless and towering over her, grins wickedly. "Just warmin' up, Cupcake."

He lunges forward with surprising speed for his size, aiming a controlled but powerful jab at her midsection. Scout twists away, using his momentum against him as she hooks her foot behind his ankle and shoves. Brayden stumbles but recovers with practiced ease.

"Someone's getting slow in his old age," Scout laughs.

I lean against the doorframe, captivated by their dance. She didn't lie about being a scrappy street fighter. There's nothing polished or technical about Scout's style. It's pure instinct and survival, dirty moves and quick reflexes. She fights like someone who learned in back alleys rather than a state-of-the-art gym.

Brayden dwarfs her by comparison, all muscle and controlled power, but Scout holds her own. She ducks under his arm, lands two quick jabs to his ribs, and dances away before he can counter.

"Fuck!" Brayden grunts, rubbing his side. "Those lil' raccoon hands of yours fucking hurt."

"Aww, you got a boo-boo?" Scout teases, bouncing on her toes, seemingly tireless.

I should walk away. This isn't helping my resolution to keep a distance between us. But I can't tear my eyes from her. The fluid way she moves, the fierce determination in her eyes, and the sheer life force radiating from her small frame.

Brayden catches her with a sweep of his leg, sending her tumbling to the mat. She lands flat on her back with a loud thud. Before she can roll away, he's on her, pinning her with his weight.

I stand frozen in the doorway, watching as Scout struggles beneath Brayden's weight. She twists her hips, trying to buck him off, but he's too heavy, too strong. Her small hands fly toward his face, aiming for his eyes or nose, a classic street fighter move, but Brayden catches both wrists in one large hand.

In a smooth motion that sends ice through my veins, he pins her arms above her head against the mat.

Just like I did to her against the wall in Chicago.

Scout's chest heaves with exertion, her sports bra barely containing her breasts as she pants. The position is too familiar, her arms stretched above her, body arched, completely at the mercy of the man above her. A man who isn't me.

Brayden's eyes suddenly flick up, locking with mine across the gym. A slow, deliberate smile spreads across his face as he registers my presence. He holds my gaze for one beat, two, then looks back down at Scout, who's still squirming beneath him.

His free hand slides to her hip, fingers splaying possessively across the exposed skin between her shorts and sports bra. His thumb traces a small circle on her hipbone, the gesture unmistakably intimate. He ducks his head low, his lips almost brushing her ear. Whatever he whispers makes Scout go completely still.

Something in me snaps.

My vision narrows to a crimson haze. Everything peripheral fades away, the gym equipment, the walls, the space between us, until all I see is Brayden's hand on Scout's skin and her body pinned beneath his.

I move before conscious thought can stop me. One moment I'm at the doorway, the next I'm crossing the mat with silent, predatory strides. The same cold precision that guides my knife when I hunt takes over.

Twenty-Eight

Scout

I'm trapped beneath Brayden's weight, my wrists pinned above my head, his grip just tight enough to be annoying but not painful. This is how our sparring sessions always end, with him using his giant ass to his advantage, forcing me to figure out how to escape when my opponent has 100 pounds and over a foot of height on me. I'm about to try the hip twist he taught me last week when his fingers suddenly trail down my side in a deliberately suggestive caress. The unexpected touch makes me freeze, my brain short-circuiting as his hand brushes my hip with slow, sensual pressure. *What. The. Fuck.*

"Get off me, fuck face," I grunt, trying to buck him off as I glare at him. He's never done anything like this to me before.

His eyes suddenly flick toward the door as a slow grin spreads across his face. His hand lingers on my hip, thumb brushing against the exposed skin where my tank top has ridden up. He leans down, his lips nearly brushing my ear.

"Lit the fuse for ya, Cupcake. You can thank me later."

Before I can ask what the hell he means, a blur of movement catches my peripheral vision. A large hand appears out of nowhere, clamping down on Brayden's throat and shoulder. In one fluid motion, Brayden's massive body is ripped off me as if he weighs nothing.

Holy. Shit.

I blink up in shock as Deacon looms over me, his face transformed. Gone is the carefully controlled mask he always wears. His steel-gray eyes have darkened to obsidian, his pupils are blown wide with rage. His jaw is clenched so tight I can see the muscle twitching. He stands between me and Brayden, shoulders tense, hands curled into fists.

He looks ready to kill.

"Whoa there, Deacon," Brayden says, hands raised in surrender while his smirk stays firmly in place. "Just teachin' our girl how to handle herself."

Deacon doesn't respond. He doesn't even blink. He just stares at Brayden with the same cold, calculating intensity I've seen him direct at his prey.

"Well, hell," Brayden continues, his drawl deliberately sharp with challenge. "Didn't realize she was yours. Better mark it before someone else does."

A low growl rumbles from Deacon's chest, an actual fucking growl, and I scramble to my feet, suddenly worried I might have to stop Deacon from killing him.

Brayden just laughs, backing toward the door with a knowing grin. "Looks like my work here's done. Don't do nothin' I wouldn't do, kids."

The door swings shut behind him, leaving me alone with a feral Deacon who still hasn't taken his eyes off the spot where Brayden was standing.

"Deacon?" I ask cautiously.

He whips around to face me, and the intensity in his gaze knocks the breath from my lungs. There's something primal there, something possessive and hungry that makes heat pool low in my belly.

Deacon's eyes lock onto mine, something untamed and dangerous swimming in their depths. The air between us crackles with tension as he takes a step forward. I instinctively back away, my body reacting to the predatory energy radiating from him.

"Deacon," I whisper, my voice catching in my throat. "What are you—"

He doesn't respond. His face remains eerily expressionless, but his eyes. God, his eyes burn with something I've only seen glimpses of from him before. Raw, unfiltered want.

I continue retreating, my heart hammering against my ribs. For each step I take backward, he matches with a stalking advance. There's no hurry in his movements, just the confident patience of someone who knows their prey has nowhere to go.

My back suddenly collides with the weight rack. Cold metal presses against my shoulder blades, stopping my retreat. Deacon closes the final distance between us in two swift strides.

His hand shoots out, wrapping around my throat. Not squeezing, not cutting off my air, just holding me in place with unmistakable authority. His thumb rests against my pulse point. I can feel it racing beneath his touch.

"Mine," he growls, the single word reverberating through his chest.

His other hand grips my hip, fingers digging in hard enough to bruise. The pain mingles with pleasure, sending a jolt of electricity straight to my pussy. I gasp, my lips parting.

"This," he says, squeezing my hip harder, "is mine."

My breath comes in shallow pants as his hand slides up, roughly palming my breast through my sports bra. He kneads the flesh with pressure, his thumb flicking over my nipple until it hardens beneath the fabric.

"These," he continues, voice dropping lower, "are mine."

I whimper, arching into his touch despite myself. The hand at my throat tightens just enough to remind me it's there.

He moves his grip to my ass, squeezing hard enough to make me rise onto my tiptoes. "This is mine."

His thigh wedges between my legs, pressing against my pussy. The friction against my already sensitive flesh makes me moan. He dips his head, his breath hot against my earlobe, his lips brushing the sensitive skin.

"This," he growls next, rocking his thigh upward with each word, "Is. Mine."

I bite my lip to keep from begging. His hand leaves my ass, trailing up my side before tangling in my hair. I gasp as he yanks my head back, exposing my neck to him.

"Every sound you make," he whispers against my throat, "is mine."

His teeth graze the sensitive skin below my ear, and I shudder uncontrollably. The hand at my throat slides up to grip my jaw, turning my face toward his.

"These lips," he murmurs, thumb tracing my bottom lip roughly, "are mine."

His eyes bore into mine, as if searching for something. I'm not sure what he finds, but whatever it is makes his pupils dilate further.

"And these eyes," he says, voice suddenly softer but no less intense, "when they look at anyone else the way they're looking at me right now..." His grip tightens momentarily. "Remember, they belong to me."

I hold Deacon's burning gaze, my chest heaving with each breath. The weight of his hand on my throat, the heat of his body pressing against mine, it's intoxicating. Dangerous. Perfect.

Slowly, deliberately, I run my tongue across my bottom lip, watching his eyes track the movement with predatory focus.

"Yes," I whisper, my voice husky with need. "Yours. Only yours."

Something fractures behind his eyes, that final thread of control he's been clinging to since Chicago snaps like a garrote pulled too tight. His hand releases my throat so quickly I barely register the movement before both hands are gripping my thighs, fingers digging into the soft flesh as he hauls me up against his chest.

My legs wrap around his waist, as my pussy presses against the hard ridge straining against his jeans. I'm not just some passive doll to be manhandled. My fingers tangle in his dark hair, yanking his head back with enough force to make him hiss through clenched teeth.

"And you're mine," I growl against his mouth, nipping his bottom lip hard enough to draw blood. "Don't you fucking forget it."

He slams me back against the weight rack, metal clanging as barbells and plates slide off the ends and crash to the floor. The noise echoes through the gym, but I couldn't care less if the entire house hears us.

I roll my hips against him, grinding down on his erection with shameless need. His hands slide under my ass, squeezing roughly as he supports my weight.

"Fucking dangerous," he mutters against my neck, teeth scraping over my pulse point.

I laugh, breathless and wild. "You have no idea."

In one fluid motion, he turns and drops me onto the training mat, following me down with his body. His weight pins me exactly as Brayden's had minutes before, but everything about this is different. Electric. His hands capture my wrists, dragging them above my head and holding them there with one large palm.

"This is how he had you?" Deacon asks, voice deadly quiet.

I arch beneath him, deliberately rubbing against the hard length pressed against my center. "Jealous?"

His free hand grips my jaw, forcing me to look at him. "Answer me."

"Yes," I gasp as his hips grind down. "But he doesn't make me wet like you do."

Something dark and primal flashes in his eyes. His hand slides from my jaw down my throat, between my breasts, over my stomach, until his fingers hook into the waistband of my shorts.

"Show me," he commands.

I lift my hips, allowing him to yank my shorts and underwear down in one rough motion. Cool air hits my exposed skin, but I'm burning everywhere he touches. He releases my wrists only long enough to pull my sports bra over my head, leaving me completely naked beneath him while he remains fully clothed.

The power imbalance makes me dizzy with arousal.

My newly freed hands don't stay idle. I grab his shirt, ripping it up and over his head, my nails raking down his chest hard enough to leave angry red trails. He hisses, catching my wrists again and slamming them back above my head.

"Behave," he growls.

I bare my teeth in a feral grin. "Make me."

He pins me with his weight, his strength evident in the way he holds my wrists with just one hand. His eyes devour every inch of my exposed skin, and I can feel his cock pressing against me through his pants.

I'm not some conquest to be claimed without a fight.

I arch my back, pushing my breasts toward him. His eyes immediately drop to follow the movement, his grip on my wrists loosening just a fraction. That's all I need.

"You want me?" I purr, rolling my hips beneath him. "Then earn me."

With a sharp twist of my wrist, I break his hold on one hand. Before he can react, I grab a fistful of his hair and yank hard to the side, momentarily throwing him off balance. In that split second, I hook my leg around his, plant my free hand on his shoulder, and use the momentum to flip our positions.

The move is fluid, practiced. It's one of the first moves that Brayden taught me for taking down larger opponents. Deacon's back hits the mat with a satisfying thud, surprise flashing across his face before his expression settles into something darker, hungrier.

I straddle his chest, knees pinning his arms to his sides. My nakedness is a weapon now, my power. I lean forward, grabbing his jaw with bruising force, my nails digging into his skin hard enough to leave crescent-shaped marks.

"Not so easy, is it?" I hiss before crashing my mouth against his.

There's nothing gentle about the kiss. It's all teeth and tongue, a battle for dominance that neither of us is willing to lose. I bite his lower lip hard enough to draw blood, the metallic taste mixing with our shared breath. He growls into my mouth, the vibration traveling through my body straight to my core.

I break the kiss, sitting up straight on his chest. His eyes are wild now, pupils blown so wide there's barely any gray left. I rock my hips forward, dragging my slick folds across his bare skin, marking him with my arousal.

"Feel that?" I whisper, grinding down harder. "That's how wet you make me. But if you think I'm just going to roll over and let you take what you want," I lean down, my lips brushing against his ear. "You're going to have to fight harder."

His chest rises and falls rapidly beneath me, his skin growing slick where I'm rubbing my pussy against him. I can feel his heart hammering against my inner thigh, matching the frantic rhythm of my own.

"Fucking dangerous," he repeats, but this time there's something like awe in his voice.

I flash him a wicked smile. "Think you can handle me?"

His muscles tense beneath me, and I know he's about to make his move. I tighten my thighs around him, preparing for the counterattack I know is coming. The air between us crackles with tension and raw desire.

This is no longer just about sex. It's about power, control, and who's willing to surrender first.

And I have no intention of making it easy for him.

I feel his muscles coil beneath me, tension building like a compressed spring. His eyes lock with mine, a silent warning of what's coming. I tighten my thighs, ready for his counterattack, but nothing prepares me for his speed.

In one fluid motion, his arms break free from beneath my knees. His hands grip my hips, fingers digging into my flesh as he lifts me like I weigh nothing. Before I can react, he's jerking me forward.

"Fuck—" The curse dies in my throat as I realize my new position.

I'm straddling his face, my knees on either side of his head, my pussy hovering inches above his mouth. His strong arms wrap around my thighs like steel bands, pulling me down until there's no space left between us.

There's no hesitation, no gentle exploration. His mouth claims me with savage intensity, his tongue parting my folds in one long, firm stroke that tears a gasp from my lungs. My hands fly out to steady myself, one palm slapping against the mat, the other instinctively fisting in his dark hair.

"Oh god," I moan as his tongue circles my clit with firm pressure.

His grip on my thighs tightens, holding me firmly in place as he devours my pussy. There's something primal in the way he feasts, like a man starved. His tongue dips inside me, fucking into my entrance with relentless rhythm, then flattens to lick a broad stripe from my opening to my clit.

I try to squirm away from the overwhelming sensation, but his arms lock me in position, forcing me to take everything he gives. My thighs tremble with the effort to stay upright, pleasure building so quickly I can barely breathe.

His teeth graze my sensitive bud, followed by the hot suction of his mouth. The contrast of sharp pain and intense pleasure sends lightning up my spine. I cry out, my fingers tightening in his hair. He grunts as I pull at the dark strands.

He growls against my soaked folds, the vibration traveling through me, as he retaliates by sucking harder, drawing my clit between his lips and flicking it rapidly with his tongue.

"Fuck, Deacon!" I gasp, my hips rocking involuntarily against his face.

He releases one of my thighs, his hand sliding up to palm my breast roughly. His fingers find my nipple, pinching and rolling the sensitive peak in time with the movements of his tongue. The dual assault is almost too much to bear.

I look down and nearly come undone at the sight, Deacon's eyes locked on mine, watching my every reaction as he consumes me. His gaze is possessive, triumphant, challenging me to deny how completely he owns this moment.

Instead of fighting it, I surrender to the sensation. I grind myself shamelessly against his mouth, using my grip on his hair to guide him exactly where I need him.

"Right there," I pant, rolling my hips in tight circles. "Don't stop."

His tongue is relentless as it lashes my clit. His free hand slides from my breast down my stomach, then slips underneath my thigh, until his finger is pressing against my entrance alongside his tongue.

He pushes it inside me, curling upward to hit that perfect spot while his mouth continues its assault on my clit, the pleasure crests so suddenly I can't even scream. My body goes rigid, thighs clamping around his head as waves of ecstasy crash through me.

But he doesn't let up. His arms lock around my thighs, holding me firmly against his mouth as he works me through my orgasm and pushes me toward another. His tongue is merciless, alternating between broad strokes and precise flicks that have me sobbing with overstimulation.

Any protest I might have dissolves into incoherent moans as a second climax builds impossibly fast on the heels of the first.

My fingers tighten in his hair, torn between pulling him closer and pushing him away. The pleasure borders on pain, too intense, too much, but I can't get enough. I rock against him with desperate abandon, chasing the release I know only he can give me.

I'm lost in the thrumming pleasure building between my thighs, my body trembling as Deacon's tongue works magic against my sensitive flesh. My second orgasm hovers just out of reach, a coiled spring ready to snap.

His hands suddenly grip my ass with bruising force, shoving me forward. I tumble onto the mat, landing flat on my stomach with a startled yelp.

"What the fuck?" I snarl, twisting to glare at him over my shoulder.

Deacon rises to his knees behind me, eyes burning with primal hunger. His chest heaves with each breath, lips glistening with my arousal. He hooks his thumbs into the waistband of his jeans as he pops the button free, shoving them down around his knees.

His cock springs free, thick, hard, and intimidating. My mouth goes dry at the sight.

"You don't get to cum again," he growls, gripping my hips and pulling me back onto my hands and knees, "until it's on my cock."

A shiver runs down my spine at his words. "Then what are you waiting for? Fuck me already." I challenge, arching my back.

His fingers dig into my flesh as he positions himself behind me. I feel the blunt head of his cock pressing against my entrance, teasing but not entering.

"Beg for it," he commands, his voice dark with desire.

"Fuck you," I spit back.

He chuckles, the sound sending heat pooling between my thighs. "That's the idea, kitten."

Before I can retort, he grips my hips and pulls me back as he thrusts forward, spearing me in one swift motion. The sudden intrusion tears a strangled cry from my throat. He's bigger than I expected, stretching me in a deliciously painful way.

"Fuck," he hisses, holding still for a moment. "So fucking tight."

His thrusts start short but hard, working himself deeper with each stroke. My fingers claw at the mat beneath me, searching for purchase as he rocks into me with increasing force.

"Such a good girl," he groans, one hand sliding up my spine to fist in my hair. "Taking my cock so well."

He yanks my head back, forcing my spine into a deeper arch. The new angle lets him hit spots inside me that make my vision blur.

"Is this what you wanted?" His voice is rough against my ear as he drapes his body over mine, never breaking his rhythm. "To be fucked like the little killer you are?"

"Yes," I moan, pushing back to meet each thrust. "Harder."

He obliges, his hips snapping against my ass with enough force to drive me forward on the mat. One hand releases my hip to slide around to my front, fingers finding my clit.

"Such a perfect little cunt," he praises, circling the sensitive bundle of nerves. "So wet for me."

His words are as filthy as they are appreciative, each syllable punctuated by a thrust that drives him deeper inside me. The dual stimulation of his cock filling me and his fingers working my clit has me climbing rapidly toward release again.

"That's it," he encourages, feeling my inner walls begin to flutter around him. "Squeeze my cock just like that."

His thrusts become more erratic, his breathing harsh against my neck. "Tell me you're mine," he growls.

My back arches, and a raw, guttural sound tears from my throat, coherent speech dissolving into primal need. His fingers vanish from my throbbing clit. The sudden absence of his touch leaves me whimpering, only for his palm to slap against my wet, swollen pussy a heartbeat later. Electricity shoots from my core up my spine.

"Say. It." His voice is granite-hard against my ear.

"I'm yours," I gasp, teetering on the edge of oblivion.

With a guttural sound, he slams into me one final time, burying his dick to the hilt. The feeling of him bottoming out inside me triggers my second orgasm, more intense than the first. I scream as pleasure explodes through my body, my inner walls clamping down on his length as wave after wave crashes over me.

Deacon's grip on my hair tightens, pulling my head back until my throat is exposed. His other hand digs into my hip, fingers pressing deep enough to leave marks I'll find tomorrow. Each thrust is harder than the last, the sound of skin slapping against skin echoes through the gym.

He growls, his voice rough with desire. "You take my cock like you were made for it, kitten."

I can barely form words, each punishing thrust driving the air from my lungs. He's relentless, his pace increasing until I'm struggling to stay on my hands and knees.

"Fuck—Deacon—" I manage between gasps as he adjusts his angle slightly.

The new position hits something deep inside me that makes my vision blur. I cry out, my arms giving way until my cheek presses against the mat.

"That's it," he praises. "Face down, ass up. Perfect little killer."

His hips snap forward brutally, each thrust pushing me closer to another peak. The friction is exquisite, his thick length stretching me in ways I've never felt before.

"You feel so good," I moan, pushing back to meet his thrusts. "So fucking deep."

He leans over me, his chest pressing against my back as he fucks into me harder. His breath is hot against my ear, each exhale punctuated by a grunt as he bottoms out inside me.

"Going to fill this tight pussy," he promises, his words sending shivers down my spine. "Mark you from the inside."

The possessiveness in his voice makes me clench around him, drawing a hiss from between his teeth.

"Yes," I beg, desperate for more. "Fill me. Want to feel you cum inside me."

His rhythm falters for just a moment, then he's pounding into me like a man possessed. One hand snakes around to find my clit, rubbing tight circles that have me seeing stars.

"You're mine," he growls, his fingers working my sensitive bud as his cock stretches me open. "Say it again."

"I'm yours," I gasp. "All yours, Deacon."

His thrusts become more erratic, his breathing harsh against my neck. I can feel him swelling inside me, thickening.

"Nobody else gets to see you like this," he commands, as he thrusts deep. "Nobody else gets to fuck you like this."

"Just you," I breathe out as my inner walls clench around him. "Only you."

The pressure builds low in my belly, a coiling tension that threatens to snap at any moment. I'm so close, teetering on the precipice of what promises to be the most intense orgasm I've ever had.

"Cum for me," he demands, his fingers pressing harder against my clit. "Cum on my cock, Scout."

His use of my name, not kitten, not little killer, pushes me over the edge. My orgasm crashes through me like a tidal wave. I scream his name as my body convulses, inner walls clamping down on his thick cock with rhythmic pulses.

"Fuck," he groans, his hips stuttering as my orgasm triggers his own.

With one final, brutal thrust, he buries himself inside me. I feel the hot rush of his release, filling me. His body shudders against mine, cock pulsing as he empties himself.

For several moments, we stay frozen in position, both of us panting and trembling from the intensity. His grip on my hair loosens, hand sliding down to stroke my back in an unexpectedly tender gesture.

When he finally pulls out, I feel the evidence of his release trickling down my inner thigh. The sensation is oddly satisfying, a physical reminder of being thoroughly conquered.

Well, fuck. This wasn't supposed to happen. I was supposed to be the one doing the conquering, not melting into a puddle of satisfied woman beneath Deacon fucking Thorne. But as I lie here, feeling deliciously used and completely his, I can't bring myself to care. Some battles are worth losing.

Twenty-Nine
Deacon

I watch her sleeping on my chest, her wild curls spilling across the dark fabric of my shirt that barely covers her thighs. The rise and fall of her breath is hypnotic, steady, trusting. Vulnerable in a way I never thought someone like her could be.

Someone like us.

The gym floor wasn't exactly the ideal location for what happened between us, so I'd scooped her up afterward. She protested weakly, still boneless from multiple orgasms, as I pulled my t-shirt over her head.

"I can walk," she'd mumbled against my neck.

"I know you can," I'd replied, lifting her anyway. Her strong legs coiled around my waist like a vise. Her core pressed flush against my stomach, our combined release trickling between us, turning my abs into a slick, glistening canvas.

Now she's curled against me like she belongs here, one leg thrown over mine, fingers loosely gripping the sheet. The fierce little killer reduced to soft breaths and occasional murmurs.

I trace my fingertip along the curve of her shoulder, marveling at how someone so deadly can feel so delicate beneath my hands. The contradiction of her fascinates me. How she giggles over sprinkles and squeals about pink things, then kills with expert precision and ruthlessness.

Scout shifts in her sleep, pressing closer. Something in my chest tightens, an unfamiliar feeling I've spent years avoiding.

Attachment. Connection. Weakness.

Except it doesn't feel like weakness anymore. It feels like certainty.

This is what Tristan meant on the terrace. When he asked how far I'd go for her, I didn't have an answer then. Now I do.

I'd burn down the world for her. I *would* become the monster if she needed me to.

The realization should terrify me. I've spent my life avoiding connections, convinced they were liabilities. People who care become people who hesitate. People who hesitate die. That's what I've always believed. I've lost everyone I've ever loved. Why would this be any different?

Scout, with her untamed nature and her complete disregard for my carefully constructed walls, has changed the equation.

She makes me want impossible things. A future. A partnership. Her feral moods first thing in the morning and her soft snores at night. I want it all.

My hand finds her hair, fingers threading through the silky strands. She makes a sound of contentment in her sleep, nuzzling closer.

I've been alone for so long I forgot what it was to want someone near. To crave not just their body but their presence. Their everything.

I press my lips to the top of her head, breathing in the scent of her shampoo mixed with sweat and sex. Our scents mingled together.

The cold, logical part of my brain tries to intervene. Reminds me that attachments are dangerous in our line of work. That caring makes you vulnerable, and I can't protect her from everything.

But for once, I silence that voice.

Because I understand now that there's nothing that could drag me away from this woman. Not The Hollow's rules. Not my own demons. Not the Glass Gardener or whatever threat comes next.

Nothing except death itself would be enough to separate us now.

And even then, I'd fight my way back from whatever hell they sent me to if it meant returning to her.

"Deacon," she murmurs, lost in sleep.

Something primitive and possessive flares inside me. My name on her lips, even in sleep, feels like claiming. Like belonging.

A hunger rises in me, different from the frantic need that consumed us in the gym. This is something deeper.

Carefully, I roll Scout onto her back, her body pliant in deep sleep. She doesn't stir as I slip from the bed, my eyes never leaving her form. The shirt I'd given her has ridden up, exposing the curve of her hip.

I retrieve my knife from my discarded jeans, the metal cool against my palm. With surgical precision, I slide the blade under the hem of my shirt that covers her body. The fabric parts like water, falling away from her skin without leaving a mark.

She's magnificent. All soft curves and deadly strength. Scars tell stories across her skin, evidence of a life lived dangerously, violently. Each one makes me want to press my lips against it, to honor the pain that created it.

I start at her feet, taking one delicate arch in my hand. I press my mouth to her ankle, tasting the salt of her skin. My lips trail up her calf, worshipping each inch. Her legs are strong, capable of running down prey or wrapping around my waist with bruising force.

Working up to her thighs, I take my time. My mouth leaves a trail of heat across her skin, alternating between soft kisses and gentle scrapes of teeth. I whisper against her flesh, words too raw to say when she's awake.

"Perfect." Kiss. "Mine." Bite. "Beautiful." Lick.

I deliberately pass over the apex of her thighs, though the scent of her arousal mixed with the remnants of our earlier activities makes my cock throb painfully. This isn't about my need. Not yet.

My mouth continues its pilgrimage across the soft plane of her stomach, tongue dipping into her navel. Her skin tastes like salt and something uniquely Scout. Sweet and deadly.

When I reach her breasts, I pause to admire them. Full and perfect, tipped with dusky nipples. I take one peak into my mouth, sucking gently.

Scout moans in her sleep, her back arching slightly off the bed. The sound encourages me, stokes the fire burning low in my gut. I lavish attention on her other breast, my hand sliding up to caress the first so it isn't left wanting.

Her body responds even in sleep, a light sheen of sweat forming on her skin. I work my way back down, tracing the line between her breasts to her navel, then lower.

Her legs fall open, an unconscious invitation I can't resist. I settle between her thighs, my breath ghosting over pussy. The sight of her glistening folds, still bearing evidence of my claiming, sends a jolt of possessive pleasure through me.

I lower my mouth to her, my tongue making a soft pass through her folds. The taste of us combined explodes across my tongue, her sweetness mixed with my salt. I moan against her, the vibration causing a slight buck of her hips.

"You taste like heaven," I murmur against her center, eliciting a shiver from her. "Like mine."

My hands slide beneath her thighs, lifting them slightly to give me better access. I'm methodical and thorough. The same focus I bring to a kill is now focused entirely on her. Her soft, sleepy moans are the only sound I can hear.

I return to my worship, placing feather-light kisses along her inner thighs, occasionally nipping at the tender skin there. I drag my tongue through her center, the contact is barely there, just a ghost of pressure. I watch as her hands fist in the sheets.

I pull away and move up her body. My lips trail over her stomach, between her breasts, along the elegant column of her throat until I'm hovering above her.

I lower myself between her legs, supporting my weight on my forearms. One hand reaches down to cradle her thigh, guiding her calf to rest loosely over my arm. It opens her to me completely, her soaked cunt my nirvana.

I position my cock at her entrance, the head slipping through her folds, gathering her wetness. I push forward, entering her in one slow, continuous motion until I'm buried to the hilt. Her eyes fly open, liquid amber pools with pupils so wide they nearly swallow the color, reflecting the hunger I know she can see in mine.

The sensation is overwhelming. Her swollen folds are tight around me in a way that borders on painful, but the pain mingles with pleasure, creating a heady cocktail that makes my vision blur at the edges.

"You're everything," I whisper against her lips, the words are inadequate for what I'm feeling.

I kiss her then, soft and slow. Her mouth opens beneath mine, our tongues meeting in a languid dance. She tastes herself on my lips, moaning softly into my mouth.

"Fuck," I groan against her neck. "So tight. So perfect around me." My body stills, allowing her time to adjust.

Scout's nails dig into my shoulders, her back arching slightly. "Move," she demands, though her voice lacks its usual authority.

I withdraw almost completely before sliding back in with the same measured pace. There's no urgency now. No frantic race to claim or possess. This is different. It's a slow-burning fire rather than an explosive inferno.

Her pussy grips me like a vise with each withdrawal, as if it's reluctant to let me go. The friction is exquisite, heightened by her swollen folds.

"Your pussy was made for me," I murmur against her ear, maintaining my unhurried rhythm.

Her hands slide down my back, fingers tracing the muscles that flex with each thrust. "Deacon," she breathes, my name sounds like a prayer on her lips.

I capture her mouth again, pouring everything I can't say into the kiss. Words like "love" don't exist in my vocabulary; they're too dangerous, too vulnerable. But I can show her with every stroke, every touch, every kiss.

"I've never wanted anyone the way I want you," I confess against her lips, the closest I can come to the truth burning in my chest. "Never needed anyone before you."

Scout's lips find mine, soft yet demanding. Her kiss is different now, not the frantic clash of teeth and tongue, but something deeper. Something that feels dangerously close to surrender.

"I've never needed anyone either," she whispers against my mouth. "But I need you, Deacon. I need this."

Her words hit me, cracking something open inside my chest. I maintain my steady pace, each stroke deliberate and deep, watching her face as pleasure washes over her features.

"You're perfect," she breathes, her hands sliding up to cup my face. "So fucking perfect inside me."

I drop my forehead to hers, our breath mingling as I continue the slow, measured rhythm with my hips. Her walls flutter around me, squeezing with each withdrawal.

"That's it," she says, her voice a husky whisper. "Just like that."

Her praise is intoxicating. I've never cared what anyone thought of me before, but hearing any kind of praise from her lips makes something inside me preen with satisfaction.

"You were made for this," I murmur, rotating my hips slightly to hit that spot that makes her gasp. "Made for me."

Her nails dig into my shoulders as her breathing quickens. I can feel her building toward release, her inner muscles beginning to tighten rhythmically around my cock.

"I'm close," she admits, her voice breaking on the words. "So close, Deacon."

I maintain my pace, refusing to rush despite the fire building at the base of my spine. I want to watch her fall apart slowly. Beautifully. Completely.

"Let go for me," I say as I press my lips to the pulse point beneath her ear.

She arches beneath me, her body a perfect bow of tension. "Cum with me," she pleads, her hands sliding down to grip my ass, urging me deeper. "I need to feel you cum inside me."

Her words nearly shatter my control. "You want my cum?" I growl against her neck, my hips never faltering in their steady rhythm.

"Yes," she moans, her walls clenching around me. "Cum for me, Deacon. Cum in me."

I slide one hand between us, my thumb finding her clit. I circle it with gentle pressure, matching the rhythm of my thrusts. Feeling my own release building. It's almost impossible to hold back now.

Her eyes lock with mine, wide and vulnerable in a way I've never seen before. "I'm yours," she whispers, and those two simple words push me over the edge.

My balls tighten, electricity shooting up my spine. A groan falls from my lips as I bury myself deep inside her, as the first pulse of my release goes through me.

Scout comes with a soft cry, her body clenching around me in rhythmic waves that milk every drop from my body. I continue to move inside her, drawing out our pleasure until we're both trembling with oversensitivity.

I collapse beside her, gathering her sweat-slicked body against mine. Her head finds the hollow of my shoulder, fitting there as if the space was carved just for her.

We lie in silence, our breathing gradually slowing, our heartbeats finding a synchronized rhythm. My hand traces lazy patterns on her back, unwilling to break contact even for a moment.

I should be planning my exit strategy. I should be calculating the safest distance to maintain. Instead, I'm memorizing the weight of her against my chest and the way her breath fans across my skin.

There's no going back from this.

THIRTY

SCOUT

I wake slowly, my body deliciously sore in all the right places. The digital clock on Deacon's nightstand reads 4:17 AM. His arm drapes heavily across my waist, his breath warm against my neck.

For a moment, I just lie here, soaking in this delicious feeling. I've had my share of one-night stands. Quick, meaningless hookups where I could be the fun, wild girl without worrying about explanations or morning-after conversations. The kind that are easy to slip away from before anyone started asking questions about scars or why I never talk about my job.

But this feels different. Bigger. Like maybe all that chaos and glitter I throw around finally landed on someone who gets it. Who gets *me*.

I've always figured normal people get the white picket fence dreams. They get to have relationships, connections, and someone to come home to. People like me? We get satisfaction from a solid kill and really good orgasms if we're lucky.

But Brayden's words keep echoing in my head about Deacon not being normal either. Maybe... maybe that changes things.

I trace my fingers lightly over the arm holding me captive, feeling the corded muscle beneath warm skin. Last night was... different. Not just the sex, though holy hell, the man knows what he's doing, but the way he looked at me. Like I mattered. Like I was something precious rather than just convenient.

Ugh. I'm lying here at four fucking AM having *feelings* instead of sleeping like a normal person. This is exactly why I hate being up early. My brain does weird shit when it's running on fumes, turning perfectly good post-sex satisfaction into some kind of emotional crisis.

I'm pissed at myself for even letting these stupid, ridiculous thoughts swirl around in my head like glitter in a snow globe that someone won't stop shaking.

I carefully extract myself from his grip, watching as he shifts but doesn't wake. Standing beside the bed, I take a moment to appreciate the view, his broad shoulders, the sheet draped low across his hips, the scattered scars telling stories of survival.

My body feels sticky with dried sweat and other fluids, a reminder of the way he possessed me. A shower. That's what I need. Hot water to wash away my bullshit and hopefully steam out whatever sappy nonsense is clogging up my thoughts. Then maybe I can crawl back into that bed and sleep like a normal person.

I pad silently to the bathroom, closing the door with a soft click before turning on the water. Steam quickly fills the space as I step under the spray, sighing as hot water cascades over my tender muscles.

My mind drifts back to Deacon's hands on my body, the way he claimed me with such fierce possession yet touched me with unexpected tenderness. The contrast between the man who efficiently slit a monster's throat and the one who whispered my name like a prayer against my skin.

I'm halfway through washing my hair when my phone chimes from the counter. Probably Roman with more Glass Gardener updates. I quickly rinse the suds from my hair and step out, wrapping a towel around myself before checking the screen.

Unknown number.

I swipe to open the message, water dripping onto the screen.

UNKNOWN SENDER

No Hollow. Come alone or he dies.

Below the text is a photo that makes my stomach drop. Brayden, his face bloodied and swollen. He's chained to what looks like a concrete wall. His head hangs forward, but I can see he's conscious from the tension in his shoulders.

Another message appears as I stare at the image.

> Coordinates attached. You have 90 minutes. Tell anyone and I'll send you his teeth one by one.

I grip the counter, suddenly light-headed. Brayden. The annoying, overprotective asshole who's been like a brother to me since I joined The Hollow. The man who gave me pink bunny slippers and comfort when I needed it.

The bathroom suddenly feels too small, and the steam is suffocating me. I force myself to breathe, to think.

My phone chimes again. Another message.

Another photo. Broken mirror shards are scattered across a concrete floor, arranged in what looks like the beginning of a sunburst pattern. The jagged edges reflect dim light, creating an eerie kaleidoscope effect.

Ding.

> Clock's ticking, Stitcher. Better hurry before I finish my masterpiece.

My blood turns to ice. The Glass Gardener. The psycho who's been haunting our steps, leaving bodies arranged in mirror shards with sun symbols carved into their chests.

And now he has Brayden.

I check the coordinates on my phone. It's a rural farm area, a little over an hour from the manor. If I leave now, I can make it.

I wrap the towel tighter around myself, my mind racing through options. I should wake Deacon. Tell Roman. Alert the entire Hollow and storm the place with backup.

But the threat rings in my head: *Tell anyone and I'll send his teeth to you one by one.*

I've seen enough of the Glass Gardener's work to know this isn't an empty threat.

I slip out of the bathroom, pausing at the bedroom door. Deacon lies exactly as I left him, one arm still stretched across the space where my body had been. His face, usually so guarded, looks peaceful in sleep. Vulnerable, even.

Something twists in my chest, sharp and painful. Last night changed things between us. We crossed a line neither of us can uncross.

And now I have to go kick some Glass Gardener ass to save Brayden. The picture of his bloodied face flashes through my mind, and rage burns hot in my veins.

Part of me wants to wake Deacon, but I've seen enough of this psycho's work to know he's not bluffing.

Fine. He wants to play games? I'm about to show this mirror-obsessed piece of shit exactly why you don't fuck with my family. He thinks he's so clever with his little ultimatum, but he clearly doesn't know who he's dealing with.

Brayden needs me, and I'll be damned if I let some wannabe artist with a glass fetish hurt him.

I turn away, slipping silently through the door and padding across the hallway to my room. Once inside, I dress quickly in my dark cargo pants, fitted black top, and combat boots. I quickly plait my hair into box braids and grab my embroidery kit from the closet, fingers lingering momentarily on the tapestry inside.

So many monsters. So many victims avenged.

I slip a switchblade into my boot and another into my sleeve. I consider leaving a note, some explanation for when he discovers I'm gone, but what would I even say?

Hey, babe. Went to rescue Brayden from a psycho. If you're reading this, I'm probably elbow deep in blood and having the time of my life. PS - last night was amazing, wish we could do it again, but I'm busy being a badass. XOXO, Scout.

Fuck it, there's no time for this. Every second I waste here is another second that bastard has with Brayden. I need to move my ass now.

The manor is silent as I make my way downstairs, avoiding the creaky third step from habit. The security system recognizes my fingerprint, disarming long enough for me to slip outside.

The night air is cool against my face as I cross to my car. Yeah, I'm totally going rogue here, but when some mirror-obsessed freak threatens my family, rules can kiss my sparkly ass. Sometimes you have to break them to save the people who matter.

Brayden would do the same for me. Has done the same, pulling me out of situations I never should have survived.

I start the engine, wincing at the sound that seems deafening in the pre-dawn quiet. As I pull away from the manor, I check my mirrors, half-expecting to see Deacon's tall figure emerging from the shadows.

There's nothing but darkness behind me.

I press the accelerator, the car surging forward as I head toward the coordinates. My mind keeps bouncing between wanting to process whatever the hell happened with Deacon last night and the very real problem of how this bastard managed to take down Brayden.

Brayden's not some helpless victim. He's six-and-a-half feet of pure Southern destruction who can charm his way out of anything or fight his way through it. If the Glass Gardener got him, what the fuck does that say about what I'm walking into?

My hands tighten on the steering wheel. I've got my blades, my embroidery kill kit, and a whole lot of pissed-off determination, but is that enough? What if I'm not enough?

No. Fuck that noise. Brayden is family. The one who gave me pink bunny slippers and bad jokes when I needed them most, and I'll be damned if I let some artsy serial killer keep him.

As the manor disappears from my rearview mirror, I shove down the flutter of panic trying to claw its way up my throat. When. Not if, when I get back, maybe I'll finally figure out what the hell these Deacon feelings mean.

But first, I have to save Brayden and probably commit some beautifully violent murder in the process.

THIRTY-ONE
DEACON

I wake to cold sheets where Scout's warmth should be. The digital clock on the nightstand glows 5:47 AM in harsh red numbers. My arm stretches across the empty space beside me, finding nothing but the lingering scent of her on the pillow.

Something's not right.

Scout isn't a morning person. The woman I've come to know would sooner fight a man twice her size than voluntarily leave a warm bed before sunrise, especially after last night.

Last night changed everything. The walls I'd built around myself for years crumbled under her touch, her whispers, her surrender. And my own.

I sit up, scanning the room. Her clothes from yesterday are gone. The bathroom door stands open, light off. No sound of the shower running.

"Scout?" My voice echoes in the empty room.

Nothing.

I dress quickly, pulling on jeans and a black t-shirt, not bothering with socks as I pad barefoot into the hall. Maybe she's just gone to her own room. Maybe she needed space after everything that happened between us.

The thought sits like lead in my stomach as I cross the hallway to her door. I knock twice, then try the handle when I don't get an answer.

Her room is empty and her bed looks untouched.

I check the bathroom, the closet, looking for any sign of where she might have gone. Everything looks normal, but something feels off. Scout wouldn't just disappear.

Unless she's avoiding me, unless last night was a mistake she's already regretting.

I step back into the hallway, mind racing. Where would she go at this hour? My fingers curl into fists as dread settles in my stomach. Maybe she needed space after everything that happened between us. Maybe she's already running from what we started.

The floorboards creak at the end of the hallway, and Roman appears at the top of the stairs, steaming coffee mug in hand. His eyebrows lift in surprise when he spots me.

"You're up early," he says, taking a sip from his mug. "I thought I was the only one who couldn't sleep past five."

"Have you seen Scout?" I ask, not bothering with pleasantries.

Roman frowns. "Scout? No. She's never up this early. You'd need an earthquake or the promise of donuts to get her moving before nine."

"I can't find her."

The casual slouch vanishes from Roman's posture. "What do you mean you can't find her?"

I hesitate, then decide there's no point in being coy. "She's not in her room. Her bed hasn't been slept in." I pause, running a hand through my hair as I sigh. "She left my bed sometime before dawn."

Roman's expression shifts from confusion to concern. He balances his coffee in one hand while pulling his phone from his pocket with the other. His thumb moves rapidly across the screen.

"Let me pull her location."

I lean against the wall, trying to ignore the knot in my stomach. There are a dozen innocent explanations. She could be in the gym. The garden. Anywhere in this massive house.

So why does every second she's gone feel like confirmation that I've already lost her?

Roman's phone pings with an alert. His eyes narrow as he reads the notification.

"What is it?" I demand.

"The system just flagged Scout's GPS. All her devices have been disabled for over an hour."

"What does that mean?"

Roman's jaw tightens. "It means the tracking on her phone, watch, car, and the chip in her ID card are all offline. The system alerts me if any Hollow member goes dark on all devices for longer than sixty minutes."

My blood runs cold. "That doesn't happen accidentally."

"No." Roman pockets his phone. "It doesn't." He studies my face with that uncomfortable intensity of his. "Maybe she doesn't want to be found. You two have been working through some things."

The words hit like a blade between the ribs. Maybe he's right. Maybe she finally got past my walls, only to realize there wasn't anything worth finding.

"But," Roman continues, rubbing his temple, "with the current security lockdown, it does give me some concern."

I clench my jaw to keep from snapping at him. Space is one thing. Disappearing during a security lockdown is another.

"Come with me to the data room," Roman says, not waiting for a response. "I'll dig deeper into this, just to give myself some peace of mind. And from the looks of it, you need some too."

I follow him down the stairs, trying to force myself not to panic. If she left without telling anyone, she had a reason.

"Has this happened before?" I ask as we descend to the lower level. "Scout going dark?"

Roman continues walking down the hallway towards the data room. "Not without prior notice. Even on solo missions, she's big on check-ins."

Once inside, Roman gestures to an empty chair as he slides into his own at the central console. "Take a seat."

His fingers fly across multiple keyboards, bringing new screens to life. "Let me check something."

I stare at the screens around me, tension coiling tighter with each display that flickers to life.

One large monitor on the wall already shows a map dotted with markers in different colors. The red, yellow, and green pinpoints are scattered across the country. I recognize it immediately as the Glass Gardener tracking data Roman's been obsessing over.

Roman's fingers dance across the keyboard at a workstation to my right. "I'm pulling up everything on Scout now. Her phone locations, credit cards, car movements, and her active burner phones."

"How many does she have?" I ask, watching the list of devices grow on a secondary monitor.

"More than she needs." He shakes his head. "Call me paranoid, but I like to make sure everyone has backups of backups."

The data cascades across the screen beside the Glass Gardener display. A new map materializes, showing Scout's digital footprint, blue dots for general movements, red dots for confirmed kills through The Index.

"That's Scout's movement pattern for the past year," Roman explains without looking up, his focus entirely on narrowing down her recent activity. "If I can just pinpoint her last known location before everything went dark..."

I find myself studying both maps, something nagging at the edges of my consciousness. The Glass Gardener's pattern on the left, Scout's movements on the right. Side by side like this, they look... familiar somehow.

Roman zooms in on Scout's timeline, focusing on the past two days. "If we narrow it down to recent activity, I should be able to—"

The nagging feeling intensifies as I stare at the displays. My eyes move between the two maps, tracing the flow of markers across state lines.

"Wait." I stand abruptly, moving closer to the wall displays. "Zoom back out. Show me Scout's full year again."

Roman gives me a questioning look, but complies, returning to the broader view while still typing commands to track her current location.

The realization steals the breath from my lungs.

"They match," I whisper, stepping closer to the displays.

"What matches?" Roman's chair swivels toward me, his hands finally stilling on the keyboard.

"The movement patterns." I trace my finger along Scout's blue dots, then gesture to the Glass Gardener map. "Look at the overall flow, the clustering in specific regions at specific times."

Roman looks toward the screen, his attention fully shifting from finding Scout to understanding what I'm seeing.

"The patterns match," I continue, my voice growing hoarse. "Everywhere Scout travels, the Glass Gardener appears shortly after. Same cities, same regions, following her path across the country."

Roman's face goes pale. "Shit. I can't believe I missed this." He runs his hand through his hair as he stares at the maps for a long moment, the weight of realization settling over both of us. "I was tracking the Glass Gardener against everyone's kills. I never even considered pulling Scout's broader travel data."

My mind races through the implications. Someone has been tracking Scout, following her movements, learning her patterns. For how long? Months? The entire year?

Roman spins back to his keyboard, his movements sharp and urgent. "I need to check something."

My heart pounds in my chest for what feels like an eternity, even though it's literally just seconds.

"She left the property."

My world stops. Everything freezes except the thundering of my pulse in my ears.

Roman jerks forward in his chair, his fingers attacking the keyboard in a violent staccato of clicks. My ragged breaths punctuate the digital symphony, harsh inhales and shaky exhales merging with his frenzied typing in the suffocating silence.

"What do you mean she left the property?" My voice sounds distant, like it belongs to someone else.

The security footage appears on the center monitor. I watch as Scout slips through the front door at 4:32 AM, dressed in black with a small bag clutched in her hand that I recognize as her embroidery kit.

"Why?" I demand, leaning closer to the screen, searching for any clue in her body language, her movements.

"She disabled the proximity alerts." Roman's voice is tight. "Let me check her last known GPS location."

I think of her warm body curled against mine just hours ago. The way she whispered my name in her sleep. The vulnerability in her eyes when she looked at me after I'd made love to her, slower, deeper.

"Last ping was at 4:39 AM, two miles southeast of here, then everything went dark." Roman pushes back from his desk.

A harsh electronic wail blasts from his phone, pulsing three times before falling silent.

"What's that?" I ask as the same sound erupts from my pocket.

"Emergency check-in protocol." Roman's voice is tight as he pulls up a secure messaging system. "Everyone has five minutes to confirm their location and status."

I pull my phone out to silence and confirm my location, which I thought was weird since I was standing right next to him, but whatever.

My mind races through possibilities, each one worse than the last. Scout wouldn't just leave. Not after last night. Not without telling me.

Unless she's running from me.

The door flies open, and Ivy rushes in, her dark hair wild around her face, wearing flannel red pajama pants and an oversized grey t-shirt. "What's wrong?

"We're not completely sure yet," Roman says, eyes fixed on his screen. "Lucien just checked in from his quarters."

Tristan steps in, eyes immediately drawn to the data sprawled across the wall. He doesn't speak, just appears to be absorbing the information with that eerie focus of his.

"It's been five minutes, where's Brayden?" Ivy asks, looking around the room as if expecting to find him hiding in a corner. "And Scout?"

My stomach drops at the question. Roman taps quickly through his tablet, pulling up a tracking program.

"Brayden's in Nashville on a hunt," Roman says, his frown deepening as he stares at the screen. "But he hasn't responded to the emergency check-in." He pulls up a timeline, pointing to a blinking dot. "His last communication was at 7 PM last night when he confirmed he'd landed at the airstrip."

The room falls silent. Two people are unaccounted for. Even if Brayden's absence has an explanation, the timing feels too coincidental.

I shake my head, trying to piece it together. "She was with me until at least 3 AM. Everything was fine, better than fine. She wouldn't just leave without saying anything."

Tristan, who's been silently studying the data, speaks. "Obviously, she didn't want to be followed."

We all turn to look at him.

"What? Am I wrong?" he says, as if it should be obvious to everyone. "This is interesting, though," he continues, pointing to the screen displaying both location maps. "Looks like the Glass Gardener has been following Scout."

The color drains from Ivy's face. "Can you track her car? She has no idea she's being hunted."

"It's been disabled too," Roman says. He inhales deeply as his hands rake through his hair.

The room falls silent as we all process what this means. Scout is alone, and we have no way to track her.

"Why would Scout leave with her kill kit and not keep her location on?" Ivy asks as she points to the monitor showing the security feed.

Roman turns back to his computer, typing rapidly. "I'm checking for any communications that came through our security systems."

"Check her burner phones too," Tristan suggests. "All of them."

"And security footage outside of her room," I add. "From about 4 AM onwards."

As Roman works, I try to control the rage and fear threatening to overwhelm me. I should have felt her leave the bed. I should have woken up. I should have known.

I clench my fists so hard my knuckles turn white. "We need to find her. Now."

THIRTY-TWO

SCOUT

The GPS coordinates lead me to a narrow dirt road winding through dense Georgia pines. My hands grip the steering wheel like I'm choking the life out of it as I follow the final turn, revealing a small farmhouse nestled against a backdrop of overgrown woods.

I kill the engine and sit for a moment, taking in the scene. The house looks abandoned. White paint is peeling from worn boards, and the porch is sagging at one corner. What might have once been carefully tended flower beds line the front walkway, now choked with weeds and saplings. Nature is reclaiming what the owners left behind.

Brayden is in there. Or at least, that's what the Glass Gardener wants me to believe.

I check my phone one last time. No new messages beyond the three that dragged me here:

The attached photo shows Brayden as a bloodied, chained, and possibly unconscious mess.

Well, this is stupid. Should've told Deacon, should've woken Roman, should've done literally anything besides storm off into the obviously a death trap woods alone. But here we fucking are.

Instead, I slide my Smith & Wesson out for a quick magazine check before tucking it back home. Throwing knives against my thigh, switchblade at my wrist. Yep, all my pointy friends are accounted for. At least I'm not going in naked.

The gravel crunches under my boots as I creep closer, staying low, moving from tree to tree. No cars visible. No movement in the windows. The whole place screams "abandoned creepy-ass shack," but my neck is practically buzzing with warning bells.

I do a wide loop around the property, eyes peeled for cameras, motion sensors, trip wires. All the fun toys serial killers love. Nothing. Which is either really good or really, really bad.

This farmhouse looks like every horror movie cliché rolled into one big nope sandwich. My gut's screaming "TRAP" in neon letters, but whatever. Traps are just death puzzles, and I've always been good with my hands.

I press my back against the weathered siding, breathing in the scent of rotting wood and damp earth. My weapons settle against me like comfort items, each one exactly where I need it. Thirty-two kills don't happen by accident.

"Hang on, Bray," I whisper, even though I know he can't hear me. "The cavalry's only a five-foot-two menace, but I'm here."

I peer through a grimy window. The interior is shrouded in shadows, the furniture draped in dusty sheets like pale ghosts. No movement, no sound except the distant call of birds stirring with the dawn.

Someone went through a lot of trouble to get me here. The whole "kidnap your bestie" routine isn't exactly subtle. This isn't some random psycho. This is personal, but I have no fucking clue why.

I run through my options. Front door? Too obvious. Back entrance? Likely watched. Basement access? Worth checking.

The side of the house offers better cover, and overgrown bushes provide shadows as I creep towards the back. A broken window. A cellar door is hanging open on rusted hinges. Too obvious. Too easy.

I pause at the corner, listening. Nothing but crickets and the distant call of a whippoorwill. My breath catches as I peer around to the backyard.

Fuck. Fuck, fuck, fuck.

There's a body kneeling in the center of the lawn, surrounded by what looks like a thousand mirror pieces arranged in some sick sunburst pattern. Blood catches the morning light, turning everything into a nightmare kaleidoscope.

My whole world tilts sideways. The shoulders, the frame. It's him! It's fucking him! Brayden's build, Brayden's hair color, all of it wrong and bloody and still.

Blood and dark hair fall across his face like a gruesome veil, hiding his features completely. But I know that jacket. God, I know that stupid leather jacket. I gave him that fucking leather jacket last Christmas. He wore it everywhere after that, said it made him look like a "badass biker with daddy issues." He never left the manor without the damn thing.

"No, no, no, fuck no," I breathe, stumbling forward with my gun half-raised like it's going to somehow fix this.

I crash into the clearing, spinning around like a maniac, looking for someone to shoot, someone to blame. But there's nothing. Just me and Brayden and all this fucking blood.

"Bray?" His name cracks out of my throat like a sob. "Brayden, please..."

I have to know. Have to see. My feet move without my permission, carrying me closer even though every smart part of my brain is screaming to stop, to think, to fucking pay attention.

The mirrors. God, there are so many more than the other scenes. This isn't just murder. This is a fucking declaration. And my gut says it's aimed right at me.

Something shifts behind me. Barely a sound, just air moving wrong.

I whip around, gun coming up, but my hands are shaking and my vision's blurry, and I'm too goddamn slow—

Sharp pain stabs into my neck. A needle, shit, a fucking needle. I catch a glimpse of black fabric and gloved hands. They've probably been behind me the whole time I was staring at his body like an idiot.

I try to pull the trigger, but my arm goes limp, the gun tumbling from useless fingers. My legs give out completely.

"Son of a—" I slur, but the word comes out like mush.

Everything goes fuzzy around the edges. Gray eyes. Calloused fingers tracing my skin. The way Deacon said my name when he thought I was asleep.

He's gonna lose his absolute shit when he finds out about this. Then everything goes black.

CONSCIOUSNESS CREEPS BACK like a hangover from hell. Everything feels wrong. Something's cutting into my wrists, plastic, zip ties maybe? And this chair feels like it was designed by someone who hates spines. Birds are making way too much fucking noise for... what time is it?

My eyelids weigh about a thousand pounds each, but I pry them open anyway. Big mistake. The world does this fun little spinning thing, like a really shitty carnival ride. Everything's got doubles. Triples.

Fuck, I think I'm gonna be sick.

My tongue feels like sandpaper soaked in bleach. Whatever cocktail they gave me was top shelf. The good kind of pharmaceutical-grade shit I keep in my own kit for special occasions.

Great. I'm strapped to a deck chair that probably came from someone's garage sale circa 1987. The wooden deck looks like it's competing with my current situation for "most likely to collapse." To my right, some asshole's made a little museum out of my entire arsenal. My gun, throwing knives, boot blade, and even my wrist switchblade are all arranged neatly on the rusty table.

Well, shit.

The zip ties are digging into my wrists hard, and being completely disarmed makes me feel like I'm sitting here in my underwear. Whoever did this knows their shit. They found every single hiding spot I thought was clever.

Twenty feet away, the psycho is hunched over Brayden's body, completely absorbed in their twisted hobby.

Well, hello there, Glass Gardener.

Wearing all black tactical gear, very "mysterious serial killer" aesthetic. They're fussing with those mirror pieces like they're arranging flowers for Sunday brunch instead of whatever the hell this is supposed to be.

Each shard gets placed just so, catching sunlight and throwing little rainbows across the bloody mess. It's almost pretty, in a "completely unhinged" kind of way.

Fury starts clawing through me, but it's tangled up with something raw and broken. Brayden. God, I can't stop looking at his broken body. The rage wants to burn everything down, but grief keeps choking it out before it can really catch fire.

I test the zip ties, trying to focus on something other than Brayden's still figure.

"You know," I say, my voice cracking around the edges, "if you wanted a chat, you could've just slid into my DMs like a normal stalker."

The figure goes rigid, mirror shard frozen halfway to the ground. Slowly, they turn.

A gloved hand reaches up and tugs off the black balaclava, shaking out blonde hair that's been pulled into a tight ponytail. A woman with pale skin, hollow cheeks, eyes so light blue they're almost white, stares back at me. She looks young, maybe thirty, but something about her gaze feels old and hungry.

"You're finally awake." Her voice is weirdly gentle. "I was beginning to worry I'd given you too much."

"Yeah, well, I'm disappointingly hard to kill." I test the zip ties again, meeting her gaze directly. "Glass Gardener."

She tilts her head like I'm some fascinating bug under glass, as a small smile creeps across her mouth.

"You don't recognize me, do you?"

I search her face, running through every mark, every witness, every collateral damage from the past three years. Nothing.

"Can't say I do."

She moves closer, and I notice she's still holding that mirror shard. Her Blood wells where the edge bites into her skin, and there's something hungry in those ice-chip eyes.

"Eliza Morgan." She says it like it should mean something. Like it should break me.

"Well, that's nice. I'm Scout. We having a tea party now, or...?" I cock my head."

"Three years ago," she continues, voice getting softer and more dangerous, "you killed Henry Voss in Seattle. Took your sweet time with that pretty little flower of yours."

Memory clicks. Voss was a Pediatric dentist with a trail of four dead women, all from the same street corner. My twenty-sixth kill.

"Good for me. Guy was a monster who needed putting down." I roll my eyes. "What's your point?"

"Yes, he did." Her voice turns sharp as the glass in her hand. "But you were too late."

She gestures toward the mirror pattern, and something cold starts spreading through my chest.

"My sister, Caitlin, was his last victim. You killed him three days after he murdered her."

The world tilts. Caitlin Morgan. One of my girls. Her name was carefully stitched into that black dahlia on my tapestry, preserved forever in red thread.

But it's not enough, is it?

The knowledge hits differently when there's a face attached to the failure. A sister who's been carrying this grief for three years. I'd tracked Henry Voss for weeks. I methodically and carefully built the perfect case, like I always do. Gathering evidence, studying his patterns, and making sure I had everything just right.

And while I was being so fucking thorough, he was out there hunting Caitlin.

My stomach churns. I can feel the bile rising in my throat. I've always told myself the process matters. Doing it right, making sure they can't hurt anyone else, that's what separates me from them. But what good is being right when being fast could have saved a life? Her life?

My fingers twitch automatically, desperately reaching for the needle and thread that isn't there. The familiar weight of tools that make everything make sense, that turn pain into careful, controlled stitches. But there's no control here. It's just me, zip-tied to a chair, staring at the reality that all my careful justice came three days too late.

Too late, always too late, wasn't I?

"The sun was our thing," Eliza continues, shifting the mirror shard to her other hand and touching her wrist. I catch a glimpse of black ink on her skin, part of a tattoo. "Matching sun tattoos we got on her eighteenth birthday. 'You are my sunshine.' That's what I always told her when things got dark."

Her voice cracks on the last word, and something twists in my chest. A sister who sang lullabies. A girl who was someone's sunshine before she became one of the victims I carry in my stitches.

"I was in pharmacy school when she started using. Couldn't do much to help her then, I was barely keeping myself together." Eliza's grip tightens on the mirror shard. "By the time I graduated, got established, she was already on the streets. I was trying to get her clean, get her into a program. I was so close."

The weight of it crushes down on me. Not just another victim, she was someone's baby sister. Someone who was loved, who was being saved, who had a future that got snuffed out while I was taking my sweet time playing detective.

"Three days," she whispers, and her eyes meet mine. They're empty of everything but raw, bottomless pain. "If you'd been three days faster, she'd still be alive. Still be my sunshine."

Her words slice through me deeper than any blade ever could.

"You were too slow, Stitcher. You failed her."

Thirty-Three

Deacon

I pace the length of Roman's data room, each step a thunderclap of rage and fear. Scout is out there alone, and I have no idea where or why she left, and every second that passes is another second she might be—

"Got something," Roman announces, his voice slicing through my spiraling thoughts.

My boots freeze against the floor as the wall monitor flickers to life, Scout's burner phone messages suddenly illuminating the darkness.

> **UNKNOWN SENDER**
>
> No Hollow. Come alone or he dies.
>
> A photo of Brayden, face bloodied and swollen, chained to what looks like a concrete wall. Head hanging forward.

Behind me, Ivy's sharp intake of breath cuts through the silence like a blade.

> **UNKNOWN SENDER**
>
> Coordinates attached. You have 90 minutes. Tell anyone and I'll send you his teeth one by one.

A photo of broken mirror shards scattered across a concrete floor, arranged in what looks like the beginning of a sunburst pattern. The jagged edges reflect dim light, creating an eerie kaleidoscope effect.

"Open the coordinates," I demand, my voice barely recognizable to my own ears.

Roman clicks on the attachment, but instead of a location, an error message flashes across the screen.

"Shit," Roman mutters, immediately pulling up code windows. "It's encrypted to the device's unique identifier. The coordinates will only decrypt on Scout's actual burner."

I turn to Roman. "Can you bypass it?"

"I can clone her device from a backup," Roman says, fingers already flying across his keyboard. "Trick the attachment into thinking it's opening on Scout's phone."

"Do it."

Roman glances up, dark circles forming beneath his eyes. "It'll take about thirty minutes. Without her physical burner—"

I slam my palm against the desk, making the monitors shake. "Make it fifteen."

"Deacon—"

"She doesn't have thirty minutes." My voice drops to something dangerous, even to my own ears. "Brayden might not have thirty minutes. Make. It. Faster."

Roman holds my gaze for three seconds before nodding once. "I'll make it work."

I pace the edges of the room. I feel like a caged tiger with nowhere to channel the murderous energy coursing through my veins. My gaze snaps to Ivy, who stands perfectly still at the edge of the monitors.

To anyone else, she might look composed. Her back is straight, shoulders squared, face impassive. But I've spent enough time watching people to recognize the subtle tells of someone fracturing beneath a carefully constructed mask.

Her breathing is too measured. Too deliberate. The kind of breathing someone does when they're one ragged inhale away from falling apart. Her fingers, usually fluid and graceful, remain completely motionless at her sides, not natural stillness but the rigid paralysis of someone afraid that the slightest movement might shatter their control.

Tristan shifts his position, the movement so subtle it would be easy to miss if I weren't paying attention. He positions himself slightly behind her left shoulder, and after a moment's hesitation, his pinky hooks around hers with the lightest pressure. The contact lasts maybe three seconds before he releases it, but Ivy's rigid posture softens almost imperceptibly.

Ivy doesn't acknowledge the touch, doesn't turn to look at him, but some infinitesimal tension leaves her shoulders. Her breathing evens out just a fraction.

It's a protective gesture, understated but unmistakable. The kind of contact between two people who understand exactly what comfort looks like in their shared language of careful distances and unspoken support.

"Eleven minutes," Roman announces, his fingers creating a symphony of keystrokes. "That's how much longer I need."

Ivy's breathing hitches. It's so slight I almost miss it.

"If they have Brayden, they knew exactly how to manipulate her," Tristan says without looking away from Ivy's profile. "They knew which button to push."

"Family," Ivy whispers, the single word barely audible.

It's the first thing she's said since reading the messages on the screen, and it hangs in the air between us, heavy with meaning. Scout would walk into hell itself for any member of this strange, murderous family, especially Brayden, who seems to occupy a special place in her chaotic heart.

Just like she would for me.

The realization hits me with stark, brutal clarity. Whatever this is between us, this raw, dangerous thing we've barely begun to understand means that Scout would put herself in the same danger for me that she's facing now for Brayden.

Tristan takes half a step closer to Ivy, and this time his pinky finds hers again, holding the contact longer than before. When she doesn't pull away, he lets their fingers intertwine properly. It's still subtle, still careful, but undeniably there.

"We should prepare to move," I say, needing action, needing to do something besides stand here watching Roman's countdown. "I'm not waiting. You said she was headed Southeast, so that's the direction I'll start. Call me the second you get the coordinates."

I LEAVE THE DATA ROOM, the voices of the Hollow fading behind me as I stride down the hallway. My bare feet slap against the marble floors, each step propelling me closer to what I need to do.

My room is exactly as we left it this morning. The sheets tangled from where Scout's body had been pressed against mine just hours ago. Her citrus and sunshine scent still lingers.

I grab my go-bag from under the bed and dump its contents across the mattress. Ammunition. Burner phones. Cash. Fake IDs. The tools of a life spent hunting monsters.

I pull on socks and lace up my boots, the familiar ritual grounding me. Every movement has a purpose now. No wasted motion, no hesitation.

My fingers close around cold metal as I retrieve my knife from the nightstand. The weight feels right in my palm, familiar and deadly. I slide it into its sheath at my ankle.

At the bottom of my duffel lies my mask. The black skull that transforms me, my armor against the world. My fingers close around it, feeling each ridge and contour. When I wear this, I become something else. Something untouchable. Something that doesn't feel pain or fear or doubt.

Something that can save her.

I slip the mask into my jacket pocket and head for the garage. No time for goodbyes or plans. Every second matters now.

The engine of my Charger roars to life, the sound reverberating through the cavernous garage. My phone rings through the car's speakers, Roman's name flashing across the dashboard.

"Tell me you have something," I answer, not bothering with greetings. I punch the accelerator and shoot down the long driveway, gravel spitting beneath my tires. The manor grows smaller in my rearview mirror until it disappears completely.

"Almost. But you need to know you have a communication device in your glovebox," Roman says. "I put it in there while you were on the hunt with Scout."

Southeast. It's not much, but it's something. Better than standing still while Scout faces whatever nightmare awaits her. Better than doing nothing while someone who matters, fuck, who am I kidding, while someone who has become everything to me walks into danger alone.

I hit the main road and push the speedometer past ninety, weaving through sparse early morning traffic. The world blurs around me, but my focus has never been sharper. My phone rings through the car's speakers, Roman's name flashing across the dashboard.

"We've got the coordinates," Roman says, his voice tight with urgency. "I'm uploading them to the Index navigation system now. They should appear on your display in three... two... one..."

My dashboard screen refreshes, a pulsing red dot appearing on a map.

"What am I looking at?" I demand, pressing harder on the accelerator.

"Old farmhouse," Roman replies. "Property records show it's been vacant for a few years. Tax foreclosure. Sits on about ten acres, mostly overgrown fields. There's a main house, a detached garage, and what looks like a barn or large shed structure."

"Satellite imagery?"

"Sending it now. The buildings appear intact but deteriorating. Lots of cover with trees surrounding the property on three sides. Open approach from the north only."

I take the next exit at nearly a hundred miles per hour, the car drifting slightly before I correct its path.

"Deacon," Roman's voice cuts through my concentration, "Ivy and

Tristan are fifteen minutes behind you. Lucien and I are coordinating from the manor. We're coming for both of them."

Both of them. Brayden and Scout. I haven't allowed myself to consider that the photo of Brayden might be genuine. That this isn't just about Scout. The Glass Gardener might have two of them.

"I'm not waiting," I say, my voice flat and final.

"We're not asking you to," Roman replies. "But you need to know what you're walking into. This isn't random. Nine kills in nine cities, each one following Scout's movements. This is personal."

"I know." The words come out as a growl.

"The profile suggests someone with a vendetta. Someone who's been tracking her specifically. Be careful and keep the line open once you're on site."

I end the call without responding. The navigation system estimates twenty-two minutes to arrival. I'll make it in fifteen.

As fields and farmland flash past my windows, I slip my hand into my pocket, fingers brushing against my mask. For years, it's been my shield. The thing that separates the man from the monster, that allows me to compartmentalize the violence from the rest of my existence.

But for the first time, I'm not putting it on to protect myself from the world.

I'm putting it on to protect the world from what I'll become if anything happens to her.

I KILL the Charger's headlights half a mile from the coordinates, creeping the final stretch in darkness. Dawn's first hint of gray barely lightens the eastern sky as I pull off onto a dirt access road, concealing the car behind a cluster of overgrown bushes.

Scout's Audi sits abandoned fifty yards ahead, parked haphazardly with the driver's door left ajar. My chest tightens. She either got out in a hurry or she was dragged from the vehicle.

I slip out of my car, the fall morning air cold against my face. For a moment, I stand motionless, listening. Nothing but crickets and the distant call of an early bird.

The mask slides over my face, familiar and grounding. I become something else when I wear it. Something without hesitation or mercy. Something that will tear apart whoever has taken her.

I tap the communication device in my ear. "I'm here."

"Got it," Roman's voice responds, unnaturally calm. "Ivy and Tristan are twelve minutes out."

"Scout's car is here. It's empty."

My hands wrap around the hilt of the blade at my side as I move toward the property, staying low in the tall grass. The farmhouse looms ahead, a two-story structure with peeling paint and partially boarded windows. A detached garage sits to the left, and beyond that, the silhouette of a barn against the lightening sky.

No lights are visible from any building. No movement.

I circle wide, approaching from the east where trees provide cover. The ground slopes downward toward a creek bed, offering a natural path to the rear of the property.

"Checking the perimeter first," I murmur into the comm. "No sign of activity from the main house."

I move like a shadow through the tree line, every sense heightened. The wind whispers through the branches.

As I near the back of the house, voices drift through the stillness, faint at first, then clearer. A woman is speaking, her tone is oddly gentle.

I drop to a crouch, edging closer until I can see into the clearing behind the house.

"I see them," I breathe into the comm. "Behind the house. There's a wooden deck overlooking the yard."

The scene unfolds before me like a nightmare. In the center of the clearing, a bloody body kneels amid a perfect circle of mirror shards, arranged in a sunburst pattern. Blood glistens black in the dim light. A man's body. He's broad-shouldered, wearing what looks like Brayden's leather jacket.

"There's a body," I report, my voice barely audible. "It's male and wearing Brayden's jacket. It's surrounded by mirror shards."

My eyes shift to the wooden deck where Scout sits bound to a chair, her posture unnaturally straight.

Standing over her is a slender woman dressed in black, her back to me. She moves with precise gestures as she speaks to Scout, one hand casually holding what appears to be a glass shard.

"I can see Scout," I whisper. "She's restrained on a deck. There is a female standing over her and she's got a glass shard in her hand."

"Status?" Roman demands.

"Scout appears ok." I edge closer, using a fallen tree trunk for cover. "The woman is talking to her, but I can't hear clearly."

The woman shifts, and I catch a glimpse of her profile. She's young, maybe mid-thirties, with blonde hair pulled back from her face. Nothing remarkable about her appearance, but her movements have the practiced efficiency of someone dangerous.

"She's distracted," I murmur. "And focused on Scout. I can get close from behind the deck."

"Wait for backup," Roman orders. "Ivy and Tristan are ten minutes out."

I don't respond. Scout's life isn't measured in minutes. It's measured in the twitch of that woman's finger on the glass.

"Deacon, goddammit! Don't go in alone." Roman screams into my earpiece, but I don't hear him.

I silence the comm with a tap and look for the best approach. Twenty yards to the edge of the deck. Another five to reach the woman. Scout's eyes haven't spotted me yet, which means I'm still invisible in the shadows.

The woman gestures with the broken glass, pointing it toward Scout's chest, then toward the body surrounded by glass. Whatever this is, it's personal. Methodical. Planned.

And I'm about to unplan it.

Thirty-Four

Scout

The zip ties dig into my wrists, the sharp plastic edges biting into my skin like angry little teeth. I shift in the wooden chair, testing the restraints for any wiggle room. Nada. Zero. Zilch.

"You know what I found interesting, Stitcher?" Eliza paces in front of me, the mirror shard catching morning light between her fingers like some twisted fairy wand. "How you talk about 'your girls' like you're some kind of guardian angel."

She practically spits the words at me, her face all twisted up with disgust. I keep my expression as neutral as possible, even though my heart's doing this crazy tap dance against my ribs.

"But here's the thing about guardian angels," Eliza continues, her voice dripping with venom. "They're supposed to *save* people, not let them die."

I can't help myself. Even tied to a chair with a psycho waving glass at me, my mouth runs on autopilot. "Yeah, well, last I checked, stopping monsters from killing *more* women was still guardian angel territory, sweetheart."

"You claim to avenge them. To speak for them." She crouches down, bringing her face level with mine like we're about to have some twisted heart-to-heart. "But you're always too late, aren't you?"

The accusation slams into me like a freight train loaded with guilt. I flinch before I can stop myself. Fuck. So much for keeping my poker face.

"My sister was already dead when you found Henry Voss." Her voice cracks just a little, and for a hot second, I almost feel sorry for her.

She screeches, "Caitlin had been dead for three days before you finally killed him!"

I swallow hard, my throat suddenly feeling like sandpaper.

"You were too late!" she screams, completely losing her shit now. "That's my point! You're always too late!"

She straightens and appears to get her crazy back under control. "You stitch your pretty little flowers over their hearts like it means something. Like it helps them. But they're still dead. They're still gone."

My chest squeezes tight like someone's got a fist around my lungs. Every word hits like a blade sliding between my ribs because God help me, I've whispered these exact same things to myself in the middle of the night when the guilt gets too heavy.

"And now your friend is gone too." She waves toward the body, surrounded by all those mirror shards like she's presenting some sick art project. "Another person you've failed."

Brayden. My eyes start burning with tears, I refuse to let fall as I stare at that fucking leather jacket, those broad shoulders that have carried me through so much shit. He's kneeling in this awful, twisted position, head hanging forward, blood covering every inch of him like some damn nightmare painting.

"It was too easy, you know." Eliza walks toward the body, glass shard still in hand like some demented surgeon. "All it took was a small threat against you, and he came running."

The tears start spilling down my cheeks like a dam broke somewhere inside me. Brayden, who never lets me give up on anything, who wraps me up in those ridiculous bear hugs when the world gets too dark and twisty, who's been more of a brother to me than anyone with actual shared DNA.

"Don't," I choke out as she kneels beside the body like she's about to pray or something equally twisted.

"Don't what?" She flashes me this sick, satisfied smile that makes my skin crawl. "Don't finish my work? But honey, I *always* finish what I start."

While she's busy being a complete psycho, I twist my wrists against the zip ties, hunting for any tiny bit of give. The plastic bites deeper into my skin. It hurts like a bitch, but I keep working at it because what else am I gonna do? Sit here and watch the fucking show?

Eliza positions herself beside the body, clutching that mirror shard like it's some precious family heirloom.

"This is the part where I make it mine," she says, shifting his body around to get better access to the chest. "My mark. The sun that Caitlin and I both wore."

She presses the tip of the shard against his chest, dragging that sharp point through the blood-covered skin right over his heart. My breath gets stuck somewhere in my throat as I sit here completely frozen, unable to tear my eyes away from her sick little art project. God, is this karma? Is this the universe showing me that I truly am a monster? Making me watch someone carve their mark into someone I love, the way I've stitched mine into so many others?

Eliza shifts to get a better angle, and his head flops to the side like a broken doll. I catch a glimpse of his face through all the blood.

It's not Brayden.

The relief slams into me so hard I actually sob out loud. This dead guy is a complete stranger. He's just some poor middle-aged dude with broad shoulders like Brayden's, and the same hair, but this guy is more weathered, and the nose is totally wrong.

Eliza's face whips toward me, her lips stretching into this twisted grin that makes my stomach turn inside out. Her eyes are practically glowing with this predatory gleam that turns my blood to ice water. "Oh, did you think this was your precious friend?" She lets out this awful laugh that sounds like nails on a chalkboard. "No, no, no. This is just some unfortunate truck driver who made the mistake of stopping to help a damsel in distress. Your friend is somewhere else entirely. But don't you worry your pretty little head, you'll be joining him real soon."

I feel something warm and sticky trickling down my fingers. Blood. I've been twisting my wrists so hard against these damn zip ties that I've basically given myself matching bracelets of cuts. The slickness might actually help me slip out of these things.

"You're right about one thing," I say, needing to keep her yapping while I work. "I was too late for Caitlin. I'm sorry for that."

"Sorry?" She looks up from her sick little craft project, rage practically shooting sparks from her eyes. "Sorry doesn't bring her back!"

"No, it doesn't." I twist my wrists harder, feeling the plastic slide just a tiny bit in all this blood. "Nothing brings them back. That's why I do what I do. It's not to save the ones already gone, but to stop these psychos from taking more."

"Noble speech," she sneers, going back to her carving like she's working on some twisted masterpiece. "But hollow. Just like your promises to protect 'your girls.'"

She pauses, looking directly at me with this cruel smile. "Tell me, Stitcher. How many more women died while you were planning your perfect little revenge fantasy? How many screamed for help while you were always one step behind?"

The words hit me like a sledgehammer to the chest. Oh God. How many times have I spent weeks, sometimes months, researching, planning, making sure I had the right guy? How many women died while I was being so damn careful?

I think of my tapestry hanging in my closet. Each flower represents not just justice delivered, but lives that were already lost. Lives that maybe, just maybe, could have been saved if I'd moved faster. The weight of all those failures crashes down on me like a building collapsing.

Eliza's words cut deeper than any of her glass shards could. She's standing over me now, with the morning sun creating this halo effect behind her that makes her look almost angelic, which is seriously messed up considering she's got blood all over her hands like some demented finger paint.

"Caitlin was everything to me," she says, her voice going all soft and tender like she's talking to a child. "She was my baby sister. She was mine to protect."

The mirror shard catches the sunlight as she twirls it between her fingers.

"Do you know what it's like to lose the one person that makes your life worth living, Stitcher? To wake up every single morning and feel that gaping hole where someone should be?"

My chest squeezes tight because yeah, I do know. I've been carrying that exact emptiness around like a lead weight since I was eight years old when my parents died and again when I lost my gran at seventeen.

"She was so bright," Eliza keeps going, and I swear I see an actual tear sliding down her cheek. "So full of life and possibilities."

My chest feels like someone's squeezing it in a vise.

"Henry Voss took all of that away. He stole her future. He ripped my heart right out of my chest." Her voice goes hard as concrete. "And you! You who claim to protect women were too busy playing detective to save her."

"I didn't know—"

"You should have!" she screams, so loudly, so suddenly that I actually jump in this stupid chair. "That's your whole damn purpose, isn't it? To find these sick fucks before they destroy more lives?"

She drops down in front of me, getting so close I can smell the crazy on her breath.

"Caitlin was the only precious thing I had left in this entire screwed-up world. The only thing that made any of this worth it." Her voice drops to this creepy whisper that makes my skin crawl. "And you failed her. You failed me."

Something just... snaps inside me. Like this wall, I've built up to keep all my worst thoughts locked away, all those middle-of-the-night doubts that what I do is basically pointless, that I'm just playing dress-up as some avenging badass while women keep dying anyway.

I sink back in this chair, my whole body going limp like a deflated balloon.

She's right.

For all my pretty little embroidery, all my perfectly stitched flowers, and my obsessiveness at being accurate, I'm basically the world's most useless janitor. Just cleaning up messes after they've already happened. The women I "avenge"? They're already cold in the ground. Their families have already been destroyed.

"I know," I choke out, tears streaming down my face like I'm some broken faucet. "I know I failed her."

Eliza's expression falters, confusion flickering across her features, like she was expecting me to keep throwing sass at her instead of just... breaking.

"I failed all of them," I keep going, and the words just won't stop spilling out like I'm bleeding truth all over the place. "Every single woman on my tapestry is someone I was too damn slow to save."

I can see my needlework clear as day in my head, thirty-two black dahlias with those bloodred-tipped petals, each one representing a woman I couldn't save. Thirty-two epic failures with my signature stitched right over their hearts.

"I tell myself I'm some kind of justice warrior, but what good is justice when they're already dead?" My voice cracks like I'm thirteen again. "What good did any of it do Caitlin?"

For a moment, Eliza just stares at me, the mirror shard hanging loose in her grip.

"You're right to hate my guts," I tell her, and I actually mean it. "You're right about all of it."

For the first time since I woke up zip-tied to this freaking chair, I actually look her straight in the eyes. "So go ahead. Do whatever twisted thing you've got planned. I probably deserve it."

And God help me, I actually believe that. Sitting here with all these what-ifs and should-have-beens eating me alive, with Brayden probably bleeding out somewhere because of me, with the crystal-clear knowledge that no matter how many psychos I take down, there's always gonna be more women screaming for help while I'm too slow to reach them. Yeah, maybe I do deserve whatever hell she's planning to put me through.

Maybe this is karma finally catching up. Maybe this is the universe saying, "Hey, Scout, time to pay the bill."

I squeeze my eyes shut, waiting for that mirror shard to slice into me, waiting for some actual physical pain that might finally match the mess inside my chest.

"Look at me," Eliza snaps like I'm some disobedient kid.

I crack my eyes open to find her staring at me with this weird mix of disgust and fascination.

"You really believe that, don't you? That you deserve to die for failing her?"

I manage one pathetic little nod because there's this giant lump stuck in my throat that feels like I swallowed a golf ball whole.

"Good," she says, and her face goes all hard and cold again, like someone flipped a switch. "Because you absolutely do."

The fight goes out of me completely. I stop working on the zip ties, stop planning, stop hoping. I just sit waiting for whatever comes next.

THIRTY-FIVE

DEACON

I move through the overgrown field, keeping low enough that the tall grass gives me cover. My mask feels like a second skin now, a thin barrier between the man I pretend to be and the monster I am.

Scout is zip-tied to a chair on the deck, her face streaked with tears. A blonde woman stands over her with a jagged mirror shard gripped in her hand like she's just waiting for the perfect moment to use it.

I'm close enough now to catch pieces of their conversation.

"Caitlin was the only precious thing I had left in this entire screwed-up world."

"Eliza, please—" Scout's voice cracks. "I know you're hurting, but this won't bring her back."

I pause, listening, waiting for the right moment to make my move. This isn't about random killing, it's personal. And personal means distraction. Means she's not thinking clearly, which gives me an advantage.

"And you failed her. You failed me."

I watch Scout's reaction, something I've never seen before. She crumples, all that bright, sparkling defiance just... gone, like someone flipped a switch and turned off the light inside her.

"I know," Scout's voice breaks. "I know I failed her."

What the hell? This isn't the woman who stormed into my kill site and called it art, who crawled under my skin in Chicago, who faced down a doctor with nothing but thread and righteous fury. She sounds broken, defeated.

"I failed all of them. Every single woman on my tapestry is someone I was too damn slow to save."

Her words hit something raw inside me. How many children did I avenge after they were already broken beyond repair? How many cotton candy signatures did I leave after the damage was already done?

I grip my knife tighter, edging closer. Just a little more and I'll be able to get a jump on her.

"I tell myself I'm some kind of justice warrior, but what good is justice when they're already dead? What good did any of it do Caitlin?"

I recognize this poison. I've tasted it myself, standing over graves and wondering what good any of it did. Eliza is feeding Scout the same venom that I've fed myself, questioning if it makes a difference if they're already gone.

"You're right to hate my guts. You're right about all of it."

No, she's not. This lunatic doesn't understand what Scout is. What we both are. We're not saviors. We were never meant to be. We're just the balance that comes after, the scales even out.

"So go ahead. Do whatever twisted thing you've got planned. I probably deserve it."

I freeze mid-step. She's completely given up. Scout Prescott, who never backs down from anything, is surrendering to death like she's welcoming it.

Not on my fucking watch.

Rage builds inside me, a familiar darkness that usually comes before a kill. But this is different. This isn't the cold, calculated fury I unleash on predators. This is primal, protective, the need to shield what's mine.

Because she is mine.

All of her belongs to me in a way no one ever has.

And I belong to her.

I watch as Scout closes her eyes, waiting for death. Waiting for this psycho to punish her for crimes she didn't commit, for failures that aren't hers to bear.

Eliza orders Scout to look at her.

"You really believe that, don't you? That you deserve to die for failing her?"

Scout nods. A single, defeated movement.

"Good. Because you absolutely do."

I've heard enough. I slip from shadow to shadow, moving closer without alerting her to my presence. My fingers flex around the hilt of my knife, the weight familiar and comforting. I can take this bitch from behind before she even knows I'm here.

But Scout's eyes suddenly widen. She's spotted me. Just a fraction of a second, a micro-expression Eliza doesn't seem to catch, but it's enough.

Don't react, I silently plead. Don't give me away.

Scout drops her gaze immediately, but something changes in her posture. The tiniest straightening of her spine. The faintest return of that fight I've come to know.

I'm only a few feet away now, moving silently as death across the weathered boards of the deck. Eliza is so focused on Scout that she doesn't hear me.

"Do you know what I'm going to do to you?" Eliza asks, turning the mirror shard so it catches the morning light. "I'm going to carve my sun into your chest. But I'll do it slowly. I want you to feel every—"

I move without conscious thought. Three steps and I'm behind her.

She senses me too late, starting to turn as my arm locks around her throat in a practiced hold. The mirror shard drops from her hand, shattering on the wooden planks.

"Not today," I whisper against her ear, my voice distorted through the skull mask.

She struggles against my grip, but it's pointless. No one hurts what's mine.

Scout's eyes widen in shock, hope flickering across her tear-stained face.

"Deacon," she whispers.

I tighten my grip on her as Eliza struggles, careful to keep her restrained without cutting off her air completely. Not yet.

"Did you really think I wouldn't come for you?" I ask Scout, my eyes never leaving hers, despite Eliza's thrashing. "Did you think I'd let you face this alone?"

"But Brayden—" Scout's voice breaks. "She's got Brayden. I had to save him."

Eliza claws at my arm, but I've restrained people a lot stronger than her.

I tighten my arm against her throat. "Where's Brayden?" I demand.

She thrashes against my grip, her body tense with rage and desperation. I can feel her pulse hammering against my forearm, the telltale rhythm of someone who knows they're in deep shit.

"Where's Brayden?" I repeat, tightening my hold just enough to make breathing uncomfortable.

A harsh laugh escapes her throat. "You'll never find him," she spits, venom dripping from each word. "And even if you do, he'll be dead before you can get to him."

My blood runs cold. Scout's eyes meet mine, terror replacing the defeat I saw moments ago.

"You're lying," I say, though doubt creeps into my voice despite my certainty.

"Am I?" Her lips curl into a cruel smile. "The clock's been ticking since before the little bitch arrived. Tick. Tock."

I press the knife against her throat, feeling her swallow against the blade. "Where. Is. He."

"You're both going to die here," Eliza hisses, her body trembling with rage against my grip. "Just like Caitlin died. Just like they all died."

I keep my knife steady against her throat, feeling her pulse hammering beneath the blade. My eyes flick to Scout, still bound to the chair, her face a mask of horror and guilt.

"Deacon," Scout warns, her gaze dropping to Eliza's right hand.

I catch the subtle movement, her fingers inching toward the pocket of her black vest. Too late, I realize my mistake. I've been so focused on controlling her that I missed the slight bulge in her pocket.

"Get off me!" Eliza screams, thrashing with the blade. "She destroys everything she touches! First Caitlin, then Brayden. You'll be next!

She drives the blade backward and down, sinking it deep into my thigh. White-hot pain explodes through my leg as the serrated edge tears through my skin.

"Deacon!" Scout screams, struggling against her restraints.

Blood soaks through my pants, warm and sticky against my skin. The pain sharpens my focus rather than dulling it. This is what I was made for. To function through injury, to destroy a monster regardless of what it costs me.

She lets out a breathless laugh of triumph as she twists the knife deeper, her body practically vibrating with satisfaction.

"Tick tock," she whispers. "Everyone who loves you dies. Brayden's learning that right—"

I don't let her finish. In one fluid motion, I drag my blade across her throat, opening her neck wide. Blood sprays in an arc, spattering across the wooden deck. Some of it hits Scout's face and chest, droplets of crimson stark against her tan skin.

Eliza's eyes widen in shock, her hand releasing the knife still embedded in my thigh. She tries to speak, but only a wet gurgle emerges as blood fills her throat. Her body goes slack in my arms, and I drop her to the side, forgotten.

The pool of blood spreads rapidly across the weathered wood, seeping between the planks and dripping onto the dirt below. The metallic scent fills the air, mixing with the earthy smell of the surrounding fields.

I stagger forward, leaving Eliza's body to cool on the deck. Blood continues to flow from my thigh wound, but the knife stays where it is, acting as a plug. Removing it now would be stupid.

"Hold still," I tell Scout, my voice rough with pain.

Her eyes are wide, fixed on the knife protruding from my thigh. "Deacon, you're—"

"I'm fine." The lie comes easily. I've worked through worse. "Let's get you out of these."

I move behind her, fighting the dizziness that threatens my vision. The ties around her wrists are industrial zip ties, not something she could have worked free from without tools. I use the blade still covered in Eliza's blood and carefully slide it between the plastic and her skin.

"Don't move," I murmur, focusing on the task despite the pain radiating from my thigh.

I carefully angle the blade away from her skin and cut through the plastic. Scout immediately brings her freed hand to her face, wiping away tears and Eliza's blood.

I cut the second tie, then the ones binding her ankles to the chair legs. As soon as she's free, I drop to my knees in front of her, partly from intention and partly because my legs won't hold me any longer. I push the skull mask up, letting it rest on top of my head.

Her wrists are torn up. The cuts are deep where the zip ties bit into her skin, dried blood coating her forearms. She must have fought against them hard enough to slice herself open.

"Brayden," she chokes out, fresh tears streaming down her face. "She said—"

"I know." I reach up and cup her face, wiping away the mixture of tears and blood. And then I gently take her hands, avoiding the worst of the cuts as I examine them. "But first, we need to take care of you."

Scout shakes her head, pulling her hands from mine. Her entire body trembles as she wraps her arms around herself. "This is my fault. All of it. She was following me, killing because—" Her voice breaks. "I created The Glass Gardener. Every person she murdered... that's on me."

"No." I grip her chin, forcing her to look at me. "Listen to me. You didn't create her. You didn't make her kill anyone."

"But Caitlin—"

"Was murdered by Henry Voss," I finish firmly. "Not by you."

Scout's face crumples. "I was too late, just like I was too late for all of them. Just like I was too late for Brayden."

The guilt in her voice is raw, visceral. A wound deeper than any knife could create. She's drowning in it, and I can't let that happen.

"Scout." I brush my thumb across her cheek, smearing the mixture of tears and blood. "This isn't on you."

The sound of running footsteps pulls my focus from Scout. I tense, ready to defend her despite my injury, but it's Ivy and Tristan who burst onto the deck, weapons drawn.

Ivy's eyes sweep across the scene: Eliza's body, the blood-soaked deck, the knife in my thigh, Scout's tear-streaked face. Her expression immediately hardens.

"Where's Brayden?" she demands, her voice tight with fear.

Scout sobs, fresh tears spilling.

"I don't know. She wouldn't tell us." My voice is hard. "She said the clock's been ticking since before Scout got here."

Tristan moves to the body, checking for a pulse, we all know isn't there. He looks up at me, his eyes darting to the knife in my thigh. "I'll grab my pack."

TRISTAN RETURNS MOMENTS LATER, a black tactical medical kit clutched in his hand. He kneels beside me, his movements controlled as he unzips the bag.

"Ivy," he says, pulling out supplies and setting some aside. "Take these for Scout's wrists." He hands her gauze, antiseptic wipes, and medical tape. "Clean the cuts and wrap them. Some of them look deep."

Ivy takes the supplies and moves to Scout, who sits hunched in the chair, arms wrapped around herself, staring at nothing. Her face is blank, eyes vacant like she's retreated somewhere deep inside herself.

"This is going to hurt," he warns, examining the knife protruding from my thigh. "I can't take it out. I'm pretty sure it didn't hit any major arteries, but I can't be sure until we get back."

"I know. Just handle it." I say.

Tristan nods, his face grim. He pulls out gauze pads, medical tape, and antiseptic. He tears open packets of gauze with his teeth and packs them carefully around the knife's entry point. The pressure sends fresh waves of pain radiating through my body, but I don't flinch.

"She said the clock's been ticking," I tell him, my eyes fixed on Scout.

She sits hunched in the chair, arms wrapped around herself, staring at nothing. Her face is blank. Her eyes are vacant like she's retreated somewhere deep inside herself. Ivy crouches in front of her, speaking in low, soothing tones, but Scout doesn't respond.

"Looks like she's in shock," Tristan murmurs, securing gauze around the knife. "She's completely shut down. What the hell happened here?"

"Scout," Ivy pleads, as she wraps gauze around her wrists. "Look at me. We'll find him. We'll bring him home."

No response. Not even a blink.

Tristan secures the last piece of tape across my thigh, immobilizing the knife. "That'll hold until we get you to medical, but don't move it. You've already lost a decent amount of blood."

"I'll be fine," I mutter, pushing myself to my feet. The world tilts dangerously for a moment before steadying. "We need to search the property."

"Don't be a dumbass. You can barely stand," Tristan observes. "Stay with Scout. Ivy and I will search."

Ivy stands, her eyes sweeping the property beyond the deck.

"She could have him anywhere," she says, her composure cracking just enough to reveal the fear beneath.

"He's most likely not here," Tristan says, as he looks at Scout. "Based on the concrete floor in that photo that Scout received, if he is on the property, it would be the cellar or barn. But we'll check anyway to be sure."

He's already moving toward the farmhouse door. "Ivy, take the barn. I'll check the house and cellar."

"What about her?" I nod toward Eliza's body.

"Roman will handle it," Ivy says. She hesitates, looking at Scout. "She's in shock. And you're bleeding through the gauze. Wait here, I won't be long."

I move to Scout's side, crouching despite the pain it causes. "Scout." I keep my voice soft, steady. "I need you to look at me."

Nothing. Her eyes remain fixed on some middle distance, seeing things I can't.

"We're going to wait here until they get back," I tell her, settling beside her chair.

She doesn't respond, doesn't even acknowledge that I've spoken. I keep watch on the farmhouse and barn, listening for any sounds from Ivy and Tristan's search.

Minutes pass before they return, Ivy from the barn, shaking her head, and Tristan from the farmhouse with the same result.

"Nothing," Ivy says as they approach. "No sign of him anywhere."

"I doubt he was ever here," Tristan says. He looks at me and Scout. "We need to get you both back to the manor. You've lost too much blood, and she's completely shut down."

Ivy moves to Scout, gently taking her arm. "Come on, we're going to the car now." Scout allows herself to be guided up from the chair. She moves mechanically, like a doll with broken joints.

"We'll take Tristan's SUV," Ivy says, looking back at the other vehicles. "Roman will have to send people for the rest."

Tristan slides his arm under my shoulder, taking most of my weight as I struggle to my feet. "Easy," he murmurs. "Don't put pressure on that leg."

The walk to Tristan's SUV is slow and painful. Every step sends fresh waves of agony through my thigh, and I have to lean heavily on Tristan to keep from collapsing. He adjusts his grip, practically carrying me the last few yards.

Ivy helps Scout into the backseat first, then Tristan eases me in beside her. Scout stares straight ahead, unblinking, while I fight off another wave of dizziness.

Once we're settled, I pull out my phone and call Roman.

"What the fuck happened? You went dark on me," Roman answers immediately.

"We're alive," I cut him off, keeping my voice low. "The Glass Gardener is dead. Scout's in shock. I took a knife to the thigh."

"And Brayden?"

"Nothing concrete. Ivy and Tristan searched the property. There's no sign of him anywhere. She said the clock's been ticking since before Scout arrived.

"She?" Roman asks.

"Eliza Morgan. The Glass Gardener. Her sister was a victim of Scout's kills." I keep my voice low. "She blamed Scout for failing to save her."

"I'll start scanning for properties connected to Eliza Morgan within a fifty-mile radius," Roman says, keyboard clicks audible in the background. "How's Scout?"

I look at her. She's still staring blankly, unmoving. "Not good. She's not speaking."

"Get her back here. I'm already dispatching teams for the vehicles and cleanup."

As Tristan starts the SUV, Scout doesn't acknowledge my presence, doesn't even seem to register the movement of the vehicle as we pull away from the farmhouse.

Ivy sits rigidly in the front passenger seat, her shoulders tense. Tristan drives with silent intensity, his eyes constantly checking the rearview mirror.

The silence in the car is suffocating. No one speaks as we leave behind the property where we'd hoped to find Brayden. The clock is still ticking, and we're no closer to finding him than we were before.

I reach for Scout's hand, half-expecting her to pull away. She doesn't. Her fingers remain limp in mine, her eyes fixed on nothing.

"We'll find him," I promise her, though I'm not sure she hears me.

THIRTY-SIX

SCOUT

I trace my finger over the delicate red stitching, following the curve of a petal. Caitlin Morgan. Her name flows beneath my touch, perfect and permanent in crimson thread.

Too late. Always too late.

It's been five days since we returned to the manor without Brayden. Five days since I've spoken to anyone. Five days locked in my bedroom with only Tank and my failures for company.

My tapestry sprawls across my bed, a chronicle of death that once brought me pride. Thirty-two black dahlias, each with bloodred-tipped petals bearing the names of the women I avenged. Above each flower is the date I removed their monster from the world.

Now all I see is failure.

"I'm sorry," I whisper to Caitlin's name, my voice rough. My throat burns from days of crying, and a dull headache pounds behind my swollen eyes. "I should have found him sooner."

Henry Voss. My twenty-sixth mark. The man who raped and murdered Caitlin Morgan, because I needed proof instead of trusting my gut. He was too good at blending in. The perfect neighbor, helpful coworker, the kind of guy who'd help you carry groceries. The Index had him dead to rights, but seeing him in person made me doubt. So I drove hours away, spent weeks building a case that would make me feel better about the kill. While I was playing it safe, second-guessing what I knew in my gut was true, he found Caitlin. If I'd been faster, smarter, better, she might still be alive.

My fingers drift to a different Dahlia and another petal. Naomi Winters. One of Dr. Stanton's victims.

"Too late for all of you."

Every name accuses me. Every perfectly stitched letter reminds me that I only arrived after they were already broken, already gone. What good is vengeance to the dead?

Someone knocks at my door. I ignore it, just like I've ignored every knock for the past five days.

My phone lights up on the nightstand. Probably Roman with another update that isn't an update at all. No sign of Brayden. No leads. Nothing.

The Hollow is falling apart without him. Ivy tells me bits and pieces when she brings food. Roman and Tristan are constantly searching. Everyone is running on fumes and desperation.

And Deacon...

I don't know what Deacon is doing beyond the texts I ignore and the gentle knocks I pretend not to hear. He tried to stay with me that first night, but I couldn't bear it. Couldn't stand to see the concern in his eyes or listen to him try to console me, to tell me this wasn't my fault when I knew, I *knew*, it was.

If I hadn't been so careless, Eliza wouldn't have tracked me. Wouldn't have found us. Wouldn't have taken Brayden to punish me for failing her sister.

My new bunny slippers sit on the foot of my bed, but I can't bring myself to wear them. Tank is lying on the floor next to my bed. I've kept him with me since we returned.

"I'm sorry, Tank," I whisper, reaching down to pet his head. "I'm so sorry."

Another knock, more insistent this time. I ignore it again.

I lean back against my headboard, surveying the expanse of my life's work spread before me. All those flowers. All those names. All those failures.

The Stitcher. What a joke. I don't bring justice; I just clean up messes after it's too late to matter.

Eliza was right. What good am I if I can't protect the people who matter? What good is vengeance when they're still dead?

I grab a handful of my once-prized fabric, bunching it in my fist. Part of me wants to tear it apart, to shred this monument of failures. But I can't. These women deserve to be remembered, even by someone who failed them.

Instead, I smooth it back out, tracing the pattern of the very first dahlia I ever stitched. Randall McGinnis. Three victims, including Brittany, his wife, whose murder finally exposed him.

Too late for her, too.

A soft knock at my door interrupts my spiral. I ignore it, just like I've ignored every knock for the past five days.

The soft beep of the biometric scanner makes me tense. Only one person has been programmed to access my room other than me. The door opens slowly, and Ivy steps inside, carrying a tray with soup, crackers, and tea. Her eyes are rimmed with red, her usually perfect makeup absent. Her hands tremble slightly as she sets the tray on my nightstand next to yesterday's barely touched sandwich.

"You need to eat more than a few crackers," she says, her voice gentle but strained, eyeing the picked-at remnants of the last meal she brought me. "It's been five days, Scout."

I stare past her at the wall. Tank shifts, lifting his head to sniff hopefully at the fresh food, his tail giving a half-hearted wag.

"Roman's still searching." Ivy sits on the edge of my bed, careful not to disturb my tapestry. "We have people looking in four states now. Tristan's analyzing Eliza's digital footprint. We'll find him."

Her voice breaks on the last word. I know she's trying to convince herself as much as me.

I say nothing, but I know I should be out there with Roman, driving him crazy with theories and demands. But what if I'm wrong again? What if I lead us down another dead end while Brayden suffers? I can't trust myself anymore.

Ivy reaches out, hesitates, then places her hand over mine. "This isn't your fault."

The lie hangs between us. We both know better.

"Scout, please. Talk to me." She squeezes my hand. "Scream at me. Throw something. Just... do something."

I turn to look out the window. The sky is gray, threatening rain. Fitting.

Ivy sighs, a sound so heavy with exhaustion and grief it should bring walls down. "Deacon's basically living outside your door. He's worried about you."

My chest tightens at his name. Another person I've endangered. Another person I'll lose.

"He cares about you," she continues. "We all do. And we need you. Brayden needs you."

My phone buzzes again on the nightstand. Probably Deacon. I've ignored all his texts, his calls, his knocks. It's better this way.

Ivy stands, defeated. "The food's there if you want it. I'll come back a little later to check on you and take Tank outside."

She pauses at the door. "He's still alive, Scout. I can feel it. And we're going to bring him home."

The door clicks shut behind her. Tank whines softly, nudging my hand with his nose. I scratch behind his ears, finding comfort in his warm, solid presence.

"I can't lose him, Tank," I whisper, finally giving voice to the fear that's been choking me. "I can't lose any of them. But especially not him."

Tank tilts his head, listening with those soulful brown eyes.

"If losing Brayden hurts this much... losing Deacon would destroy me." The admission feels like ripping open my chest. "I can't. I just can't."

My phone buzzes again. I glance at it, seeing Deacon's name on the screen.

> Please talk to me. I'm right outside your door. Let me help you.

I turn the phone face down, leaving him on 'read'.

"It's better this way," I tell Tank, who looks thoroughly unconvinced. "Distance. Space. Walls. That's how I survive."

Another knock at the door, firmer this time. Deacon.

"Scout." His voice is muffled through the wood but still sends a shiver down my spine. "I know you're in there. I'm not going anywhere."

I close my eyes, willing him to leave. Willing myself not to run to the door and throw myself into his arms.

"I'll be here when you're ready," he says after a long silence.

Tears burn behind my eyelids. Tank seems to sense my distress and jumps up onto the bed, his weight making the mattress dip. I reach for Brayden's leather jacket, which Roman had brought back from the farmhouse. It still smells like him. His cologne and that stupid cinnamon gum that he's always chewing.

I curl around it, burying my face in the worn leather. Tank shifts to press against my back, a warm, solid comfort.

"Come back," I whisper into the jacket. "Please come back."

The tears come then, hot and relentless. I cry until exhaustion claims me, dragging me down into fitful sleep with Brayden's jacket clutched to my chest and the weight of everyone I've failed pressing down on me.

THIRTY-SEVEN
DEACON

I 've memorized every crack in the wall across from Scout's door. Every chip in the paint. The exact pattern of the wood grain beneath me. Five days of sitting here, leaving only when absolutely necessary.

Five days of her silence is cutting me deeper than Eliza's blade ever could.

I passed out from blood loss somewhere between the car and the Manor. When I woke up the next day, Roman was sitting in a chair beside my bed, laptop balanced on his knees, his keystrokes soft and measured.

"Welcome back," he said without looking up. "How much do you remember?"

My throat felt like sandpaper. "Farmhouse. Eliza. Scout tied up." I tried to sit up as pain shot through my thigh. "Fuck."

"The emergency doctor came last night. You got 29 stitches in your thigh, two units of blood." Roman finally looked at me, his expression clinical. "You lost a lot."

"Scout?"

"Physically, she's fine. Mentally..." He shrugged. "That's why I need to know exactly what happened in there."

I gave him the rundown on Eliza Morgan, the Glass Gardener. Sister to Caitlin Morgan, one of Henry Voss's victims. She blamed Scout for being too late to save Caitlin, convinced Scout that she'd created a monster by failing her sister and how Scout destroys everything she touches. Roman asked questions and took notes. When he finally closed the laptop and stood to leave, I swung my legs over the side of the bed.

"Where are you going?" he asked.

"To check on Scout."

Roman nodded once, understanding but not optimistic. "Good luck."

The moment he left my room, I limped across the hallway to Scout's door and knocked softly.

"Scout? You okay?"

No answer. I tried the handle, it was unlocked. I pushed the door open slowly.

She was curled on her bed, back to the door, still wearing the same clothes from the farmhouse. She didn't move when I entered.

"Scout?"

"Please go." Her voice was hollow, distant.

"I just want to make sure—"

"Please." The word cracked. "Just go."

I stood there for a long moment, wanting to fight her on it, wanting to crawl into that bed and hold her until the haunted look left her eyes. Instead, I backed out and closed the door.

The soft click of her lock engaging from the inside hit harder than any hit I'd ever taken.

That hollow "please go" has been echoing in my head ever since.

I've texted her. Called her name through the door. Even fucking begged, which is something I've never done for anyone.

"Scout, please. Let me in."

"Just tell me you're okay."

"I'm not leaving until you talk to me."

Nothing but goddamn silence in return.

The others walk by occasionally, their faces a mix of pity and concern. Ivy brings food to Scout's room three times a day, using her biometric access to get through the locked door. Each time she emerges with the same defeated expression, Scout won't speak, won't eat much, won't acknowledge anyone. She also stops by to let Tank out and feed him, the bulldog's confused whining echoing my own frustration. Roman updates me on the search for Brayden, but there's still nothing concrete.

I press my palm against Scout's door for the hundredth time. "I know you can hear me," I say, my voice rough. "You don't have to talk. Just... let me sit with you. Please."

The silence on the other side feels permanent now, like a wall she's building between us.

"You know what's fucked up?" I say to the empty hallway. "I spent my whole life keeping everyone out. Built walls so high nothing could get through." I lean my forehead against the door. "Then you came along and tore them all down without even trying. And now that I finally know what it feels like to need someone..." My voice cracks. "You won't let me in."

I hear movement inside, just the slightest shift of weight on the floor. My heart hammers in my chest.

"Scout?" I whisper, pressing my ear to the door. "I'm right here. I'm not going anywhere."

More silence.

I close my eyes, remembering how she felt in my arms just days ago. How her body fit against mine like she was made for me. How her eyes lit up when she laughed at something I said. How alive she was.

This silence... this absence... it's worse than anything I've ever felt. And I've felt a lot of fucking pain in my life.

"You know what?" I say, louder now. "You're allowed to be broken. You're allowed to hurt. But you don't get to disappear. Not from me." My voice cracks on the last word. "We find Brayden together. We fix this together."

The silence stretches between us, again. I slide down to the door to sit, back leaning against the wall. I'll wait forever if I have to.

Ivy appears with a tray of food. She hands me a sandwich and a bottle of water from the tray. A sad smile on her lips. She knocks lightly and walks inside, shutting the door behind her.

I lean my head back against the wall, listening to the muffled voice inside. Ivy's gentle pleading. Scout's absence of response. The sound of footsteps approaching the door makes me straighten, but I don't stand. I know the routine by now.

Ivy emerges, closing the door softly behind her. Her eyes meet mine, red-rimmed and exhausted.

She shakes her head. "She's shutting everyone out. Won't eat, barely responds when I talk to her." Ivy's voice cracks. "She's drowning in guilt and I don't know how to pull her out."

I nod, understanding completely. I've felt that kind of suffocating weight before, when guilt becomes so heavy it crushes everything else.

"You should get some rest," I tell her. "I'm not going anywhere."

Ivy studies me for a moment, something unreadable in her expression. She opens her mouth like she wants to say something, then thinks better of it.

"She needs you," she says simply, then walks away.

I send Scout another text she won't answer, telling her I'm still here, still waiting. I watch as my message changes to 'read' but no response comes. I close my eyes, letting my head fall back against the wall again.

"Still maintaining your vigil, I see."

I open my eyes to find Roman standing over me, tablet in hand, expression unreadable.

"I'm not leaving her," I say simply.

"Admirable. Ineffective, but admirable." He gestures for me to stand. "Come with me. I need your help with something."

"I'm not—"

"You sitting here isn't helping her, and it certainly isn't helping Brayden." His voice is sharp but not unkind. "But there's something you can do that might actually make a difference."

I glance at Scout's door, torn.

"She's not going anywhere," Roman says. "And neither is her guilt. But maybe we can give her something else."

I rise slowly, muscles stiff from sitting so long as my thigh throbs. "What do you need?"

"I need your brain. And your perspective." He starts walking, expecting me to follow. "I've been digging into Eliza Morgan's background."

I cast one last look at Scout's door before slowly following Roman down the hallway.

His data room. The technological fortress... multiple screens, servers humming quietly, keyboards arranged with military precision. Maps, timelines, and data points fill every monitor. It still wasn't enough to stop Eliza before she destroyed Scout.

"What have you found?" I ask, scanning the information.

"Eliza Morgan, thirty-two. Pharmacist by trade." Roman pulls up images on the main screen. "Older sister to Caitlin Morgan, who was—"

"Henry Voss's victim," I finish. "Scout's twenty-sixth."

"Correct." Roman brings up photos of the sisters together. "After Caitlin's death, Eliza had a complete psychological break. Three hospitalizations over six months."

He pulls up another document. "Charles Morgan, their father. Found dead in his home about a year after Caitlin's death. Multiple stab wounds, while Eliza was in the hospital."

Roman closes the file and turns to face me. "All of this got me thinking about Scout's research methods. She's meticulous about gathering intelligence before a kill, victim patterns, timelines, potential targets."

He gestures to another set of monitors that are loading new data. "So I started digging deeper into the files she compiled on all twenty-six of her targets. Cross-referencing police reports, victim statements, surveillance footage."

"What for?"

"To find out what she stopped," Roman says, pulling up another screen. "Based on what you told me about the farmhouse, and what Ivy's been reporting from her visits, Scout's spiral isn't just about Brayden. She's convinced herself that she's a failure. That she's never saved anyone, only arrived too late to matter."

Roman continues bringing up more files. "She's drowning in the belief that her work is pointless. That every kill she's made was just cleanup after the real damage was already done. She's got tunnel vision and is only focusing on the victims she was too late to save. She's ignoring the ones who are alive because of her."

Roman points to three specific files. "Marcia Chen, Scout's seventh kill had been watching her for three weeks, had already broken into her apartment twice. Sarah Williams, Scout's fifteenth target had detailed plans for her abduction, down to the hour. The Rodriguez daughters, both of them, were on Scout's nineteenth kill's list, complete with surveillance photos and schedules."

He closes the laptop and hands me a thick folder. "All the evidence is in there. Names, timelines, what these people have accomplished since Scout saved their lives without them ever knowing it."

I take the folder from him, scanning the thickness of the documentation. "Roman..."

"Don't thank me yet," he says, already turning back to his screens. "I've added your biometrics to Scout's door access. Just make sure she sees it. All of it."

I nod and head for the door.

"Deacon."

I turn back, "Yeah?"

"She needs to know her work matters. That folder proves it does."

I MARCH BACK toward Scout's room, folders clutched in my hand.

"Scout," I call, knocking firmly. "Open the door."

Nothing. Just like the last forty-eight attempts.

I press my forehead against the wooden door. "I know you can hear me."

Still silence. My patience finally snaps.

"I'm coming in," I announce, as I place my thumb against the scanner to unlock her door. "Whether you like it or not. You can yell at me all you want once I'm inside."

I push the door open slowly, light spilling into the room from the hallway.

I pause at the door and look around. Her room is a total disaster. Clothes and pillows are scattered across the floor. The scent of unwashed sheets and stale air hits me immediately. The blinds are drawn tight, blocking out any hint of daylight. A small lamp on the nightstand offers the only light in what could be called a pit of despair.

Scout lies curled on her bed, back to the door, clutching what looks like Brayden's leather jacket. Tank is pressed against her back, the bulldog serving as a living anchor. Her hair is a tangled mess, her body small beneath the rumpled sheets.

"Get out," she rasps.

I step inside and close the door behind me. "No."

"I don't want company."

"I don't care."

She shifts slightly, still not facing me. "Go. The. Fuck. Away."

"I'm not going anywhere." I move toward her bed, stepping over discarded clothes and an empty water glass.

"Leave me alone, Deacon. I don't want you here."

I sit on the edge of her bed, the mattress dipping under my weight. "Not happening."

She finally turns, and the sight of her hurts my soul. At least, what little soul I have left. Dark circles shadow her eyes. Her face is pale, drawn. Those vibrant eyes that normally sparkle with mischief are dull and lifeless.

"What the fuck do you want?" she asks.

I hold up the folder Roman prepared. "To show you something."

"I don't care about hunting or anything you or Roman want to show me right now. Unless it's about Brayden."

"It's not about hunting." I open the folder, placing the first photo where she can see it. "It's about your seventh kill."

Scout looks at me like I've lost my mind, "What? Why would you want to talk about Lester?"

"Because of her." I place a graduation photo of a young woman in a nursing cap in front of her. "Marcia Chen. Lester had been stalking her for three weeks, had already broken into her apartment twice."

Scout's eyes flick toward the paper despite herself. "Doesn't mean anything."

"She graduated from nursing school last year," I continue, laying down more documents. She works in the pediatric ICU now. Saves kids every day because you saved her first."

"What's your point?" she whispers.

I pull out another file. "Sarah Williams. Your fifteenth target had detailed plans for her abduction, down to the hour." I place a wedding photo in front of her, followed by a hospital photo of a woman holding a newborn. "She got married last spring. Had her first baby three months ago."

Scout stares at the photos, her fingers trembling slightly.

"That child gets to exist because you stopped a monster before he could take their mother," I say quietly. "A husband gets to hold his wife and baby every night because you were there when it mattered."

I spread the rest of the files across her bed. "Here are more just like them. How many lives have you saved without even knowing it?"

Scout stares at the files scattered across her bed, her breathing becoming shallow and uneven. I watch her fingers hover over the photos, trembling slightly as she picks up Sarah's wedding picture, then sets it down as if it burns.

Her eyes dart between the documents, and I can see her trying to reconcile Eliza's poison with what's right in front of her.

"I..." she starts, then stops, her voice catching. She picks up one of the files again, this time holding it longer. "I can't get her voice out of my head. Everything she said about me being too late, how I destroy everything."

"She was wrong," I say firmly.

Scout looks up at me, and for the first time in days, I see a crack in the wall she's built around herself. Not healed, not even close, but something has shifted.

"I still feel like it's my fault," she whispers. "About Brayden. About everything."

"I know." I reach out, tucking a strand of greasy hair behind her ear. "But feeling guilty and being guilty aren't the same thing."

She doesn't respond, but she doesn't pull away either. Instead, she looks down at the photos scattered across her bed, evidence of lives saved, futures protected, children who get to grow up because of her.

"None of this changes what happened to Brayden," she says, her voice hollow. "I saved all these strangers, but I let someone take the person who—" She stops, unable to finish.

"We're going to find him, Scout. I don't care what it takes, how long it takes, or who we have to go through. Brayden is coming home."

THIRTY-EIGHT

SCOUT

I stare at Deacon's face, his eyes intense and unwavering. The conviction in his voice wraps around me like a lifeline in the darkness I've been drowning in.

"You really believe that?" I whisper.

"I know it." His thumb traces my cheek, gentle despite the strength in his hands. "I've never been more certain of anything."

Something cracks inside me... the wall I've been desperately trying to maintain since the farmhouse. Since seeing Brayden's jacket on that stranger's body. Since realizing how deeply I care for the man kneeling before me.

"I can't lose anyone else," I snap. "Especially not you. I won't fucking survive it."

"You won't."

"You can't promise that." I clench my hands into fists. "No one can promise that. Look what happened to Brayden. One second he's here, the next he's gone, and I'm sitting here like a useless—"

"Scout."

"Don't." I shake my head, fury burning through my exhaustion. "Don't tell me it's not my fault. Don't tell me we'll find him. Just... don't walk away from me. Whatever happens, don't you dare walk away."

"I won't," he says. "Not by choice. Never by choice."

The exhaustion finally wins, and I sag against him, letting Deacon pull me to his chest. My hands fist in his shirt as days of pent-up rage make my whole body tremble. His arms tighten around me, one hand cradling the back of my head, the other solid against my spine.

"I hate this," I bite out against his shirt. "I hate feeling helpless. I hate that someone has him, and I'm just sitting here doing nothing."

"I know." His voice rumbles through his chest against my ear. "But you're not alone anymore. You don't have to carry this by yourself."

I pull back to meet his eyes. "Promise me we'll find him."

"We will."

"Say it. Promise me."

"I promise." His expression hardens. "I have to. I owe him."

"Owe him for what?"

A corner of his mouth almost lifts. "For forcing my hand."

A surprised laugh breaks out of me despite everything. "Explain."

Deacon's jaw ticks, like he's deciding how much to admit. "Seeing him pin you down in that gym, his hand on your hip..." His eyes darken with the memory. "I wanted to rip his throat out. Not because he was hurting you but because he was *touching* you."

"Deacon..."

"I'd never felt anything like that before. That... territorial rage." His voice drops lower. "Brayden knew exactly what he was doing. He saw it before I did."

The weight on my chest lightens just a fraction. "Do you remember how he whispered to me right before you threw him off?"

Deacon's jaw tightens. "I remember."

I reach up to touch his face, my thumb brushing across his cheek. "He said, 'Lit the fuse for ya, Cupcake. You can thank me later.'"

Deacon stares at me for a long moment before a short laugh escapes him. "That manipulative bastard."

I shake my head, a small smile tugging at my lips despite everything. "I had no idea what the fuck he was talking about."

"And now I really owe him," Deacon says, his expression growing serious again. "We're going to find him, Scout. I swear it."

I nod, feeling something shift inside me. The paralyzing guilt and grief don't disappear, but they loosen their grip enough for me to breathe. Enough for me to think.

Deacon takes my face in his hands, his thumbs brushing across my cheekbones. His eyes search mine, something intense and unspoken passing between us before he leans in. His lips find mine, and the kiss is different from the others we've shared, not desperate or claiming, but a promise. A vow between two broken people who somehow fit together.

My body responds instantly, heat flaring low in my belly as I press closer, my fingers curling into his shirt. The kiss deepens, his tongue sliding against mine as his hands move from my face to my waist, pulling me tighter against him.

For a moment, I lose myself in him, in the way he makes everything else fade into background noise. But as his hand slips beneath my shirt, the heat of his touch against my skin makes me suddenly aware of how long it's been since I've showered. Since I've changed clothes. Since I've done anything but exist in this grief-stained bubble.

I break away, breathing hard, and look around my bedroom for the first time with clear eyes.

"Holy shit," I mutter. "This place is gross."

The room is a disaster. Discarded clothes litter the floor, and empty mugs and plates are stacked on every surface. My bedsheets are tangled and stained with what might be chocolate or coffee or both. The air smells stale, like grief and unwashed skin.

"I need to get out of this filthy room," I say, wrinkling my nose. "And I desperately need a shower."

Deacon nods, studying my face for a moment. He stands slowly, favoring his injured leg slightly, and extends his hand to me.

"Come on," he says simply.

I take his hand, letting him pull me to my feet and guide me out of my room. He moves with a limp as we cross the hall to his room.

His room is immaculate, like, scary clean. The bed's made with hospital corners, and not a damn thing is out of place. It's so perfectly Deacon, it makes my chest twist. He doesn't even pause, just pulls me straight through to his bathroom and stops in front of this massive claw-foot tub..

My body relaxes as Deacon's fingers gently trace down my arm. He leans over to turn the ornate brass faucet, and water thunders in my ears as it fills.

Deacon's eyes stay focused on the rising water as he tests the temperature with his wrist. He reaches for a glass bottle on the marble shelf, uncapping it to pour that sandalwood and cedar scent that's uniquely him into the steaming water. The scent fills the bathroom, earthy and masculine, perfect.

"Arms up," he says, his voice gentle but firm.

I comply without thinking, letting him pull my stained t-shirt over my head. His eyes never leave mine as he unhooks my bra, slides my sweatpants down my legs. There's nothing sexual in his movement. Just care, protection, and a tenderness about him that makes my throat tight.

When I'm completely naked, he guides me into the tub with a hand at the small of my back. The water is hot enough to make me hiss as I sink in, but the heat immediately begins melting the tension from my muscles.

"God, that feels so good," I murmur, sliding down until the water reaches my shoulders.

Deacon grips the side of the tub to steady himself as he carefully kneels beside it, his corded forearms flexing with the movement. He reaches for a soft washcloth, soaking it before adding body wash that smells like him.

"Close your eyes," he instructs.

I obey, feeling the cloth glide across my forehead, down my cheeks, along my neck. His touch is methodical but gentle as he washes away days of tears and neglect. The cloth moves to my shoulders, my arms, my back as he guides me to sit forward.

"Lean back," he says after rinsing the soap from my skin.

I lean back into the water, studying his face while he works. The way he's caring for me is so fucking gentle, so careful, that it makes my throat tight.

"Tilt your head back."

I do, and warm water cascades over my scalp as he uses a pitcher to wet my hair. His fingers work shampoo into a lather, massaging my scalp with firm, circular motions that draw an involuntary moan from my lips.

"You're really good at this," I murmur, eyes closed in bliss.

His hands freeze for a heartbeat before continuing more slowly. "My sister had hair like yours."

I open my eyes to find his expression distant, lost somewhere I can't follow.

"You said had," I say, turning in the water to face him better. "What happened to her?"

He continues rinsing my hair, his movements gentle but suddenly mechanical. When he reaches for the conditioner, his jaw is tight, eyes focused somewhere beyond me.

"Deacon," I press, not willing to let this slide. "Talk to me."

"Her name was Sarah," he finally says, his voice low as he works conditioner into my hair. "She was seven years younger than me."

Now I'm getting somewhere. I keep my voice soft but encouraging. "Tell me about her."

"For her eighth birthday, my parents threw this ridiculous circus-themed party. We had actual circus performers, a custom-built carousel in the garden, cotton candy machines everywhere." A muscle in his jaw twitches. "The whole thing was obscene. Hundreds of guests, half of them were strangers that my father invited for networking, and my mother never missed an opportunity to host all of her friends."

He falls silent as he rinses my hair again, his touch impossibly gentle despite the tension radiating from him.

"I was fifteen, thought I was too cool for a kid's party. I spent most of it hiding in my father's study with a stolen bottle of scotch." His voice drops even lower. "I should have been watching her."

My heart clenches as I realize where this is going. I reach up, catching his wrist as he pulls away. "Deacon..."

"She disappeared during the magic show." His eyes finally meet mine, haunted by memories I can see playing behind them. "Security footage showed her being led away by a man in a staff uniform. By the time anyone noticed she was missing, it was too late."

I tighten my grip on his wrist, feeling his pulse hammering beneath my fingers.

"They found her body three days later." His voice is hollow now. "The things he did to her before he killed her..."

He doesn't finish the sentence. He doesn't need to.

He clears his throat, "The last time I ever saw her was next to the Cotton Candy machine as the party was starting. She wanted to get a pink one to match her dress."

"Fuck," I breathe, everything suddenly making sense. "That's why the cotton candy."

He nods once, sharply. "It was her favorite part of the party. I left to hide away as her friends were surrounding her."

I stare up at Deacon, the water cooling around me as he continues his story, his voice hollow with memories.

"They caught him eventually," Deacon says, reaching for a towel. "Charles Emerson. A freelance photographer who'd been hired for the party. He had a history of minor offenses, peeping, and public indecency. My parents didn't even check before hiring him."

He stops, his jaw working. I reach up and touch his forearm, giving him an anchor.

"The police found evidence linking him to three other missing girls." His eyes darken. "They arrested him, but he posted bail and disappeared before trial. Just vanished."

"Damn," I breathe, my chest tight, thinking about him as a kid, helpless and watching his world fall apart.

"Six years later, he died in a single-car accident on a mountain road in Colorado." Deacon's voice is flat, emotionless. "His brake failed and his car went over a cliff. They ruled it an accident."

The implication hangs between us. I search his face, finding no remorse, only a cold certainty.

"Please tell me you killed that bastard," I say quietly, my eyes locked on his.

He nods once, sharply. "I was twenty-one. I used my trust fund to track him down. Spent six months watching him, learning his routines."

"Did it help?" I ask, genuinely wanting to know. "Did it make it hurt less?"

"No." His honesty is brutal. "Nothing could fix what happened to Sarah. Nothing could bring her back." He meets my eyes. "But it stopped him from hurting anyone else."

Deacon leans back from the tub, gripping the edge as he carefully stands, favoring his injured leg. He reaches his hand out to me, and I grab it, pulling myself to stand. He releases my hand and holds the towel open for me, water cascading down my body as I step out of the tub. He wraps the towel around me, his movements gentle but efficient.

"My parents..." He hesitates, his hands lingering at my shoulders. "They were never the same. My mother started drinking heavily. My father buried himself in work. They stopped talking, stopped looking at each other. It was like living with ghosts."

"Where are they now?" I ask.

"My mother overdosed when I was nineteen. Pills and wine." His voice is flat. "My father had a heart attack six months later. The doctors said it was stress, but I think it was guilt."

"I'm sorry," I say, knowing how inadequate the words are.

He shrugs, the movement almost imperceptible. "They died long before that. The day we lost Sarah, we all died in different ways."

I reach up, placing my palm against his cheek. He leans into it slightly, his eyes closing for a brief moment.

"After they were gone, I inherited everything. The house, the businesses, the fortune." His mouth twists. "My father had a cabin and property in the Rockies. I moved in there and then sold everything else. I stop there from time to time when needed to recover or get access to funds. As far as anyone is concerned, I'm the same recluse I became after Sarah died."

"And that's when you started hunting full-time," I say.

He nods, guiding me to sit on the edge of the tub as he reaches for another towel to dry my hair. "I couldn't save Sarah. I couldn't stop our family from falling apart." His hands are gentle as they work through my wet curls. "But I could stop other monsters. I could prevent other families from experiencing what mine did."

I sit quietly as he towel-dries my hair, his movements methodical and soothing. There's something incredibly intimate about this moment... more intimate than the sex we've shared. This is Deacon letting me see the wounded core of him, the broken pieces he's transformed into deadly purpose.

"The cotton candy is a reminder of destroyed innocence." His voice is quiet. "And a promise that they won't hurt anyone else."

When my hair is mostly dry, he helps me stand and wraps a robe around me, his robe, soft and smelling of him. It's enormous on me, the sleeves hanging well past my fingertips, the hem pooling on the floor.

"That's why I understand what you're feeling about Brayden," he says, his eyes intent on mine. "The guilt. The responsibility. The helplessness of not being able to protect someone you care about."

I nod, my throat tight.

"But Scout," he continues, his hands coming up to frame my face, "love isn't what puts us in danger. It's what makes us dangerous."

THIRTY-NINE

DEACON

The dining room feels too formal for the gravity of our situation. I stand by the window, staring out at the property as the wind blows the multi-colored leaves from the trees. Scout sits at the table, her fingers wrapped around a mug of tea she hasn't touched. The dark circles under her eyes match my own. No one has been sleeping much these past few weeks.

Lucien sits at the head of the table, his usual afternoon tea relocated here to accommodate everyone. His face is drawn, the lines around his eyes deeper than usual. Even in crisis, he maintains his ritual, though there's nothing ceremonial about this gathering.

"Any updates?" I ask as Roman enters the room, laptop tucked under his arm.

Roman's expression gives me my answer before he speaks. "Brayden's last check-in was at 7 PM when he landed in Nashville," Roman says, pulling up files on his laptop. "His phone GPS went dark eight minutes later. Vehicle GPS shows it was in an alley shortly after behind Murphy's Bar on Broadway."

"And?" I prompt, though his expression already gives me the answer.

"ATM camera across the street caught part of it," Roman continues, turning his screen toward us. "Two figures moving someone into a black van. I've already had the vehicle picked up. It was extremely clean."

Ivy sits across from Scout, her posture rigid. Her face is a mask of controlled emotion. I've noticed she doesn't let herself break, at least not where anyone can see. The only indication of her distress is the slight tremor in her hands as she lifts her teacup.

"Tristan is still combing through surveillance footage," Ivy says. "He's been at it for sixteen hours straight."

"He was alone," Scout whispers, her face draining of color. "He was on a hunt, alone, and I didn't even know he was in trouble until..."

"Until she sent you the texts," I finish. "She already had him when she contacted you."

"Yes," Lucien confirms, his voice grave. "It appears she knew the fastest way to get to Scout was through Brayden."

"What about Eliza's properties?" I ask. "Family connections? Known associates?"

"We've checked everything," Roman says, frustration evident in his voice. "The farmhouse was her only property. No family left alive. No connections we can trace."

"There has to be something," Scout insists, her voice cracking. "She couldn't have just vanished with him."

"We're looking at everything," Roman assures her. "Traffic cameras, satellite imagery, property records under aliases."

"What about her victims?" I ask. "Is there a pattern to the locations? Something that might indicate where she'd take a captive?"

Roman shakes his head. "The only pattern was Scout. Eliza only killed in cities where Scout was at."

Scout pushes away from the table abruptly, her chair scraping against the floor. "This is pointless. We're just talking in circles while Brayden is—" She cuts herself off, unable to finish the thought.

I cross to her, placing my hand on her shoulder. She doesn't shrug it off, which I count as progress.

"We'll find him," I say with more certainty than I feel.

"I should be doing something," Scout says, her voice small but determined. "I can't just sit here drinking tea while he's out there."

"You are doing something," Lucien says firmly. "You're providing information, helping us understand Eliza's motivations and methods."

"It's not enough," she insists.

"Scout," Ivy says quietly, "you know how this works. We gather intelligence, we form a plan, we execute. Rushing blindly won't help Brayden."

She shakes her head and looks up at me, her eyes fierce despite the exhaustion. "Every minute we wait is another minute he might not have."

"I know," I say, squeezing her shoulder. "But we'll find him. All of us together."

Lucien nods. "Roman, I want you to-"

"I found something," Tristan says as he walks into the room.

Everyone turns as he enters, his tablet clutched in his hand.

"It's not much, but I found something," he says, moving directly to the table.

I rub my thumb in soothing circles as I feel the muscles in Scout's shoulder tense. "What is it?"

Tristan places his tablet on the table, and we all crowd around. On the screen is a grainy black and white image from what appears to be an ATM camera. The timestamp shows it was taken at 11:08 pm the night before Scout received Eliza's texts.

"This is from a traffic camera about twenty miles west of Nashville," Tristan explains, his voice measured despite the tension.

Scout leans in closer, her shoulder pressing against mine. "Is that—"

"A van," Tristan confirms. "Black Ford Transit, 2019 model. No visible plates."

Roman immediately takes the tablet. "Same model as the one in the alley?"

"Consistent with what we could see, yes," Tristan nods. "It's a common work van, used by contractors all over the country."

I study the image, focusing on the driver's side window. There's a blurry figure behind the wheel.

"Can you enhance that?" I ask, pointing to the driver.

Tristan taps the screen, and the image zooms in, becoming even grainier but revealing enough to see blonde hair.

"Female driver," Ivy notes, her voice tight. "Blonde."

Scout's fingers dig into my arm. "But it's impossible for it to be Eliza."

"Exactly," Tristan says firmly. "That's what caught my attention. The timestamp."

"Eliza was already dead," I finish. "Scout and I were at the farmhouse with her body at that time."

A heavy silence falls over the room as everyone processes this information.

"So Eliza wasn't working alone," Scout whispers, her face pale.

"Or she was working for someone else," I add, the pieces starting to rearrange in my mind.

Tristan nods. "That's my theory. She wasn't working alone."

Roman moves back to his laptop. "I'll run facial recognition on the driver, but with this image quality..."

"It's a start," I say, feeling the first flicker of hope since this nightmare began. "At least we have a direction now."

Tristan nods. "And a vehicle to track."

"I'll alert our contacts at traffic enforcement agencies," Roman says. "Get them looking for black Ford Transits heading west in Tennessee."

"Good," Lucien says, rising from his chair. "Ivy, verify we have all possible medical supplies stocked and ready. We don't know what condition Brayden will be in when we find him."

"When," Scout repeats, clinging to the word like a lifeline. "When we find him."

I squeeze her hand. "Yes. When."

The room falls silent as we process what we've learned. Eliza wasn't working alone. Someone else has Brayden. Someone who's still out there while we've been focused on a dead woman.

Roman closes his laptop with a decisive click. "I'll alert everyone the moment I find anything new on the van or its driver." His eyes sweep across our faces, lingering on Scout's. "In the meantime, we need to return to business as usual."

"Business as usual?" Scout's voice rises in disbelief. "Are you fucking kidding me, Roman? I'm not fucking around with Murder-gram or any other bullshit until Brayden is found, one way or another."

I place my hand on her lower back, a silent request for patience.

Roman holds up his hand. "Hear me out. If Eliza was working with someone, or for someone, they're watching us. They'll know we found her and that we know the body at the farmhouse wasn't Brayden's. They'll expect us to be in crisis mode."

"But we are in crisis mode," Ivy says, her voice icy.

"Exactly," Roman nods. "And that's what they want. They want us distracted, emotional, making mistakes."

Lucien sets down his teacup. "Roman's right. We need to give the appearance that we're in control. The lockdown restrictions are officially lifted as of now."

Scout turns to me, eyes wide with betrayal. I keep my expression neutral, but the look on her face makes it difficult. My instinct is driving me to tear apart every inch of the countryside until we find Brayden. I would do anything to keep that look off her face.

"We'll implement tighter security protocols," Roman continues. "But outwardly, we need to appear functional. Operational."

"You want us to pretend everything's normal while Brayden is out there somewhere?" Scout's voice breaks on his name.

"I want whoever has him to believe we've given up," Lucien says firmly. "I want them to believe we're moving on."

Roman nods in agreement. "People get careless when they think they've won. If they believe we've given up searching for Brayden, they might relax. Make a mistake."

"And if they don't?" Scout demands.

"Then we lose nothing," I tell her quietly. "We'll still be searching, just not where they can see us doing it."

Scout pulls away from my touch, wrapping her arms around herself. "So what does 'business as usual' look like exactly? We just start taking assignments again? Killing like nothing's wrong?"

"Yes," Lucien says simply. "The Index remains active. There are still monsters out there that need removing."

"I'll continue working on tracking the van and identifying the driver," Roman adds. "But I'll also maintain regular operations, approving claims, managing communications, the works."

"And the rest of us?" Ivy asks.

"You'll choose assignments through The Index as normal," Lucien says. "Though I suggest pairing up for now. No solo hunts."

I move closer, drawn by the exhaustion written across her face. She's holding herself together through sheer will.

"What if we took something local?" I suggest quietly. "Close enough that we could be back here in hours if Roman finds anything."

Her eyes flash. "You want me to go kill someone while Brayden is—"

"I want you to have something to focus on besides the waiting," I interrupt. "Something that isn't sitting in this room, drinking tea, going insane."

She stares at me, and I can see her weighing it. The need to act warring with guilt at the thought of doing anything other than searching.

"Together," I add. "We'd go together."

Her eyes meet mine, but there's no gratitude there, only raw pain. "You'd babysit me while I pretend to function?"

The words sting, but I understand the anger behind them.

"I'd hunt with you," I correct. "Because sitting here isn't working for either of us."

"Nothing's working," she snaps, then immediately deflates. "This is my fault. I should have—"

"Don't."

"He's gone because of me, Deacon. Because I couldn't see what Eliza was doing, because I—"

"Scout." My voice cuts through her spiral. "We'll find him."

She laughs, but it's bitter. "Will we? Or are we just going to kill some random asshole so I can feel like I'm doing something useful instead of fucking everything up?"

The others continue discussing logistics, but Scout's words hang between us like a challenge.

"Maybe," I say honestly. "But falling apart won't bring him back either."

Her jaw clenches. "I'm not falling apart."

"No?" I gesture to her untouched tea, the way she's been picking at her cuticles until they bleed.

She looks away, caught.

"A hunt gives us something concrete," I continue. "Someone who deserves what's coming. And it keeps us moving instead of sitting here drowning."

Scout's silence stretches long enough that I wonder if she'll refuse entirely. Around us, the others continue planning, their voices a low hum of strategy and logistics.

Finally, she looks up at me. "Okay." Her voice is barely above a whisper. "We'll go on a hunt. Together."

The relief that floods through me is immediate, though I keep it off my face.

"Local," I confirm. "Close enough that we can be back here in a few hours if Roman finds anything."

She nods, then glances toward the others still discussing surveillance and security measures. "How do we even pretend this is normal?"

"One step at a time," I tell her. "Starting with finding a claim."

She picks up her tea, finally taking a sip. It's probably cold by now, but she doesn't seem to notice.

"Deacon?" Her eyes meet mine again, and this time, there's something steadier there. "Thank you. For not letting me sit here and rot."

I nod, unable to trust my voice with anything more substantial than, "Always."

FORTY
SCOUT

I stare at my embroidery kit for a full minute before slowly pushing it aside. The delicate needles and spools of crimson thread, my constant companions to every kill, stay on the bed as I zip up my suitcase.

"Not today," I whisper, running my fingers over the worn case.

It feels wrong leaving it behind, like walking out without my skin. But stepping back into normalcy feels impossible when Brayden is still missing. Honestly though, I still haven't been able to stitch anything since the farmhouse. The Dahlia for Dr. Stanton's death still sits unfinished. I'm not ready to be the Stitcher. Hell, I can barely manage to be regular Scout right now, and she's supposed to be the easy version of me.

It took two days of me stress-scrolling through the Index before I finally admitted defeat and handed it over to Deacon. Sure, there were plenty of creeps who deserved a visit from yours truly, but apparently, my brain decided to go on vacation right when I needed it most. Turns out worrying makes even picking which asshole to murder feel impossible. Kinda hard to channel your inner killer when your chest feels like it's being crushed and every worst-case scenario about Brayden keeps playing on loop.

I toss extra clothes, makeup, and surveillance gear into the bag instead. My hands work mechanically while my mind drifts to Brayden. Is he hurt? Alive?

Tank whines from his spot on my bed, his wrinkled face somehow more sorrowful than usual.

"I know, buddy. I miss him too." I scratch behind his ears. "But we're going to find him. Promise."

A soft knock interrupts my packing. Deacon leans against the door-frame, arms crossed. His steel-gray eyes scan my room, landing on the embroidery kit still sitting on my comforter.

"You're not taking it?"

I shake my head, setting my suitcase on the floor with more force than necessary. "Don't feel like stitching right now."

He doesn't push, just nods. Thank God for that. I'm not sure I could handle a pep talk right now, even a well-meaning one.

"Car's packed. Ready when you are."

"Almost." I grab my phone, checking for any updates from Roman. Nothing. "Any updates?"

"Nothing new. Roman's monitoring traffic cams along the Tennessee border."

I nod, throat tight. "And we're just supposed to go hunt some former frat boy while Brayden is—"

"We're making it look like business as usual," Deacon cuts in, voice firm. "Anyone watching will think we've moved on. That's when they get sloppy."

He's right. I hate that he's right. But logic doesn't make the guilt sitting in my chest any lighter.

"Tell me about the perv again," I say, pulling the handle from my rolling case. Maybe if I focus on someone else's nightmare, I can stop drowning in my own.

"Harrison Westfield. Thirty-four. Real estate developer in Tuscaloosa. Likes to hang around his old fraternity house, where he drugs and assaults college girls."

"And the university looks the other way because..."

"He donated the money for their new business school. Golden boy alumni." Deacon's jaw tightens. "Three girls tried to report him. One transferred schools, one dropped out entirely, and one," His voice hardens. "Suicide. Last month."

I follow Deacon downstairs, where Ivy waits by the front door. Her eyes are shadowed, her skin pale.

"Roman packed you some supplies." She hands me a small box. "Burner phones, cash, new IDs.

I nod, not trusting my voice. Ivy pulls me into a fierce hug.

"We'll find him," she whispers. "You focus on your hunt. Stay safe."

"You too."

The drive to Alabama stretches before us, four hours of highway and silence. I climb into Deacon's Charger, settling into the passenger seat as he starts the engine.

"You good?" he asks, hand hovering over the gearshift.

I'm not. I'm nowhere near good. My family is fractured, my closest thing to a brother is missing, and I'm driving to Alabama to kill a man without my needles and thread. Everything feels wrong and backward and completely screwed up.

"Let's just go," I mutter, grabbing my phone and shoving it in my pocket.

Deacon says nothing as he shifts the car into gear. Smart man. Right now, I've got all the conversational charm of a rabid honey badger.

The Charger purrs as we pull away from the manor. I watch our home get smaller and smaller in the side mirror, feeling like I'm abandoning Brayden all over again.

My leg bounces uncontrollably. I tap my fingers against the door handle, then my thigh, then the dashboard. I can't get comfortable. Can't get still.

"You want music?" Deacon asks after twenty minutes of my silent fidgeting.

I shrug, which he correctly interprets as yes. He connects his phone and scrolls through a playlist.

The opening notes of a classical piece fill the car, something with violins that's probably fancy and cultured. I immediately reach over and hit skip.

"Not today," I say. "I need something with a pulse."

Deacon raises an eyebrow but says nothing as he selects something else. Heavy drums and electric guitar blast through the speakers. Better.

I still can't settle. My hands keep moving, tapping, twisting my rings, playing with my hair. I crack my window, then close it. Adjust my seat. Check my phone for the hundredth time.

"He's going to be okay," Deacon says quietly.

"You don't know that," I mutter.

"No, I don't. But Brayden's tough."

I close my eyes. "Tough doesn't matter when someone has you tied up somewhere."

Deacon reaches across the console and takes my hand, stilling my restless fingers. His palm is warm against mine.

"We're going to find him."

I squeeze his hand once before pulling away. "I need to pee. And snacks."

We stop at a gas station. I pace the aisles while Deacon pumps gas, grabbing snacks I don't want and energy drinks I definitely don't need. When I return to the car, Deacon eyes the four different caffeinated beverages in my arms.

"You sure that's a good idea?"

"Nope." I crack one open and take a long pull from the can.

Back on the highway, I channel-surf through radio stations, never settling on one for more than thirty seconds. Deacon says nothing, just keeps his eyes on the road.

"Tell me about Harrison again," I say, needing something to focus on that isn't the anxiety tornado in my stomach.

"Former fraternity president turned real estate developer. Made his money flipping houses in college towns. Thirty-four, never married, apartment life, posh office downtown."

"It's a fairly decent drive, so I figure we can just settle in tonight and do some reviews. The fraternity's hosting a party this weekend. Figured it would give us a few days to dig into his file."

I nod, my mind already racing through scenarios. It's weird planning a hunt without my embroidery kit, like showing up to a gunfight with a water balloon.

"We need to get word to his victims," I blurt out. "After. They deserve to know that piece of shit can't hurt anyone else."

Deacon glances at me. "I'm sure we can do something about that."

I drain my second energy drink and crush the can. My heart hammers in my chest, partly from caffeine, mostly from anxiety. I switch positions again, tucking one leg under me.

"You're going to wear a hole in my seat," Deacon says.

"Can't help it." I drum my fingers on the window. "I feel like I'm going to crawl out of my skin."

"Can't imagine why," Deacon says dryly, eyeing the crushed energy drink can. "Maybe it's time to switch to decaf."

He exits the highway, turning onto a rural road. "We're about twenty minutes out from the safehouse."

I check my phone again. Nothing from Roman or Ivy.

By the time we pull up to the small cabin that serves as our safehouse, I'm practically vibrating like a phone on silent. Yeah, turns out chugging energy drinks when you're already a human stress ball was about as smart as bringing a knife to a gunfight. I jump out before Deacon fully stops the car, pacing the gravel driveway while he unloads our bags.

"I can't do this," I blurt out. "I can't just pretend everything's normal when Brayden is—"

"Scout." Deacon sets down the bags and approaches me slowly, like I'm a wild animal that might bolt. "Take a breath."

"I don't need to breathe, I need to find my friend!"

"And we will. But right now, we need to focus on what we can control."

My hands are shaking. I clench them into fists, nails digging into my palms.

Deacon reaches for me, and I let him pull me against his chest. His heartbeat is steady under my ear, grounding me.

For a moment, he says nothing, just holds me while I fall apart. His silence is more comforting than any empty promises could be.

I close my eyes and breathe him in, clean laundry and subtle cologne. For just a moment, I let myself be held.

He strokes his strong hands along my back as he says, "I know you're worried about Brayden. I am too. But right now, the best thing we can do is focus on exactly what we're doing."

I let myself lean into Deacon's embrace for one more breath before pulling away. The warmth of his chest against my cheek lingers even as I step back.

"Okay," I say, squaring my shoulders. "Let's get to work."

The safehouse is smaller than our Chicago location, just a two-bedroom cabin with basic furnishings. Rustic but functional, like a Pinterest board titled "Serial Killer Hideaway: Cozy Edition." I drop my bag in the first bedroom I see, not bothering to unpack properly. Just dump the essentials in the bathroom and toss my clothes onto the bed like I'm twelve and my mom just told me to clean my room.

When I emerge, Deacon is already setting up in the dining area, laptop open and files spread across the wooden table.

"That was fast," I comment, sliding into the chair across from him.

"Don't have much to unpack." He doesn't look up from the screen. "Roman sent over the floor plans for the fraternity house and Harrison's apartment building."

I reach for the stack of papers nearest me. Crime scene photos from the suicide last month. Emma Donovan, nineteen, pre-med student. She was found hanging in her dorm room after filing a complaint against Harrison, which was promptly buried by the university's administration.

My stomach turns. I set the photos aside and grab another file.

"The fraternity's hosting their annual 'Cider & Sin' party on Friday," Deacon says, turning his laptop so I can see the social media post. "Perfect cover for us to get close to Harrison."

🍎 *Cider & Sin*
A Fall Frat Affair
Date: *Friday, October 21st* **Time:** *9 PM 'til the fire dies*
Location: *Delta Rho Lawn & Basement*
Dress Code: *Flannels, Fishnets & Everything Forbidden*
Pumpkin punch, hard cider on tap, apple pie shots at midnight. *Live DJ. Bonfire. Bad decisions are encouraged.*

"Jeez. Even their party name screams, 'this is where bad things happen to good people.'" I scan the details. "He'll be there?"

"According to his calendar, which Roman helpfully accessed. He never misses these types of events." Deacon's voice hardens. "Likes to pick his victims there."

I spread out the papers, creating a makeshift timeline of Harrison's predatory behavior. Three formal complaints, all dismissed. At least seven other incidents were documented in text messages and social media posts where girls warned each other about him.

"He has a type," I note, looking at the victims' photos. "Brunette, petite, usually a freshman."

"Which is why you'll be perfect as bait," Deacon says, eyes meeting mine. "You fit his victim profile."

I raise my eyebrow at him even though I'm already mentally cataloging what I'll wear. "Are you sure you're going to handle that, Candy man?"

"I still don't like the idea of you being alone with him," Deacon says, jaw tightening. "Shocking, I know."

I roll my eyes. "I won't be alone. You'll be watching." I tap the fraternity house blueprint. "We need to get access to their security system."

Deacon nods. "Roman's already working on it. The house has cameras at all entrances and in common areas. Not in bedrooms or bathrooms, thankfully."

"Thank God for small favors," I mutter. "So you'll have eyes on me until we get to his apartment."

I chew my bottom lip, thinking. "We'll need earpieces. Something discreet."

Deacon reaches for a small black case and slides it across the table. "Roman thought of everything."

Inside are two flesh-colored earpieces, practically invisible once inserted. "Gotta love App Daddy, he's got all the best toys." I grin across the table at him.

"These have a range of about half a mile," Deacon explains. "I'll be parked across from the fraternity house, monitoring the video feeds. Once you leave with Harrison, I'll follow at a distance."

"Think he'll go to his apartment?"

"Not sure. It could be his apartment or one of the spec houses in his development. But the second you leave with him, I'll be right behind you."

I nod, studying the layout of Harrison's apartment building. "We should do some basic recon tomorrow. Get a feel for his routines, the security at his building."

"Already planned on it. His office is downtown. We can start there, then check out the apartment complex and fraternity house."

I gather the photos of Harrison's victims, looking at each face. Young women who trusted the system to protect them and were betrayed. Women who are still out there, carrying the weight of what he did to them.

"We need to be clean on this one," I say. "High-profile victim, college campus. Too many eyes."

"Agreed. We can take him back to his apartment, make it look like a robbery gone wrong."

I tap my fingers on the table, thinking. "No signature this time?"

Deacon studies me for a moment. "You okay with that?"

I shrug. "Not like I've been in a stitching mood lately anyway." I push back from the table, stretching my arms above my head. "I'm going to shower, then we should get some sleep. We've got an early start tomorrow."

"I'll finish setting up the equipment."

I pause in the hallway. "Deacon?"

He looks up.

"Thank you. For being here. For helping me through this."

A small smile touches his lips. "Always, Kitten."

I walk toward my room, and for the first time since this nightmare started, I feel steady on my feet. The crushing weight of helplessness is still there, but now it has somewhere to go. I'm not drowning in my own head anymore. I have a target, a plan, something to channel all this rage and fear into. Time to hunt down a motherfucker.

FORTY-ONE

DEACON

The past three days blur together in a haze of surveillance and preparation. We've followed Harrison Westfield through his daily routine, morning runs along the university's outer track, business lunches at upscale restaurants where he orders scotch neat regardless of the hour, and afternoon meetings with university officials who laugh too loudly at his jokes. Every night, he hits a different bar near campus.

Scout and I documented each location, mapped entry and exit points, and cataloged security measures. We've verified his apartment, office, and the three spec houses he uses for his private "meetings." All potential kill sites, all with vulnerabilities we can exploit.

Tonight, Harrison becomes a statistic.

But Scout's been off her game. During yesterday's surveillance outside his office building, she checked her phone seventeen times in two hours. Each buzz made her shoulders tense, each blank screen left her deflated. She's trying to hide it, but I see everything, the way her fingers hover over the screen, the micro-expressions of disappointment when there's no news about Brayden.

It's becoming a liability.

I park the Charger across the street from Delta Rho's sprawling house. Music already pulses through the neighborhood, bass vibrating through my steering wheel. Students stream toward the party in packs, dressed in flannel and denim, girls in skirts despite the October chill.

"Testing, testing. Can you hear me, Flossie?" Scout's voice comes through my earpiece, playful despite everything.

"Loud and clear, Kitten." I check the laptop, confirming the fraternity's security feed is up. Six camera angles fill my screen. The front entrance, back door, main floor, basement, stairwell, and upstairs hallway. "I've got eyes on all the common areas."

Scout steps out of the passenger side, and my mouth goes dry.

Her denim skirt barely covers the curve of her ass, fishnet-clad legs drawing my eye from thigh to ankle. That damn pink glitter belt catches the streetlight, winking like a promise. Her cropped pink top wraps across her chest, showcasing cleavage that would stop traffic. She looks like the perfect college freshman out for a good time.

Irresistible bait for a predator like Harrison.

"How do I look?" She does a little spin, and I force my hands to stay on the steering wheel.

"Like trouble." My voice comes out rougher than intended.

She grins, leaning into my open window. "That's the idea, right?" Her scent of citrus and sunshine fills my senses. "Don't worry, I've got this. You just keep those sexy eyes on the screens."

"You good?" I squeeze her hand. "Remember, don't drink what he gives you."

"Not my first rodeo, Candy Man." She winks, though her phone buzzes and she reaches for it. "I'll get him talking, then suggest we go somewhere private. You follow us."

"The moment you leave, I'll be thirty seconds behind you."

Scout straightens, adjusting her top. "See you on the other side." She pulls her phone from her pocket, checks the screen, and immediately tucks it back in her pocket. A discouraging pout on her lips as she shakes her hands. She turns on her heel and heads to the party.

I watch her walk away, hips swaying with deliberate provocation. Every male gaze on the street follows her, exactly as planned. Heat crawls up my neck as I tighten my grip on the wheel.

"Still with me, Flossie? Or are you too busy looking at my ass?

"Always. Hard not to." I shift focus to the laptop, watching as she approaches the fraternity house. The front lawn teems with students holding red cups, gathered around fire pits and strung lights. "Harrison is by the punch bowl, just to the right of the front porch."

I watch as Scout stops to pull her phone from her pocket and puts it back... *again*. She's been doing this since we left the Manor. Constantly checking for updates about Brayden that never come. Her focus is shot, and that's dangerous.

Through the camera feed, I spot Harrison Westfield holding court near a massive bowl of something unnaturally red. At thirty-four, he's easily fifteen years older than most attendees, but his designer clothes and cultivated charm let him blend in as the cool alumnus who bankrolls these parties. The perfect cover for a predator.

Scout enters the frame, immediately drawing attention. Two frat boys offer her drinks, which she accepts with a giggle, which I can hear through the earpiece. She makes her way toward Harrison, appearing to stumble slightly, just enough to look like she's already had a few.

"Showtime," she whispers, and I feel it like a breath against my ear.

My stomach knots as Harrison notices her, his smile widening in a way that makes my trigger finger itch. He says something to the boys around him, and they part like obedient soldiers, clearing his path to Scout.

I watch him approach her on my screen, his confidence making my jaw clench. He touches her arm in greeting, leaning close to speak over the music.

"Hiiii," Scout draws out the greeting, voice pitched higher and breathy. "I'm Brooke. You're really cute. Are you running this whole thing?"

I watch Harrison circle Scout like a shark that's caught the scent of blood. His practiced smile never reaches his eyes as he leans closer, one hand coming to rest on the small of her back.

"What brings a beautiful girl like you to our little gathering?" His voice carries through Scout's mic.

Scout tosses her hair, playing the part of flattered freshman perfectly. "My roommate knows someone who knows someone." She giggles, leaning into his space. "I literally just transferred here, and everyone said I had to come to this party."

"Well, we're certainly lucky to have you." Harrison's gaze drops to her cleavage without any subtlety. "What are you studying?"

"Psychology." She takes a sip of her drink, maintaining eye contact over the rim. "I'm really good at reading people. It's kind of my specialty."

Harrison steps closer, eliminating what little space remains between them. "Really? What can you read about me?"

Scout bites her lip, pretending to concentrate. "You're the type who sees what he wants and just... takes it. And..." she giggles, "you're probably really good at convincing people to give it to you."

Scout's phone buzzes in her pocket. Her fingers twitch, and I can see the momentary break in her character as she reaches for it.

"Sorry," she mutters, glancing at the screen before tucking it away. "My mom is like super overprotective."

Harrison's smile tightens fractionally. "Freshman year can be tough on parents. Let me get you something better than that watered-down punch."

He takes the cup from her and guides her toward a private bar setup in the corner where a student in a Delta Rho shirt guards a collection of premium liquor bottles.

"Jake, fix my friend Brooke something special," Harrison instructs, his hand still possessively on Scout's back.

"Coming right up, Mr. Westfield."

I shift in my seat, watching the bartender mix something with vodka and a splash of cranberry. When he turns to grab a lime, Harrison slips something from his pocket, a small vial, and empties its contents into the glass.

"He just drugged your drink," I warn through the earpiece. "Clear as day on camera."

Scout's phone buzzes again. This time, she pulls it out immediately, breaking contact with Harrison to check the screen.

"Everything okay?" Harrison asks, irritation flickering across his face.

"Yeah, sorry." Scout looks genuinely distracted, not the calculated performance we planned. "My friend's going through something and I promised to be available."

Harrison's predatory focus wavers. He hands her the drugged drink, which Scout accepts with a smile that doesn't quite hit her eyes.

"College life," he says smoothly. "Always some drama happening. Drink up, sweetheart, it'll help you relax."

Scout lifts the glass toward her lips but doesn't actually drink, distracted by another buzz from her phone. She immediately pulls it out, her attention completely diverted from Harrison.

"Oh my god, sorry," she says, staring at the screen with obvious disappointment. "My friend is going through like, major drama."

Harrison watches her with the drink still untouched in her hand, his smile tightening. "Maybe you should focus on the people who are actually here with you tonight." His tone stays friendly, but there's an edge underneath.

Scout looks up from her phone, "You're right, sorry. I'm being so rude." She raises the glass again but gets distracted by yet another buzz, immediately checking her phone instead of drinking.

Harrison's jaw clenches almost imperceptibly. His eyes flick to the untouched drink in her hand, then back to her face buried in her phone. His gaze is already drifting across the room, cataloging other potential targets who might be more... cooperative.

"Excuse me for a moment," he says, stepping back smoothly. "I need to check on something with the fraternity president. Don't go anywhere."

I watch him walk away on the camera feed, his posture rigid with frustration.

"Scout, you're losing him," I murmur into the mic. "He's already looking for someone else."

"No, I can get him back," she insists, but her voice wavers with uncertainty. "He's just... I can fix this. Roman promised to text if they found anything about Brayden, and I thought maybe..."

She's standing alone now, looking small and out of place among the partying students. Her phone comes out again, screen illuminating her face as she checks for messages.

"He's moving toward the back stairs," I report, tracking Harrison through the camera feeds. "Looks like he's heading to the second floor with the fraternity president."

Scout doesn't respond, still staring at her phone.

"Scout!" I drop her name into the mic with the same tone I'd use to stop a man from pulling a trigger. Hard. Final. A verbal slap.

She jumps, head snapping up from her phone. I watch her on the screen, see the moment my voice cuts through her spiral.

"Get your ass back to the fucking car. Now." I don't try to hide the anger in my voice. "We've got to fix this clusterfuck."

For a second, she looks like she might argue, that defiant tilt of her chin I've come to recognize, but then her shoulders slump.

"I'm coming." Her voice is small through the earpiece.

I watch her thread through the crowd on the camera feed, no longer the confident predator but something diminished. She dumps the drugged drink in a potted plant on her way out, moving with none of her usual swagger.

A few minutes later, the passenger door opens. Scout slides in beside me, smelling of cheap beer and too many bodies in too small a space.

"I fucked up." She stares straight ahead through the windshield. "I know."

"Where were you?" I keep my voice level, not accusatory. "Your body was in there, but your mind was somewhere else."

"I can't stop thinking about him." Her fingers twist together in her lap. "Every time my phone buzzes, I think it might be Roman with news about Brayden."

"And every minute you're distracted is another minute Harrison has to find a new victim."

She flinches like I've struck her. "I can fix this. Let me go back in—"

"It's too late." I nod toward the fraternity house. "Harrison's already moved on."

Scout follows my gaze just as Harrison emerges from the front door. He has his arm around a petite blonde who can barely stand upright. Her head lolls against his shoulder as he guides her down the steps.

"Jesus." Scout's breath catches. "She's completely out of it."

We watch in silence as Harrison helps the girl into his SUV, then moves around to the driver's side. The car pulls away from the curb.

"Oh fuck." Scout's voice breaks. "This is my fault."

"Yes."

She turns to me, eyes wide with hurt, but I don't soften.

"You want me to lie to you?" I hold her gaze. "Tell you it's okay? That girl is about to become his next victim because you couldn't stay focused."

Scout's face crumples. She presses her palms against her eyes, shoulders shaking. "I just keep thinking about Brayden. What if we don't find him?"

"We're looking for Brayden." I start the car, pulling away from the curb to follow Harrison's SUV at a distance. "But we can't let it consume us to the point where others get hurt."

"I know." She drops her hands, revealing eyes bright with unshed tears. "I'm sorry."

"Don't apologize to me." I nod toward the SUV three cars ahead. "She's the one who would be paying for your mistakes. Make it right."

Scout straightens in her seat, wiping roughly at her eyes. "Where are they going?"

"Based on the direction we're going, one of his spec houses would be most likely." I change lanes, keeping his vehicle in sight. "We have about ten minutes to come up with a new plan."

"I won't screw up again." Her voice hardens with resolve. "That girl doesn't deserve what he's planning."

"No, she doesn't."

Scout pulls her phone from her pocket, stares at it for a long moment, then turns it off completely.

"Brayden would kick my ass if he knew I let someone else get hurt because I was too busy worrying about him." She tucks the phone away, out of sight. "He's the toughest person I know. If anyone can survive until we find him, it's Bray."

I reach across the console, taking her hand in mine. Her fingers are cold, trembling slightly.

"We will find him," I promise. "But right now, that girl needs us more."

Scout squeezes my hand, her grip strengthening. "Let's go get this pervy motherfucker."

The SUV stops outside of a house in an unfinished development. We watch as he helps the stumbling girl inside, his arm around her waist, supportive to any casual observer. Only we know what waits for her inside.

"I'm going in first," Scout says, voice steady now. "He's seen me already, so I'll create a distraction. You get the girl out."

I nod, pulling into a parking space across the street. "And then we deal with Harrison."

FORTY-TWO

SCOUT

I stare at my reflection in the car window. Mascara is smudged beneath my eyes from rubbing them earlier, giving me raccoon rings that somehow make the amber look more intense. My foundation is still flawless from the sorority girl act, but underneath the perfect makeup, I can see the exhaustion, the sleepless nights, the guilt eating away at me. This isn't the Stitcher. This isn't me.

I've been so wrapped up in my own guilt and fear that I've forgotten why I do what I do. That poor girl inside doesn't deserve what's coming to her because I couldn't keep my shit together.

Deacon's already moving toward the back of the house. Maybe five to ten minutes, and he'll be inside through whatever window or door he can access on the lower level. All I have to do is keep Harrison's attention locked on me and away from any sounds Deacon might make getting in.

"Pull it together," I whisper to my reflection. "Stop being a bitch." I leave the car and cross the street to stand before the only finished house in the area.

I square my shoulders and feel something inside me shift. Without my embroidery kit, I can't be the Stitcher tonight. But I can still be Scout Prescott, chaos incarnate.

"Time to play," I murmur, feeling the switch flip inside me.

I lean on the doorbell like it owes me money, holding it down until it makes that angry, sustained screech that could wake the dead. When that doesn't work fast enough for my liking, I start pounding on the door with both fists like I'm trying to beat down the gates of hell.

"Harrison! Baby, open up!" I screech, my voice echoing down the empty street. "I know you're in there!"

I hear movement inside. Cursing, shuffling. Good. I've got his attention.

The door cracks open, Harrison's annoyed face appearing in the gap. Behind him, I catch a glimpse of the blonde girl sprawled on the couch, barely conscious.

"What the fuck?" he hisses, keeping the chain on the door. "Brooke?"

I wedge my foot in the door before he can close it, my eyes wide and unblinking. "Where did you go, baby? I've been looking everywhere for you!"

"Look, whatever happened at the party—"

"No, no, no." I shake my head frantically, pushing against the door. "You left me at the party. I saw you leave with her." I point past him toward the couch. "But that's okay. I forgive you. I missed you."

His face shifts from confusion to recognition to barely concealed panic. "Look, I think there's been some kind of misunderstanding—"

"I'm ready to play with you now," I whisper, tilting my head at an unnatural angle. "I've been waiting so patiently."

Harrison's face pales. "You need to leave before I call the cops."

I slam my body against the door, the chain straining. "But I brought my special toys!" I reach into my pocket and pull out nothing, pretending to hold something precious. "Don't you want to see?"

His eyes dart to my empty hand, then back to my face. I can see the panic cross his face. The girl on his couch, the crazy woman at his door. He's trying to figure out which problem to solve first.

"I'll scream," I say, my voice dropping to a whisper. "I'll scream and tell everyone what you do to girls like her." I nod toward the couch. "How many others have there been, Harrison? Ten? Twelve? I've been counting."

The color drains from his face. "You don't know what you're talking about."

"Oh, but I do." I smile wider, showing too many teeth. "I know everything about you. I've been watching you for so long."

Harrison glances back at the girl on his couch, then to me.

I catch a flicker of movement behind Harrison, a shadow passing by the living room window. Deacon. My pulse quickens, but I keep my face locked in this manic expression I've crafted.

"You know what's funny about stalking someone, Harrison?" I giggle, high-pitched and unnatural. "You learn all their little secrets." I tap my finger against the door frame, one-two-three. "Like how you take them to empty houses. How you slip something in their drinks when they're not looking."

His jaw tightens. "I don't know what you think you saw—"

"I saw everything!" I shriek, making him flinch. "I see everything you do!" My eyes go wide as I push hard against the door. "I've been watching you for months. I know where you live. I know where you work. I know how your mother takes her coffee."

Through the crack in the door, I glimpse Deacon slipping into the living room behind Harrison. He moves like a ghost, silent and purposeful, lifting the unconscious girl from the couch.

Harrison starts to turn his head.

"I CUT OFF ALL MY HAIR FOR YOU!" I scream, slamming my palm against the door. His attention snaps back to me, eyes widening. "Do you like it? I did it just how you like it."

"You're out of your goddamn mind," he says, looking genuinely terrified now.

I need to keep him distracted just a little longer. Deacon is carrying the girl toward what must be a back bedroom, her limp form cradled against his chest.

"I wrote you poems," I whisper, abruptly shifting my tone. "Do you want to hear them? I wrote them in my blood."

Harrison's hand reaches for his phone. "Look, I'm calling the police—"

"NO!" I throw my body against the door again. The chain rattles but holds. "They'll take me away from you again! They always try to keep us apart!"

Deacon has disappeared from view with the girl. I need maybe thirty more seconds.

"Did you fuck her already?" I ask, my voice suddenly flat, eyes narrowing. "Did you fuck her like you fucked the others?"

His face hardens. "That's it. I'm calling—"

I reach through the gap in the door, grabbing his wrist before he can react. My nails dig into his skin, and he jerks back, eyes widening in shock. "I forgive you," I whisper, tears suddenly streaming down my face. "I forgive you because I love you. But you have to let me in now."

"You're fucking insane!" He yells as he tries to push the door closed.

Deacon reappears in the hallway behind Harrison, giving me a subtle nod. The girl is safe. Time to finish this.

My face goes completely still. The tears vanish like they were never there. My eyes widen until the whites show all around my irises, and my head tilts at that unnatural angle again, like a doll with a broken neck.

"Harrison," I whisper, voice flat and empty. "You need to let me in now."

"Get the fuck away from my house," he hisses, backing away from the door.

My lips stretch into a smile that doesn't move the rest of my face. "But that's not fair. My friend gets to come inside and play without me."

Harrison's brow furrows. "What friend?"

"The one behind you."

Harrison turns, just enough to catch a glimpse of Deacon pulling his black skull mask down over his face. The eye holes frame cold steel grey eyes that seem to glow against the darkness of the mask. For a moment, Harrison's mouth opens in a perfect O of surprise.

I pull my foot out of the door gap as Deacon's hand shoots out, grabbing Harrison by the hair and slamming his face into the doorframe with a sickening crack. Blood sprays from his nose, spattering the white-painted wood.

The door slams shut.

I wait, rocking back and forth on my heels, humming a nursery rhyme under my breath. Inside, I hear the sounds of a brief struggle, a thud, and then silence.

The chain lock slides open with a metallic rattle. The door swings wide.

Deacon stands there, skull mask in place, Harrison's unconscious body crumpled at his feet. Blood trickles from the man's broken nose, pooling on the hardwood floor.

I step over the threshold, glancing down at Harrison's form. "Aww, you started the party without me." I pout, tapping my finger against the skull mask's cheek. "Rude."

Deacon just grunts, bending down to grab Harrison by the armpits. He drags the unconscious man across the hardwood floor, leaving a thin smear of blood behind. The developer's expensive loafers scrape against the floor as Deacon positions him on the couch, his head lolling to one side.

I close the door behind me, making sure to wipe the doorknob and frame where I touched it. "How's our sleeping beauty?" I ask, nodding toward the back bedroom.

Deacon tilts his head in that direction, then gives a thumbs-up.

"Perfect." I circle around the living room, taking in the half-staged furniture and the smell of fresh paint. "Typical spec house. Everything looks nice, but nothing's built to last."

I tap my chin, considering our options. "We could still make it look like a robbery gone wrong," I suggest, but even as I say it, I'm shaking my head. "But that doesn't feel right."

Deacon walks to the back of the room, where a staircase leads to the second floor. He pulls off his mask and tucks it into his back pocket. "I think the stairs would be our best bet." He says as he points upward.

"Stairs?" I follow his gaze, understanding immediately. "That's perfect. He's drunk, he's in an unfamiliar house, he falls down the stairs and breaks his neck." I clap my hands together. "Clean and simple." I grin at him. "Look at you getting all creative. I'm so proud."

My grin fades slightly, the weight of responsibility settling back on my shoulders. "Can we check on the girl?" I ask. "I just need to make sure she's okay."

I follow as Deacon moves towards the bedroom. After I confirm she's still out cold, he arranges her on her side in case she throws up from the drugs Harrison gave her.

"She'll wake up with a hell of a headache, but she'll be alive," I say, looking up at him. "That's better than what he would have given her."

We return to the living room, where Harrison is starting to stir, groaning as he shifts on the couch. Blood has dried around his nostrils, crusting in his perfectly groomed beard.

"Wakey wakey," I sing-song, perched on the coffee table directly in front of him. "Time to rejoin the party."

Harrison's eyes flutter open, unfocused at first, then widening as he registers me sitting inches from his face. He tries to lunge forward, but Deacon's hand clamps down on his shoulder, pinning him to the couch.

"What the," Harrison's voice is thick, confused. "What the fuck is happening?"

"Community service," I reply simply. "In an unorthodox manner."

His eyes dart between Deacon and me, panic setting in. "If this is about money, I can pay."

"It's not about money." I lean in closer, my voice dropping to a whisper. "It's about *my* girls. It's about Melissa Carter. And Tanya Washington. And Emma Donovan."

Harrison's eyes go wide with shock.

"And Bethany Klein, Sophia Martinez, Jessica Taylor..." I continue, counting off on my fingers. "Should I go on? Because I can. I know all their names."

"I don't know what you're talking about," he stammers.

I tsk. "Liar. Liar." I tilt my head, studying him like a curious specimen. "You drugged them, just like you drugged that poor girl in the bedroom."

His eyes widen further. "How could you possibly know?"

"We know everything about you, Harrison. The donations to the university that make the administration look the other way." I tap my finger against his knee. "The hushed settlements with the two girls who tried to come forward."

Sweat beads on his forehead. "Look, whatever you think happened..."

"Ten girls, Harrison. Ten young women whose lives you've damaged forever." I stand up, looking down at him. "And you were never going to stop because number eleven is waiting in the bedroom."

"Please," he whispers, voice cracking. "I have money. A lot of money."

"We don't need your money." I smile, and it's not a nice smile. "We just want you to understand why this is happening to you. It's only fair, don't you think? That you know exactly why you're about to die?"

Deacon moves with terrifying efficiency. One moment, Harrison is sitting on the couch, begging for his life, and the next, Deacon's muscular arm snakes around his throat in a perfect choke hold, cutting off circulation to his brain.

Harrison's eyes bulge as Deacon pulls him from the couch. His expensive shoes scrabble against the hardwood floor, seeking purchase, finding none. Deacon's grip is harsh, not crushing his windpipe, just restricting blood flow to the brain. Harrison's arms flail uselessly, fingers clawing at Deacon's forearm.

"God, that's sexy," I purr, following behind them as Deacon drags Harrison toward the staircase. "Nothing hotter than a man who knows how to move a body."

Deacon grunts in acknowledgment, his face a mask of concentration. Harrison's struggles grow weaker, his movements more uncoordinated as oxygen deprivation sets in. Just as his eyes begin to roll back, Deacon eases the pressure slightly, not enough to let him recover, just enough to keep him conscious.

I trail behind them up the carpeted stairs, watching Harrison's feet bump against each step. The carpet will show the drag marks, but that works perfectly for our scenario. A drunk man, stumbling up the stairs, then falling to his death.

"Did you check the security system?" I ask, suddenly remembering. "These new builds sometimes have cameras."

Deacon nods once, not breaking his stride. Of course, he checked. Deacon never misses details.

Harrison makes a gurgling sound, his face turning an alarming shade of purple. Deacon adjusts his grip again, allowing him just enough air to stay conscious but not enough to fight back effectively. Harrison's expensive dress shirt is coming untucked, his designer watch catching the light as his arm flops uselessly at his side.

At the top of the stairs, Deacon pauses, still holding Harrison in that implacable grip. He turns him around so he's facing back down the staircase, his toes just at the edge of the top step. From here, it's a straight shot down to the hardwood foyer below. Fifteen stairs. More than enough to break a neck if you land wrong.

"You're going to have a terrible accident tonight, Harrison," I step closer as I continue conversationally. "A drunk man in a mostly empty house, taking a tumble down the stairs while his date sleeps it off in the bedroom. Such a tragedy."

Deacon eases his grip slightly, allowing Harrison just enough air to speak. Harrison gasps, sucking in desperate breaths, tears streaming down his face. "Please," he pants, voice hoarse and broken. "Please don't do this."

"Did any of those girls say please?" I lean in and whisper. "Did you stop when they begged you to?"

Harrison's eyes are wide with terror now, comprehension dawning. He tries to speak again, gulping air between words. "I'm sorry, I'm—"

I step to the side, out of the way.

Harrison's eyes dart frantically between Deacon and me, realization dawning that these are truly his final moments. His fingers scrabble weakly at Deacon's arm, a final, futile attempt at survival.

Deacon's face remains impassive as he repositions one hand to cup Harrison's jaw and the other to grip the back of his skull.

A quick, sharp twist.

Crack.

Harrison's body goes limp immediately. Deacon releases him with a shove that sends his body cascading down the carpeted steps.

I watch dispassionately as Harrison's body bounces and twists, limbs akimbo, each impact making a sickening thud against the wooden steps. He lands in a crumpled heap at the bottom, neck bent at an unnatural angle, eyes open but unseeing.

For a moment, the house is completely silent.

I grin at Deacon as he rubs his thigh, "Well, that was fun." I pause, tilting my head thoughtfully. "Though now that I think about it, we could've just snapped his neck downstairs and saved ourselves the cardio."

He glares at me as he stretches his still-healing leg.. "Maybe next time you can share that brilliant observation *before* you have me haul a body up stairs."

FORTY-THREE

SCOUT

The engine purrs beneath us as Deacon navigates the empty streets back to our safehouse. My fingers tap an erratic rhythm against my thigh, excess energy coursing through my veins like electricity. The adrenaline high after a kill never gets old. That rush of power, of vengeance, of playing God for just a moment.

I can't stop staring at Deacon's profile. The sharp line of his jaw. The steady concentration in his eyes. The way his hands grip the steering wheel with perfect control. Those same hands that just ended Harrison's life.

"Take a picture," Deacon says without looking at me. "It'll last longer."

I shift in my seat, crossing and uncrossing my legs. "Maybe I will. Your murder face is extremely photogenic."

His mouth twitches, almost a smile. "My murder face?"

"Mmhmm." I lean closer, invading his space. "That look you get when you're about to end someone. All focused and intense. It's hot."

He gives me a sideways look, one eyebrow barely raised. "You have concerning taste in men."

"Says the serial killer to the serial killer." I laugh, the sound filling the car with manic energy. "We're quite the pair, aren't we?"

The streetlights flash across his face in rhythmic patterns, high-lighting those steel-gray eyes that miss nothing. I want to climb into his lap right here, right now, consequences be damned. The need pulses through me with each heartbeat.

"You're vibrating," he says flatly.

"Post-kill high." I drum my fingers against the dashboard. "Some people crash after. I go the other direction."

"I've noticed."

His tone is dry, but I catch the way his gaze flicks to my bouncing knee, my restless hands, my lips. The air between us crackles with tension thick enough to cut.

"We should be back in less than ten minutes," he says, his voice controlled. Too controlled.

I slide my hand onto his thigh, feeling the muscle tense beneath my touch. "That seems like a long time."

"Scout," he warns.

"What?" I trace small circles on his leg, inching higher. "I'm just saying, ten minutes is..."

His hand captures mine, stilling my movement. "Ten minutes is exactly how long it takes to drive back and finish wrapping up Harrison."

I pout but withdraw my hand. "Fine. Be responsible."

The corner of his mouth quirks up. "One of us has to be."

"Boring," I sing-song, but lean back in my seat.

The safehouse cabin comes into view, dark wood and shadows blending into the forest around it. Deacon pulls into the garage, the door closing behind us with mechanical finality. The moment the engine cuts off, I don't wait for him. I'm out of the car in seconds, prac-tically bouncing on my toes as he methodically collects his things.

"Could you move any slower?" I complain as I watch him meticu-lously check that nothing incriminating remains in the vehicle.

Deacon glances up, eyes darkening as they take in my impatience. "Some things shouldn't be rushed."

I tilt my head, studying Deacon's methodical movements as he checks the car one last time. My skin feels too tight, my blood racing with adrenaline that demands release. Watching Deacon kill does something primal to me. I love seeing those controlled hands that just ended a life, knowing what he's truly capable of beneath his calm exterior. The rush of taking justice into our own hands, of being his partner in this dark dance. I need him. Now.

"Are you sure you need to take your time with *everything*?" I ask, my fingers finding the hem of my shirt.

Deacon glances up, freezing mid-motion as I slowly peel the fabric upward, revealing inch by inch of my skin. His eyes track the movement like a predator locked on prey, pupils dilating as I pull the shirt over my head and let it drop carelessly to the garage floor.

I stand before him in just my short denim skirt, fishnet leggings, and black lace bra. The cool air of the garage raises goosebumps across my exposed skin.

"What do you think you're doing?" His voice drops an octave, rough around the edges.

I run my fingers along the waistband of my skirt, hooking one thumb beneath it as I kick off my shoes. "Just getting comfortable. You're taking forever."

Deacon's expression shifts, something primal replacing his careful control. He straightens, abandoning whatever he was checking, and takes one deliberate step toward me. Then another.

"Scout." My name is a growl on his lips. "If you keep this up, I'm going to devour every. Single. Inch. of you."

Heat pools low in my belly at his words. I back up slowly, matching his stalking advance with teasing retreat.

"Promises, promises," I taunt, my heart racing as his eyes darken. "You'll have to catch me first."

I spin on my heel and dart through the door into the house, laughter bubbling up from my chest. I hear his heavy footsteps behind me. He doesn't rush. He knows, we both know, there's nowhere I want to run that isn't straight to him.

But the game is too delicious to end so quickly.

I race through the kitchen, bare feet silent on the tile, and pause at the entrance to the living room. I glance back over my shoulder just as Deacon appears in the doorway, filling the frame with his imposing presence. His eyes are molten silver, burning with intent.

"Running only makes it worse for you," he warns, voice deadly calm as he advances.

"Worse?" I laugh, backing away. "Or better?"

The tension between us is a living thing, electric and dangerous. I feel it in every heartbeat, every breath. My skin hums with anticipation, nerve endings alive with want.

"There's nowhere to go," Deacon says, stalking forward. His movements are controlled, like a hunter who knows his prey is already cornered.

I bump against the back of the couch, momentarily trapped. "Maybe I don't want to go anywhere."

His smile is slow, predatory. "Then why run?"

"To see that look on your face," I admit, breathless. "The one you're wearing right now. Like you're going to destroy me."

Deacon closes the distance between us in two long strides. His hand slides into my hair, gripping firmly at the nape of my neck. Not painful, just controlling, possessive.

"Is that what you want?" His voice is barely above a whisper. "To be destroyed?"

I lift my chin, defiant even as my body melts against his. "I want everything you've got, Candy Man. Every dark, twisted bit of it."

Deacon's eyes lock with mine, dark with hunger. His hand slides from my hair, tracing a slow path down my neck until his palm rests against my throat. His fingers curl around the sides, thumb pressing against my pulse point. The pressure isn't threatening; it's possessive, a living collar that makes my breath catch.

"Mine," he growls, and the single word sends a shiver down my spine.

I swallow hard against his palm, feeling the slight constriction as his grip tightens just enough to remind me who's in control. My head falls back slightly, surrendering to his touch.

"Say it," he demands, voice rough with desire.

"Yours," I whisper, the word barely audible.

His other hand reaches behind him. My eyes widen as his knife appears between us, the black metal catching the dim light.

"Don't. Move." He growls.

The cold flat of the blade touches my thigh at the hem of my skirt. Deacon slides the blade upward, the sharp edge slicing through denim like it's nothing. The sound of fabric tearing sends another rush of heat through me. He repeats the motion on the other side, never once breaking eye contact.

My skirt falls away in two pieces, pooling at my feet. Deacon's gaze drops, his expression darkening when he discovers I'm wearing nothing underneath except the torn fishnet leggings.

"Fucking hell, Scout." His voice is strained. The hand at my throat tightens momentarily in warning. "You're playing with fire."

"Good thing I like getting burned."

Deacon's knife disappears back into his pocket before both hands grab the waistband of my fishnets. With one powerful movement, he tears them apart, the delicate mesh giving way easily. The ripping sound echoes in the quiet room as he shreds them from my body, leaving me in nothing but my bra.

His hands move to my hips, fingers digging into my flesh as he lifts me onto the back of the couch. The position leaves me exposed, vulnerable.

"Look at you," he says, voice dropping to a dangerous whisper. "So fucking perfect. These hips." His hands squeeze possessively. "This perfect ass." One hand slides around to cup me roughly. "All mine to mark. To devour."

His thumb traces the curve where my thigh meets my hip. "Every inch of this body belongs to me now. Do you understand?"

I nod, breathless.

"Say it," he demands, his hand returning to my throat. "Tell me who owns this body."

"You do," I gasp as his grip tightens slightly. "It's yours, Deacon. All yours."

His smile is dark, satisfaction personified. "That's right, kitten. And I'm going to make sure you never forget it."

His free hand slides between my thighs, finding my folds slick with desire. "So wet for me already," he growls, satisfaction evident in his tone. "This sweet cunt is mine. Nobody else gets to touch it. Nobody else gets to taste it. Just me."

The crude words from his usually controlled mouth send another flood of heat through me. I arch against his hand, desperate for more contact.

"Please," I whimper, beyond pride now.

"Please, what?" His fingers trace teasing circles, never quite where I need them. "Tell me exactly what you want, Scout. I want to hear those filthy thoughts."

"I want you," I tell him, my voice raw with need. "All of you, Deacon. The real you, even the darkest parts. Especially those. Don't hold back. Not with me."

Something shifts in his expression, like a final barrier crumbling. The careful control he maintains shatters like glass.

"You have no idea what you're asking for," he growls, eyes flashing dangerously.

"Show me." I dare him.

His hand shoots out, fingers tangling in my hair and yanking my head back. The sudden movement forces a gasp from my lips, pain and pleasure blurring together as he exposes my throat.

"You want the monster?" His voice is barely recognizable, rough and primal. "I'll give you the monster."

He spins me around roughly, bending me over the back of the couch. One powerful hand presses between my shoulder blades, pinning me down while the other grips my hip hard enough to bruise. The manhandling sends electric currents of arousal through my body, making me whimper.

"Fuck, Kitten," he says, voice dark with appreciation. "You like being handled roughly, don't you? Like being put in your place?"

"Yes," I gasp, my cheek pressed against the couch cushion.

His palm comes down hard on my ass, the sharp crack of skin on skin making me cry out. The sting blooms into heat that races through my veins.

"Fuck, Deacon!" I moan, pushing back against him.

"That's it, kitten. Let me hear you."

"I've wanted to do that since the first day I saw you," he confesses, rubbing the reddened skin. "Wanted to see my handprint on this perfect ass."

I've never been this turned on in my life. Every nerve ending is alive, hypersensitive to his touch. The mixture of pain and pleasure is intoxicating, my body responding in ways I've never experienced before.

I feel him drop to his knees behind me, his hands spreading me open. The vulnerability of the position should make me uncomfortable, but instead, it only heightens my arousal.

"So fucking beautiful," he murmurs, his breath warm against my pussy. "And all mine."

The first swipe of his tongue has me clawing at the couch cushions. He's relentless, alternating between broad strokes and fast flicks that have me seeing stars. His fingers dig into my thighs, holding me open and immobile for his assault.

"You taste so sweet," he growls against me, the vibration of his voice adding another layer of sensation. "I could feast on this pussy all day."

His crude words make me practically purr. Who knew the strong, silent type had such a filthy mouth?

"Please don't stop," I beg, rocking back against his face shamelessly.

He chuckles darkly, the sound vibrating against my sensitive flesh. "Not until you come all over my tongue, kitten."

Two long fingers thrust inside me without warning, curling to find that perfect spot while his tongue continues its merciless attention. The dual sensations are overwhelming, pushing me rapidly toward the edge.

"That's it," he encourages, feeling my inner walls begin to clench around his fingers. "Give it to me. Let me feel you come."

"Deacon, I'm—" My words dissolve into a cry as the orgasm crashes through me, my body convulsing around his fingers.

He works me through it relentlessly, drawing out every last tremor until I'm gasping for breath. I cry out at the loss as he withdraws his fingers.

Something slick circles my back entrance, and my breath catches.

"You wanted everything," he reminds me, his voice dangerously soft as one slick finger breaches me slowly. "Everything means everything, Scout. This perfect ass? Mine. This tight little hole? Mine."

The intrusion burns slightly, but the discomfort quickly melts into pleasure as he works his finger deeper with exquisite patience.

"Oh god," I whimper.

"No god here," he says darkly. "Just me. And when I'm done with you, there won't be a single part of your body that doesn't belong to me."

The pressure of his finger inside me creates a delicious burn, a new sensation that has me gasping against the couch cushions. My body is still pulsing from my first orgasm when I feel Deacon shifting behind me. The finger remains, stretching me open as he rises to his feet.

"Don't move," he commands, his free hand working at his jeans. I hear the metallic scrape of his zipper, the rustle of fabric as he pushes his pants down.

"Deacon," I whimper, not even sure what I'm asking for.

"Shh," His voice is rough velvet. "I'm going to fill you up so good, kitten."

I hear him spit, then feel the press of a second finger alongside the first. The stretch intensifies, burning in the most exquisite way as he works both digits in a scissoring motion.

"So tight," he groans. "Your perfect little ass is going to take my cock so well."

The filthy promise sends a fresh wave of arousal through me. I've never wanted anything more.

"Please," I beg, pushing back against his hand.

"Greedy little thing," he chuckles darkly.

The blunt head of his cock presses against my pussy. He pushes forward in one slow, relentless thrust until he's buried to the hilt.

"Fuck," I cry out, the sensations of his fingers in my ass and his thick length stretching my pussy overwhelming my senses.

"That's it," he growls, beginning to move his hips in measured strokes. "Take it all."

His fingers continue their stretching motion in rhythm with his thrusts, preparing me. The combination is mind-bending, pleasure bordering on pain, each sensation heightening the other.

"Were you made for me, Scout?" he praises, his voice strained with restraint. "Taking my cock and my fingers like you were made for it. This tight pussy, this perfect ass, were they made for me to claim?"

"Yes," I gasp, beyond pride or shame now. "All for you. Only you."

His pace increases, hips snapping forward with more force. The fingers in my ass press deeper, scissoring wider. The stretch burns but in the most delicious way, a counterpoint to the pleasure building low in my belly.

His free hand slides around to find my clit, circling the sensitive bud. All of this stimulation, his cock filling me, his fingers stretching my ass, his touch on my clit, sends me spiraling toward another peak.

"That's it," he encourages, feeling my inner walls begin to clench around him. "Come on my cock. Let me feel it."

My orgasm crashes through me like a tidal wave, more intense than the first. I cry out his name, my body convulsing around him as waves of pleasure wash over me.

"Fucking perfect," he growls, continuing to thrust through my climax.

Just as the aftershocks begin to fade, he withdraws completely, both his cock and fingers, leaving me empty and aching. Before I can protest the loss, I feel the slick head of his cock pressing against my other entrance.

"Breathe for me," he instructs, one hand stroking soothingly down my spine while the other grips his length, guiding it against me.

I inhale deeply, trying to relax as he pushes forward. The pressure is intense, the stretch more significant than I had anticipated. My head jerks up during a moment of sharp discomfort as the head breaches me.

"That's it," he praises, his voice strained. "So fucking tight. Taking me so well."

He pauses, allowing me to adjust to the intrusion. His hands move to my breasts, cupping them roughly as he leans over me. His fingers find my nipples, pinching and rolling the sensitive peaks.

"Mine," he growls in my ear. "Every. Fucking. Inch." He thrusts with each word.

The thrusts gradually deepen as my body accommodates his size. The initial discomfort gives way to a pleasure so intense it borders on overwhelming.

One hand abandons my breast to slide between my legs, finding my clit still swollen and sensitive from my previous orgasms. His fingers circle the bundle of nerves.

"Want to feel you come with my cock in this perfect ass," he demands, his voice rough with exertion. "Can you do that for me, kitten? Can you come again?"

His hips maintain their relentless pace, each thrust pushing me further into the pleasure-pain that's consuming me. His fingers work my clit while his other hand roughly kneads my breast, pinching my nipple hard enough to make me gasp and cry out.

"Answer me," he demands, punctuating the command with a deep thrust.

"Yes," I moan, barely recognizing my own voice. "Yes, I can come for you."

The burn of his invasion morphs into something transcendent, pleasure so sharp it borders on pain, pain so exquisite it becomes pleasure. I can't tell where one ends and the other begins anymore.

"You feel that?" Deacon growls, his pace relentless as he drives into me. "Feel how perfectly you take my cock? Like you were made for this. Made for me."

I can only respond with broken sounds, my vocabulary reduced to gasps and whimpers. My fingers claw desperately at the couch cushions, seeking purchase as he pounds into me.

"Every. Fucking. Inch. Scout." He punctuates each word with a brutal thrust that sends sparks shooting up my spine. "This ass? Mine. This pussy? Mine. These perfect tits?" His hand roughly squeezes my breast. "All fucking mine."

His hand on my pussy, his cock in my ass, his other hand torturing my sensitive nipples. The stimulation is overwhelming, my nerve endings firing signals of pleasure so intense they short-circuit my brain.

"You're going to come like this," he demands, voice rough. "Come with my cock buried in this perfect ass. Show me how much you love it."

The command in his voice triggers something primal in me. My body responds instantly, convulsing around him as the orgasm crashes through me like a tidal wave. I scream his name, the sound tearing from my throat as my vision whites out at the edges.

"Fuck," he growls, his rhythm faltering as my body spasms around him. "That's it. Squeeze my cock with that tight little ass."

My inner walls clench and release in waves as I ride out the most intense climax of my life. I'm vaguely aware of begging, pleading words spilling from my lips, though I couldn't say what I'm asking for.

"I'm going to fill you up," Deacon promises, his voice strained. "Mark you from the inside. Make you mine in every way."

His hips snap forward with renewed vigor, each thrust harder than the last. His fingers dig into my hips with bruising force, holding me exactly where he wants me.

"Take it," he commands, his voice breaking. "Take every fucking drop."

With a guttural groan, he slams into me one final time, burying himself to the hilt as his release pulses inside me. The sensation of his hot seed filling me triggers aftershocks that ripple through my oversensitized body.

For several moments, we remain frozen in place, both of us panting. His weight presses me into the couch, his chest against my back, his breath hot against my neck. Slowly, carefully, he withdraws from me, and I whimper at the loss.

"Shh," he soothes, his hand stroking down my spine.

His warm cum trickles down my thigh as it leaks from my body. Before I can move, his fingers are there, gathering his cum from my thighs.

"No, no," he murmurs, almost to himself.

I gasp as his fingers press back into my sensitive entrance, pushing his cum back inside me. The intrusion stings slightly against my tender flesh, but the possessive gesture sends a fresh wave of arousal through me.

"You're going to keep my mark inside you," he says, voice low and commanding as he works his fingers deeper. "I want you to feel me and remember who you belong to."

A low moan escapes me, the sound barely human as his words sink in.

He hums in satisfaction, his fingers still working inside me. "That's right, kitten. All mine."

I whimper softly as Deacon's fingers press deeper, ensuring every drop of his cum stays inside me. The possessiveness of the gesture makes my heart race. No one has ever claimed me so completely.

"Perfect," he murmurs, withdrawing his fingers. His hands move to my waist, and before I can catch my breath, he's lifting me up. "Let's get you to bed."

He carries me effortlessly, one arm under my knees and the other supporting my back. My head lolls against his shoulder, my body utterly spent. The sensation of his release inside me creates a delicious reminder with every movement.

"Deacon," I mumble against his chest, not even sure what I'm trying to say.

"Shh," he soothes, pressing a kiss to my forehead.

He lays me down gently on the bed, the cool sheets a welcome relief against my overheated skin. I watch through heavy-lidded eyes as he walks to the bathroom, his movements still predatory and graceful despite our exertions.

The water runs briefly, and he returns with a warm washcloth. He sits beside me on the bed, and with unexpected tenderness, begins to clean me up. The warm cloth passes over my inner thighs, between my legs, everywhere his hands and mouth have been.

"You're beautiful like this," he says softly, his eyes tracing over my body. "Marked by me. Claimed."

I shiver at his words, a fresh wave of desire washing over me despite my exhaustion.

"Turn over," he says, his voice gentle yet commanding.

I roll onto my stomach, wincing slightly at the tenderness between my legs. The washcloth moves over the small of my back, my thighs, cleaning away the evidence of our passion while somehow making me feel even more thoroughly possessed.

"How do you feel?" he asks, his free hand stroking my hair back from my face.

"Like I've been thoroughly fucked by a very possessive man," I reply, a small smile playing at my lips despite my exhaustion.

He chuckles, the sound warm and rich. "As it should be."

Once he's satisfied I'm clean, he tosses the washcloth aside and pulls the covers over me. The weight of the blanket is comforting, cocooning me in warmth.

Deacon stretches out beside me on top of the covers, propped up on one elbow as he gazes down at me. His fingers trace lazy patterns on my shoulder, each touch sending little sparks across my skin.

"I fought this," he says quietly, his hand cupping my face. "Fought wanting you this much."

"And now?"

His eyes are intense, final. "Now I'm done fighting. You're stuck with me, Scout. Forever isn't long enough."

His thumb presses harder against my lip. "You don't face anything alone anymore. Not Brayden's disappearance, not your guilt, not your nightmares. Nothing."

The intensity of his declaration steals my breath. I've never had someone want to consume me.

His hand slides down to my throat, resting there. "You don't run from me. Ever. Not physically, not emotionally."

I swallow against his palm, feeling my pulse quicken beneath his touch.

I nod slowly, unable to look away from the fierce possession in his eyes. My lips quirk as I tease, "Are you *sure* you don't want me to physically run from you? Because I distinctly remember someone getting very excited about chasing me through the house earlier. That whole hunter-stalking-his-prey vibe you had going?" I bite my lip playfully. "It was extremely hot, just saying. But if you insist on no more running games, I guess I'll have to find other ways to get you all growly and possessive. Challenge accepted, Candy Man."

He arches his eyebrow. "Very funny, you know what I mean. Say it."

"Yours," I breathe. "Completely. But you're stuck with me, too."

His eyes flash with something wild and tender. That slow, satisfied smile spreads across his face.

"Damn right," he murmurs, pressing his lips to mine in a kiss that's surprisingly soft. "Mine. Always."

FORTY-FOUR
DEACON

I sit on the terrace, watching the sunset. It's been three weeks since Scout and I returned from Alabama. Three weeks of searching, waiting, and hoping for news about Brayden.

The news broke about Harrison Westfield's "tragic accident" two days after we returned to the Manor. The girl we'd saved was found unharmed but with no memory of the evening, which honestly was a mercy, considering what Harrison had planned for her. Roman, ever the meticulous operator, anonymously sent the broadcast to each of Harrison's victims with a simple message: "Justice served. You are not forgotten." A small comfort for those women, perhaps, but sometimes that's all we can offer.

Scout has been... different since we returned. Stronger in some ways, more vulnerable in others. She no longer locks herself away when the guilt becomes too much, instead seeking me out. Progress, even if it's small. She still checks her phone regularly for updates on Brayden, but the frantic desperation has given way to a steadier determination.

Every night, she curls against me in sleep, sometimes whispering his name. On those nights, I hold her tighter, reminding her that she's not alone in this.

Roman has been working tirelessly, tracking every lead, every whisper that might point to Brayden's location. Ivy spends hours in the gym, her controlled violence a physical manifestation of her worry. Tristan retreats further into his wing, emerging only for family meetings where we discuss any new developments, which have been frustratingly few.

Lucien maintains his calm facade, but I've caught him standing in Brayden's empty room, staring at the rumpled bed sheets as if they might offer some clue we've missed.

The French doors open behind me, and I don't need to turn to know it's Scout. Her scent, citrus, sunshine, and something uniquely her, reaches me before her footsteps do.

"Hey," she says softly, settling into the chair beside mine.

I glance over, taking in the sight of her. She's wearing cupcake pajama pants and one of my hoodies, specifically, that one that I haven't been able to find for a month. The hem hits mid-thigh, her curls piled messily on top of her head. In her hands, she holds an embroidery hoop, the black dahlia for Stanton's victims finally taking shape after weeks of sitting untouched.

"Where did you find that?" I ask, tugging at the hem.

She examines the hoodie like she's seeing it for the first time. "This old thing? Must've been mixed up in my laundry. You know how these things happen."

Right. Just like how my entire bedroom "happened" to relocate itself the day we came home from Alabama while I was working with Roman. I'd returned from the data room to find my space completely gutted, not even a sock left behind.

Scout had been waiting in the hallway, bouncing on her toes like she'd just pulled off the crime of the century.

"Surprise! You've been evicted," she'd announced cheerfully. "But don't worry, I found you a much better place. You're welcome."

No discussion, no warning. She made a decision and went with it. Not that I'm complaining, except the menace had just thrown all my clothes into random drawers like some kind of beautiful hurricane. Apparently, organization is optional in her world. But it's classic Scout logic: act first, let Deacon deal with it later.

"How does it feel?" I ask, nodding toward the embroidery hoop. "Working on it again?"

She shrugs, adjusting the fabric in the hoop. "Better, I think. At least I can work on this now."

I nod, understanding the significance. After Eliza, Scout couldn't bring herself to touch her embroidery. The fact that she's working on Stanton's flower means she's healing, slowly reclaiming pieces of herself.

"Any news?" she asks, the same question she's asked every day since we returned.

"Nothing yet," I tell her honestly.

Scout nods, her needle moving steadily through the fabric. "We'll find him."

"We will," I agree, my certainty absolute, because failure isn't an option. Not when it comes to Scout's happiness.

We sit in comfortable silence for a few minutes, Scout working on her embroidery while I watch the sunset deepen into twilight. This has become our routine, these quiet moments together, grounding each other in this life we've chosen.

Scout sets her embroidery aside and moves to sit on my lap, her legs dangling over the arm of the chair. I wrap my arms around her waist, holding her close.

"We're going to find him, Scout," I promise, pressing my lips to her temple. "I don't care how long it takes or what we have to do. We won't stop looking."

She nods against my chest, her fingers tracing patterns on my arm. "I know. I just hope..."

"He's alive," I finish for her. "And when we find him, I'm going to kick his ass for making you worry."

She laughs softly. "Get in line. Ivy's already called dibs."

I tighten my hold on her, watching as the first stars appear in the darkening sky. In this moment, with Scout in my arms and the promise of a future with her, I allow myself to hope that maybe, just maybe, we'll find a way through this darkness together.

I wrap my arms tighter around Scout as she nestles against me, both of us watching the stars emerge one by one. The weight of her in my lap grounds me, keeps me from spiraling into the dark places my mind wanders when I think about all the what-ifs.

"What are you thinking about?" she asks, her fingers tracing the scar on my forearm, a souvenir from a kill gone sideways in Detroit.

"About how I'd like to introduce the person who took Brayden to my favorite knife," I answer honestly.

Scout tilts her head up, studying my face. "Just your knife? I was thinking more along the lines of a full medieval torture rack."

"We could do both." I brush a curl from her face. "Start with the rack, finish with the knife."

She smiles, but it doesn't reach her eyes. Something else is weighing on her mind.

"What's wrong?" I ask, running my thumb along her jawline.

Scout takes a deep breath, shifting slightly in my lap to face me more directly. "I need to tell you something, and I need you to just... listen. Okay?"

I nod, suddenly tense. In my experience, nothing good follows that kind of introduction.

"When I went after Eliza, I thought..." She pauses, collecting her thoughts. "I thought I might not make it back. And the only thing I regretted was not telling you how I felt."

My grip on her tightens instinctively.

"I've spent my whole life thinking I didn't deserve good things," she continues. "That someone like me, someone who does what we do, doesn't get to have normal relationships or happiness. And then you came along with your stupid cotton candy and your brooding silences..."

I almost interrupt, but she places a finger against my lips.

"I love you, Deacon." The words fall between us, simple and devastating. "I'm in love with you. And that terrifies me more than any killer I've ever hunted."

My heart hammers against my ribs. I've known this, felt it in the way she reaches for me in sleep, seen it in her eyes when she thinks I'm not looking. But hearing her say it aloud shatters something inside me.

"You don't have to say it back," she adds quickly. "I just needed you to know. If anything happens..."

"Nothing is going to happen to you." The words come out harsher than I intended, my voice rough with emotion. "Not while I'm breathing."

Scout studies my face, waiting. I've never been good with words, especially not these words. They feel too small, too ordinary for what I feel for her.

I cup her face between my palms. "The day I saw you in that cafe, I was planning to disappear after Lorre. New identity, new hunting grounds. Just like I have every other time." I stroke her cheek with my thumb. "But then you walked into the warehouse like a goddamn hurricane with that crazy smile that lit up the whole room, and I couldn't look away."

She leans into my touch, her eyes never leaving mine.

"I've spent my entire life alone, Scout. By choice. Because people are liabilities, they get hurt. They die." I swallow hard. "But you... You're the exception to every rule I've ever made."

I pull her closer, pressing my forehead against hers. "I would burn this world to ashes if you needed me to. I would hunt down anyone who tried to take you from me and show them what their organs look like while they're still breathing. Death would be a mercy I'd make them earn."

A tear slips down her cheek, and I catch it with my thumb.

"If that's not love, I don't know what is," I whisper against her lips.

Scout makes a sound between a laugh and a sob. "That might be the most romantic death threat I've ever received."

I smile against her mouth. "I love you, Scout Prescott. God help anyone who tries to change that."

She kisses me then, fierce and desperate, her hands clutching at my shoulders like she's afraid I might disappear. I kiss her back with equal intensity, pouring everything I am into the press of my lips against hers.

When we finally break apart, both breathing hard, she rests her head against my chest. I can feel her heartbeat against mine, our rhythms syncing.

"I was so scared you wouldn't say it back," she whispers.

I press a kiss to the top of her head. "Like you would have given me a choice anyway."

EPILOGUE

BRAYDEN

old. That's the first sensation that registers as I claw my way back to consciousness. Cold concrete against my cheek. Cold metal biting into my wrists. Cold dread settles in my gut as my memory returns.

My head throbs with each heartbeat. Blood has dried in a tacky trail from my temple to my jaw. I catalog my injuries with clinical detachment. Possible concussion. Check. Three cracked ribs on the left side. Check. Dislocated right shoulder that's been roughly shoved back into place. Check. Check. The copper taste in my mouth suggests internal bleeding. Awesome.

Nothing fatal. Yet.

I test the iron shackles binding my wrists. Industrial grade. No give. The chain between them rattles against concrete as I shift position, sending echoes through what I now recognize as a basement. The earthy smell of dirt and mildew hangs heavy in the stale air. A single bulb dangles from exposed wiring overhead, casting harsh shadows across bare walls.

"Fuck," I mutter, my voice scraping raw against my throat.

The last clear memory I have floods back with sudden, sickening clarity.

Landing in Nashville. Checking in with Roman as required to hunt Marcus Webb. Walking to the SUV parked and waiting for me.

I'd just gotten into the SUV when I felt it. A sharp pinch in my neck, like a bee sting. I reached up to swat whatever it was away, but my hand felt heavy. Wrong.

"What the hell..." The words slurred as they left my mouth.

The world tilted sideways. My vision blurred, darkness creeping in from the edges. I tried to fight it, tried to reach for my weapon, but my limbs wouldn't obey.

Then nothing until this basement.

I pull myself into a sitting position, ignoring the protest from my ribs. The room is maybe twelve by twelve. Cracked concrete floor, rock walls. A wooden door with no handle on this side. No windows. The only light comes from that single bulb.

From where I'm sitting, I'm fucked. No weapons. Old thick iron chains bolted to the floor. No idea where I am or who has me.

I strain against the shackles again, feeling the metal bite deeper into my wrists. Blood slicks my hands, but the restraints don't budge.

"Well, ain't you a stubborn son of a bitch," I grunt, straining against the metal.

But the chains hold, and eventually I slump back against the wall, breathing hard.

I don't know how long I've been here. Hours? Days? The hunger gnawing at my stomach suggests at least a few days.

A metallic scrape slices through the silence. My muscles tense, every sense on high alert.

The door swings open, flooding the room with blinding light. I squint against the sudden assault, my eyes watering as they struggle to adjust after hours in dim lighting. All I can make out is a silhouette framed in the doorway, slim, feminine, confident in its stillness.

Footsteps echo on concrete. Deliberate. Unhurried. The cadence of someone who knows they hold all the power. I brace myself, muscles coiling despite the pain radiating through my body. Whatever's coming, I won't make it easy.

As my vision clears, I get my first look at my captor.

She's beautiful in the way a venomous snake is beautiful. All sleek lines and deadly promise. Long blonde hair cascades over shoulders clad in a fitted black blazer. Expensive jeans hug curves that would be distracting under different circumstances. Her smile reveals perfect teeth, too white, too sharp.

But it's her eyes that lock me in place. Cold. Calculating. The eyes of someone who enjoys the suffering of others. I've seen her before. My memory is fuzzy trying to place her.

"Who the fuck are you supposed to be?" I snap, tasting copper.

She clicks her tongue, disappointed. "Such language. I expected a little more softness from the infamous Tooth Fairy. Hasn't Lucien taught any of the Hollow members manners?"

Ice shoots through my veins. She knows my signature. She knows Lucien's name. She knows about The Hollow.

Fuck. How the hell does she know about The Hollow?

Her voice drips with honey-coated venom, seductive yet dangerous. A soft British accent triggers something in my memory, but I'm too busy trying to figure out how much this bitch knows. Does she know about Scout? About the manor?

"Allow me to properly introduce myself," she says, crouching down to my level with practiced elegance. "Vivienne Sterling. Yes, *that* Sterling. The Sterling Institute." She watches my face for recognition, savoring the moment. "I see you know who I am. How flattering."

My mind races as the pieces click into place. The Sterling Institute. Glossy commercials of smiling children in third-world countries, humanitarian awards, and global news segments about revolutionary medical breakthroughs. The perfectly styled blonde with the dazzling smile, accepting awards, shaking hands with presidents and prime ministers. Vivienne Sterling, the golden girl of global philanthropy, is the darling of humanitarian circles.

And apparently, a fucking psychopath.

"Well, I'll be damned," I drawl, voice rough. "The saint herself. How's that halo fitting, sugar?"

Her smile widens, pleased I recognize her public persona. "My work extends far beyond what the cameras capture, Mr. Lockwood. The Institute has... diverse interests."

"Well now, I don't recall seein' the kidnappin' and torture part in your little TV commercials."

"We all wear masks," she says, standing to smooth invisible wrinkles from her blazer. "Mine just happens to be exceptionally profitable. And useful."

"Well now, darlin', what exactly are we doin' here? This seems like a lot of work just to chat."

She reaches out, trailing perfectly manicured fingernails along my jaw. I jerk away, chains rattling.

"Straight to business. I like that." She stands, smoothing invisible wrinkles from her blazer. "What I want is simple. I want The Hollow eradicated."

A laugh scrapes its way out of my throat, sharp and humorless. "Well, honey, that's one hell of an ambitious to-do list you got there."

"You'd be surprised how manageable it becomes when you have the right leverage." Her smile widens. "I have you."

"Honey, I hate to break it to ya, but I ain't worth trading the whole damn kingdom for."

"Not the whole kingdom. Not yet." She begins to circle me slowly, like a shark. "But they'll come for you. Scout first, I imagine. She's so predictably loyal. Then the Reaper and her shadow. Then the new one, what do they call him? Mr. Floss?" She laughs, the sound like breaking glass. "How ridiculous."

"Honey, you have no idea what kind of hornet's nest you just kicked," I growl, tracking her movement as best I can without turning my head.

She stops and looms in front of me. "No, you don't know who *you're* dealing with. But I know exactly what I'm dealing with. I've had you in my sights for a while now. Learning your patterns. Your weaknesses." Her breath is warm against my skin. "Your family."

The threat hangs in the air between us. I lunge forward, chains snapping taut, teeth bared in fury. She dances back on her heels, laughing.

"There he is! The Tooth Fairy in all his glory." She claps her hands together like a delighted child. "I was beginning to think they'd exaggerated your temper."

"Darlin', you better hope these chains hold, 'cause when I get free..."

"You'll what? Pull my teeth? Add them to your collection?" She tsks. "So predictable."

She moves to a small table I hadn't noticed before, picking up what looks like a cell phone.

"Your friends are getting closer," she says, scrolling through something on the screen. "They found my little decoy at the farmhouse sooner than expected. That Deacon is quite resourceful."

The mention of the farmhouse connects the dots. "You're workin' with the Glass Gardener."

Her smile falters for the first time. "Working with? Ha! No, Eliza Morgan was a useful tool, nothing more. A damaged girl with a vendetta against your precious Stitcher. Easy to manipulate." She shrugs. "Disposable."

"You used her."

"Of course I did." She says it like it's the most natural thing in the world. "Just like I'm using you."

She turns toward the door, pausing with her hand on the frame. "Rest while you can, Mr. Lockwood. Tomorrow we begin the real work."

"Listen, my family's gonna come for me," I drawl, voice steady despite the pain. "And darlin', you ain't gonna like what happens next."

"Oh, I'm counting on it." Her smile is all teeth now, predatory and cold. "That's exactly the point."

The door slams shut behind her, and I'm back to staring at these four walls. Sitting here in the dark, chained up like some kind of animal. Most people would call this fucked.

But then again, I'm not most people.

She thinks she knows The Hollow.

I lean my head back against the cold wall and actually smile.

Because this psycho just made the biggest mistake of her life.

Acknowledgments

To my husband, thank you for the unwavering support, the horrified looks, and every "Are you sure you're okay?" Each one confirmed I was writing in the right direction.

To my girls, you are my world and greatest inspiration. Thank you for loving me through the late nights and really weird questions. May you both always chase your wildest dreams, no matter how impossible (or terrifying) they seem.

To the Core Four, you know who you are. My lifeline through plot holes, mental spirals, and imposter syndrome. This book exists because you believed in me even when I didn't and because you never flinched when I said, "So, I've got an idea..." right before things got twisted.

Connect with me

If you made it to the end, you're officially one of us. Follow me for updates, behind-the-scenes chaos, and entirely too much dark romance energy.

TikTok: @leannastone

Book Two coming soon. Brace yourself.

ABOUT THE AUTHOR

Leanna Stone is a dark romance author with a soft spot for broken heroes, unhinged heroines, and love stories that refuse to stay in the lines. When she's not plotting morally questionable love stories, she's wrangling her two daughters, overanalyzing dialogue, and surviving on caffeine and sarcasm. *The Hollow* marks her debut into the world of morally gray romance, where justice is messy, passion burns deep, and happy endings come with body counts.

www.ingramcontent.com/pod-product-compliance
Lightning Source LLC
Chambersburg PA
CBHW030228120726
47903CB00005B/1403